EMBERS OF TRUTH

THE PESHTIGO FIRE CHRONICLES
BOOK ONE

AVRIE SWAN

To Mema,
who read my stories from the beginning.

ACKNOWLEDGMENTS

Thank you to my dear Mema for supporting my writing journey from the very beginning. I no longer send her little books written on scrap paper and stapled together like I did when I was small, but that's only because I don't have staples that are large enough to hold all the pages!

Thanks to Evie for listening to my ideas and offering advice when I found myself stuck with writer's block. I am forever grateful to have you as my sister.

Thank you to my parents for being the best support team I could have asked for. I never would have come this far without their continual support and encouragement. To Mum—thanks for always believing in me, for listening when I most needed it, and for assuring me I could overcome any struggles that came my way. And to Teddy—thank you for pushing me out of my comfort zone and helping me get involved in the writing community.

Thanks to the wonderful team at Wild Heart Books for helping me bring this book to life. A special shout out to my editor, Denise Weimer, for all her hard work and assistance.

And finally, thanks to the One who inspired this book and gave me the strength to pursue it. The same God who moves mountains and parts seas gave a story to a young woman, and I am grateful for that every day.

CHAPTER 1

*C*arina Clarke wasn't normally prone to violence, but at the moment, she was strongly considering it.

"Move, you lazy animal!" She grunted, giving the tan-and-white cow another hard shove as she struggled to push it away from her. The warm scent of alfalfa and corn swirled around her, the usually comforting smell now stifling in the cramped shed. The animal had shifted to the side as Carina was attempting to squeeze past with an armful of hay, effectively pinning her against the inner wall. As she gave Gertrude another push, the cow finally stepped away from her with a plaintive moo.

Taking a much-needed breath of air while brushing a stray curl behind her ear, Carina leveled a glare on Gertrude. "What on earth was that for? I was trying to feed you. Now look at me —my dress is ruined! Not to mention, I dropped your dinner. You're going to have to eat off the floor, silly beast."

The cow gave Carina a single cursory glance, her brown

1

eyes droopy beneath white lashes. Then, without further comment, she lumbered around and presented Carina with her back end.

Suppressing a sigh, Carina shimmied out of the tiny shed and into the sunlight. While it was the middle of October, the air was surprisingly warm and dry, and she took a moment to soak in the sunlight before she assessed the damage done to her garments. With her skirt ripped in multiple places and her apron smeared with mud, she was in no state to go into town.

Letting out a groan of frustration, Carina rubbed at her eyes with one hand. How was she going to speak with the landlord now?

"If only Mother hadn't asked me to feed the cow." She scrubbed at a brown smudge on her dress. "I should have gone to visit Mr. Howard directly after work. It was foolish of me to come home and change." She sniffed and dropped the fabric. No use in complaining. The damage had already been done.

Treading slowly through the grassy lawn, Carina made her way toward the back door of the house. She paused just before entering, surveying the humble place she called home. Her heart hurt at the realization that without a very persuasive conversation with the landlord, she could very likely lose the place she loved most.

The frame house boasted a fragrant array of autumn flowers that sprouted from the garden and waved a greeting from the window boxes. While it had been painted white once upon a time, the paint had begun to wear and crack, giving the structure the feel of a tired old woman. It had only a single level, with three bedrooms and a small kitchen. All things considered, the house wasn't much. To Carina, however, it was her whole world.

As she clambered up the wooden steps, she plucked a few half-wilted zinnias from the nearest window box before opening the door. After shedding her boots inside, she made her way down the hall to the nearest bedroom. "Mother?" She tapped softly on the door.

"Come in, dear," a cheery voice with a faint Irish lilt responded, the sound of movement echoing from within.

Carina opened the door and found her mother attempting to scrub every square inch of the room with a washrag.

Mary Clarke was and had always been an industrious woman, ready to push her sleeves back and do whatever needed to be done. After her husband's untimely passing, it had fallen to her to keep the household running. While another woman might have balked at the task, Mary had simply taken a deep breath and continued on. Currently, her curly red-and-silver hair was pulled into a tight bun at the nape of her neck while her simple gingham dress was buttoned up at the elbows.

"Mother, I brought you some zinnias." Carina held out the hastily made bouquet, causing several of the flowers to bobble and droop. "They won't last much longer, so I decided to bring them in."

Mother took the plants from her and gave them a sniff, her face brightening into the smile Carina so loved. "Oh, these are wonderful. Would you mind setting them in the vase on the kitchen table while I finish up in here?" She eyed her daughter's state of dress with a raised brow. "You may want to change into something fresh, as well. Did you slay a dragon to get those flowers?"

Carina couldn't contain a snort of amusement. "Only the cow, I'm afraid. She didn't like me trying to get past her to refill the food trough."

Mother sighed and plopped her hands on her hips, the corners of her mouth twitching up in barely concealed laughter. "That cow is going to be the death of us all. I don't know why your sister insists on keeping the creature around when we could just as easily get milk from the neighbor's farm."

Carina let out a short laugh. "You know as well as I do that Charlotte is too soft-hearted to ever get rid of the cow."

"You aren't wrong, my dear." Mother stepped forward and brushed a speck of dirt from Carina's shoulder. "It is good of her to be so kind and caring, and I know she will mature as time goes on, the same way you did." She swatted at Carina with the cleaning rag. "Now, go and change while I finish wiping down the furniture. I'm fixing up a nice chicken soup for dinner, and I won't have any muddy waifs sitting at my table."

"Yes, Mother," Carina said with a grin, scurrying from the room amid her mother's soft laughter.

After depositing the zinnias in the vase, she hurried to her small bedroom to freshen up. Though the room contained naught but a bed, dresser, and mirror, Carina had gone to lengths to make it feel like her own. A red-and-green quilt her mother had given her at Christmas decorated the bed, while a few of her favorite books lay stacked on the dresser. The rest were tucked safely in the closet so Charlotte wouldn't find them and tease Carina mercilessly for reading romance novels.

Stepping up to the dresser mirror, Carina winced. It was worse than she had thought— her hair had become unpinned in several places, leaving red curls to spill down around her shoulders, and dirt adorned her nose. Taking several pins from the top dresser drawer, she went to work. Once the curls had been pinned back into something presentable, she wiped the dirt from her nose and switched her ruined dress for a slightly cleaner one. She smoothed the green fabric. "Much better." She turned to leave but paused just before the door.

Reaching into the top dresser drawer, Carina pushed aside a bundle of stockings and grabbed the item underneath. As she pulled the paper from her drawer, guilt assailed her. She opened it and scanned the words written upon the page, skipping over the terse greeting and going straight to the heart of the letter.

I regret to inform you that you have failed to pay your rent on the agreed upon date. If you do not send the payment within two weeks, I will be forced to take further action. Though the word was not mentioned, there was no doubting what Mr. Howard meant by *further action.*

Eviction.

Carina plopped down on her bed and dropped her head into her hands. While she had taken a job at the local laundry, the pay wasn't enough to see them through the month. Even her mother's work as a seamstress combined with Carina's efforts wasn't sufficient. The only options left were for Carina to either find a different job entirely or ask her younger sister, Charlotte, to work at the laundry with her. Looking at her hands, which had become chapped and red from long hours of labor, Carina despised the thought of asking her little sister to join. Yet what other options did she have? Her mother wasn't even aware of their dire straits, or if she was, she didn't let on.

Carina battled between wanting to hand her mother the letter and continuing to hide it. Eventually, the desire to spare her mother additional stress won, and she put the envelope back in the dresser.

Voices caught her attention as she slid the drawer closed. Turning toward the window above her bed, Carina spied Charlotte and Edwin, Charlotte's friend, walking in the grass along the side of the house. Their conversation appeared serious, for Charlotte was frowning and Edwin had wrinkles between his brows. Cracking the window open, Carina listened to their voices rise and swell.

"I still think it would be a good idea," Edwin was saying, his dark eyes intense and solemn. "If you marry me, I can help provide for your household."

Carina stifled a gasp. Edwin, marry Charlotte?

"Edwin, you and I both know we don't see each other romantically. We've always been friends and nothing more." Gone was the joy that usually infused the twenty-one-year-old's tone. Instead, Charlotte looked troubled as she attempted to politely turn her friend down.

"That was before you found that letter in Carina's drawer." Edwin spread his hands. "Now you know things are more serious than you originally thought. Let me help you, please."

Carina clapped her hands over her mouth to prevent a groan of dismay from escaping.

Charlotte had seen the letter?

Charlotte released a soft sigh. "Give me some space to think about it. I'll give you an answer in a day's time."

Edwin nodded and enveloped Charlotte in a quick hug. "Whatever you think is best, Lottie. I only want to help you, your mother, and your sister. If you don't believe this will work, we'll find a different way. I simply think it's the best option considering the time you have left before the next payment is due." With a quick wave, he trotted off.

Turning from the window, Carina charged to the front door and out onto the porch. She grabbed her sister from the front step before the young woman could react and propelled Charlotte into her room, sliding the door shut behind them.

"You can't marry Edwin." Carina fought to keep her voice low.

Charlotte narrowed her eyes and lowered herself to the bed, fluffing her brown skirts around her. "For your information, I wasn't planning on marrying him. Why were you listening in on our conversation, anyway? It was no business of yours."

Carina crossed her arms and glared at her younger sister.

"How funny it is that you should accuse me of prying when it was you who clearly went rummaging through my drawer."

Charlotte deflated at the harsh comment. "I suppose you're right. I was only looking for hairpins—truly, I was. I saw the letter and glanced at it out of curiosity. Oh, Carina, why didn't you tell Mama that we're going to lose the house?"

"We aren't losing the house, nor are we losing anything else." Carina spoke with as much conviction as she could muster, but her sinking heart told a different story. "I'll find a way to pay Mr. Howard without worrying Mother and without you marrying for the sake of money."

Charlotte sighed. "There's nothing wrong with Edwin. He's a fine, upstanding man, and I wouldn't be horrified to marry him."

"Lottie, we both know perfectly well that you don't love Edwin. Mother always said marriage should be about more than just a union. Not being horrified by someone is hardly good criteria."

"So saith the one who seems to abhor men." Charlotte raised a brow in a passable imitation of their mother. Lottie looked like her, with an innocent face, button nose, and sky-blue eyes. The only thing she had inherited from their father was her chestnut-brown hair, long and straight.

Father. Carina scowled. "You know why I feel the way I do. Father should have listened to Mother, but instead, he left her. That isn't love."

"Carina, you know Father only went into the forest because he needed time to calm down after they got into that argument." Charlotte gestured to the window. "He never would have left us. The fact that he got lost was no fault of his."

Carina folded her arms against her chest. "If he had listened to Mother's pleas, he never would have gone out in the cold. Instead, he did, and now we've been left to fend for ourselves." There was another reason she held such hard feelings toward her father, but it was nothing Carina would ever admit to Charlotte. She didn't need her sister's innocent heart to become tainted with such ugly memories. Seeing that Charlotte was beginning to formulate an argument, she raised a hand. "I'll hear no more of Father. You won't marry a man you don't love. There was never any sense in rushing into decisions, especially when it comes to marriage. We'll find a different way."

Charlotte sighed and slowly nodded, the corners of her mouth drooping. "If you say so, Carina."

Carina patted her sister gently on the shoulder. "I know so. I'll sort this out, Lottie. I promise. Please, give me some time."

At their mother's call from the kitchen, they rose and exited the room. Upon entering the dining room, they found the table adorned with spoons, bowls, and napkins. The bowls were chipped, and the spoons had several dents, but that was part of what made them comforting.

Mother appeared beside Carina and placed a steaming pot on the table, using her ladle to gesture to the chairs. "Go on and take a seat. We'll pray and then enjoy the soup."

After sliding into a seat alongside her sister, Carina held out the chair next to her for her mother. Once she had been seated, the three of them bowed their heads.

"Dear Lord," Mother began, "thank You for giving us the provisions for this lovely meal. Give us the energy we need to accomplish our work and always remind us when we are being led astray to find our way back to You. For it is by You alone that we have strength to endure, Lord. In Your name we pray, amen." A smile crossed Mother's face as she finished. "Well then, let's eat! I didn't spend nearly all day cooking for this meal to simply sit and smell good."

Carina ladled soup into her bowl, blew on it, and took a dainty sip. It was bursting with exceptional flavor, the cooking a feat of talent that only their mother seemed to possess. She let out a sigh of contentment as the soup warmed her from within, loosening a fraction of the stress that had held her captive throughout the day. It was almost enough to make her believe everything would turn out for the better. It would have been even more enjoyable had Mr. Howard's words not been hanging close in her mind.

Finishing her stew only a few moments later, Carina excused herself and removed her dishes to the washtub. She tidied the table with her sister before retreating to her room for the evening.

After changing into the comfort of her nightgown, Carina slid beneath the quilt on her bed and extinguished the lamp on the dresser. The thick mattress was a blessing to her tired muscles, which ached after hours spent stirring tubs of dirty clothing. Carina tugged the quilt tighter around her in a habit she had begun during her childhood, when the cold winter nights made her shiver in bed. Mother had wrapped the blankets tightly around her to keep her warm. *"My little butterfly,"* she had whispered. *"All wrapped up in your little cocoon."* Even now, at the age of twenty-three, the snugness of the quilt made her feel warm and secure.

"Goodnight, Mother! Sweet dreams, Charlotte," Carina called. Smiling at the returning chorus of goodnights, she closed her eyes and leaned back against her pillow.

She would rise early tomorrow morning and pay a call to Mr. Howard. And she must be very convincing, for if they lost their house, where could they go?

CHAPTER 2

*I*t was the smell that woke her. Carina rubbed her nose and sneezed. The sweet scent of smoke permeated the air, though that was nothing unusual. Farmers often slashed and burned the fields during the day, and the thick haze from their controlled fires hung in the air late into the night. Yawning, Carina closed her eyes and attempted to fall back asleep. Despite her fading consciousness, the woodsy smell persisted. If anything, it seemed to be growing stronger by the second. And was that shouting she heard, or was it simply the wind rattling her window?

An alarm sounded somewhere in the back of Carina's mind. She unraveled from her cocoon, dragged herself from the bed, and glanced out the window. What she saw nearly made her scream aloud.

Peshtigo was on fire!

Flames lashed at the buildings, long tongues of flame climbing into the sky and turning the air a sickly orange. The blaze spread like a hungry beast, swiftly advancing through town and racing toward the outskirts where their home was located. Their *wooden* home.

Carina ran down the hall and ripped open the door to her sister's room. "Charlotte, fire! Wake up. We have to get out of the house before it reaches us!" There was no time to think of saving the building. The blaze was spreading far too quickly for them to counteract it.

Her sister let out a murmured complaint before bolting upright, realization dawning on her face. "Are you certain?"

Carina nodded. "Move fast, Charlotte. I must go wake Mother."

She ran back into the hallway and burst into her mother's room a moment later. "Mother, the town is ablaze! We must leave before the fire reaches us!"

Her mother pushed herself upright with one hand while rubbing at her eyes with the other. "Is Charlotte awake?"

"Yes." Warning bells clanged in her mind, growing ever louder as smoke began to seep through the cracks in the windows.

"Go get her." Mother's voice was steely calm. "Leave the house together, and do not lose sight of one another. I will fetch some things and join you outside in a moment."

"Yes, Mother," Carina answered, racing back into the hall. Running to her sister's bedroom, she found Charlotte trying to stuff a blanket full of clothing.

"There's no time, Charlotte. Quickly, follow me!" Carina gasped, coughing in the smoky air. Grabbing her sister's hand, she propelled Charlotte out the front door and into what could only be described as hell on earth.

A wall of pure fire had descended upon town, carried forward by vicious gusts of wind that tore at buildings and sucked trees from the ground, propelling them into the path of the blaze. The spiraling wind even dragged several birds into the flaming inferno. Embers from the fire rained down on the people fleeing the town and caught on their garments, setting them ablaze. Screaming rent the air in a terrible cacophony, an unearthly chorus of fear and pain.

"Where are you, Mother?" Carina whispered into a night as bright as day, the stars and moon having been obscured by the unearthly orange glow of the blaze. Horror rose within her and she watched, frozen, as flames began to lick at the sides of the home she so loved. *No!* Mother's prized flowers turned into blackened ash as the fire made its way up the sides of the house. The beams shuddered and groaned, threatening to collapse as the structure weakened from within.

Something brushed past Carina, and she watched in a daze as a figure ran back toward the burning house. Charlotte? It couldn't be. The woman's dress was a deep mahogany, not the white of her sister's nightgown. But, if so, who was running back into the house? The strange sight was enough to dispel the haze in her mind, freeing her limbs from the terror that had been holding them hostage.

She had to get her mother out. Carina launched herself toward the house. Before she had ran more than a few feet, arms grabbed her from behind, preventing her from advancing farther. Turning, Carina found her neighbor and friend Willow behind her. The girl's face was so covered in soot that it had turned a corpse-like gray, and ash dusted her ebony hair.

Willow shook her head, tears leaving pale tracks on her cheeks. "Carina, you can't go back in there. The roof is collapsing!"

Whirling back around, Carina screamed as the roof shuddered and groaned. With a sickening crack, it slowly crumbled in on itself and thundered to the earth in a shower of sparks.

Hot tears ran down Carina's face as she clutched her hands to her mouth, her breathing ragged.

Willow coughed and began dragging Carina through the clearing, her hand tight on Carina's arm. "We must get to the river! It's the only way we'll survive."

Blinded by smoke and tears, Carina allowed herself to be led toward the river. Beside her, she could make out the blurry forms of Willow and another woman who must be Lottie, also racing to beat the flames. At the edge of the river, they met a great wall of people and animals struggling to enter the water. Children screamed and animals bawled as they jumped into the frigid river, creating a terrible noise that battled with the crackling of flames.

Finding an opening, Willow plunged in and dragged Carina behind her. The cold water was in direct contrast with the heat in the air, leaving Carina shivering as she forced her freezing legs to swim. Turning, she searched the river for anything she could use to escape the ice-cold water. There—an empty crate floating nearby! She swam to it and hefted herself over the top.

"Willow? Charlotte? Where are you?" Carina cried, her voice hoarse. She saw neither her sister nor her friend as the flames burned on. There...a woman with long chestnut-colored hair treaded water a few feet from a crate. Carina's heart skipped a beat. "Lottie!" She waved her arms. "Lottie, is that you?"

The figure turned slowly, revealing a face so marred by burns as to be nearly unrecognizable. Carina fought back the horrified gasp that rose in her throat and lowered her arm. *Not Lottie. At least it's not Lottie.*

As Carina continued to peer across the river in search of her sister, the wind rose until it reached a terrifying roar. A noise like thunder split the air, causing her to jolt and turn her attention toward town. Just visible through the thick smoke, railcars and burning wood were being picked up by the flaming gale and tossed through the charred remains of the town, ever closer to the people taking refuge in the river. Bowing her head, Carina began a fervent prayer, hoping against hope that she would make it through this living hell.

After what seemed like ages, the screams and crackling of

flames finally began to taper off. Cracking her eyes open, Carina scrubbed at her face with the wet sleeve of her nightgown and pushed a few limp strands of hair behind her ears. Her body was shaking violently in the cold, and her eyes felt as though they were covered in sand. The smoke obscuring the sky made it impossible to tell whether it was day or night. Destruction littered the water all around her—a mixture of charred wood, dead animals, and personal belongings. While some people remained in the water, others had begun venturing back to land, their legs wobbling as they made their way up onto the beach.

After sliding off the crate that had been her safety throughout the fire, Carina swam and then waded slowly to the riverbank. Reaching a hand down, she found the sand was still warm. Trembling from exhaustion, she stretched out on the beach in an attempt to soak up as much of the heat as she could. All around her, conversation and cries echoed in the air as people searched for family members and friends.

Once Carina felt strong enough to sit up, she pushed herself onto her elbows and shook her head to remove the sand from her hair. She ripped a long strip of cloth from the hem of her dirty nightgown and tied it around her nose and mouth to block the smoke. With that accomplished, she pushed herself slowly to her feet and glanced around for any sign of Charlotte or Willow. No matter how many times she wiped her eyes, her vision remained blurry, making it hard to look for familiar faces amongst the dead and living on the beach.

As she stumbled aimlessly along the beach, Carina spotted a head of midnight-black hair she knew all too well. Edwin crouched next to a badly burned woman with a piece of fabric wrapped around his face to protect his mouth. Carina attempted to call his name, but her voice was faint after inhaling so much smoke. Instead, she settled for stepping up behind him and tapping him on the shoulder.

As he looked up, Edwin's eyes widened, and he leaped to his feet. "Carina! You're alive!"

Carina nodded weakly. "It would appear so." Her voice sounded like gravel in her throat, making her wince and cough.

Edwin patted her shoulder and handed her a canteen. "Here, have some of this. It isn't completely clean, but we did our best to filter it."

After taking a few sips of the cold river water, Carina let out a grateful sigh of relief. It wasn't nearly enough to quench her thirst, but there were others who needed the water more. Wetting her lips, she handed the water canteen back to Edwin and gave him a tiny smile. "Thank you." Her voice was still raspy, but at least it was a bit louder. "Have you seen Willow or Charlotte?"

Edwin's brow furrowed, his brown eyes reminding Carina of Willow's as they darkened with worry. "No, I'm afraid not. The last I saw of Willow was when we both ran out of the house. We made it as far as the front lane, but I lost sight of her after that."

Carina gulped, anxiety filling every pore of her body. "What of Charlotte?"

Edwin shook his head. "I didn't see her. When I reached the house, you were both gone. I thought the two of you were at the river."

Carina massaged her temples. She had assumed Charlotte ran to the river beside her, but what if it hadn't been her sister at all? Had she run back into the blazing house? With a groan, Carina sank to the ground, burying her face in her hands. She was too parched to cry, but ragged sobs and coughs escaped her chest and leaked from between her fingers. Her mother was gone, and now it seemed as though her sister could be too.

As she continued to mourn, a gentle hand patted her shoulder and draped something heavy over her back. Opening her eyes, Carina wrapped the smoky blanket tighter over her shoulders. "Thank you," she croaked.

Edwin nodded, his blurry face lined with exhaustion and worry. "I'm going to help the rescue team carry victims to the hospital in Marinette. You stay here and rest."

Carina managed a faint nod before falling asleep right on the beach. She drifted in and out of consciousness for a short time before being shaken awake by small hands. "Ma'am?"

Blinking, Carina sat up and rubbed at her eyes.

A young boy stood before her, his brown hair tousled and his blue eyes stark against an ash-streaked face. Holding out a tiny bundle, the boy gave her a gap-toothed smile. "Food came from another town." His small chest puffed out with pride. "I've been put in charge of passin' it out to the folks on the beach. Here's some for you."

Carina thanked the boy and sank her teeth gratefully into the cheese and bread. A pang went through her chest as she recalled the dinner she had shared with her mother and sister. Had it really only been a few hours since they had all sat around the table? What if that had been their last dinner as a family and she hadn't even realized it?

There were fewer people on the beach now. Many had begun boarding wagons that were trundling northward, up what remained of the road.

"Excuse me," Carina called to the nearest group of people migrating toward the wagons. "Where is everyone going?"

A man pointed to the road. "They're heading a few miles north to Marinette. Some of the buildings there were damaged by the fire, but not nearly as many as Peshtigo. We received word that hospitals and temporary shelters are being erected there. Most folks are leaving to try and find a place to stay while they wait for the fire to burn itself out."

"Damaged by the fire, you say?" Carina shook her head in disbelief. "How far did it spread?"

"Nobody knows. All we know is, Marinette is the closest

town that's safe." The man smiled grimly. "Everything else is gone."

Thanking the man, Carina stood and wrapped the blanket around her shoulders. If Charlotte and Willow had survived the night, perhaps they were on a wagon bound for Marinette. Edwin had said that was where the rescue team was bringing the fire victims. Besides, nobody who had remained in town could have survived the horrible blaze. Carina shuddered at the thought. Going to Marinette certainly seemed like her best option. If all else failed, she would regain her strength at one of the shelters and renew her search when the confusion died down.

Finding a space in the nearest wagon proved impossible, so Carina settled for walking alongside the strange caravan. What had once been a dirt road was now a path of charred ash and smoldering embers. Several times, Carina used her bare heel to stomp on patches of orange that still glowed on the ground, taking a small bit of satisfaction from snuffing the embers out despite the pain it caused her.

Eventually, the group of wagons reached Marinette, where the unburned portion of town had been converted into dozens of makeshift hospitals and shelters. After seeing the dire condition of the wounded who awaited treatment outside of one of the hastily constructed infirmaries, Carina decided to forgo getting treatment for her burned heels and instead began looking for the nearest shelter. This proved to be a small house with shuttered windows and a sagging porch. Inside the kitchen of the tiny building, a kind woman gave her a dry dress and instructed her to use one of the two bedrooms to change.

Once dressed in the clean, warm clothes, Carina approached the woman who had helped her and tapped the kind lady on the shoulder. "Excuse me?"

The woman paused from where she was folding wet garments and fixed Carina with tired gray eyes. "Yes, miss?"

"My name is Carina Clarke. I was wondering if you've seen my sister, Charlotte Clarke, or my friend Willow Deeran?"

The woman shook her head, the corners of her mouth turning down. "I'm afraid not, miss. Even if I had, I couldn't have told you. There are far too many people here to keep track of."

Shoulders slumping in defeat, Carina released a breath. "Very well. Thank you for your help, ma'am."

The woman nodded, an idea brightening her gaze. "Perhaps you might check with the doctor that set up a hospital in the Palmer House." She pointed toward the right. "It's the brick building two doors down. I know he delegated where many of the patients went when they first arrived."

"I'll try. Thank you again."

Hope infused Carina with new energy, speeding her steps outside and down the street. It didn't take much for her to locate the building the woman had referred to as the Palmer House. It was a large square structure made of brick, with dark gables that seemed to glare down at her as she pushed through the door and made her way down a long hallway. People of all ages lined the foyer, some leaning against the walls and others sitting on the floor. Nearly all were injured. Carina shivered as several glanced her way, giving her a view of their disfigured faces and blistered hands.

The sooner I leave this place, the better.

The end of the hall opened into a large dining room that had been cleared of all but the long table, which had been covered with a tablecloth. It was at this makeshift examination table that the doctor stood. The poor fellow appeared extremely frazzled as he spouted commands to the man waiting next to him, whom Carina could only guess to be his assistant. Every time someone new sat on or was lifted onto the table by a group of stretcher bearers, the assistant jotted something in a large book that the other people in the room were clamoring to see. Carina elbowed her way through the group clustered around the book and found it was a list of the wounded. When the doctor turned away, she flipped a couple of pages, and her heart jolted painfully in her chest. *Charlotte Clarke.*

She was here.

"Doctor? Doctor, please!" Carina moved into the man's line of vision and waved her arm to draw his attention. "Where has Charlotte Clarke gone?"

The doctor glanced up from the child whose arm he was wrapping with gauze. "If the person you're searching for isn't here, they've most likely been sent to one of the hospitals in Milwaukee for better treatment. We can't treat them all here."

Milwaukee? Carina nearly recoiled in shock. If that was true, her sister was currently heading to a city over a hundred miles away. "Which hospital or hospitals are you sending them to?"

The doctor shook his head. "Any that have space. I'm sorry, but I don't know more than that."

Defeated, Carina trudged through the hallway and back to the shelter. She found an empty spot in the cramped sitting room and lowered herself to the floor, gazing up at the cracked ceiling and blinking back the tears that burned hot behind her eyes.

Oh, Mother, why didn't you leave the house? Where have Charlotte and Willow gone? What do I do now?

As though a voice quietly whispered in her ear, a single word appeared in her mind. *Trust.*

Carina blinked. *How can I trust anyone or anything when my sister is missing?*

There was no response save the sound of her ragged breathing.

Carina pulled her knees tight to her chest as a woman rushed past her and tearfully embraced a young girl. Could there really be a chance she would never hug her sister again?

No. Carina straightened, pushing the terror away. She couldn't give up, not when there was still hope she might someday hold her sister in her arms again. She would find Charlotte, no matter how long it took. And it seemed like Milwaukee was the best place to begin.

CHAPTER 3

"Come in, Mr. Ramhurst." The masculine voice echoed from behind the closed mahogany door.

Detective Oliver Randolph Ramhurst turned the brass knob and entered the office of Allan Pinkerton. After closing the door softly behind him, he hastened across the carpeted floor and took a seat in a leather chair. On the opposite side of the desk he now faced sat the head private investigator of the Pinkerton Agency.

Pinkerton was on the early side of fifty, with a thick beard and piercing blue eyes. His ruddy cheeks gave him a deceptively jovial appearance, though the man was capable of disarming a criminal within seconds. At the moment, Oliver's boss relaxed against his cushioned chair with a cigar in one hand. His black jacket lay across the back, and the black cravat around his neck had been loosened, leaving it dangling atop his gray waistcoat. "Good day, Mr. Ramhurst." Pinkerton straightened and extinguished his cigar in the snuffer on the desk. "I trust you are faring well?"

"Indeed, I am, sir. The Springfield factory investigation went smoothly. I'm glad I was able to prevent that labor strike before it became dangerous. That being said, I was more than happy to leave, especially after three months undercover." Oliver gave an easy laugh.

Pinkerton nodded sagely, leaning back in his chair and steepling his hands across his stomach. "You seem incredibly adept at handling factory cases, Ramhurst. That became my deciding factor in the topic of your next investigation."

Oliver sat forward. "Sir?"

"You will be traveling to Milwaukee, Wisconsin, where you will be conducting an undercover investigation of the Jamieson and Browning Textile Mill. The Pinkerton Agency was hired to investigate after the mill owners noticed a steady stream of wage money disappearing from their company safe. Someone is stealing worker's wages before they can be distributed, and the company employees are beginning to get restless after several months without full pay. The mill owners are convinced that the thief is someone working in the mill, as nobody else would know where the pay envelopes are kept. This is where you come in, Ramhurst. You will be joining the mill as an employee in the hope that you will be able to gather enough evidence to bring the thief to justice."

Oliver tapped his finger on his knee, his mind whirling. "When do I depart?"

Pinkerton chuckled. "I like your enthusiasm, Ramhurst. You will depart from the Chicago station in two days, leaving at nine o'clock sharp and arriving sometime around noon. You'll have the rest of the day to find accommodations and suitable work clothing. You will report at the mill at six-thirty the next morning." Pulling a piece of paper from the top desk drawer, he handed it to Oliver. "This map details the directions to the mill, along with a sketch of the interior. You'd be wise to memorize all the routes a person could take to and from the office where the wages are kept."

After studying the map for a moment, Oliver folded it with a decisive nod. "Is there anything else I should know before I make preparations for travel?"

"No. I've gone over all the information I was given. As always, report the minute you have new information."

Oliver rose. "Yes, sir."

Standing, Pinkerton rounded the desk and clapped him on the back. "Good man. Now, go and collect your things. I want this thief facing a judge before the week is out."

~

*A*t the edge of the snowy boardwalk outside the agency, Oliver stopped to remove a mint from the tin in his coat pocket and popped it into his mouth. As the bittersweet scent of peppermint filled his nostrils, carriages and people raced to and fro, some in fine suits and others in little more than rags. It was rather remarkable considering that a fire had burned down a large portion of the city only a year ago. There were still hundreds of people without homes.

After walking down the street for several blocks, Oliver turned right and entered the lane where his family's residence stood. While it was considered a mansion by most people's standards, the building was rather humble in comparison to the opulent homes that surrounded it. Clean white brick made up the exterior walls, and black shingle covered the roof. Oliver's mouth turned up in a wry grin. Come to think of it, the only pop of color in the whole place were the green fir boughs and red silk ribbons that decorated the front porch in preparation for Christmas. His mother had most likely spent hours ensuring they were positioned exactly right so as to impress the many guests that called upon her over the winter season.

Oliver passed through the iron gates and made his way up the cobblestone drive and onto the porch. Stepping inside, he found himself face to face with the family butler. "Hello, Jack."

"Hello, sir. I apologize. Had I known you were coming, I would have opened the door for you." Disgruntlement was evident on the man's wrinkled face.

"No need to apologize. I'm more than willing to open the door for myself every now and then." Oliver slid the coat from his shoulders and handed it, along with his hat, to the butler. "That being said, I do need you to pack my portmanteau. A few plain sets of clothes and my pair of work boots should do the trick."

The butler raised a brow. "Preparing for another case, are you?"

Oliver grinned, adjusting his cravat. "Yes. Is my mother nearby?"

"She's in the parlor, sir."

"Thank you, Jack." After taking a moment to wipe his shoes upon the rug lest his mother scold him for tracking snow into the house, Oliver strode through the foyer and entered the parlor.

Seated upon the floral chaise to the left of the room, his mother was fully absorbed in her newest sewing project. She was the picture of elegance in a trim, lacey day dress and shawl. Her black hair, similar in color to Oliver's, was braided and gathered at the back in the latest fashion. While lines had begun creeping around her eyes and mouth, her face retained a youthful glow. She was the perfect image of a lady. It was to be expected, for society accepted nothing less from the wife of a judge.

Upon seeing Oliver, his mother set aside her sewing and placed her hands demurely in her lap. "Oh, Oliver, it is so good to see you. What brings you home at such an early hour? Are you unwell? Come, sit with me."

Oliver accepted the invitation, though he chose to lower himself onto the worn chair next to her rather than sit on her spotless floral couch. "I am well, Mother. I have been sent home early to prepare for my next assignment. I depart for Milwaukee in two days."

Mother deflated slightly, reaching for the handkerchief on the tabletop next to her. With a mournful sigh, she dabbed at her temples. "Oh, Oliver, I do wish you would choose a different occupation. This detective business of yours makes me worry so."

"I know, Mother. I promise I'll be careful." Oliver spoke soothingly, leaning over to pat her pale hand. "I'll be home before you know it."

His mother released another long breath. "So I hope. Your father expects you to join him at several upcoming society events, you know."

Oliver grimaced. "Two was more than enough for my liking, Mother. Besides, you and I both know that Father only wants me join to him so I can select what he deems a suitable wife. He all but shoved me at the visiting heiress during the last ball I attended. The poor girl was already being swamped by males and didn't need me to add to the fray."

Mother sniffed, folding her handkerchief into a neat square. "As well he should have. You're getting to the age where you should be settling down to start a family, Oliver. Twenty-eight years old is a perfectly respectable age to get married. How do you expect to take over for your father if you have no family and no money with which to do so?"

Oliver stood. "I'll marry when I find the proper woman. I'll not join in a lifelong union just to increase the family coffers."

His mother studied him for a moment before inclining her

head resignedly. "As you wish. Your father only wants to see you happy and settled, you know."

Though Oliver murmured an agreement, his heart pounded painfully in his chest. If his father wanted him to be happy, then why did he constantly voice his displeasure about Oliver's choice of occupation? *Why has he never told me he's proud of me?*

Perhaps this time would be different. After all, his previous cases had focused on assisting small groups of people, not an entire factory. Even his case in Springfield had been for the benefit of the factory owner and not the workers themselves. Maybe this time, his father would finally see that his work was about more than simply catching criminals. If he was successful at this assignment, dozens of people would regain their wages, money they needed to feed their families and keep a roof over their heads.

Oliver smiled as the image of the judge congratulating him filled his head. *Yes.* This job was just what he needed. All he had to do was catch a thief, and that meant getting to Milwaukee as soon as possible.

Two days later

Oliver stepped off the train platform and onto the streets of Milwaukee with his portmanteau in hand. His parents had done the proper thing and accompanied him to the Chicago station to bid him farewell. While his mother had given him a tremulous smile and a flutter of her pristine handkerchief, his father had remained stone-faced and silent. His dour expression remained in the back of Oliver's mind as he clutched his heavy suitcase tighter and began searching for a streetcar that would take him into the heart of the city. Spotting one that was slowing to a stop farther down the road, he trotted to it and hopped aboard.

After handing the conductor the proper amount of change, Oliver slid into one of the wooden seats near the front of the car and deposited his luggage near his feet, sighing in relief as the weight left his arm. "What did Jack put in here? Half my wardrobe?" he murmured in amusement, tapping the dusty leather with one foot. It certainly felt like it.

As the streetcar rolled slowly into motion, Oliver took the opportunity to study the city he would be calling home for the foreseeable future. Milwaukee was as full of life as Chicago, with vendors hawking wares and horses pulling carriages along crowded lanes. A variety of smells filled the air, from the warm pretzels a man sold from a cart to the small piles of manure left behind by carriage horses. Tall warehouses and factories rose behind a variety of storefronts, spewing smoke high into the air. Behind the buildings lay the expansive Lake Michigan, one of the main methods of transportation for most of the industries in Milwaukee. During the summer months, steamers would stock up on steel, coal, and other goods before carrying them to other cities.

As he tilted his head to gaze out the window at yet another towering building, Oliver shifted and nearly fell back onto the person next to him. Turning, he murmured a quick apology, the words dying on his lips when he caught sight of his bench mate.

Next to him sat a young woman, her vibrant red hair pulled back in a work-ready bun, with a few curls springing loose to dangle around her face. Blue eyes regarded him quizzically from behind a pair of round spectacles with thin silver rims. Though simple in design, the woman's gingham work dress was clean and neatly pressed, and a deep-green capelet covered her shoulders. What was she doing on a streetcar by herself?

Returning from an errand, if the basket by her side was any indication.

"Pardon me, miss. I didn't mean to bump into you." Oliver offered an apologetic smile.

The woman favored him with a quick nod. "No harm done." Her voice was quiet with a slightly raspy quality that reminded Oliver of leaves brushing against the ground.

Oliver opened his mouth to ask her name, but the streetcar began to slow.

The woman glanced out the window, the corners of her mouth turning up in a smile. "If you'll excuse me, sir, this is my stop." With that, she shook out her dress, collected her basket, and leaped deftly to the sidewalk.

As she began walking away, Oliver realized it was also the stop where he had meant to disembark. Thanking the driver, he snatched his bulky suitcase from the floor and hurried from the streetcar, nearly losing his wool derby in the process.

Upon catching up with the young woman, he tipped the hat in her direction. "Pardon for the intrusion, but do you know of any boardinghouses in this area?"

The woman studied his fine attire, her brow raising. "Sir, I think you're on the wrong side of the city. Apartments for the business class can be found back the way you came. We passed them not long ago."

Oliver shook his head. "No, I'm quite certain I'm in the right place."

The woman gazed at him for a moment before shrugging delicate shoulders. "As you wish. The most reputable men's establishment I know of is up this street a block. If you continue walking straight, you should eventually see a sign for Lucy's boardinghouse."

Oliver thanked her and made to leave. Pausing after just a few feet, he turned back to the woman. "You know, miss, you really shouldn't be traveling these streets alone. It's dangerous for a young woman such as yourself."

The lady bristled as though thoroughly insulted. "Sir, I am fully capable of handling any danger that comes my way. Between the two of us, I believe it is I who knows these streets, not a newcomer in a fancy suit. With that said, I bid you farewell." Huffing, she gathered her skirts and turned the corner onto a side street.

Oliver blinked. How curious. With a shrug, he continued down the sidewalk. Women were a mystery he had never quite been able to solve.

∾

*A*fter securing a room at the boardinghouse, Oliver ventured out to locate a few more pairs of clothing that would be suitable for working in a mill. It wasn't long before he found several pairs of trousers, simple cotton shirts, and a flat cap to top the ensemble off. He paid for his selections, gathered the items into a paper bag, and headed back toward his temporary home. Just before reaching the boarding-house, he paused at a nearby telegraph office to send Pinkerton a telegram, confirming that he was prepared to begin work on the morrow.

With all his duties for the day accomplished, Oliver wound his way back to the boardinghouse. There he sat down at the table for supper, which Lucy had informed him began promptly at eight each evening. He was soon joined by a cluster of men, each clearly worn out from a hard day of work. They regarded him curiously as they slid into chairs around the table. Oliver had been quick to change into his new clothes before dinner, as they would be more likely to stare if he appeared in a full suit and tie. Still, the arrival of a newcomer was enough to spark everyone's notice, and Oliver found himself being nudged in the side as he began eating.

"So where do you hail from, stranger?" the man next to him asked. He seemed friendly enough, with dark brown hair and a dimpled grin.

Oliver took a moment to swallow before answering. "I'm from Chicago,"

The young man whistled. "Illinois, eh? Got some folks down that way myself. They're still working on rebuilding the house since it burned down with everything else in that fool fire." Holding out a hand, he waited until Oliver gave it a firm shake. "My name's Timothy Baker. My companions sitting around you are Joseph, Wallace, Frank, Reuben, and Arlo."

Each man waved in turn, which Oliver returned with a nod of acknowledgment. "Nice to meet you all. I'm Oliver... Bricht." It would take time to adjust to the false surname, but it was important for him to do so. Having his name connected to the powerful Judge Ramhurst of Chicago could ruin his chances of uncovering the factory thief.

"What brings you to Milwaukee, Oliver?" Lucy bustled into the dining room, plopping a plate of sliced turkey onto the table. She was a pleasant older woman, with curly gray hair that fluffed around her face like a fuzzy halo. Oliver had instantly decided he liked the woman when she welcomed him into her boardinghouse with a beaming smile and a free molasses cookie.

"I came here looking for work," Oliver explained. "I plan on beginning my job as a picker at the Jamieson and Browning Textile Mill tomorrow."

Timothy clapped Oliver on the back, nearly making him spit out his bite of diced potatoes. "You're in luck, chap, because I work there as well. I'll show you the ropes tomorrow." He raised a brow. "Would you be up for meeting me at six o'clock in the morning, out on the porch? We can walk there together."

Works there as well? This fellow could be a fine source of information. Oliver studied the young man for a moment before inclining his head. "That'll do just fine."

"Good. Get some rest tonight. You're going to have a long day's work ahead of you. Lucy serves breakfast and hands out paper sack lunches at a quarter to five."

Oliver smiled, finishing the last of his dinner. "All right. I'll see you tomorrow, friend."

If only Timothy knew his true reason for being there. What would he think of Oliver then?

CHAPTER 4

*T*he next morning, Oliver rose before dawn to dress and study the map of the mill. It took him several yawns and a good scrub of his eyes to fully awaken his brain, but once he did, he was able to memorize the mill's layout fairly quickly. With that accomplished, he slid his boots on and clomped down the stairs.

Pots clanked as he moved into the dining room, and the smell of bacon, griddle cakes, and eggs wafted through the air, creating a tantalizing scent that even the most stubborn souls wouldn't be able to resist. Oliver took a seat and waited with the other men while Lucy laid breakfast out on the table. Once she stepped back, he wasted no time in piling food onto his plate and wolfing it down. Having satisfied his appetite, he stacked his dirty dishes and moved quickly toward the door.

"Oliver, wait!" a voice called from behind him. Lucy bustled up and handed him a paper sack with a smile. "Don't forget your lunch. You won't want to go hungry after working all morning."

Oliver accepted the sack and tipped his hat. "Thank you, Lucy. I'll see you this evening."

Lucy wiped her forehead with a washcloth, blowing a lone curl from the side of her mouth. "Certainly. I'll be in the kitchen, same as always."

After waving in farewell, Oliver stepped out into the indigo-colored dawn and closed the door behind him. He took a deep breath of the crisp morning air as it swirled around him, smiling in amusement when his exhale created a puff of white fog.

"So you kept up with the hustle and bustle this morning, did you?"

Oliver jumped, turning toward the source of the voice. "Timothy! And here I thought I was faster than you."

Timothy stepped forward and clapped Oliver on the shoulder. A flat cap similar in style to Oliver's concealed the man's tousled brown hair, and a pair of worn suspenders peeked from underneath his thick jacket. "Trying to beat the master at his craft, are you? Another time, perhaps." Hopping down the steps, he motioned for Oliver to follow.

As Oliver caught up and began walking beside Timothy, the man cast a side glance at him. "I have to admit, you chose a pretty poor time to start working here, my friend. Especially if you have someone back home to support."

"And why is that?" Oliver feigned curiosity.

"There's been a thief at the mill for the past few months." Timothy blew on his hands. "Whoever it is has been taking our wages. We've been getting less and less of our normal monthly pay. I think there'll be a strike soon if they don't find the culprit. They've tried to keep outsiders from getting in, but the thefts haven't ceased."

Oliver frowned, pretending to give the manner some thought. "In that case, I would guess the thief is someone working from within the mill. Someone who would know where the wages are kept."

Timothy nodded. "So the gossip vine thinks as well. The

workers on the first floor think the thief is someone from the second floor, and the workers on the second floor think the thief is someone from the first floor. It's caused division between us all."

"Who do you think did it?" Oliver asked, this time in genuine interest.

"Well, the opening room and the picker room are on the first floor of the mill. If one of us were the thief, I think it would be obvious because we don't have much of a reason to be wandering around upstairs. That's why I believe it must be someone from the second floor. The wages are kept up there, you know. It would be easy for a worker to access the office when nobody else was looking."

Oliver hummed and tapped his hand against his leg, his brain whirling with the new information. He knew where the wages were kept, but the division between the workers was something new. "What does the second floor have to say?"

Timothy shrugged. "I couldn't tell you. True to what I just said, we don't interact with them much. The only time we meet is over lunch break, and I'm not one to argue about the identity of a thief. I just want to see whoever it is caught so I can start sending my wages back home to my parents. They need it to afford repairs on the house."

Before Oliver could question Timothy further, they arrived at the gate to the mill. After giving their names to the guard, they crossed into the courtyard and made their way toward the large building at the center of the cobblestone clearing.

"There didn't used to be such high security." Timothy gestured toward the gate they had walked through. "After the thefts continued for several weeks, however, Mr. Browning decided to hire guards in the hopes that anyone masquerading as an employee would be caught. It hasn't done us a whole lot of good, unfortunately. The money is still disappearing, and employees are still getting angry."

Oliver made a sympathetic noise, though his attention focused on the building they were entering. The mill loomed over them, cold and stately, its brick walls stained with dirt and grime. The snow on its eaves gave it the look of a gingerbread house, though there would be no candy wonderland inside. A smokestack protruded from the back of the building, spewing smoke that spiraled up into the air and stained the sky gray. The place was a strange mixture of ugly and beautiful.

As they entered the interior of the massive building, deafening noise filled the air. Men shouted to one another as they cut open large bales of cotton and sent them into a machine, where the cotton was torn apart and sucked into a large tube that ran across the ceiling. Large clumps of lint and fiber drifted through the air, causing Oliver to sneeze as Timothy motioned him into the next room. Here it was slightly quieter. Cotton dropped from a chute in the ceiling and onto a large table, where workers plucked debris from the mounds of white fuzz and pulled it through metal racks to form rough sheets that almost resembled blankets.

"Once the pickers are done making the cotton into sheets, they send it off to the card hands. From there, the cotton is twisted into yarn and woven into cloth. It's a long process, with dozens of workers at each station." Timothy explained over the sound of the men working. "For you and me, however, this is the end of the road. Come on, let's get started on this next load." Marching over to the table, he waited until Oliver joined him and then began picking refuse from the cotton.

Rolling up his sleeves, Oliver took a deep breath. He had a feeling that he was about to regret taking on this case.

∾

*B*y the time lunch break rolled around, Oliver was all too glad to leave the picker room. The floating lint made him sneeze constantly, and his hands were red and sore from maneuvering the scratchy cotton for hours. As he took up the sack lunch he had left at the back of the room during the start of the shift, he reviewed his mental map of the mill. Lunch break would be a prime hour for the thief to steal wages. Everyone was off duty and wandering about unsupervised, making it easy for someone to slip in and out of the office unnoticed.

Oliver slid from the room with a promise to Timothy that he would return shortly and strode through first the first floor of the factory. Pinkerton's maps had showed that each room was devoted to a different area of production. From the picker house, the cotton went through a variety of carding machines and drawing frames that spun it into thin strands of thread. Then the thread went on to rooms of spinning and spooling frames, where it was twisted and spun into single strands of yarn. As Oliver passed through each room, he couldn't help but marvel at the machines. While currently still, the spinning frames contained dozens of wooden bobbins that could spin thread at incredible speeds.

After locating a staircase in the central room, Oliver entered the upper level of the factory. Here was the area for cloth production, where noisy power looms wove thread into cloth of all sorts. While the machines were certainly interesting, it was the back of the second floor that held his attention, for that was where the office lay.

Oliver moved quickly through the rooms until a scuffling noise sounded nearby, leading him to duck behind one of the looms. The office door lay within sight, making this area an excellent hiding place for a thief. Indeed, a shadowy figure crept along the outskirts of the room, moving directly toward the loom where Oliver was concealed.

Gathering his courage, Oliver leaped from his hiding spot and tackled the thief, bringing them both to the floor. "Aha! Wait...it's you?"

Lying underneath him with a growing expression of bewilderment and anger on her face was the woman from the railcar.

Hopping off her, Oliver folded his arms across his chest and fixed her with what was meant to be an intimidating stare. "What are you doing outside the wage office at this hour? Shouldn't you be at lunch?"

The young woman stood and brushed lint from her skirt, her spectacles hanging from one ear and irritation plain on her face. "I, good sir, was attempting to fetch my friend's birthday present from where I left it underneath one of my looms. I work in this room and therefore have every right to be here. If anything, I should be asking what *you* are doing here."

A brightly colored package lying near Oliver's feet, now squashed, drew his notice. Guilt washed over him. "Ah. I believe I owe you another apology, miss." Holding out his hand, he gave her his most charming smile. "Allow me to introduce myself. Oliver Bricht, at your service."

The woman pursed her lips as she stared at his hand, keeping her own planted firmly on her hips. "Carina Clarke. You still haven't answered my question, Mr. Bricht. What are you doing up here during the lunch hour?"

Oliver groaned internally. This woman was going to be a heap of trouble.

~

*N*ot only had this Bricht fellow smashed Ella's birthday gift, but he also had the audacity to demand to know why Carina was in her own workspace. Why, it was enough to make her blood boil! Readjusting her spectacles so she could look him clean in the eye, Carina waited for the man to give her his excuse. What was a rich fellow like him doing in a textile mill, anyway? Only a day ago, she had seen him step off the railcar in a finely tailored suit. Even now, dressed in a cotton shirt and trousers, his soft hands and elegant stature labeled him as someone unaccustomed to hard labor.

The man seemed to consider his words for a moment before responding. "I heard this morning that there was a lot of theft occurring at the mill. I figured the only way to calm everyone down would be to catch the thief in action. That way, we can all get our full wages."

Carina narrowed her eyes, mentally berating her foolish spectacles for making her look less intimidating. The doctor had told her she only needed to wear them until the aftereffects of the smoke wore off, but a year had gone by and she was still half blind without them. "Those are bold words coming from someone who just began work today."

Mr. Bricht held up his hands in a silent plea. Before he could say more, however, the bell in the courtyard clanged. Lunch hour had ended, and voices began echoing through the building as workers returned to their stations.

Carina crossed her arms over her chest. "I believe you ought to be returning to your station, Mr. Bricht, lest your supervisor reprimand you for being tardy."

Mr. Bricht muttered something under his breath, his gray eyes rising to meet hers a moment later. "So it would seem. Good day, Miss Clarke."

Carina gave him a stiff nod as she bent to collect Ella's

misshapen birthday gift. "Good day, Mr. Bricht. Do look before you tackle unsuspecting women next time."

As the strange man waved a hand in farewell and presented her with another brilliant smile, Carina began formulating a plan. This Mr. Bricht was concealing something, and she was going to discover what it was. There would be no hiding behind smiles or charms once she was on the trail.

~

"*W*here were you during lunch?" Carina's friend Ella approached the looms next to the ones Carina supervised. They operated five of the large, noisy machines each. "It was cold, and I was lonely, you know."

Elizabeth Weston was a thin, frail girl who had never fully recovered from a childhood illness. Her blond hair was tied back with a faded ribbon, and her brown eyes reminded Carina of a sad puppy dog. Despite the girl's sallow appearance, however, she was very bright, and Carina had become fast friends with her after moving to Milwaukee.

"I'm sorry, Ella." Carina had to lean close to the girl for her voice to carry over the sound of the looms. "I was trying to get something for you and ran into a strange man. He very nearly ruined what I was attempting to find." She rolled her shoulders back. "Luckily, I did manage to salvage it." Presenting the gift to her friend, she smiled. "Happy birthday, Ella."

The girl squealed as she took the lumpy package. Peeling back the paper, she gasped at the blue linen dress Carina had saved for months to get for her. Within the dress was a crushed chocolate chip cookie wrapped in wax paper.

"I'm sorry for the condition of the gift." Carina studied the rumpled fabric with a frown. "It was neatly folded this morning, I assure you."

Ella laughed. "Oh, Carina, no harm done. This is positively

splendid. Just look at these wonderful lace flowers along the collar! It's absolutely beautiful. Thank you."

As their rather strict supervisor, Mrs. Farley, entered the room, Ella quickly tucked the package away. Carina and Ella began a detailed inspection of their looms, though they occasionally cast a smile each other's way. Carina pushed aside her thoughts of Mr. Oliver Bricht and his strange behavior for the time being. Today was Ella's day, and she wouldn't let sour thoughts of the imposter ruin it.

CHAPTER 5

$\mathscr{I}$t was dark by the time Carina finally started for home. While she had finished work with the rest of the mill employees at six-thirty, she had remained out a bit later than usual. The catalyst for her nighttime jaunt was the envelope she clutched in one hand, the paper nearly folding in her tight grip. Excitement mingled with doubt. The paper could contain a hint to her sister's whereabouts...or another dead end. Either way, she would toughen up and take the news gracefully. It wouldn't be the first time she had been disappointed by false leads.

After what felt like hours but in reality was only a few minutes, Carina arrived at her boardinghouse. She rushed through the foyer and past her proprietress, Mrs. Fields, with the briefest of greetings.

Carina closed the door to her room and leaned back against the solid wood, turning the envelope around. Heart beating in her chest, she ripped open the letter and viewed the contents. A sigh escaped her at the sight of yet another *we're sorry* at the top of the page.

"No," she whispered dejectedly. And yet, no matter how she

wished it wasn't true, there was no denying the typed words. It seemed as though her sister would remain missing for at least another week...or however long it took for the next response to arrive.

Carina set the letter on the chest of drawers beside her bed, trudged down the stairs, and wandered into the kitchen, where she met Mrs. Fields's raised brow with a soft laugh. "Sorry, Mrs. Fields. I thought I had exciting news, but it turned out to be nothing of import."

Mrs. Fields chuckled and waved a spatula at Carina. "No harm done. In the future, a warning would be nice, though. I very nearly jumped out of my skin when you came running through like that."

Carina let out a full laugh. "You have my word, Mrs. Fields. How was your day?"

"Oh, fine enough, dear. Come and sit at the table, now. Dinner's nearly ready."

After eating a hearty meal with the thirteen other boarders, Carina excused herself and retired to her bedroom. There she changed into her winter nightgown and flopped ungracefully onto her cot. She reached into the chest beside her bed, pulled out the hospital letters, and fanned them out on the bed. Five rejections. Five false leads since she had moved to Milwaukee a year ago. Yet there were still so many doctors in the city Carina had yet to visit. With luck, one of them would have records of her sister. Otherwise, Carina could very well be chasing false hope.

"The doctor can't have been wrong," she whispered to bolster herself. He had been the one to tell her that her sister was most likely transferred to Milwaukee for better care. Had she been foolish to trust his word?

Carina returned the letters to the chest and rolled onto her back, lacing her hands across her chest. Her thoughts turned to the odd behavior Mr. Bricht had displayed earlier that day.

Even if he had the best of intentions, no new employee should have been wandering around the building during the lunch hour. Carina frowned. Especially when he had been walking around the floor he didn't work on.

Mr. Bricht's appearance made it clear he didn't come from a life of labor. With that in mind, what was he doing at a textile mill? Even if he *was* in dire straits, there was surely a better job he could have chosen. Yet Mr. Bricht took up work at a mill that was clearly having trouble with robbery. The whole thing struck Carina as being very odd. However, her mother had always told her to give people grace until they were proven guilty. So Carina would... though that certainly didn't mean she wouldn't try and discover what the man was hiding.

～

*T*he next morning, Carina dressed swiftly and was out the door at a quarter to six. Turning the corner onto the main road, she narrowly avoided groaning aloud at the sight of none other than Mr. Bricht, who was striding toward her with another young man following in his wake. Though she quickly turned her back on the duo, the sound of her name being called informed Carina her traitorous red hair had given her away.

"Miss Clarke! Do wait up!"

She would simply have to devise an alternate route to the mill.

Though she was tempted to ignore the irritating man, Carina pasted a smile on her face and spun to face him. "Good day, Mr. Bricht."

"Good day. How do you fare? For a moment there, I thought you were going to run straight past us." Mr. Bricht fell into step beside her. The gleam in his eye told Carina he knew she had been trying to ignore him.

"Splendid. Or I was doing well, before you appeared," she mumbled. "Who is your friend?"

Mr. Bricht smiled, crinkles forming around his eyes. "I heard that." He turned to his brown-haired companion. "This fine fellow is Timothy Baker. He works in the picker house alongside me. He's been showing me the ropes, so to speak."

Carina acknowledged the man with a nod, which he returned with a shy smile. At least all men weren't prone to tackling a lady on sight.

As they walked along, Mr. Baker and Mr. Bricht fell into an easy conversation, leaving Carina to further study the enigma of a man. Truly, if he hadn't insulted her so, she might have said Mr. Bricht cut a fine figure. He stood a good six inches above her five-foot-three, with wavy black hair that peeked out from underneath the front of his cap. His skin was surprisingly tan considering the season, with gray eyes that warmed as he laughed at something Mr. Baker said. Yes, it truly was a shame that he was so inconsiderate.

She glanced over again to find the man staring back at her with an expectant expression. Wait... had he asked her a question? "I'm sorry. Might you repeat your question?"

"I asked what the top floor thinks of the robberies." Mr. Bricht tilted his head slightly like a curious dog. "Timothy works on the bottom floor, so he already informed me of their opinion."

Carina adjusted the scarf around her shoulders. "The workers on the top floor are adamant the thief is someone from the lower floor. They believe the top floor is too busy for someone to sneak away and steal money. In their defense, our supervisor is incredibly strict. It would take nothing short of a miracle for someone to get past her."

Mr. Bricht's eyes narrowed by a fraction. "You do not agree with them?"

"I prefer to make my own conclusions, free of what the rumors may be."

Both men nodded at her declaration. "A wise decision, miss," Mr. Baker agreed. "You remind me of my younger sister, Emmy. She's the same way, always trying to be fair to everyone."

As Carina smiled her thanks, an idea sprang into her head. If Mr. Bricht was trying to catch the thief, who was to say she couldn't as well? A thrill ran through her. Imagine, impersonating a detective! She nearly laughed aloud at the thought.

"You have a lovely smile, Miss Clarke. It's a shame you don't show it more often."

Carina glanced up to see Mr. Bricht staring at her, his eyes sparkling with mirth. If only he knew what she was smiling about. She gave another soft laugh. Oh, this would be most fun.

It would also keep her mind off the depressing matter of her sister.

~

*W*hen lunch break rolled around once more, Carina took her time packing up her things. As each person left the room, she scrutinized them, making a mental catalog of what she knew about them. Upon first glance, she couldn't identify anyone she suspected of thievery. Then again, the culprit was far too clever to be so obvious. As Carina considered whether it was worth hiding behind her loom to see if someone would sneak in during lunch, a voice interrupted her thoughts.

"Carina, did you hear a word of what I just said?" Ella planted her hands on her slim hips.

Carina offered her friend an apologetic grin. "I'm afraid not. Care to repeat it? I'm listening."

Ella laughed, her face relaxing. "Oh, never mind. Are you coming?"

Carina took one last look around the room, nibbling on her lower lip. "Yes, I suppose so."

She followed Ella down the steps, and they emerged into the courtyard. Workers milled about on the snow-covered ground, eating and conversing in groups of two and three. Ella and Carina wasted no time in making for their favorite spot under one of the large oak trees that covered the property. While it normally possessed huge leaves that could shade one from the sun, it was currently dry and barren. Still, it made a good resting spot, and Carina and Ella carefully brushed the snow from the trunk before taking a seat.

Looking around the clearing as she ate her ham sandwich, Carina silently listed every person she knew. Everyone seemed present and accounted for...everyone except for Mr. Bricht, that was. Spotting Mr. Baker standing with a group of men near the front of the building, Carina excused herself from Ella and walked over to him. "Mr. Baker? Sir?"

The young man turned, the tips of his ears reddening when he saw her. "Oh, hello, Miss Clarke. What can I do for you?"

"I was wondering if you knew where Mr. Bricht has gone off to."

Mr. Baker frowned and glanced around the clearing. "Well, I'll be. He *is* gone! Oliver was standing right next to me only a second ago. Perhaps he went back inside to look for something? I don't believe he was carrying his lunch when we walked outside. He might have left it in the picker room."

A triumphant smile momentarily creased Carina's face. So... the man was supposedly investigating again, was he? "Thank you, Mr. Baker. I'll go and find him. I have something to give to him."

Mr. Baker nodded and waved as Carina turned away. Moving at a fast clip, she advanced through the mill door and up the steps. Once at the top, she paused and listened for any signs of movement. The only sound was two male voices, and coming from the office, no less! Carina crept through the room, then paused just outside the door.

"I cannot say how happy I am to have you working on this case," Mr. Browning, the mill owner, was saying.

Carina frowned. A case?

"The theft has been steadily increasing, and when even our guards failed to stop the ruffian, I knew I had to take drastic measures. Things haven't been this bad since Jamieson's passing all those years ago. The Pinkerton Agency is said to be the best, so I do hope you will be able to catch this scoundrel before any more employees walk out the door."

Mr. Bricht's deep voice resonated from within the room. "I will do my best, sir."

A quiet gasp escaped Carina, and she clapped her hands over her mouth. A Pinkerton detective? No wonder the man had been so finely dressed. He wasn't a common laborer at all!

"The only thing I ask is that you do not single me out for any reason," Mr. Bricht said. "I cannot allow the employees to cast any suspicion on me if I am to earn their trust."

Hmm. So Mr. Bricht wanted to get closer to the employees, did he? No wonder he had been trying to make conversation with her earlier.

"You have my word, Mr. Bricht. I do believe that concludes our meeting. You have my permission to examine the office so long as you do not remove anything. There are thirty minutes till the end of lunch break."

The sound of footsteps made Carina dive behind the nearest loom. She waited until Mr. Browning had left before standing and making her way to the office door. Inside, Mr. Bricht was bent over the office desk with his back to her, examining the papers spread across the top.

Carina folded her arms across her chest. "I don't believe it. A detective, and a Pinkerton at that. Why didn't you simply tell me that before? It would explain a lot of your oddities."

Mr. Bricht jumped and whirled around. "Miss Clarke! What are you—wait, what did you just say?" His gaze sharpened. "You overheard my conversation? What were you doing, snooping around like that?"

Carina huffed. "For your information, I was trying to find out why *you* were snooping. You weren't at lunch, so I knew you must have been looking around. I wanted to know why a supposed employee was investigating the building. Now that I know you're a detective, it makes far more sense."

"Listen, Miss Clarke. You seem a smart woman, so I appeal to your better sense when I ask you not to reveal my identity. Secrecy is extremely important to the success of this case." Mr. Bricht spread a hand across his chest. "If word of my identity as a detective gets out, the thief will go free. Therefore, it is imperative that I remain unnoticed."

An idea began to bloom. *Charlotte.* Carina smiled. "Very well, Mr. Bricht. I will keep your secret, on one condition." She set her hands on her hips. "You must allow me to assist you in your investigation."

CHAPTER 6

*T*here were very few times in Oliver's life when he could confess to being really and truly surprised, and now was looking to be one of them. He blinked a few times before words finally arrived at his lips. "I beg your pardon?"

Miss Clarke sighed and adjusted her spectacles, squinting as she stared at him. Because she was irritated with him? She was rather adorable, really.

"Don't smirk at me, sir! You heard me. I wish to become a part of your investigation." Miss Clarke straightened her back.

Oliver leaned back on the desk, crossing his arms in front of his chest. "Why?"

Miss Clarke blinked. "Why?"

"Yes, do tell why you wish to involve yourself in extreme danger, danger that most people would go to great lengths to avoid. This is no children's game, Miss Clarke. Things could become ugly if the thief decides to resort to violence."

Miss Clarke lifted her chin, her blue eyes glinting with indignation. "I am well aware of the dangers associated with such work, Mr. Bricht. I can provide you with information that's just as good as any other detective. I work on the top floor and know most of the employees fairly well. As such, I can get information from them while you collect information from the bottom floor."

Oliver raised a brow. "You aren't wrong, but you still haven't answered my question. Why would you help me? It would be foolish of me to assume that you're doing it because you like me."

The woman seemed to wilt a bit. "I suppose it's because I need my full wages." She let out a delicate sniff. "Perhaps I also need a bit of help with a problem of my own."

Oliver frowned. "What kind of problem?"

Before Miss Clarke could respond, the distant sound of the bell ringing made them both glance toward the door.

"That is something we can discuss at a later time. So, Mr. Bricht, what will it be?"

"Very well, Miss Clarke. You may assist me at a minimal level." He held up a hand to block her protest. "Having you gather information is more than enough danger for my conscience to handle. I can't watch you and work on the investigation simultaneously. Now, if you discover anything of interest, report it to me during lunch or at the end of your shift. I'll keep you updated with new information as well."

Miss Clarke nodded resignedly. "Very well. I look forward to catching a thief, Mr. Bricht." She held out a hand, which Oliver shook. Grinning, she turned in a swish of skirts and fairly sashayed to the office door.

"I pity the man who marries you," Oliver muttered under his breath.

Miss Clarke swiveled back to face him with a glare that could have melted metal. "At least I'll have someone willing to marry me. With your personality, I doubt you'll ever be able to say the same."

Oliver sighed as she left the room. He was going to have to

ask Lucy for a very strong cup of coffee when he was finished with work.

∽

"Welcome back. Where were you off to during lunch?" Timothy asked as Oliver returned to his spot at the cotton-picking table. "Miss Clarke was looking for you, and I had half a mind to join her. It's dangerous to wander around the mill alone, you know. People could suspect you. If someone did report you, Browning would have you out of here in two winks."

Oliver gave his new friend an easy smile. "Calm yourself, Timothy. Browning himself requested to see me over lunch. I suppose he wanted to ensure that he had hired an honest employee. Miss Clarke located me shortly after, and we had a quick chat."

Timothy's frown eased at Oliver's words, and he shrugged. "I suppose it's wise of him to ensure that his employees are of good moral standards. You don't suppose he's going to bring us all in one at a time and interview us, do you?"

Oliver shook his head. "I don't imagine so. That would take an incredibly long time. Besides, it could cause workers to walk off the job if they thought their overseer suspected them of theft." However, that didn't mean Oliver wouldn't speak with everyone. The most important thing during his subtle interviewing would be keeping the workers from becoming suspicious. If the thief got so much as an inkling that Oliver was trying to catch him, he would go into hiding, leaving Oliver back where he began.

"What did Miss Clarke want to give you?" Timothy refocused on the cotton in his hands.

Oliver recalled the spunky woman's reaction to finding him in the office. "A piece of her mind. She isn't exactly fond of me."

Timothy raised a brow. "What did you do to make her dislike you? She was perfectly civil when I spoke to her. As a matter of fact, I thought she was very nice."

A grin teased Oliver's lips. "I haven't the faintest clue. I suppose her dislike may have begun during our first meeting, when I almost fell over her. That or the fact that when I mentioned she shouldn't have been traveling alone, she became quite irritated and stormed off."

Timothy pressed a hand to his forehead. "You're a fool, Bricht. Didn't anyone ever tell you to mind a woman's feelings? They're sensitive creatures, you know. Why, my younger sister once cried over a frog she found squashed on the road."

Oliver tugged on a particularly stubborn bramble that had become ensnared in the cotton, not responding until it was free. "I'm not sure I would describe Miss Clarke as being overly sensitive. The woman could fell a warrior with her evil eye."

Timothy sighed. "You're hopeless."

Oliver chuckled and clapped Timothy on the back. "That's why I'm friends with you, Timothy. You can ensure that I don't make a complete mess of things."

As they continued picking cotton, Oliver studied the men working the table around him. Reuben and Arlo from the boardinghouse would make good starting points for his questioning. They were standing relatively close, so he sidled around the table until he was within their hearing range.

"Good day!" Oliver shouted over the noise of machines and chatter.

Both men responded with nods, their attention focused mostly on their work. Reuben was a tall fellow who looked to have Swedish roots, with light-blond hair that shone in the lamplight and a muscular structure that suggested frequent trips to the boxing club. On the other hand, Arlo was small, with golden hair that fluffed around his head like a dandelion. The two workers were incredibly fast at their job. Their nimble fingers quickly cleaned debris from the cotton, moving it down the line in the blink of an eye.

Oliver edged a bit closer and selected his own clump of cotton to pick through, albeit at a much slower rate. "How long have you gentlemen been here?" He kept his gaze on his work as he spoke. "You're quite adept at this."

"Four years," Arlo called over the noise.

"Three." Reuben's muscles bulged as he hefted a huge pile of cotton in front of him.

Oliver whistled. "Well, I'll be. That's a long time. I suppose you've seen quite a bit of change in these last few months, haven't you?"

"Sure. Not good changes, though," Arlo said. "Our hours have increased, but we're still getting minimal pay. I think we're being cheated. Browning has enough money in his coffers to buy himself a new carriage but not enough to give us proper wages."

Oliver grunted, mentally filing away Arlo's dislike for the current mill wages.

Next to him, Reuben made a noise of agreement. "These robberies certainly aren't helping." His deep voice boomed over the noise of the machinery. "If the theft continues, I may walk out with some of the others."

Oliver's throat ran dry. "Well now, I don't think there's any reason to be so hasty. The thief can't continue on forever, can he? We'll get our wages back in time."

Reuben snorted, hefting a large pile of cotton closer. "How long will that take? I would rather take my chances with another job."

A chorus of agreement rang around the room. "You said it, Reuben," a man called.

Oliver resisted the urge to sigh. He had to stop the thefts before the workers decided it was no longer worth it to stay.

Hours passed and Oliver still had no new leads. Most of the

men he talked to expressed opinions similar to those of Reuben and Arlo—they were tired of getting low wages and were prepared to go on strike if the theft continued. Luckily, there were several like Timothy who were willing to wait until the robber was caught. Tomorrow he would further question the same workers to see if he could detect any motives they might have to steal. In the meantime, however, he was without suspects.

Rolling his tight shoulders, Oliver began to follow Timothy out the door but froze when he noticed Miss Clarke standing near the back of the crowd. She tilted her head in his direction, motioning him over. Releasing a breath, he turned to Timothy. "I'll meet you back at the boardinghouse. There's something I have to take care of first."

Timothy followed Oliver's gaze to where Miss Clarke was standing, tapping her foot. He grinned cheekily. "I understand. I'm not nearly as pretty, after all. Shall I tag along and ensure that you don't cause each other bodily harm?"

Oliver adjusted his hat with one hand and pushed Timothy with the other. "Go home, Timothy." Moving to where Miss Clarke stood, he held out an arm. "Shall we take a walk on this fine evening?"

Miss Clarke squared her shoulders as though preparing for battle. "I suppose we shall."

As she took his arm, a petite blond girl at her side snickered and whispered something to Miss Clarke that made her blush. She murmured something sharp and grasped Oliver's elbow. He couldn't help but notice how rough and callused her hands were, most likely from years of work. It made him realize just how soft his own were.

They left, the tiny girl's tinkling laugh drifted out the door behind them. Miss Clarke huffed a sigh. "Ignore Ella. She likes to think that every male I interact with will be standing at the altar with me by the end of the month."

"Rest assured, Miss Clarke, I prefer women who have enough sense to keep their nose out of other people's business."

She glowered at him. "Well, then, you'll be glad to know you would be the last man on my list of marriage candidates."

"Last?" Now *there* was a challenge. Oliver glanced at the prickly woman, an idea taking root. Perhaps, if he had time...

"Indeed. Now, putting matters of the heart aside, I wanted to speak with you about my findings."

"Ah. I don't suppose you had more luck than I," Oliver muttered.

Miss Clarke gave him a look that could almost be mistaken for sympathy. "You couldn't find anything?"

He glanced at his shoes, noting the scuff marks that had appeared in the leather. "No. I talked to the picker house men, but not one of them mentioned anything that would lead me to believe they're the thief."

Miss Clarke frowned. "What do you believe would cause someone to steal?"

"Many things. Debt, for one. Having a family to support is also a motivator, as is plain old greed."

The young woman next to him seemed to have become lost in her head, for she fell silent as they strolled along the cobblestone sidewalk. The brightly lit streetlamps illuminated her fiercely tented eyebrows and downturned lips, making Oliver aware of just how close they were walking. A bit disconcerting, that.

What was the reason behind the woman's expression? "Penny for your thoughts?"

She gasped. "Oh, pardon me. I was reviewing my conversations from today. I tried to ask what the workers around me thought concerning the theft. Considering what you just told me, I didn't find anyone who seemed as if they might be guilty."

"Well, I suppose it's only fair. Nothing groundbreaking ever occurred on the first day of investigating," Oliver said with a wry chuckle.

Miss Clarke studied him out of the corner of her eye. "Yes, that does make sense. What is your plan for the next few days, then?"

"Starting tomorrow, I'll question the men about their home life and interests." Oliver shifted closer to his coworker to make room for a couple walking in the opposite direction. Once they passed, he cleared his throat and quickly stepped away from Miss Clarke, who smelled quite nicely of lavender. "Not only will that draw me closer to them, but it will also give me a list of any potential motives they might have."

Miss Clarke smoothed her skirt with one hand. "A fine idea. I will do the same with the workers in the cloth department."

Oliver smiled. "Very good. I await any discoveries you may make."

For a moment, they walked in silence, content with listening to the noise of the city as it filtered through the night air.

Miss Clarke drew in a breath. "So, Mr. Bricht, what led you to become a detective?"

Oliver arched a brow. "Being civil, are we? I was under the impression you disliked me."

"Well, considering that you don't think a woman should travel alone, I don't foresee myself getting free of you until we arrive at the boardinghouse. I've decided to make polite conversation to pass the time. For your benefit, of course. If you would rather quarrel, that can be arranged."

Oliver held up a hand in defense. "No, no. We shall call a truce for the being. I'm too tired to throw jabs, and besides, this is far more pleasant."

Miss Clarke huffed. "Returning to my question..."

"Right. I began work as a police officer at the age of twenty-four." When Miss Clarke tilted her head, Oliver added, "I'm twenty-eight now, so it was four years back."

She nodded. "Continue."

"I enjoyed the work—not to mention, it kept me out of the war. However, when the Pinkertons rose in popularity, I found I was better suited at solving crimes than handling criminals. I decided to join the detective agency and leave guarding prisons to the police department. I've never looked back."

Miss Clarke perused him with a look that Oliver could have sworn almost resembled approval. "That's admirable. Doing what you like, I mean. Where have you gone in the course of all your detective adventures?"

Oliver shrugged. "Oh, here and there. Springfield, Louisville, Pittsburgh, Washington DC, and several other cities. My most recent case even took me all the way down to Austin."

Miss Clarke released a startled gasp. "My goodness! I've never left Wisconsin."

Oliver winced as shame burned a hot streak through his chest. He had entirely forgotten that the young woman at his side was nowhere near rich and most likely had no means by which to travel. He could almost hear his mother berating him for bragging to someone who had far less than him. "Forgive me, Miss Clarke. It was not very well done of me to boast."

Miss Clarke simply shook her head. "No harm done. I've always wanted to travel around the States, but between the war and work, I never had time to visit other places." Her face brightened. "Oh, do tell me about your adventures. I'm sure you have so many exciting tales."Oliver obliged and launched into one of his favorite stories, a case in which he had tracked down a murderer in Pennsylvania. Just before they reached the fork that separated their boardinghouses, he drew to a halt. "Wait here for just a moment, please."

After running into the drugstore across the street, he paid for a sheet of paper on which he could write a more detailed account of his findings. In addition, he purchased two pieces of caramel from a jar on the cashier's counter.

Back outside, he presented the candy to Miss Clarke. "A gift for you. Consider it an apology of sorts for knocking you over."

She gave him a slight smile as she took it. "Thank you, Mr. Bricht. Perhaps you aren't hopeless, after all."

Oliver grinned. "Am I no longer last on your list?" His mile faltered slightly. Where on earth had that come from?

Miss Clarke laughed as she unwrapped the candy. "No, and perhaps, in time, you will even be promoted above second-to-last."

Oliver choked on his forced chuckle and adjusted his too-tight collar. Only an hour ago, he had told Miss Clarke he would never marry her. Perhaps it was simply the thrill of a challenge that had made him speak in that flirtatious manner. No matter. Challenge or not, he would be leaving as soon as he finished the case, which meant second-to-last would have to do.

CHAPTER 7

$\mathcal{S}$omething was wrong. Dead silence prevailed when Carina entered the mill the next morning. She had hurried to work a bit earlier than she normally would, but not nearly early enough to be the first one there. The reason for her dash rested with the desire to avoid Mr. Bricht.

Last night had shown her a different side to the previously contemptible man, and it left her a bit confused. It had been easy to handle him when he was disagreeable, for all she had to do was hold her ground. But kindness? She wasn't entirely sure what to make of it. It wouldn't have been the first time a man had seemed kind, only to turn around and lie to her.

Carina rolled her shoulders back. Yes, that was it. She wouldn't risk being lied to again. It was better to keep her distance from Mr. Bricht and focus on the true task at hand—finding her sister.

Unfortunately, only a second after Carina's arrival, the man appeared at her elbow. "Good morning, Miss Clarke. Is there a reason you're standing in the doorway? I suppose it would be foolish for me to hope you were waiting for my appearance."

He chuckled, tugging the brim of his cap lower. He was close enough that Carina could smell the faint scent of peppermint coming from his breath, a realization that made her cheeks grow warm despite her best efforts.

Clearing her throat, Carina held herself rigid and refused to make eye contact. "Hardly."

The smile fell from Mr. Bricht's face. "Have I offended you again in some way? If so, I apologize. I thought we were past feelings of absolute hatred for one another."

A tiny sliver of guilt poked at Carina. While the man could be irritating, he didn't deserve such sudden cold treatment. "No, it's nothing you've done. I'm simply a bit on edge this morning. Ella wasn't waiting downstairs for me as she usually is, and it sounds as though the machinery hasn't been turned on. It's altogether a bit too quiet for my liking."

Mr. Bricht frowned as he took in the lack of people on the first floor. "I see. Shall we look upstairs and see if we can locate your friend?"

Carina nodded.

Making their way up the stairs, they hastened at the sound of quiet voices coming from the top floor. As they reached the last step, Carina spotted Ella near the office door. Her friend stood amid a large circle of whispering men and women, their expressions taut.

"Ella!" Carina rushed toward the group.

Mr. Bricht joined them at a more sedate pace, his gaze moving from one side of the room to the other as he took in each detail of the scene before him.

"Ella, what's happening? Why is nobody working?" Carina set a gentle hand on her friend's shoulder.

Ella turned, fear written plainly on her thin face. "There you are, Carina. There's been another theft, and now some of the workers have left. There are more threatening to leave within the week if the thief isn't caught. Oh, Carina, what if the mill gets shut down?"

A chorus of nervous murmurs punctuated the air. The chatter rose in volume as some of the ladies seemed to grow slightly hysterical, fluttering their hands in front of their faces. "I can't lose my job!" one woman cried.

Carina stomped her foot, effectively halting the noisy conversation. "The mill is *not* shutting down. Nobody is going to be out of work! I'll hunt down this thief myself if it ensures we keep our jobs."

Mr. Bricht sucked in a tiny breath behind her. Too late, she realized the error of her words. Turning slightly, she caught sight of him standing next to Mr. Baker, who must have joined the workers at some point. While Mr. Bricht had schooled his features into a blank expression, his eyes fairly blazed with anger. No doubt she would have quite the lecture waiting for her at day's end.

Clearing her throat, Carina straightened her spine. "By that, I mean I will talk to Mr. Browning during lunch about summoning the police. He'll sort this out. I'll make sure of it."

A chorus of agreement echoed around her as the workers seemed to take heart at her declaration. Carina deflated, sending a silent prayer upward that her words would be enough to distract the others from her previous statement.

Just then, Mr. Browning emerged from the staircase and silenced the chatter with a wave of his arm. He stepped forward, surveying the strained faces of the workers from beneath tented brows. "What's going on here? Why aren't the looms on?"

A voice echoed from the back of the circle, and the group parted ever so slightly, giving Carina a view of the speaker. "The office door was open when we came in to start work." The loom girl gestured to the door behind them, which, true to her word, sat ajar. "The safe was open, and the wage money was gone, every last dollar! Twelve of the loom workers walked out to find other jobs."

Mr. Browning turned a ghostly shade of white. "Walked out? Wages gone?" He stormed through the circle and into the office. The group waited in silence as sounds of stomping and cursing echoed from within. After a moment, Mr. Browning reemerged, wiping his brow with a white handkerchief. "Terrible, just terrible. Oh, what shall I do? Terrible, I say." The man scrubbed at his shining forehead with one hand and used the other to gesture about the room. "Who was present when the open safe was discovered?" He waited until a few of the loom girls tentatively raised their hands. "Laura, Emmaline, and Opal? I'm going to call an officer from the police department, and I'd like you three ladies to tell him precisely what you saw. In the meantime, the rest of you should continue with the workday as if nothing was amiss. I assure you, I will have this problem resolved and your wages fully compensated as soon as possible. Thank you." With that, the man backed into his office and wilted into a chair.

As the group began to disperse amid angry looks and anxious whispers, Carina met Mr. Bricht's gaze. He jerked his head toward the office, and Carina realized what he wanted her to do. She nodded and moved closer to one of her looms, pretending to do a thorough examination of the machine. From the corner of her eye, she watched as Mr. Bricht descended the steps with Mr. Baker. Once she was certain they were gone, she surreptitiously angled her head toward the open office door, where Mr. Browning was conversing with the three witnesses.

"Now, please explain in exact detail what you discovered when you entered the mill this morning."

Carina struggled to hear the girls' responses over the noise of the looms. Luckily, the other workers and even the floor supervisor must have been as hungry for information as her, for the room remained free of its normal chatter. They worked in silence, looking not at their looms, but at the door to the office.

"Well," one of the girls began, "we walked in together before the start of our shift, as we always do. Nothing seemed amiss on the first floor, but when we got to the second floor, we noticed the office door was ajar. We crept forward very quietly so as to not alert any intruders to our presence."

"That was my idea, mind you," a second voice chimed in.

"It doesn't matter whose idea it was." Mr. Browning sounded as though he was barely concealing his irritation. "Continue, if you please."

"Well, we didn't see or hear anyone, so we crossed over to the office and peered in. There was nobody inside, and the desk was undisturbed, but the safe was open. We looked closer and realized it was empty. Not a single coin remained."

A wave of murmurs rippled through the room as workers digested this information. Next to Carina, Ella was fiddling with the folds of her dress as she listened. "What are we going to do?" she whispered.

Carina shook her head. "I don't know."

Just then, the police officer arrived, his shiny revolver jangling as he marched across the room. Carina and the others listened as he greeted Mr. Browning and took statements from all three of the women, whom he then dismissed. Once they were back at their looms, the shuffling of feet informed Carina the officer was examining the room.

"The door was not broken, simply unlocked and opened. I assume there is only one key?"

"Yes. Only one. It has been with me since the beginning of the week." A note of weariness crept into Mr. Browning's voice.

Carina shared an incredulous look with Ella. It appeared their thief was quite skilled in lock-picking.

"Have you checked the drawers of your office desk to ensure nothing else was taken?" the policeman asked.

"No, I'm afraid I was too overwrought."

The opening and closing of drawers indicated they were searching through the contents of the desk.

"Everything appears to be undisturbed," Mr. Browning finally announced, relief evident in his voice.

"Good," the officer said. "Since everything seems to be in order, I'll take this information back to the station. In the meantime, please refrain from disturbing the safe. Good day, Mr. Browning."

As the police officer strode from the room, chatter rose and the gossip chain began spreading information to those who were too far back to have heard the conversation. No doubt, by the end of the day, the entire mill would be aware of the latest robbery, though by the time the news reached the bottom floor, the thief would probably be seven feet tall and have left a note written in blood upon the wall. It would be up to Carina to keep fact straight from fiction until she could relay her findings to Mr. Bricht.

"This is the first time the safe was found empty," Ella said anxiously. "Carina, our wages are completely gone! How am I going to pay rent this month?"

"Hush, Ella. The police will sort this out. We'll get our wages before rent is due, I assure you."

The rest of the morning passed in nervous conversation and half-hearted work as people speculated as to the identity of the thief. Even the floor supervisor engaged in the chatter, her normally harsh composure relaxing as she allowed the employees to speak with one another. Was she being lenient in the hopes of keeping more employees from walking away from their jobs?

By the time the lunch bell rang, rumors abounded, and three more workers had resigned. Employees hastened from the room, eager to get to the courtyard to speak with the workers on the first floor. Carina lagged behind with the intent of seeing the office for herself.

"Carina, are you coming?" Ella asked from somewhere behind her.

"No. I promised to speak with Mr. Browning, remember? I want to ensure that he is going to do something about this theft. It's spiraling out of control." Carina's stomach twinged at the lie.

"Would you like me to go with you?" Ella twiddled her thumbs, clearly ill at ease with the thought of speaking with Mr. Browning.

Carina smiled. "That's all right, Ella. You go on and eat lunch. I'll find you when I finish here."

The girl nodded and scurried from the room, obviously relieved to escape what was sure to be a difficult conversation.

Carina peered into the office, where she found Browning sitting behind the desk, his head in his hands. She spoke his name tentatively.

The man looked up, his face creasing with anxiety and suspicion. "Yes?"

Carina stepped forward. "My name is Carina Clarke. I'm working with Oliver Bricht on solving this case."

Mr. Browning frowned, causing deep lines to appear in his cheeks. "I don't recall Bricht mentioning another detective."

Carina cleared her throat. "Well, I just started investigating. Mr. Bricht can confirm my identity when he arrives. Do you mind if I look around while I wait for him?"

Mr. Browning relaxed a bit, waving a hand. "Go ahead. There's nothing left to take, anyway. All I ask is that you don't touch anything."

Carina agreed and began a cursory scan of the room. As the officer had said, it appeared to be undisturbed. There was no furniture apart from the desk and two chairs, one of which was currently occupied by Mr. Browning. A picture of the two mill founders hung on the left side of the room, while a wastebasket sat on the right. Empty. The only other object of interest was the safe itself—a large black metal box with a dial on the front. The thick door hung open, the interior of the safe barren.

"How is the safe locked?" She clasped her hands in front of her to keep from reaching out and touching it.

"It is locked using a key and then reinforced by a combination code."

Carina tapped her finger against her cheek. "The thief has evidently found a way to bypass this code. Do you have it written down anywhere?"

"It's on a piece of paper that's kept in a secret location." Mr. Browning folded his arms across his chest. "I doubt they would have been able to find it."

"I see," Carina said, her thoughts whirring. "I would agree that it seems as though the thief doesn't need the code to crack the safe. In that case, getting a different safe would most likely be ineffective."

Mr. Browning inclined his head. "Getting a different safe was the first thing I tried. Next were the guards, but the thief snuck past them as well. I'm at a loss as to what I should do."

Carina rubbed her temples. "Why don't you store the wages in a bank?"

"I do." Mr. Browning threw up his hands. "I only bring the wage envelopes here the day before I intend to distribute them. I've even begun changing the day I transfer the wages, but it still hasn't stopped the thefts."

Carina sighed. "I think it would be in your best interest to keep the wages at the bank for now. We simply cannot allow the thief to make off with any more money. We will have to devise a new method for distributing wages in the meantime."

"Yes, I suppose we will," Mr. Browning mumbled, rising from his desk. He seemed to have aged several years in the past few hours, and Carina couldn't help but feel sorry for the man.

"I'm going to take a walk and clear my head. Talk things over with Mr. Bricht, and visit me when you have reached a decision on our next course of action."

"Certainly." Carina moved to the side and watched as the man shuffled from the room. Then, she turned toward the safe, deep in thought—until a hand grabbed her shoulder from behind.

CHAPTER 8

*O*liver grunted as the red-haired woman elbowed him in the ribs. Good grief, she was like a cat—all flailing limbs and angry hissing. "Miss Clarke, it's me!"

Miss Clarke stopped struggling and whirled around. "Mr. Bricht! For goodness's sake, why didn't you announce your arrival? You surprised me."

Oliver crossed his arms. "I did call out your name."

Miss Clarke relaxed ever so slightly. "Oh. I see." She cleared her throat. "I suppose you would like to know what I heard of the conversation between Mr. Browning and the witnesses."

Oliver narrowed his eyes, irritation bubbling in his chest. "Actually, I'm not so sure I would. Perhaps you should go to lunch and forget all of this happened."

Miss Clarke gasped. "Why?"

"You announced in front of half the mill that you intend to search for the thief." Oliver pointed at her. "You put the entire investigation in peril with your thoughtless actions. To make matters worse, you also endangered yourself. The thief now knows you are looking for him, which will make it twice as hard to uncover his tracks. I cannot in good conscience allow you to continue assisting me if you cannot keep a secret."

Each harsh word he spoke made her wilt a bit more. By the time he was finished with his tirade, an embarrassed flush had covered her face. "I am aware of my error." She acquiesced with a sigh. "I regretted the words as soon as I spoke them, but I realize it doesn't matter now that the deed is done." She rolled her shoulders back and appeared to mentally bolster herself. "I apologize for my rash words, Mr. Bricht, and I will refrain from making such hasty statements in the future."

Oliver let out a deep breath. To tell the truth, he didn't mind the woman's company. It had been a long time since he had worked with a partner on a case. Still, he couldn't allow anything to reveal his involvement in the investigation. If Miss Clarke could not keep from saying anything, he would have to ask her to stop assisting him. "All right, Miss Clarke. I will give you another chance, but you must keep to your word."

"I will. I promise." She gestured to the safe. "Take a look and tell me what you see."

Oliver stepped around the desk. There was no immediate evidence of tampering so far as he could see, for the locks on the safe were unharmed. However, a closer inspection revealed something stuck in the keyhole. "Do you have a hairpin I might borrow?"

"Of course." Miss Clarke felt about in her hair for a moment before procuring a pin. She presented it to Oliver, who then used the pin to extract the mystery item from the keyhole.

It was a long, thin piece of wire that had been snapped off at the front. Oliver recognized it instantly, having used it several times during his old cases.

"What is that?" Miss Clarke leaned over his shoulder to peer at the object.

"Part of a lock-picking set." Oliver pinched the rod between his thumb and forefinger. "Judging by the broken end, it would appear that our thief was in quite a hurry."

Miss Clarke bent even closer, causing a stray lock of hair to brush against Oliver's cheek. "Do you think there are finger-prints on it?"

Oliver cleared his throat and shot to his feet, unnerved by their sudden nearness. "I doubt I would be able to get a full fingerprint off such a small object. Not to mention, the majority of thieves I've come in contact with have worn gloves." He turned to face Miss Clarke, taking a step back as he did so. He had a hard time thinking straight when the faint scent of lavender tickled his nose. "Now, did you manage to hear any of the conversation between Browning and the witnesses?"

Miss Clarke studied the ceiling as though backtracking through her memories. After a moment, she launched into an account of the women's conversation with the mill owner, including the police officer's observation about the door.

Oliver clasped his hands together. "Good. I saw that the door was untouched. The thief clearly picked the lock to get in, opened the safe, and made off with the wage money." He tilted his head, studying the door behind Miss Clarke. "The criminal was in a rush, however, so my guess is that it couldn't have been long before the mill opened for the day. I'm going to talk to the men in the picker house and see if any of them were awake early this morning."

"All right. Shall I do the same with the second floor?"

Oliver shook his head. "No. I need you to remain unin-volved for the remainder of today. You need to let your state-ment from earlier quiet down. If all goes well, you can resume collecting information tomorrow."

Miss Clarke hummed her agreement, though a frown tugged at her lips. "Very well, Mr. Bricht."

As Oliver turned to leave, a flicker of warmth in his chest

took him by surprise. How curious. He cast one last glance back at the woman, noting the determination in her eyes. There was something to be admired there, tenacious as she could be. Oliver ducked through the door before Miss Clarke could see his smile.

~

*L*ater that evening, Oliver leaned against the brick wall, waiting until Miss Clarke exited the mill. "Miss Clarke!" He waved his arm. Once he was certain she saw him, he ambled up to her and held out an elbow. "May I escort you home?"

The woman nodded and accepted his arm. When they were a safe distance from the departing workers, Oliver relaxed. "Where's your friend? Ella, was it?"

"She left for home a bit early so she could inform her landlord that she can't pay rent today." A forlorn expression crossed her face. "Mr. Bricht, if we can't catch this thief, people like Ella will lose their homes."

"I'm all too aware of that, Miss Clarke. A stakeout may be necessary."

"You mean you're going to hide in the office? What good will that do?" Miss Clarke asked incredulously.

"The next time the wages are going to be transferred to the mill, I'll spread the word so everyone knows. Then I'll wait in the office for the thief to arrive." Oliver carefully guided the woman around a large pile of slush, ignoring the way his boots became splattered with water in the process. "When he tries to open the safe, he'll find it empty, and I'll have enough evidence to place him under arrest."

Miss Clarke tugged her thin scarf over her mouth, causing her voice to emerge slightly muffled when she next spoke. "A decent enough idea, I suppose. Did you learn anything useful today?"

Oliver shook his head. "Not much. Most of the men were still asleep around the time the theft would have occurred and had fellow coworkers that were able to confirm their alibies. There are only a couple, like myself and Timothy, who wake up early to walk to the mill."

"I see. What was Mr. Baker doing?"

"He left home early to send a telegram to his parents. When I arrived at the mill, he was only a few steps behind me. Besides, I saw him in the telegraph office when I walked past. I feel fairly confident when I say it couldn't have been Timothy."

"All right. Was there anyone else?" Miss Clarke tilted her head slightly, gazing at Oliver from behind her spectacles.

"Let me think..."

A lamplighter walked the street in front of them. Though most of the streetlights glowed a brilliant yellow, one was dim. The old worker lifted his lighting pole high with gnarled hands, using the hook on the end to open the door and pull the cord below the lamp. Light sprang forth, casting a warm glow over them as they walked beneath the lamp.

Oliver tipped his cap at the man as they passed and earned a friendly nod in return. There was something far kinder, far more honest about the laborers than there was about the social elite.

"Mr. Bricht?"

"Sorry." Oliver turned his attention back to the question Miss Clarke had asked. "Arlo and Reuben were awake, but they were still at the boardinghouse when I left. If the theft did take place in the early morning, I doubt they would have been able to sneak all the way back to the boardinghouse in time." He shrugged. "I do think they'll be the next to leave if they don't receive their wages, though. Arlo seems to believe we're getting cheated out of our money. It makes me wonder if he perhaps suspects Browning of keeping the wages for himself."

"But that's preposterous. Why would Mr. Browning keep the wages if it meant losing employees and potentially his company as a whole?"

Oliver laughed. "It is ridiculous. Besides, the man is far too anxious to be a thief." He tucked his hand into his pocket and procured his tin of altoids. "Would you care for a mint? They're popular over in Europe."

"No, thank you." Miss Clarke sighed, her lips drooping. "We shouldn't continue to walk home like this, Mr. Bricht."

"Why not, Miss Clarke?" Oliver's surprise crossed his features before he could prevent it, and he dropped the tin back into his pocket.

"Well, people could get the wrong idea. Ella already believes us to be an item."

"What's wrong with that?" Oliver grinned and gestured between them with his free hand. "It makes a fine cover story. I'm not all that horrible to look at either."

Miss Clarke grimaced. "You know how I feel about you, Mr. Bricht. Besides, I prefer not to play about relationships."

Oliver dropped the smile. "I didn't mean it like that, Miss Clarke. I would never take advantage of a woman in that way."

Miss Clarke stiffened next to him. "My father once said the same thing. He lied."

Oliver fell silent, waiting for her to continue. When he caught her gaze, raw hurt shone in her eyes.

Miss Clarke took a deep breath before speaking. "When my father came back from the war, my mother was so happy to see him. She had waited three years for him to return home, you understand. We held a big party for him and even spent some of our hard-earned money to get him a fine new suit. He seemed so happy that first day home. But there was something different about him." She let out a shuddering sigh. "Not long after his return, he began leaving home for extended periods of time. He told us he was looking for a job. The first few times he left, we believed him. Then the money began disappearing, and we knew something wasn't right. My mother confronted my father, convinced he was spending our savings on drink. He denied the claims, and my mother loved him enough to believe him. Yet the money continued to disappear, and the time to pay rent continued to draw nearer."

Oliver swallowed. He had the horrible feeling he knew where the story was going, for it was one he had heard before. Still, he kept quiet and allowed her to continue, hoping she would disprove his suspicions.

"One day, I went into town to buy my mother a present. It was nearly her birthday, and I was determined to purchase the new pair of ice skates I had seen hanging in the general store window for her. I was almost to the store when I noticed someone who looked like my father at the train station nearby. I moved closer and realized that it *was* him...in the arms of another woman."

No. Oliver glanced away to cover his grimace. He was no stranger to stories of infidelity, for it was an ugly secret kept by many members of the upper class. A number of his father's cases involved an unfaithful partner. It had always pained Oliver to see the repercussions such actions had on innocent people, just as it had for the young woman beside him.

Miss Clarke toed at a rock, kicking it away as they walked. "She was clearly of wealth, for her mink coat and velvet dress were nothing my family could afford. I waited until my father had left the woman's embrace and started for home to confront him. When I accused him of seeing another woman, he first denied it. He told me he would never do such a thing to my mother. Yet when I told him what I had witnessed, I saw the shame on his face that his daughter knew the truth. Finally, my father admitted what he had done. He had been injured on the battlefield and taken to a local mansion-turned-hospital. There he met the owner of the mansion, a rich widow who told him we wouldn't love an injured man and that she would care for him instead. The worst part is, he believed her." Miss Clarke sniffled, her eyes watering.

Oliver placed a comforting hand on her wool sleeve as she carried on with telling her story.

"By the time my father came home, he was...involved with the woman. He admitted he wished he hadn't been taken in by her and said he understood if I wanted nothing else to do with him. According to him, once the woman discovered he wasn't rich, she treated him coldly. She refused to have any further contact with my father if he would not give her money. So he gave her what little wages he made."

"What did you do? Did you tell your mother?" Oliver halted in the middle of the sidewalk, waiting for the answer.

"I couldn't forgive my father's actions, nor could I let him deceive my mother. I brought him home and made him tell her. My mother was angry but willing to forgive. She begged my father to break off his relationship with the woman."

"What happened?" Oliver asked softly.

Miss Clarke gazed at the snow-covered ground. "My father said he was too broken to live with his shame. Despite my mother's pleas, he ventured out into the night. He died out in the snow." A single tear ran down her face. "I couldn't so quickly forgive what my father had done, but I never wished death upon him. Yet his actions taught me something important. Anyone can be deceived. Anyone can lie. And the rich will never marry the poor." She wiped at her face with one hand. "That woman took what little money my father had and left him in the snow. She already had everything she desired, yet she still wanted more. It's despicable. My father trusted her over his own family, as if we meant nothing to him." After letting out a small hiccup, Miss Clarke fell silent.

Gathering his thoughts, Oliver waited a moment before speaking. He wouldn't want the woman to misconstrue his words, especially in her current state. "No person is the same as the next, Miss Clarke. I know of rich people who are happily married to the less fortunate. Real love does not demand money or goods, but the whole heart. Your father may have loved your mother, but his heart was turned astray by a wicked woman. It was a truly horrible error but not indicative of all men and women. We all deserve to be judged according to our own actions—not those of others, whether good or bad. Do you understand my meaning?"

Miss Clarke studied him from beneath wet lashes. "I suppose so."

"Is that why you're helping to catch this robber, then?" Oliver smiled gently. "You know what it's like to be hurt by a thief of sorts and don't want others to experience the same thing."

Miss Clarke let out a choked laugh. "Perhaps, in a way. I cannot stand to see people take everything from those with so little."

Oliver nodded. "I agree. It's admirable how strong you are, Miss Clarke."

"Strong?"

"Indeed. Rather than let your hatred destroy you, you found a way to rise above it and use it for something good. You could be like dozens of scorned people, raging against the injustices of the world. Yet instead you chose to bring down a corrupt individual."

A blush spread across Miss Clarke's face. "Thank you, Mr. Bricht." She smiled. "Frankly, I don't even know why I told you all of this. I thought I disliked you."

Oliver chuckled. "Perhaps I'm not the evil cretin you first thought me to be."

"Perhaps not, Mr. Bricht. Time will tell." Miss Clarke presented him with a true smile, one Oliver had never seen from her before.

It warmed something inside him, knowing he had been able to bring her joy.

CHAPTER 9

$\mathcal{B}$y the time Carina entered the mill the following morning, the looms were already in motion. It was evident that despite the continual theft and loss of workers, Mr. Browning was eager to keep his employees producing the same amount of cloth as before. While it seemed to be working at the moment, it was only a matter of time before the remaining employees grew tired and overworked. If that happened, the mill could very likely close down.

Unwilling to dwell on such negative thoughts, Carina gave Ella her best smile as she approached her looms. "Up bright and early, are we?"

Ella returned her smile with a cheeky grin. "I awoke at a perfectly reasonable time. It is you who is late." She leaned closer, dropping her voice so it couldn't be heard over the noise of the looms. "Perhaps because of a certain dark-haired fellow I saw taking your arm last night, hm?"

Carina waved her hand at Ella. "It was nothing of that sort. He simply escorted me home after work because our boarding-houses are near one another."

Ella squealed. "Oh, how romantic it must be to have a handsome escort. Do you think he'll ask to court you?"

Carina chuckled, recalling her blotchy, teary-eyed appearance from yesterday. Romantic, indeed! "No, Ella, there's no romance between us. We're far too dissimilar to be in love. Why, he's from a different world than I!"

Ella set her hands on her slender hips. "Since when has that ever stopped anyone? All the stories say—"

"That's all they are, Ella—silly, fanciful stories. I've found real life to be far less glamorous."

Ella laughed. "Perhaps you're simply looking at things the wrong way."

Measuring her friend's cheerful gaze, Carina gave her a tiny smile. "Perhaps."

A sudden cracking noise had Carina swiveling. She gasped at the sight of her loom. The wooden shuttle was coming loose! Before she could jump out of the way, it snapped from the loom and shot through the air like a bullet. Diving to the side, Carina narrowly avoided getting sliced by the object as it sailed past. She hit the floor with a soft thud and remained there for several moments, willing herself to breathe. Her heart thundered in her chest, and her palms felt glued to the ground by the weight of her body.

Worried voices echoed from above, and a moment later, small hands urged her up.

"Carina, are you all right?" Ella asked.

Pushing herself up, Carina found herself facing a group of worried girls, with Ella at the front. They must have rushed from their looms when they saw her fall—a thought that cheered her a bit.

"I'm all right." She brushed her skirt off with a trembling hand. "The shuttle broke from the loom and nearly hit me, but I moved aside in time."

A collective sigh of relief traveled through the room. Broken shuttles certainly weren't unheard of, but they were unpredictable and incredibly dangerous. Had Carina not jumped to the side in time, she might have remained on the floor for good. She shuddered at the thought.

Carina accepted a new shuttle from one of the supply boys and carefully threaded it back onto the loom. Taking a deep breath to calm her racing heart, she cautiously started the loom again. Once she was sure the new shuttle was running without a hitch, she sagged against the wall and let her racing heart take over once more.

"Are you sure you don't need to see a doctor?" Ella took a step closer, twisting her hands. "That was quite a scare, and I don't want you to grow faint. I fear I won't be strong enough to prevent you from falling if you do."

Carina managed a weak laugh. "I won't faint, Ella. I simply need a moment to get my wits about me. In all the time I've worked here, I've never once had a shuttle break in such a manner."

Ella nodded understandingly and returned to her spot. The girl bent to examine the cloth one of the machines was producing, checking for any broken or loose ends in the fabric. Carina really ought to be doing the same thing, but at the moment, she was having a hard time breathing.

"You know, I had a shuttle break off only two months after I started working at the mill." Ella glanced up at Carina. "I did the same thing as you and dove to the floor. I find it an amusing incident now, but it certainly didn't seem so then."

Carina chuckled, pushing herself from the wall. To her relief, her legs remained firmly beneath her. "Well, at least I'm not the only one, then."

Ella laughed. "Not at all."

As Carina cautiously returned to checking the cloth from her looms, her mind gradually wandered to what Mr. Bricht had said about learning possible motives through casual conversation. Turning to the woman on her right, she stepped closer so she was within hearing range. "Thank you for assisting me, Jo. That was quite frightful."

The woman laughed cheerily. She had shiny brown hair that was loosely pinned around her face, reminding Carina of a woodland nymph. "But of course. When you've worked here for as long as I have, you become accustomed to seeing broken shuttles. It doesn't get any less startling, I'm afraid. I'm just glad you're unharmed."

"Thank you." Carina tried to recall her previous conversations with the woman. Had Jo ever mentioned whether she had family in the city? Or had Carina simply never asked? Though they had been loom neighbors for a few months, she couldn't recall asking the woman much of anything apart from her name. *Time to remedy that.* "Where are you from, Jo?"

"I've lived in Milwaukee all my life." Jo ran her hand over the cloth on one of her looms. "My grandparents moved here long ago, and my family has been happily situated since then."

"I see." Carina shifted one step closer and turned her gaze down to the loom in front of her. "What do you think of all these robberies, then? It must be strange after having been here for so long." She glanced at Jo from the corner of her eye, hoping to catch the woman's reaction.

Jo shrugged. "It's certainly frustrating, but there isn't much you or I can do about it. Besides, my husband makes enough to cover rent. It isn't the most comfortable living, but it will do until the thief is caught. I simply hope it happens soon. I don't know if I can eat another bowl of bone broth soup, but it's all that we can afford at the moment."

The woman on the opposite side of Jo chimed in with her agreement, and the two began a lively conversation over dinner food.

Carina sighed, having been all but forgotten by the two

women. It seemed gathering information was going to be more difficult than she had assumed.

~

*T*he workers let out a quiet cheer of relief at the sound of the lunch bell—Carina included. Picking up her tin pail, she followed Ella into the courtyard. After taking a seat beneath their snow-covered oak tree, Carina peeled the lid off her pail and reached in to grab her food. But rather than touching the thin wax paper in which her sandwich had been wrapped, her fingers instead brushed against something cold and scaly. Carina let out a short scream and tossed the pail into the snow. The contents flew from the container and scattered across the ground, revealing a misshapen sandwich, a flattened piece of cranberry pie, a small apple...and a tan snake with a diamond-shaped head and dark brown spots.

Next to her, Ella sucked in a startled breath and leapt to her feet. "A snake! Carina, are you all right?"

"I believe so. It doesn't appear to have bitten me."

The animal began to shake its tail in a menacing matter, making a rattling noise.

An exclamation led her to look up. Mr. Bricht and Mr. Baker stood over them, peering at the disgusting creature.

"You're lucky this fellow didn't bite you, Miss Clarke." Mr. Baker's expression was serious. "He's a timber rattlesnake. They're venomous." He rolled the snake over with the toe of his boot, narrowly dodging an angry dart of its fangs. In a strange sort of hopping, dodging dance, he continued to roll the snake across the yard until it slithered under the fence and away from the rest of the mill workers. The men then came to crouch next to her and Ella.

Mr. Bricht examined the lid Carina still held, his brow furrowing. "That's the lid, isn't it?"

Carina nodded. "There's no way the snake could have entered by mistake. The lid is watertight."

A dark look spread across Mr. Bricht's face. "In that case, it would appear that you've made an enemy, Miss Clarke."

Carina spread a hand across her rapidly beating heart. "Ella, you don't think…"

The young woman gasped. "The shuttle?"

"What is it?" Mr. Bricht demanded, his gaze sharpening.

"The shuttle on one of my looms broke this morning. I narrowly avoided getting hit by it. At first, I thought it was merely an accident, but now I'm not so sure."

Mr. Bricht scrubbed at his eyes with one hand, a sigh hissing between his teeth. "I'm afraid someone has made you their target. It would be in your best interest to remain cautious until the end of your shift, just in case any other traps have been set for you. I'll escort you home as soon as the mill closes. Please be careful, Miss Clarke."

Carina rubbed her arms where goosebumps had formed. "I'll do my best. Why is someone trying to harm me?"

Yet even as she spoke the question, she already knew the answer. The thief had discovered her promise to speak with Mr. Browning and was sending her a clear warning to mind her own business. But would someone really be willing to kill her over a simple promise? It certainly seemed so.

Carina's stomach twisted. "I need a moment," she muttered, stumbling to her feet and hurrying away from the concerned faces of her friends.

Just before she reached the door to the mill, a gentle hand tugged on her elbow. "Miss Clarke, slow down." Mr. Bricht's compassionate tone brought her to a halt. "You're only going to stress yourself more by running about."

"How am I supposed to stay calm when someone is trying to cause me harm?" Carina rubbed her temples, trying to relieve the pressure rapidly building in them. "And because of my own foolishness, at that!"

Mr. Bricht slid his hands into his pockets. "Miss Clarke, in my line of work, death threats are everyday business. We're hunting down unsavory characters, people who are all too willing to use violence to get their way. By my estimation, if you don't stop hunting for information, the danger will only worsen." He paused to look her in the eye. "Perhaps it would be better for me to work alone from now on. I cannot risk your life, Miss Clarke."

"No!" Carina said, her voice sharp. The sick feeling in her stomach receded as determination won out. The matter of finding the thief had gone from merely interesting to personal, and she wasn't about to back down. She took a deep breath. "I'll not be scared away because of a snake or a broken shuttle."

Mr. Bricht sighed. "I feared you would say as much." A tiny smile crossed his face. "You don't give up easily, do you?"

"No. My mother always said it was our Irish stubbornness coming through."

"I have to agree with her. If you think you can handle the danger, I will allow you to continue helping me." Mr. Bricht's face grew serious. "However, you must tread with the utmost caution, Miss Clarke. If this thief realizes you aren't letting up, his attempts to harm you may worsen."

Carina squared her shoulders. "That's a risk I'm willing to take. I don't appreciate bullies, not in the least."

"I understand. I feel the same way." Mr. Bricht offered her an arm, his lips lifting at the corners. "Shall we?"

"We shall." Carina accepted his arm, and they walked back into the courtyard together. "You know, I talked with some of the women before lunch."

Mr. Bricht raised a brow. "Did you learn anything new?"

"Not enough to be useful. Everyone seemed content with

their lives. Not one of them had a clear reason to be taking money."

"It often looks that way at first. However, if you continue to speak with them, you will eventually learn more about the things they struggle with. Then you can deduct possible culprits from true innocents." Mr. Bricht leaned closer as a group of women passed by, his voice dropping. "I've arranged for a false wage transfer in three days' time. Between now and then, I'm going to let the word out and make sure it spreads throughout the mill. If you could do the same, that would be appreciated."

Carina adjusted her annoying spectacles, which had begun sliding down her nose. "I can do that." She sniffed. "I seem to be fairly good at sharing secrets, anyways."

They were almost back to where Ella and Mr. Baker sat when Mr. Bricht halted one last time. "Are you sure you'll be all right? I still dislike the idea of sending you into potential danger."

"Yes. I feel better now that I've had a chance to think things over." Carina flashed him a teasing smile to extinguish the flicker of worry on his face. "How can I be sure that *you* didn't set the traps because you didn't want to work with me?"

Mr. Bricht choked and let out a loud cough. "Miss Clarke, I assure you that while I am capable of many things, I generally avoid using attempted murder to get my point across. Words do quite nicely."

"I should hope so, Mr. Bricht." With them only a foot from Ella and Mr. Baker, Carina detached her arm from his. "Shall I see you tonight?"

"Indeed." Mr. Bricht removed his cap and sketched a bow. "Now more than ever, I wouldn't let you walk the streets on your own."

Ella giggled from beneath the tree, making Carina huff as

she stooped down to tug on her friend's hand. "Come on, Ella. We must return to work."

"Goodbye, Mr. Bricht and Mr. Baker," Ella called as they walked away, fluttering a hand in their direction. She turned back to Carina with a smirk. "My goodness, they are positively charming."

Carina groaned. "Don't start again, Ella. They're simply concerned for our welfare."

"Oh, nonsense. Mr. Bricht doesn't look concerned for your welfare. He looks enamored with you."

Carina rolled her eyes and adjusted her scarf, pulling it up to conceal her rapidly heating cheeks. "Why don't you take your romantic fantasies and find your own beau?"

Ella grinned. "Oh, posh. It's far more fun to tease you."

As they reentered the building, murmuring from the second floor caught Carina's attention. Walking up the stairs, she pinpointed the noise as originating from the looms.

"Carina, what are they all looking at?" Ella asked as they entered the room.

Carina stood on her tiptoes, trying to see over the crowd. "I can't tell. Let me try and get closer." Upon squeezing through the group, she gasped at the sight of her loom. It had been beaten to shreds, with splintered wood and tangled thread laying everywhere. "Oh no!"

A piece of paper fluttered amongst the woodpile. She picked it up and found a few words written in nearly illegible handwriting.

Stop investigating or face the consequences.

Carina lowered the paper, set her hands on her hips, and surveyed the destruction. "No," she whispered. "I won't."

CHAPTER 10

*A*fter half an hour of walking in the dark, Carina finally arrived at her boardinghouse, her skirt hem heavy and wet from trudging through the snow. A blizzard had begun during the afternoon and continued through the end of her shift, making the journey home difficult. Luckily, there had been no more sabotage. The floor supervisor had moved Carina to a different loom, and all had gone well for the remainder of the day. Clearly, the thief was satisfied that he had gotten the point across using his scare tactics.

Carina exhaled a frosty breath and allowed herself a small smile. If only he knew how wrong he was.

Darting inside, Carina shut the door behind her and waved at Mrs. Fields. The dear woman held a feather duster in one hand, which she was using to brush off the vase and end table that sat against the wall in the foyer. "Hello, Mrs. Fields."

The boardinghouse owner gave her a cheery grin, her salt-and-pepper bun bobbing atop her head. "Good evening, dear. Would you care for a cup of warm cider?" She pointed in the direction of the parlor. "The rest of the girls are at a dance somewhere in the city, so it's just you and I for the evening. Of course, you aren't required to keep this old woman company. There's still time to attend the ball if you're so inclined." She waved the duster in the air. "But I would be glad to have a companion."

"I would love to sit with you, Mrs. Fields. Dances were never my favorite, anyway."

Charlotte was the one who had always wanted to go to a ball, though their family had never had the money. The girl had been like Ella, wishing a handsome heir would arrive to sweep her off her feet.

The memory made Carina a bit melancholy as she trudged into the parlor. She lowered herself onto a plush chair near the hearth and studied the crackling fire as she waited for Mrs. Fields to join her from the kitchen. The parlor had always been her favorite room in the boardinghouse, with its floral rugs and framed paintings of idyllic landscapes that hung along the scarlet-toned walls. It put her in mind of her old home, which was a bit silly, because it didn't resemble any of the rooms from the Peshtigo house. Perhaps it was simply the atmosphere that was familiar, that warm sort of comfort that eased the tension in her shoulders and calmed the storm raging in her head.

Mrs. Fields bustled into the room and handed her a cup of steaming cider. "There you are." She took a seat in the chair beside Carina with a cup of cider clutched in her own hands. "Now, Carina, dear, how was your day at work? Have they caught that thieving scalawag yet?"

Carina sagged against the chair, letting the warmth from the mug seep into her hands. "Not yet, I'm afraid. The theft has only been growing worse, in fact. Our monthly wages were completely stolen, so Mr. Browning must fetch more from the bank." She patted the proprietress on the hand. "I'll have the money soon, however, so there's no need to worry that I'll fall behind on my rent."

Mrs. Fields plunked her cider onto the table between the

two chairs. "Carina, you know I have no care for whether you pay your rent precisely on time or not. Why, it's no fault of yours that a thief is running loose."

Carina lifted the mug and let the steam from the liquid wash over her, thawing her nose and cheeks. "I know. It just doesn't feel fair that you should also suffer because of it." She took a sip of the cider and murmured in appreciation. "This is delightful, Mrs. Fields. Thank you."

The boardinghouse owner inclined her head, a smile spreading across her face and deepening the lines that fanned around her mouth. "You're very welcome. There are many things in life that do not seem fair, Carina. However, sitting around and complaining about them never helped. Things will turn out in time."

"I know, but sometimes it's hard to wait when you want to do everything yourself." Carina lowered her mug to the table.

Mrs. Fields laughed, placing a hand to her chest. "Trust me, dear, I know. Every once in a while, I find myself trying too hard to control the circumstances of my life. It's then that I have to stand back and let God take over." She winked. "He knows far more than I do, anyways."

Carina smiled. "Perhaps He'll know how to catch a thief."

"He does," Mrs. Fields said, her eyes sparkling with determination, "and He'll see justice served when the time is right. Perhaps not by your own hands, but by His, certainly."

"I hope so, because I haven't had much luck."

The landlady raised a brow. "You've been trying to catch the thief?"

"I've been working alongside someone to look for clues," Carina explained, carefully avoiding the use of Mr. Bricht's name. If Mrs. Fields discovered Carina was being escorted home by a man, the well-meaning older woman could very well start standing on the porch to watch for her. "So far, we haven't found anything useful. In addition, the thief has begun striking back."

Mrs. Fields frowned. "What do you mean by that?"

"This morning, the shuttle broke from my loom. Then I found a snake in my lunch pail. To top it all off, when I went back inside, I discovered that my loom had been broken to pieces."

Mrs. Fields crossed her arms, a glower on her normally jolly face. "Why, that scoundrel! Did the snake ruin your piece of cranberry pie?"

Carina grimaced. "I'm afraid so. I'm terribly sorry, Mrs. Fields. I know you worked hard to make it."

"Nonsense, dear." The woman pushed to her feet. "You wait right here, and I'll be back with a slice for you." She bustled into the kitchen, her skirts rustling, murmuring, "A snake, and on my pie, no less! Why, I'd knock that thief over the head if I had the chance."

Carina pressed her lips into a smile.

Eventually, Mrs. Fields returned, presenting Carina with a warm slice of pie on a plate. "There you are." She reached into her apron pocket. "Oh, I also have this. It was delivered here today, and I very nearly forgot about it."

Carina accepted a white envelope from her, her heart skipping a beat when she read the address. "Oh, this is splendid. Thank you, Mrs. Fields."

"Well, don't let me stop you." The boardinghouse owner chuckled. "Go ahead and open it."

Carina split the seal on the envelope, hope rising in her chest. After unfolding the paper inside, she took a moment to scan the contents. A gasp bubbled up in her throat. "She was there!"

Mrs. Fields blinked. "Who, dear?"

"My sister was there!" Carina jumped up from her seat. "I need to go to the hospital at once." She glanced again at the envelope. "Or church, rather. It seems as though they take in patients on a needs-only basis."

Mrs. Fields's hand on her arm slowed her. "Dear, I'm certain the hospital is closed to visitors this time of night. Now, why don't you sit down and explain this to me? What is this about a sister? I didn't know you had any family here. I assumed they perished in that awful fire that brought you to Milwaukee."

Carina sank back into her chair. "I suppose I do have to wait." She nibbled on her lip. "My parents are gone, Mrs. Fields. However, my little sister, Charlotte, ran outside the house with me before the fire began." She let out a long breath. "I lost sight of her that night, but I never gave up hope." She waved the paper in the air. "Now I have proof that my patience wasn't for nothing. She was here!" Carina clutched the paper to her chest, tears pricking the corners of her eyes. "She didn't perish in the fire. Lottie is alive."

Mrs. Fields smiled. "Your determination is admirable, my dear. To come all the way here without knowing if your sister survived is truly astounding. I only wish you might have told me about her sooner. I would have assisted you in your search."

Carina shook her head. "I never could have asked you to do such a thing, Mrs. Fields. This was something I could manage on my own."

The boardinghouse owner stared at her with a raised brow. "Well, that may have worked before, but certainly not now. You'll be needing an escort to the hospital tomorrow, and I'm all too glad to fill that role. You have no need to face this on your own, Carina."

Carina looked at Mrs. Fields in surprise. In all the time she had spent searching for her sister, she had never been offered help. Or was it simply that she had never asked for it? She certainly hadn't trusted Oliver with the information—not yet, at least. She couldn't risk being hurt by a man's actions once again. But there was no reason to hold Mrs. Fields under the same scrutiny, not when the woman had proven to be as kind and honest as a person possibly could be.

"Thank you," she said with a smile. "I'd like that."

~

Saturday morning dawned bright and cold as Carina and Mrs. Fields set out from the boardinghouse. While most of the girls were still sleeping after a long night of dancing, Carina had risen at dawn to prepare to go to the hospital. Anxiety warred with hope as she tucked her hands into mittens and pulled on her boots. Mrs. Fields joined her at the door a moment later, and they set off.

The hospital they were going to was halfway across the city, in one of the poorer districts. Carina and Mrs. Fields had to hop on and off of several streetcars before they were within walking distance of the building.

"My goodness," Mrs. Fields exclaimed as they jumped out of yet another car. "This is more excitement than I've had in the last three years. Do you young people really do this every day? I think I prefer a horse and carriage."

Carina laughed. "Streetcars are much faster, Mrs. Fields. They're also safer than walking. You never know what kind of scoundrels might be lurking about in dark alleys."

"I suppose you're right, dear. I'm simply growing old." Mrs. Fields paused outside a tall building with a steeple jutting out the top, studying the sign that hung over the door. "Is this the hospital you're looking for?"

The name of *St. John's Church* marched across the sign in bold black letters. "Yes, it is! Let's go inside." She tugged Mrs. Fields through the wooden doors of the small church. Once inside, the smell of antiseptic instantly assaulted Carina's nose. The front room was painted white, with chairs pushed up against two of the four walls. At the back of the room was a circular desk where a white-capped nun was writing something on a sheet of paper.

After passing by the chairs, several of which contained anxious visitors, Carina reached the desk and cleared her throat.

The sister glanced up, a smile spreading across her face. "Good morning. What can I do for you today? Are you in need of treatment, or are you simply visiting a patient?"

Carina swallowed. "Actually, I'm here to inquire about a former patient, Charlotte Clarke. I'm her older sister, Carina. I lost her a year ago and received a letter only yesterday that confirmed she was sent here. I was hoping to discover where she went after recovering."

The sister frowned. "I'm not sure how helpful our records will be since they won't indicate where she went after her treatment here. However, I'll have Vincent show you what we do know."

Carina removed her gloves, sliding them into her pocket. "I would appreciate that. Thank you."

The sister walked from the room and returned a moment later with a tall, brown-haired man. He clutched only a few papers in his hands, but the sight of her sister's name on the top one infused Carina with hope. What secrets would they hold? *Oh, please, let it show me where Lottie went.*

"Miss Clarke, was it? You're the one who sent us the letter about Charlotte Clarke?" the man asked.

Carina clasped her hands together to prevent herself from reaching for the papers. "Yes, that's me. What happened to her?"

The man, presumably Vincent, lifted the papers and flipped through them one at a time. When finished, he hummed thoughtfully. "Your sister was brought here due to hypothermia and severe burns on her arms."

Carina gasped, tears clouding her sight as she envisioned

her little sister injured. She had known Lottie would have to be hurt to get sent to a hospital, but thinking about it still made her feel ill.

Vincent apparently noticed her discomfort and attempted a smile, though it left his face rather quickly. "Not to worry. She made a full recovery and left in November of 1871. Unfortunately, that's all we know. Where she went from there is a mystery."

"Are you certain?" Carina stepped closer, peering over the top of the papers in an effort to read the page. "Did she say anything before leaving, anything about where she might be going?"

Vincent shook his head and tucked the papers close to his chest. "I wouldn't know. I'm only the record keeper. You would have to speak to the doctor who treated her, Dr. Hart."

Carina straightened and folded her arms. "Very well. May I speak with him?"

"I can ask, but you may have to wait." Vincent glanced at the hallway beside the desk. "He is busy with patients at the moment."

Carina followed his gaze to the corridor, along which echoed the faint sound of crying. She shuddered, hugging her arms closer to her chest. "I can do that. I've come this far, haven't I?"

Vincent gestured to the nun who had returned to her spot behind the desk. "Sister Wood will call you when the doctor is available." With that, he left them standing in the waiting room.

Sister Wood gave them a sympathetic smile. "I apologize for Vincent's behavior. He's prickly towards everyone, especially when his work is disturbed. Why don't you two take a seat, and I'll talk to Dr. Hart?"

Carina and Mrs. Fields nodded and moved to the chairs at the side of the room. After they sat, Mrs. Fields patted Carina's hand. "Now, don't you fret, dearest. We'll get this figured out. At least you know your sister left here alive and well."

Carina released a trembling breath. "It doesn't make the waiting any easier. I just want to see her and make sure she's all right."

"I know, dear. I know." Mrs. Fields began a quiet prayer, and a measure of peace entered Carina as she listened to the soothing words. They remained in prayer for a few minutes before Sister Wood's voice rang through the room. "Dr. Hart is ready for you now, Miss Clarke."

Standing, Carina met a white-coated doctor halfway across the waiting room. His graying hair was neatly combed back, and he wore a gentle smile on his face. At least her sister had been treated by a man who appeared to be kind and caring.

"Miss Clarke?"

Carina tucked her arms behind her back to control her nervous fidgeting. "That's me. I'm Charlotte's older sister. You treated her?"

The man chuckled. "That I did. She was quite the conversationalist, I recall. Very bright and optimistic, even when she had to stay in a hospital bed for several weeks. All of the other patients here enjoyed her company. She made a nice recovery, if I do say so."

"Did she say anything about where she was planning to go after she left the hospital?" Carina asked.

The doctor shook his head. "I'm afraid not. I recall she seemed very jumpy the day she was discharged, though whether it was from nerves or excitement I couldn't tell. Either way, we can't do much for our patients after they are gone. I wish I could tell you more, Miss Clarke. I am sorry."

Groaning, Carina put her head in her hands. "What if she went back to Peshtigo? I don't have the funds to leave Milwaukee. What am I going to do? How will I find her when she hasn't given me a clue as to where she went?"

The doctor smiled. "You will simply have to wait, Miss Clarke, and trust things will work out. One thing I know for certain is that your sister cared about you very much. In that case, I know she will find you again." He nodded to them. "I must get back to my patients now, but I am glad I got to meet you, Miss Clarke. Your sister was a good woman, and you remind me of her."

As he walked away, Carina muffled her tears in the sleeve of her coat. Gentle hands tugged on her shoulders, and before Carina could blink, she found herself wrapped in Mrs. Fields's warm embrace.

"It's all right, dear. We'll find her. As the doctor said, we simply have to trust that God has things in control."

"I feel as though we're giving up on her," Carina whispered. Sadness draped over her, leaving her silent as Mrs. Fields took her arm. They shuffled toward the door but paused when a voice rang out.

"Miss Clarke! Just a moment."

Carina turned and faced the kind Sister Wood. The nun smiled, offering her a crumpled wad of fabric. "We don't normally do this, but I'll make an exception for you. This dress was a gift from your sister to a friend she had here at the hospital. The woman she gifted it to long since passed away, but we've kept the dress in storage. I suppose we assumed we might one day have a use for it. I'm not certain if it will be helpful to you, but it's better than nothing."

Carina accepted the dress with shaking hands and turned over the soft fabric. "Oh, Lottie," she whispered. "How I miss you so." She glanced at the nun with a smile. "Thank you. This means quite a bit to me."

Sister Wood nodded. "Take heart, Miss Clarke. Do not give up when you have come so far. I am certain you will find your sister."

Carina folded the fabric and tucked it beneath her arm. "There must be something I can do," she murmured.

"What was that, dear?" Mrs. Fields glanced over at her, concern evident on her face.

"Nothing." Carina reached into her pocket to fetch her gloves but withdrew a piece of paper instead. The note from her loom. As she studied the foreboding words, her hopelessness began to recede, replaced by determination. There *was* something she could do. Now more than ever, she needed to help catch the mill thief. For if she couldn't get her wages, her sister could very well be lost to her forever.

CHAPTER 11

*T*he snow glistened in the morning sun as Oliver trudged across the courtyard toward the mill. The weekend had passed uneventfully, with the scattered winter storms preventing most of the boardinghouse residents from venturing out into the cold. While some had bemoaned the fact that they couldn't leave, Timothy had cheered the group by engaging them in a rowdy game of spades. They had remained playing card games late into the eve, and even stoic Reuben had eventually cracked a smile. Oliver couldn't help but marvel at Timothy's ability to stay optimistic. Even now as they walked along, the young man was whistling a tune.

"What's that you're whistling?" Oliver asked, sliding his chilled hands into his pockets.

"Oh, just a hymn I like to sing around Christmas. 'It Came Upon a Midnight Clear.'" A smile wreathed Timothy's face. "My mother used to hum it to my sister and me as children, and later on, we sang it in church. You should come to Christmas Eve service with me. My family attends a small chapel not far from here."

"I'd like that." It had been a while since he had made time for the Lord, a fact that disturbed something deep inside him.

A fine lady like Mother had never bothered with singing Oliver to sleep, opting instead to get a nanny who would care for him when he was young. While he certainly hadn't minded the kind Mrs. Burgess, something inside him fell flat at the thought that his mother hadn't thought it important to spend time with him as a boy. She hadn't even bothered bringing him to church until he was old enough to sit quietly in the pews and not complain about wearing a stiff suit. At least she had become more concerned with his life now that he was grown, though a part of him wondered if it was only because he was expected to follow his father's example and become a judge.

The sound of conversation echoed in the air as they entered the courtyard, some loud and others hushed. All seemed curious as they cast sideways glances at the people walking through the gates. Oliver had spent the remainder of Friday carefully spreading the word about the supposed wage transfer that would be occurring at some point Monday...today. The fake transfer would occur sometime during the morning. That way, the thief would be more likely to attempt a robbery during lunch break or at the end of the day. While Oliver wasn't particularly fond of the idea that he might have to stay in the office overnight, he was willing to do whatever it took to draw the thief out of hiding. If all went well, he would catch the criminal in the act of opening the safe and have the culprit in a jail cell by morning.

Selecting a spot at the cotton-picking table, Oliver rolled up his sleeves and got to work. After a week on the job, he was far more confident, though he still lacked the speed of more experienced employees such as Arlo and Reuben. The two men were currently positioned on his right, conversing with Timothy about the results of the latest baseball game.

Then someone at the window announced, "Mr. Browning is off to get the wages."

A round of hushed murmurs swept through the room as several workers left their duties to look out the windows and confirm for themselves that their employer was going to the bank to fetch the money.

"There goes Mr. Browning, off to fetch another round of wages that we'll never get to see," Reuben grumbled from his spot at the table.

"Come now, Reuben," Timothy said from beside him. "There's no need to be so negative. I'm sure we'll get our money safe and sound. The thief wouldn't dare be so bold as to try and sneak past the lot of us during the day."

A chorus of conflicted mutters echoed around the table as workers debated the truth of Timothy's statement.

"The thief has never stolen money during lunch," one employee pointed out. "Perhaps it'll be safe until Browning gives it to us."

Another worker shook his head. "It'll simply get taken during the night, just as it always is."

While it was true that the thief hadn't yet taken money over a lunch break, he had been bold enough to destroy Miss Clarke's loom. Oliver frowned. He had been so concerned for her welfare upon hearing of the incident that he had over-looked the circumstances surrounding it. The thief had clearly snuck in during lunch and demolished the loom.

So who had been present during lunch and who had been missing? A quick scan of his memories yielded no immediate answers. There were simply too many mill employees for Oliver to keep track of each and every one, especially when many left the mill to spend their lunch break elsewhere.

Oliver studied the hands of the picker-house men. Had they destroyed the loom with strength alone, their hands would have had cuts and scrapes due to the splintered wood. Unfortunately, while some of the men had injuries on their hands, most looked to simply be from daily work.

"Oliver, could you please grab a pair of scissors from the storage closet? Someone forgot to cut the twine on this cotton bale." Timothy gestured toward the tangled twine that ensnared the cotton in front of him. "They're lucky it didn't break the machinery."

"Sure, Timothy." Moving to the door at the side of the room, Oliver opened the picker room's tiny supply closet and peered inside. The glint of silver shone on the back wall, leading him to take a step inside the dark room and reach for the scissors hanging from a nail. Something glanced off of his foot and fell to the floor with a metallic clang.

Frowning, Oliver felt in his shirt pocket for the box of matches he kept there. Finding it, he used a match to light the supply closet's lamp, and the room was quickly illuminated. Beneath him lay a sledgehammer.

Oliver bent and carefully lifted the tool, grunting at its weight. Something black had been wrapped about the head of the sledgehammer several times. Unwrapping it, Oliver found the object to be a pair of thick work gloves—gloves that were covered in bits of wood. Suspicion rose in his chest. A closer inspection of the sledgehammer revealed several nicks and dents in the head, most likely from glancing off of metal.

Oliver twisted the tool in his hands. *Got you.*

The thief had slipped on gloves and destroyed Miss Clarke's loom with the sledgehammer, hiding the evidence in the storage closet afterward. Oliver replaced the tool in its normal spot on the wall and stepped back, picking a splinter from his hand.

With this new information in mind, it was evident the damage had most likely been done by a man from the first floor. The hammer was far too heavy to have been lifted by one of the woman, and only workers from the picker room used this particular supply closet. Judging by the almost careless manner in which the sledgehammer had been thrown upon the ground, the thief had most likely intended to return to the room and clean up their evidence within a somewhat short span of time.

After collecting the scissors from the back wall, Oliver strode from the closet and presented them to Timothy.

The man grabbed them from Oliver, a smile warming his face. "Thanks, Oliver. Are you all right? You took a long time in there."

Oliver rolled his shoulders, still in the midst of his thoughts. "I'm quite all right." He cleared his throat. "Say, do we use sledgehammers for anything?"

Timothy blinked. "Sledgehammers?"

"Yes. I found one in the supply closet. It was lying on the floor as if someone had used it recently."

Timothy hummed as he cut the twine from around the bale of cotton. "We do keep one in the supply closet for emergencies. Perhaps one of the machines needed repair. It's certainly not an uncommon occurrence."

Oliver shrugged. "Perhaps." He didn't tell Timothy about the gloves he had found. It couldn't have been Timothy who destroyed the loom, anyway, because he had been outside with Oliver for the entirety of the lunch hour.

As he filtered out of the room with the rest of the workers a few hours later, Oliver sought out Miss Clarke in the courtyard. She was under the same oak tree as before, though her friend was not with her. The blond girl conversed with a small group of women a few feet away. It was the perfect opportunity to talk to her without being overheard.

Approaching the tree, Oliver waved and called out Miss Clarke's name. She glanced up from her lunch pail, a few of the lines between her brows relaxing as her gaze settled on him.

"Good day, Miss Clarke." Oliver greeted her warmly. "How do you fare? Were there any more incidents this morning?"

Miss Clarke shook her head, a few chunks of snow falling from the shawl at her shoulders to the ground. "No. I have remained unscathed thus far," she assured him, a slight smile tugging at her lips. While she appeared alert and attentive, there was a tiredness in her eyes that hadn't been present before.

Oliver lowered himself to the ground next to her, gazing at the other workers who milled about. "I can see why you like to sit here. You have an excellent view of the people around you."

Miss Clarke nodded and scrubbed at her eyes with one hand, drawing Oliver's attention to the dark smudges under them. "It looks far better in the summer, when everything is green and the tree has leaves. It provides a lovely amount of shade on hot summer days." She fell silent, a sigh escaping her lips as she leaned back against the trunk.

"Are you well, Miss Clarke? You seem tired." Oliver blurted out the observation, forgoing all the rules that warned against commenting on a lady's appearance.

"It's nice to know I look as tired as I feel. Never fear, Mr. Bricht. I am well." Miss Clarke answered with a wry grin. "I'm simply worn out after a long day of traveling."

Oliver raised a brow. "You were traveling in the snow? Wherever to?"

Miss Clarke waved her hand. "Nowhere in particular. Are you going to be hiding in the office this evening? I noticed Mr. Browning leaving and returning with the 'wages.' The second-floor workers were quite vocal in guessing whether or not they would make it through the night."

Her vague answer made Oliver frown, but for her sake, he would play along and forgo the topic. "Yes. As soon as the mill closes for the evening, I will get into position behind the desk. With luck, the thief will try and break into the safe. If he doesn't, I'll have to formulate a new plan." He startled at the memory of his latest discovery. "Ah, I found something this morning. The thief used gloves and a sledgehammer to destroy your loom. He hid them in the picker room supply closet, which I discovered while hunting for a pair of scissors."

Miss Clarke raised both brows, surprise evident on her face. "Goodness gracious, a sledgehammer?"

"Indeed. It is my belief that the robber must then be someone from the first floor, as nobody else would have reason to open the closet."

"I suppose tonight will reveal the truth." Miss Clarke rubbed her arms with her gloved hands. "Then we can put an end to all this worry."

Oliver sighed. "So I hope, Miss Clarke. So I hope."

As they fell silent, a sliver of unease lodged in his stomach. Putting an end to the thief's reign of terror was exactly what he wanted to do. It was his job, after all. Yet, once he did, he would have to leave the life he had begun to build in Milwaukee. The people he was beginning to befriend—including the woman at his side.

He clenched his jaw. He must stay focused. As far as Miss Clarke would be concerned, he was a fraud and a liar, and he knew all too well how she felt about liars. What would she say if she knew who he really was?

There could be no risking it. Oliver would finish the case and return to Chicago, leaving Miss Clarke and Timothy to continue their lives as if he had never existed. It was better that way. Wasn't it?

～

*T*he chatter slowly grew fainter as the picker house workers left the room for the night. Oliver took his time collecting his coat and lunch pail as the flood of people thinned. Soon he was the only person left in the building.

"Oliver?" Timothy's call originated from outside the main entrance. He pushed one of the doors open, fixing Oliver with a curious look. "There you are. Are you coming? Lucy is making shepherd's pie for dinner."

Drat. "I'm all right. I'm waiting for Miss Clarke so I can escort her home. You can go on ahead."

The corners of Timothy's mouth drooped. "If you say so." He turned and glanced at Oliver over his shoulder, clearly reluctant to leave. "I'll see you back at the boardinghouse, then."

Oliver grimaced as the man left, letting the door swing shut behind him. He could only hope he wouldn't have to stay at the mill all night. Otherwise, he would have quite the excuse to manufacture for Timothy's sake.

What of Miss Clarke? Had she left? He sprinted to the nearest window, scanning the crowd in the courtyard. A sigh of relief escaped him. She must have already begun the journey home. Better that than have Timothy discover her outside and inform her Oliver was awaiting her arrival.

Oliver crept upstairs and quickly advanced to the office. After slipping inside, he closed and locked the door using the key Mr. Browning had lent him for the night. Without the light from the windows, it was pitch black in the office, and he fumbled about for a moment before locating the desk. Crouching down, he shuffled forward in an attempt to conceal himself beneath it. Unfortunately for him, there was already something—or rather, someone—there.

A feminine grunt sounded, followed by a raspy voice that he knew all too well. "Move over."

"Miss Clarke?" Oliver asked incredulously.

"Yes?"

Oliver glowered at the woman, though he knew it would be impossible for her to see his expression in the dark. "What on earth are you doing here? You were supposed to walk home with the rest of the workers."

"I wasn't about to let you do this alone. We're meant to be partners in this investigation, after all."

Oliver huffed. "Why didn't you tell me you were planning on tagging along?"

A rustle of skirts sounded as Miss Clarke shifted to the side. "You never would have allowed me to come with you if I had. Now, quit fussing and get in before you ruin the trap."

With another irritated grumble, Oliver slid beneath the desk, pressing himself as far to the side as possible. "This is highly improper, Miss Clarke."

"Mr. Bricht, I think we gave up on the rules of proper society when you bowled me over that first day," Miss Clarke stated in a fierce whisper. "Besides, you know as well as I do that we're doing nothing even remotely scandalous."

"How do you plan on explaining your late arrival to your boardinghouse owner?"

Another rustle of fabric sounded beside him. "Mrs. Fields will understand. She's a kind woman."

Oliver folded his arms across his chest, and the room fell into silence, broken only by the occasional distant noise of the city in motion. "Why were you so tired earlier today?" he whispered into the blackness.

Miss Clarke exhaled a deep breath. "I had a long Saturday, as I told you."

"You didn't tell me where you went," Oliver said quietly. "What is it that you aren't trusting me enough to tell me about?"

Miss Clarke remained silent for a moment before answering. "You don't have to be everyone's hero, Mr. Bricht. My problems are my own."

A door creaked inside the mill, and Oliver straightened. "Hush."

Footsteps sounded at the back of the loom room, causing Miss Clarke to tuck her skirts farther under the desk. The heavy tread halted right outside the door, followed by the unmistakable clinking sound of the lock being picked. There was a creak as the knob was pushed in, and someone entered the office. Oliver struggled to quiet his breathing as the steps paused for a moment and then continued. There was a moment of silence when the thief reached the safe, followed by the whirring of the dial being turned.

Oliver tensed, preparing to jump.

Unfortunately, Miss Clarke leapt to her feet first. "Stop, thief!"

With a choice word, Oliver slid from beneath the desk and raced after the fleeing robber. In the dim glow of the streetlights that filtered through the windows, he could make out the faint outline of the thief. He was dressed in a thick overcoat and a black cap that shielded his hair from view. Heavy work boots rang down the steps before the man jumped the last few stairs and fled out the door.

Following as best he could, Oliver burst out of the mill and into the courtyard, where the thief was sprinting toward the fence at the far end. He let out a cry of frustration as the man climbed over the fence, jumped to the ground in one easy leap, and crawled into a closed carriage waiting on the other side. As Oliver ran across the clearing, the driver, whom he couldn't make out in the darkness, whipped the horse into motion. The carriage raced down the road far before Oliver was at the fence, leaving him clutching the bars and gasping for air.

"Blast!" he cried, swiping the cap from his head.

The rapid tattoo of booted feminine feet behind him

informed Oliver that Miss Clarke had caught up.

"What happened?" She doubled over, clearly as winded as he was.

"The thief escaped." Oliver sighed.

Miss Clarke frowned and straightened, her face barely visible in the streetlight. "It was my fault, wasn't it? I was too hasty in springing the trap. Drat my foolish impulsiveness."

"It wasn't just that. He was far more prepared than I first assumed." He locked eyes with her. "Miss Clarke, our thief is not working alone."

CHAPTER 12

*C*arina stepped forward, surprise arching through her like lightning. "There was another person?"

"Indeed." Mr. Bricht's expression was grave. "A carriage and driver were waiting for the robber on the opposite side of the fence. The driver had the carriage in motion by the time I caught up."

Carina folded her arms across her chest as the bitterly cold night air swirled around her. "What are we going to do? Identifying one thief was hard enough, but two?"

Mr. Bricht replaced his cap, tucking the brim low over his forehead. He was undoubtedly frazzled by the chase, and no doubt Carina looked the same. "We have to investigate more carefully. I cannot believe I didn't realize the possibility of multiple thieves sooner."

Another shiver wracked Carina's frame as a gust of wind blew across the courtyard. "Might we discuss this tomorrow? There's not much more we can do tonight."

Mr. Bricht took in her shivering countenance and nodded. "As you wish. Come, let us talk to the gate guards and be on our way."

Taking her elbow, he led Carina to the front gate. There they were met by the two night guards, both of whom appeared to have been made aware of Mr. Bricht's plan.

"Any luck? We didn't hear anything," one of the two said, his dark eyes sparkling with interest.

"The thief snuck over the fence at the back left corner of the courtyard." Mr. Bricht's voice was almost harsh in its precision. "I chased him out of the building, where I discovered he had a carriage and driver waiting on the other side of the fence. It would be in our best interest, gentlemen, for you to alternate a patrol around the border of the courtyard. It may not absolve the problem entirely, but it should do the trick for now."

The men mumbled their assent, perhaps sensing that they shouldn't argue. "Have a good evening, detective."

Mr. Bricht gave them a cursory nod and tugged Carina onto the sidewalk beside him, his brow furrowed in thought.

"What is it? What are you thinking?" She tugged her hand from his so she could reach for the scarf in her apron pocket.

"The carriage." Mr. Bricht looped his arm back through her own as though by habit. "Do you know anyone here who owns one?"

Carina hummed thoughtfully as she wrapped the scarf around her neck with her free hand. "No, I don't. Do you plan on checking each house to see if anybody possesses one? That seems a bit time consuming, if you ask me."

Mr. Bricht shook his head. "In my opinion, the carriage was a rental. I'm wondering if it would be beneficial to check the liveries nearby."

"Ah, a smart thought, to be sure. As it just so happens, I know of one not far from here. I and a few of the other loom girls once pooled together our funds to rent a carriage for an injured worker. Shall we investigate it tomorrow and see what we can find?"

"Yes, that would be wise." Mr. Bricht glanced at the tips of his snow-covered boots with an intensity that made it clear he was avoiding her gaze.

Carina tapped the man's sleeve with her free hand. "Mr. Bricht? Is everything all right?"

"I feel as though I've failed."

The sudden declaration caught Carina by surprise. "Failed? In what way?"

"I didn't catch the thief. We're lucky there was nothing for him to take. If there had been, we would have lost another month's wages." Mr. Bricht sighed and toed a rock on the ground. "Now he'll be on guard for us, and it will be far harder to locate him and his accomplice."

Carina gave him a gentle bump with her shoulder. "What happened to the determined detective I met not so long ago? The man who jumps at every opportunity to prove himself? Mr. Bricht, you may not have caught the thief tonight, but you've given us clues that could very well be the missing pieces of our puzzle. That must count for something, doesn't it? I certainly believe it does. If the thief decides to make his trail harder to follow, why, we'll simply have to search harder. Don't give up yet, Mr. Bricht. Don't let the thief get away with this."

A tiny smile creased Mr. Bricht's face. "You'd do well in debate, Miss Clarke. We did find some clues, didn't we?"

"But of course! We now know there are two thieves who most likely rented a carriage to make their getaway. They avoid the guards by crossing over the fence in the back corner of the courtyard, pick the locks on the door and safe, and exit over the fence in the same manner they came." Carina fumbled in her pocket. "In addition, the thief dropped this in his haste to escape."

Mr. Bricht took the piece of paper from her. After unfolding it, he studied the words with a measure of surprise on his face. "Why, it's a receipt from Robinson's General Store. That's the drugstore right down the street from my boardinghouse. By the looks of it, our thief bought a pair of gloves."

"Is there a name on the receipt?" Carina hadn't stopped to examine the paper, but instead had grabbed it from the floor during the chase through the mill.

"No, it's only the items bought and the name of the store. The signature has been ripped from the bottom." Mr. Bricht smiled. "Still, it's a lead. Miss Clarke, you are brilliant."

Carina laughed. "Am I forgiven for sneaking along tonight?"

"Perhaps. We shall see," Mr. Bricht responded, a teasing look on his face.

At long last, they reached the turn that led to Carina's boardinghouse. "Well, it was an exciting evening, Mr. Bricht. I look forward to continuing our search tomorrow." She raised an arm in farewell.

"As do I." Mr. Bricht tipped his cap. "Goodnight, Miss Clarke."

"Goodnight, Mr. Bricht." Carina turned down the lane. Coming upon the boardinghouse door a few moments later, she fiddled with the doorknob and jumped back when it opened seemingly of its own volition.

"Just what do you think you're doing wandering around so late, young lady?" Mrs. Fields fixed Carina with a stern look. "It's far past the time when you should be in bed, as you well know."

Carina gave the woman an apologetic smile as she slid inside and closed the door behind her. "I'm sorry, Mrs. Fields. Mr. Bricht and I were investigating the thefts, and—"

"Mister?" Mrs. Fields asked, her eyes narrowing. "You were out at night with a man?"

Oh, dear. "Mr. Bricht is a perfect gentleman, I assure you. He's a Pinkerton, one of those detective fellows who travels around undercover. Why, we don't even like each other."

Mrs. Fields gave her a hard stare. "I'll believe that when I see it." She shook her head. "Now, you get on to bed. You had better be home on time from now on, or I'll be after this Mr. Bricht with a broomstick."

Carina laughed. "I give you full permission to chase him down if that is the case." She tilted her head. "Why are you awake at this hour of the night, anyway?"

"Dear, I always make sure my girls get home. I sleep better at night, knowing you're all safe and sound. Now, off to bed with you."

Something warm spread through Carina as she bade Mrs. Fields goodnight and walked up the stairs. It had been a long time since anyone had cared enough to wait for her. It reminded Carina of how her mother had been. She had always waited by the sitting room fireplace for each member of the household to return home, even if Carina worked late into the night. When she did finally arrive home, her mother would always quickly usher her off to bed.

Sliding under the covers and wrapping the quilt tightly around her to conserve heat, Carina listened as Mrs. Fields moved toward her own bed at the end of the hall.

"Girls and their young men, always off late at night," the kind woman muttered. "Dislike? I don't believe that for a second. That scalawag had better be something special if he thinks he can court one of my girls."

Carina smiled into the dark. *My girls.* It was nice to be cared for.

~

*E*lla ran to Carina as soon as she entered the building the next morning. "Oh, Carina, have you heard?"

Carina raised a brow. "No, I just arrived. What is it?"

A broad grin crossed Ella's face. "Our wages weren't stolen! Mr. Browning didn't get them yesterday, after all. He decided to wait and fetch them from the bank this morning. He's on his way there right now."

Carina chuckled at her friend's unfettered enthusiasm. "That's wonderful, Ella. Have they caught the thief?"

Ella put a finger to her cheek. "I'm not quite sure. I haven't heard anything about the robber."

With a nod, Carina turned to her looms. "We shall have to wait and see." While she continued to converse with Ella about trivial things, her mind wandered to the events of last night. What would the thief—or rather, *thieves*—do now that their plan had been foiled? Had they seen Mr. Bricht? If so, his disguise could very well be ineffective.

The thought made her frown.

Ella must have noticed her expression, because her flood of chatter instantly ceased. "Carina? What is it?"

"Oh, nothing. I was simply thinking about the thief. What if he hasn't been caught? What then?"

Ella shrugged. "I suppose the police will have to keep looking. Oh, look! Mr. Browning is back with our wages. I'll be able to pay rent tonight."

Sure enough, the man was in the process of passing out white envelopes at the back of the room. While the workers looked happy enough to be getting their money, the mill owner retained a tired expression. A twinge of guilt ran through Carina at the realization that his sleeplessness was most likely due to their unsuccessful stakeout.

When Mr. Browning reached Carina, he handed her an envelope and favored her with a quick nod. "Your wages, Miss Clarke. I apologize for the wait."

Carina accepted the envelope with a slight smile, though guilt continued to assail her. Hopefully, their search of the carriage house and the drugstore would give them something useful for identifying the thieves. Then she could put an end to the anxiety that plagued Mr. Browning. "Lord, please let us find something," she whispered under her breath.

It was a long couple of hours before the day ended and the mill closed. Carina rushed from her looms and joined the throng of people waiting to exit the building. Mr. Bricht's tall, elegant stature easily set him apart from the rest of the group. His was the bearing of a man raised far from the likes of these laborers, making Carina wonder just where the detective was actually from.

"Ella, would it be all right if I walked home with Mr. Bricht?" she asked her friend, who walked beside her.

"You know I have no problem with your escort." Ella winked saucily. "I expect a full report of what you lovebirds talked about tomorrow."

Carina gave her friend a playful push. "Oh, get on with you. I'll see you tomorrow."

"Indeed. Have a good night, Carina."

Carina waved and began elbowing her way through the crowd, grunting as she was jostled from one side to the other. Calling Mr. Bricht's name, she continued to sidle past men and women until she finally caught sight of him again. "Mr. Bricht!" She forged a path to where he stood.

As she came within a few feet, Mr. Baker turned and bumped her with his elbow, causing her to stumble. "Oh, Miss Clarke! My apologies, I-I didn't see you there. Are you all right?" He stammered, steadying her. The poor man's cheeks flared pink as he stepped back, giving her space. "I truly didn't mean to bump into you."

"No need to worry, Mr. Baker. I am quite unharmed." Carina offered a warm smile to show she wasn't irritated.

"Ah, Miss Clarke. Are you prepared to go home?" Mr. Bricht asked.

"Quite." Carina took the elbow he offered. "Good day, Mr. Baker."

Mr. Baker nodded, a shy smile crossing his face. "Good day to you as well, Miss Clarke. I'll see you at the boardinghouse, Oliver."

Walking from the warmth of the doorway to the chill of the courtyard, Carina automatically reached into her pocket to fetch her scarf. To her surprise, rather than meeting warm wool, her hand brushed across paper. Frowning, she pulled the crumpled sheet from her pocket and read the message that had been scrawled on it. *You should have listened.* Carina nearly dropped the paper. "Mr. Bricht!" She held the note out so he could see it.

Mr. Bricht drew to a halt in the middle of the sidewalk. "Where did you find this?" He snatched the paper from her hand. "It's a piece of an envelope."

"I found it in my apron pocket just now." Carina took her scarf from her pocket and wrapped it about her neck with trembling fingers.

Mr. Bricht studied the paper, smoothing it with his thumb so the words were more visible under the lamplight. "It's the same handwriting as the previous note, though I couldn't tell you who it belongs to. You didn't see or feel anyone slip their hand into your pocket, did you?"

Carina sighed. "Dozens of people jostled me as I moved across the room. It could have been any one of them."

"Timothy bumped into you." His brows tented fiercely.

Carina tilted her head to the side. "True, yet I don't see him writing something so cruel. He seems kind."

Mr. Bricht handed the note back to Carina. "People can be two-faced." He removed a small tin from his jacket and opened it, taking a mint from the inside. He replaced the container in his jacket and popped the mint in his mouth, taking a moment to chew before speaking. "While I'd like to believe Timothy is innocent, I'll still include him in the list of possible suspects. You must stay on guard. The thief clearly knows you are still looking for him. In that case, you may be in more danger than before."

"I can handle myself." Carina glanced at the street sign as they crossed the road. "The carriage house is straight ahead."

Mr. Bricht slowed his pace. "Are you certain you'll be all right?"

Forging ahead, Carina waved him off. "I will be fine. Please stop your worrying. If it's all the same to you, I would rather focus on the task at hand and not on my potential impending doom."

He winced. "As you wish. Just be careful and shout if that criminal should dare to try anything in the future. Promise me you will?"

Carina smiled softly. "I promise. We have arrived, Mr. Bricht." She gestured to the carriage house with its simple wooden siding and faded sign. The sound of horses carried from the outbuilding next door—most likely a small livery. As they approached the main building, a dim light burned within.

Mr. Bricht reached the door and held it open. "Ladies first."

Carina laughed. "Well, thank you." It wasn't often that someone held the door for her, a thought that made her cheeks heat as she entered the carriage house.

Inside, several gas lamps adorned the walls, casting a dim light over the warehouse. Carriages of all sorts lined the walls, ranging from closed to open and old to new. At the back of the room, wiping down a carriage with a wet rag, was an older gentleman with thick mutton chops whom Carina assumed owned the rental business.

Behind her, Mr. Bricht was also scanning the room. As his gaze moved to the back wall, he sucked in a sharp breath. "That carriage. That's the one that I saw last night." Moving forward, he cleared his throat. "Excuse me. Sir?"

The gentleman who had been cleaning the carriage looked up from his work. "Ah, good evening. I apologize—I didn't see you come in." Hopping nimbly from the carriage seat, he tucked his rag into his belt and extended a hand toward Mr. Bricht. "James Trout, at your service. Looking to rent a carriage for an evening drive, are you?"

"I'm afraid not." Oliver reached into his jacket and withdrew his badge, holding it out for the carriage owner to see. "My name is Oliver Bricht, official private investigator of the Pinkerton Detective Agency. Do you remember who took that carriage out last evening?" He gestured toward a black-and-gold carriage.

Mr. Trout withdrew his hand, studying Mr. Bricht with solemn eyes. "Yes, I do. What concern is it to you?"

"There's been a series of thefts at the Jamieson and Browning Mill. Last night, I came across your carriage speeding away from the mill. I believe the thieves were using it to make a quick escape."

Mr. Trout rubbed his forehead. "Well, I'll be. I'm not in the business of questioning my customer's intent, so long as they bring my vehicle back safe and sound. These folks you're speaking of have rented this particular carriage for a few weeks now. They come in sporadically and never take it out for more than a few hours. It's never returned with so much as a scratch."

"Do you remember what they look like? The people who rent the carriage, that is," Carina interjected, taking a step forward.

Mr. Trout wrinkled his nose. "Not really, I'm afraid. There was a taller fellow and a shorter fellow, both completely bundled up with scarves and the like. The taller one did most of the talking, and by talking, I mean gesturing to the carriage and handing me money. I didn't want to pry, so I simply told them the rules and let them go."

"Well, that's not much information, but I suppose it'll do." Oliver inclined his head in the direction of the carriage. "Do you mind if we inspect it?"

Mr. Trout waved his arm. "Go right ahead. Those two aren't coming back, anyway."

"They aren't?" Carina asked, her brows rising.

"No." Mr. Trout glanced her way. "Last night, when the two of them returned, they told me they wouldn't be needing the carriage any longer."

Mr. Bricht hummed under his breath. "They must have known we would come looking for them." He strode toward the carriage. "It doesn't matter. We'll still check and see if they left anything behind."

After hefting himself up into the driver's seat, he turned and held out a hand for Carina. She took it, and he pulled her up beside him. Carina blinked as the familiar scent of mint surrounded her. "I-I believe I'll examine the interior," she stammered, eager to put distance between them.

"An excellent idea," Mr. Bricht agreed. "Would you care for a hand?"

"Oh, no. That won't be necessary." Carina waved her hand and lowered herself onto the outer step of the carriage so she could reach the door to the interior. She opened it and stepped inside, making sure to keep her skirts close about her. The inside of the carriage boasted black plush cushions, each in immaculate condition. Starting with the one closest to her, Carina carefully lifted it and checked for any items beneath. Upon reaching the last cushion, she raised it and let out a startled gasp as an object tumbled to the floor.

A very large, very wicked-looking knife.

CHAPTER 13

"Mr. Bricht!" The startled exclamation came from within the carriage.

Oliver jumped down from the driver's seat and rushed to the door. "Miss Clarke? What is it?"

The woman glanced up at him, her blue eyes wide. "I found a knife!"

Pushing his way into the carriage, Oliver motioned her aside. "Here, let me take a look."

Miss Clarke moved away, giving him a clear view of the weapon. It was more of a dagger, long and thin with a razor-sharp end. Oliver gingerly lifted the knife and turned it from one side to the other. There was no decoration or inscription on the blade and only a few thin strips of leather wrapped around the hilt to provide a handle.

After sliding the weapon into his coat pocket, Oliver hopped down from the carriage and held out a hand for Miss Clarke. "Come. I believe it is time to take our investigation elsewhere."

Miss Clarke accepted his hand and stepped gracefully to

the floor. "Where will we go from here? What will you do with the knife?"

"I'll keep it for a few days and then turn it in to the police if it does me no good. For now, however, I think we should start back toward the boardinghouse. There's not much more to find here."

"What if the thieves return to look for their knife?" Miss Clarke asked, her eyes trained on his coat pocket.

Oliver shook his head. "I doubt they would take such a risk. However, I will ask Mr. Trout to watch for them should they decide to chance it." Striding to where Mr. Trout stood, he removed the dagger from his pocket and held it out in the light. "We located this in the carriage."

"Great Scott!" Mr. Trout took a step back and cast an anxious glance toward his carriage. "Those brutes could have ripped the seats."

Oliver arched a brow. "Frankly, ripped seats would have been the least of our problems had the thieves kept the dagger. Could you do me a favor and keep an eye out for them? They may decide to come back for their weapon, in which case you ought to inform me at once. I can be found at Lucy's Boardinghouse."

Though the corners of Mr. Trout's mouth drooped, he nodded his assent. "I'm not fond of the idea that they might return, but if they do, I'll send word. What should I say if they ask about the knife?"

"Say you disposed of it, as you do with all weapons found within your carriages." Oliver returned the knife to his jacket pocket. "That way they won't be tempted to search your office for it."

Trout hummed. "Yes, that may work. A fine idea, young man." He released a long breath and rolled back his shoulders. "I will make sure to send word if they come around. I still can't believe my carriages were being used for crime. What a shame it is that my business should be tarnished in such a way."

Oliver smiled his thanks. "I am in your debt, good sir. And now, we will take our leave."

Mr. Trout held up a hand. "Just a moment. I thought of something while you were examining the carriage. These thieves of yours had a horse they boarded here as well, a mare named June, if I recall. You're more than welcome to check and see if she's still here."

Oliver stood straighter at the prospect of another potential lead. "Splendid. We'll check next door before we depart." Tugging Miss Clarke by the elbow, he led her from the building and toward the barn that smelled rather strongly of horses.

"Mr. Bricht, don't you think we should wait to visit the stables? It's getting quite dark."

"Nonsense. We'll be in and out in two winks." Oliver twisted the knob of the stable's only human-sized door and pushed it in. Inside the building, the smell of horses only grew stronger, coupled with alfalfa and the faint scent of manure. A few lights illuminated the room, revealing a stone hallway. Stalls lined both sides of the hall, and at their entrance into the room, several horses draped their heads over the stall doors.

Oliver nodded toward the stalls on the right side. "You check those, and I'll check the ones on the left."

Miss Clarke drifted toward the stalls he had gestured to.

Oliver scanned the names chalked on the outside of each door. *Cricket, Rum, Apollo...* "Found her!"

"She's still here?" Miss Clarke hurried over, her eyes wide.

Oliver gestured toward the dark bay mare who regarded him curiously from the back of her stall. "It would seem as though our thieves planned on returning one more time."

Miss Clarke frowned. "What shall we do?"

Oliver tugged open the door of the stall next to June's, which was full of hay and supplies. "We'll wait for them to return." Seeing Miss Clarke's dubious expression, he gave her a reassuring smile. "We won't stay here all night. If my guess is correct, the thieves will come to collect their animal soon. They wouldn't dare leave it here for much longer, not if they suspect us of being on their trail."

"Why leave June here in the first place? Why wouldn't they take her with them yesterday?" Miss Clarke maneuvered her skirts through the door.

"They most likely needed to find a new place to board her." Oliver slid into the stall and shut the door behind him. "Assuming they found a new stable, they ought to be back for her at any moment." He gestured toward an open spot behind several of the hay bales. "You take refuge there. I'll hide behind these wheelbarrows."

Miss Clarke wrinkled her nose but moved behind the hay bales, nonetheless. "I'll be finding traces of hay in my skirt for the next five days."

"At least you won't smell like manure."

The woman laughed, her blue eyes sparkling in the dim light. "That is true."

After slipping behind the wheelbarrows, Oliver lowered himself to the ground. "Perhaps I should have chosen a different hiding spot," he muttered as the smell of manure surrounded him. "At least it's not the first time this has occurred."

"Not the first time? Do you mean to tell me you've sat behind manure before? Is it a habit of yours?" Miss Clarke asked, a note of teasing in her voice.

Oliver grinned into the low light. "No, it's only occurred one other time. You see, I was running from a madman with a revolver—"

"A revolver? Goodness."

"Yes, a revolver. I decided to take my chances by hiding in a shed. I ran straight in, slammed the door behind me, and quickly realized I was surrounded by some perfectly awful-smelling piles of manure. The smell was so strong, in fact, that it kept the man from following me in. It took me a week to smell things remotely normal again. Why, my mother nearly had a fit of apoplexy when I returned home."

"Tell me about her. Your mother, I mean," Miss Clarke said with a yawn. "She must be quite the woman to put up with all of your antics."

The smile faded from his face. "She tries her best to be a mother, though she's often more absorbed with her social calendar than she is with my whereabouts. She's sweet, however, and always frets over my welfare when I return home. I've never gone a day without clean, warm clothes in her household." He paused, and his next sentence came out a mere whisper. "But I still feel like something is lacking."

Stillness met his words.

"Miss Clarke?" Oliver peeked across the way...and chuckled.

His companion was slumped against a haystack, her breathing deep and even in sleep. Her spectacles had fallen to the ground, leaving her face looking younger and more peaceful. Probably best to let her rest for a bit before waking her for the walk home.

He, however, had stayed awake for many a mission in the past. Yes, he was quite good at stakeouts and the like. He had never fallen asleep on duty before, so he'd just watch for a few more minutes.

~

*T*he sound of birdsong drew Carina from her slumber. Yawning, she stretched her arms far overhead but snatched them back when her fingertips met something scratchy. What was this? She cracked open her eyes and gave them a good scrub while she waited for the room to come into view. Her gaze sharpened on the dark outlines of hay bales, buckets, wheelbarrows, and...Mr. Bricht?

"Good heavens!" Carina gasped, sitting upright. It *was* Mr. Bricht who lay slumped against the wall, fast asleep. Brushing the hay from her sleeves and collecting her spectacles from the floor, she pushed to her feet and made her way over to where Mr. Bricht was hiding. "Mr. Bricht, wake up. Mr. Bricht!" She shook the man awake with her hands on his shoulders.

"What's going on?" Mr. Bricht mumbled, his voice groggy and his hair mussed. "Did I miss breakfast?"

"We're still at the stables. We fell asleep! Goodness, Mrs. Fields is going to murder me." Carina stood back and twisted her hands. "Oh, what will I say? 'Sorry that I didn't come home, Mrs. Fields. I was sleeping in a barn stall next to a man I hardly know.' Of all the improper, scandalous things!"

Mr. Bricht waved his hand as he pushed himself to his feet, the grogginess clearing from his eyes. "Miss Clarke, do calm down. Our falling asleep was a simple error that can easily be resolved."

"Simple? There's nothing simple about this," Carina whispered fiercely.

Mr. Bricht suddenly wheeled about and peered into June's stall. "Thank goodness." He released a quick breath. "She's still here."

"So there was no reason to risk my reputation after all? Ugh!" Carina tossed her hands into the air. "I need to go home before Mrs. Fields sends out a search party—assuming she hasn't done so already."

Mr. Bricht had the gall to laugh. "You must admit, that would be somewhat amusing." At Carina's dark glare, his expression sobered. "Or perhaps not. I truly am sorry about all of this, Miss Clarke. I never meant to fall asleep."

"Neither of us did, yet here we are." Carina gestured to their rumpled clothes and hay-strewn hair. "Look at me! We look as though we were having a tryst, not a midnight stakeout."

Mr. Bricht studied her with a hand beneath his chin and a smile tugging at the edge of his lips. "I don't know. I find the whole look somewhat charming."

Carina rolled her eyes. "Oh, hush. Come on with you."

As they left their hiding spot, Mr. Bricht cast a forlorn glance toward the horse still in her stall. "I can't help but think we should stay. I feel as though we're terribly close to catching the thieves."

"If you want to stay, I won't stop you. I simply can't let Mrs. Fields worry about my welfare when in reality I am safe and sound." She clapped a hand over her mouth. "Not to mention work! Oh my, we're going to be horribly late. I don't want to lose my job."

Mr. Bricht grabbed her elbow to stop her from running. "Calm yourself. We still have some time. Why, the sun isn't even up. Take a moment and enjoy the morning."

Carina huffed. "What's there to enjoy about this? Our situation seems a bit dire to me."

Mr. Bricht gave her one of his charming grins. "Not a morning person, are we? It could be far worse, you know. For example, the night is clear, yet the air is not overly cold. The city is in motion, but not unbearably noisy. We could have missed work entirely, but instead, we're early. All things considered, I believe we're doing fairly well." He gazed at a nearby streetlamp, the top dusted with snow. "If only we had caught the thieves. Then the morning would truly be perfect."

Something whizzed through the air, and Carina stiffened. She choked back a cry as the white object hit Mr. Bricht in the shoulder, causing him to flinch.

"What was that? Are you all right?" Carina scanned him for injuries.

Mr. Bricht glanced up, amusement spreading across his face. "I do believe I was just accosted by a snowball."

"A snowball?" Before Carina could blink, more snowballs came sailing through the air. Ducking with a squeal, she narrowly avoided getting hit upside the head.

"Look alive, Miss Clarke. I have spotted the enemy," Mr. Bricht said in a mock whisper. "Targets are six young soldiers, spread between two sturdy snow forts. I do believe we have stumbled onto an active battlefield."

Carina followed his gaze to two mounds of snow near one of the side alleys. A tiny face with a red nose appeared behind one of the mounds before disappearing. A moment later, a gloved hand hefted a snowball over the top and sent it flying toward Mr. Bricht, though it fell flat by a few feet.

"Whoa, there. We surrender." Mr. Bricht raised his gloved hands. "May we approach?"

"Well… I suppose," a young voice responded.

As Mr. Bricht began moseying toward one of the forts, Carina grabbed his jacket sleeve. "What are you doing? We have to get home."

Mr. Bricht shrugged. "They clearly have nobody to look after them. The least we can do is give them a few moments of enjoyment."

Looking back toward the mounds, Carina softened. The boys behind the forts wore tattered jackets, trousers, and shoes. While they might have parents, they were currently absent, leaving the children to fend for themselves.

Carina released a long breath. "Only a few minutes, Mr. Bricht."

The man doffed his cap. "You have my word." Trotting up to the lads, he held out a hand. "Oliver Bricht, at your service. Who's the captain of this fine fortress?"

A gap-toothed grin appeared on the tallest lad, who

accepted the hand with a hearty shake. "I am, sir. Robert's my name."

"Well, Robert, would you and your opponents be willing to temporarily take on extra teammates?"

The boy whooped. "Sure, we would! You can stay here, and the lady can go help Jeremy at the other fort. That way it's fair 'n' square."

Carina took a step back, raising her hands up. "Oh, I'm not—"

"Splendid." Mr. Bricht saluted Robert. "May the best team win."

Carina halted and fisted her hands on her hips. "Is that a challenge?"

Mr. Bricht raised a brow, his gray eyes twinkling. "Only if you accept."

She hesitated only a moment before nodding. With that, she spun on her heel and strode to the other fort. "I am here to assist."

The young boy, whom she guessed to be Jeremy, smiled. "Oh boy, an adult to help! You sit over here. When Robert says 'fire,' we'll make snowballs and throw 'em at the other fort."

Carina peered across the alley, spotting the dimly lit outline of Mr. Bricht's black hair behind the other mound. "Very well." She compressed a wad of snow between her palms to form a ball. Then, at Robert's command, she tossed it toward the opposing fort.

Childish squeals rent the air as snowballs found their targets and the boys hurried to make more. Carina's projectile hit Mr. Bricht squarely in the chest, and she giggled, though she had to duck a moment later to avoid a flurry of snowballs being sent her way. By the time a few minutes had passed, the whole lot of them were white with snow. Yet, despite being covered by lumpy mounds of melting slush, Carina felt surprisingly warm inside. Meeting Mr. Bricht's grinning expression, she threw one last snowball in his direction and stood.

"Halt!" Robert called out across the clearing. "All soldiers at ease. The lady and gentleman have to go to work now."

There was a chorus of disgusted noises and murmurs from the children, making Carina laugh. "Thank you for letting me join in. I haven't made a snowball since I was very young," she told Jeremy, who beamed proudly.

"No problem, lady. Thanks for helpin' us."

Mr. Bricht strode across the clearing and took Carina's elbow, pointing her in the direction of the boardinghouse. As they left, small cheers and farewells echoed from the boys, followed shortly thereafter by another cry of "fire!" from Robert.

"Not bad, Miss Clarke. I do believe you soaked my jacket completely through," Mr. Bricht said with a wry grin.

"My good sir, you were the one who suggested I join in. That was hardly proper of me to do, but it was quite a bit of fun." Carina studied his face in the early-morning light. "When did you become so good with children?"

Mr. Bricht grimaced. "I wasn't always. I used to do a fairly good job of ignoring them, sad to say." His expression smoothed into something calmer. "That changed when the Chicago Fire happened. It was horrible, one of the most terrible things I've ever had the misfortune of witnessing. There were hundreds of displaced children roaming the streets afterward. As time went on and the city began to rebuild, I noticed them more and more. In a way, they reminded me of a younger version of myself. They were lonely and in need of a good friend, just as I had been. So I stopped and talked to them. I learned their names and stories and played games with them. I did my best to use my resources and find their families. Those whose parents I couldn't find, I encouraged to seek shelter at foundling homes." He shrugged. "I still miss them on occasion.

They were sweet children. I can only hope the rest of them found good, loving homes."

Carina smiled, brushing a clump of snow from her dress. "That was good of you. Helping them find their families, I mean."

What about Charlotte? Her sister was still nowhere to be found, and her efforts had thus far been fruitless. Though she had initially been unwilling to tell Oliver about her past, he had proven himself to be a good man. Carina glanced at him out of the corner of her eye. Was it finally time to tell him the real reason she had chosen to help him with his investigation?

"Your lane, Miss Clarke," Mr. Bricht said, surprising Carina from her stupor.

"Oh. Thank you." She blinked, loosening her arm from his grasp.

"I suppose I'll see you at the mill, then?"

Carina squinted at the sun, which was rising steadily over the horizon. "Yes, you'll see me very soon." Her question about Lottie would have to wait until then. "I must assure Mrs. Fields I'm all right."

Mr. Bricht bowed. "Very well. I'll see you shortly, Miss Clarke."

Carina turned down her lane, humming an old hymn and running her fingers over the snow-tipped fence that lined the walk. She was a few feet from the door to the boardinghouse when something sharp jabbed her from behind.

"Hello, girl," a deep voice whispered.

CHAPTER 14

"One wrong move and you die," the voice threatened.

The sharp pain in Carina's back intensified as a large, gloved hand pushed her toward a nearby alleyway. Was she really being held at knifepoint, just like the heroes in the fantastical tales her mother used to tell her as a child?

"You should have listened to the first warning I gave you, but instead, you chose to continue to stick your foolish little nose where it doesn't belong. Now you face the consequences."

The shock wore off, and Carina spun to try and look at her captor. She caught a glimpse of broad, black-clothed shoulders and what seemed to be a black domino mask before her arm was twisted painfully and she was forced back around.

"Nice try," the voice hissed in her ear, the smell of spirits rank on his breath. "I'm not that foolish. Now, you and I are going to take a nice walk down this alley. If you try to run from me, I'll slice your back open before you can blink."

He'll kill me. He'll kill me for knowing too much, and I'll be left alone in the alley to die. She had to get away.

Summoning all her fear and energy, Carina let out a shout

which formed words of its own accord. "Mr. Bricht! Oliver, help me, please!"

One of the thief's hands clapped over her mouth, and Carina nearly gagged at the smell coming from his gloves. What was it? Manure and sweat and something else. Alcohol, perhaps? "Shut it, stupid female. You're going to give us away!"

Carina jabbed her elbow hard into his stomach, causing him to let go with a surprised grunt. She managed to run a few feet before she was slammed face first into the brick wall, the impact snapping her spectacles and making spots dance in her vision.

"Maybe I'll just kill you now and be done with it." The heavyset man pinned Carina against the bricks.

Carina struggled against his grip. *Lord above, please give me strength.* Something the thief had said clicked in her brain, and she stilled. "You weren't going to kill me now?"

"No. We need you for something first." The thief pointed his knife at her back with his free hand, making her wince. "Though now I wonder if it was a foolish idea."

"Get off of her!" A new and thankfully familiar voice boomed through the alley.

The pressure lifted from Carina's back, and footsteps sounded as the thief took off down the alley. Turning about, she gasped as Oliver bolted past and tackled her accoster to the ground. He drew his fist back for a punch, but the thief threw him off in a mighty heave before he could make contact. Oliver hit the alley with a hard thud, landing on his back. The criminal leaped to his feet and darted down the dim passage before Carina could get another look at him, leaving the black domino mask on the ground.

The whole thing had happened in the span of only a few moments.

"Oliver, are you all right?" Carina drew herself off the wall and bent over her rescuer, who was struggling to sit upright.

"I really need to stop tackling people." Oliver groaned, rubbing his head. "I do believe that's the first time a person has thrown me, however. I don't think I like it." His steely eyes opened and sharpened on her. "What about you? That dog didn't try anything, did he? When I saw you in the alley with that knife against your back..." He shuddered. "I thought he was going to kill you. You scared ten years off of my life."

Carina released a long breath and pushed a loose strand of hair behind her ear, wincing when she brushed against the tender skin on her cheek. "Apart from a few bumps and bruises, I believe I am unharmed. The thief seemed to want to abduct me, though for what purpose I do not know. I'm simply glad you arrived when you did. Thank you, Oliver."

Oliver studied her face as though confirming the truth of her words. "You called me by my Christian name."

Carina blinked. Had she? "I apologize, Mr.—"

"No. I prefer Oliver." He smiled. "If you'll allow me to call you Carina."

A flush spread across her face. "Well, I suppose it wouldn't do any harm. Considering all we've been through, I think it's fitting."

"Your spectacles are gone," Oliver said, slowly rising to his feet.

"Yes. I lost them when that brute slammed me into the wall. My vision seems to be handling things well enough without them, however, so it's no great loss. I'll purchase a new pair when I have time."

"It's a shame they broke. Why, I'd tackle that villain again if I could." Oliver glanced around the alley. "You mentioned the thief wanted to take you. He didn't say why?"

"No, only that they needed me for something." Carina took a few steps and stooped to pick up the domino mask. "However, he did drop this."

Oliver collected the mask from her with a frown. "Blast. I

should have tried to get a closer look at him. From what I saw, he was bundled from head to toe in black, just as he was when I chased him through the mill. I couldn't even make out his hair color, covered as it was by a cap. Our thief certainly knows the art of disguising his appearance."

The rush of energy from the fight was beginning to wear off, leaving Carina tired and shaky. "Might we discuss this inside the safety of the boardinghouse? I'm leery of staying here any longer."

Oliver nodded and took her hand. "Yes, let's get you home so you can rest."

"Rest." Carina's shoulders drooped, a heavy weight settling over them. "That sounds nice."

They walked to the boardinghouse together. Oliver got one knock in before the door opened and he was thumped soundly over the head with the handle of a broomstick. "Ouch, what on earth?" he cried as the broomstick returned to jab him in the ribs.

Carina couldn't help the laugh that escaped her. "Mrs. Fields, please. He's done nothing wrong."

"Nothing wrong? Nothing wrong, indeed! You've been gone all night, had me worried sick, and now you're here with a man standing next to you on my doorstep! I suppose you've already said your vows. If not, I'll fetch the minister myself." Mrs. Fields gave Oliver another jab in the stomach for good measure.

"Madam, please." He wheezed, holding up a placating hand. "Have mercy. Carina, I mean, Miss Clarke"—he hurriedly corrected himself when a dark look spread across Mrs. Fields's face—"was just attacked in the alley nearby."

The broomstick fell from the boardinghouse owner's hands as she took in Carina's bruised face and disheveled dress. "Good heavens, dear. Are you all right? What happened?"

"The thief from the mill attempted to abduct me. Oliver saved me."

Mrs. Fields paused her examination and arched her brow. "I believe the two of you have quite the story to tell, and I expect to hear every bit of it. Come in."

A few minutes later, Carina and Oliver had finished an abridged retelling of their investigation leading up to their current state. "So you see, Mrs. Fields, we truly didn't mean to be out all night," Carina said. "We were waiting for the thieves to come fetch the horse. Then, just before getting home, I was grabbed and forced into the alley."

Mrs. Fields frowned and set her coffee cup down with a clink. "Regardless of the circumstances, you two ought to know better than to travel without an escort. It is in no way proper."

Oliver raised a hand. "Please don't blame Carina, ma'am. She did nothing wrong. It was my idea to stay."

"Young man, while I appreciate your chivalry, agreeing to stay with you puts her just as much at fault. You two are lucky nobody saw you in that barn." Mrs. Fields puffed herself up. "To prevent such things from occurring in the future, I will henceforth accompany you on your investigation."

"Yes, I am aware that... What?" Carina's eyes went wide. "Mrs. Fields, it's far too dangerous for you to come with us. Did you not listen to my retelling of the encounter with the thief?"

The stubborn old woman crossed her arms. "If you plan on continuing to go places alone with an unmarried man, then I most certainly will. Until you've married, that is."

Carina wrinkled her nose. "That isn't likely to happen."

Oliver gave her a mock look of hurt. "You wound me."

"Bottom of the list, remember?"

"I thought I was improving."

"Perhaps I *should* fetch a preacher." Mrs. Fields tapped her lips. "You two seem to suit each other quite nicely."

"Hush now, Mrs. Fields." Carina glanced at the clock on the wall and gasped. "Good heavens, we must prepare for work. We're late!" She scrambled up from the table.

"Work? You'll do no such thing! You were just attacked and need to rest." Mrs. Fields rose also.

Oliver drew to his feet and gently pushed Carina back into her chair. "She's right, Carina. You stay and rest. I'll go to the mill and come back here to talk to you at the end of the day. You won't miss a thing, I assure you."

Looking between the two people standing before her, their arms barred like soldiers preparing for war, Carina deflated. "I've been outnumbered."

"Indeed, you have. Rest well," Oliver told her with a soft nod. "Now, I must hurry if I'm going to make it in time. Ladies..." He sketched a quick bow and hurried from the room, shutting the front door behind him a moment later.

"Something tells me he was simply trying to find an excuse to escape you and your broomstick," Carina said wryly.

"As he should." Mrs. Fields leaned forward, clasping Carina's hands between her own. "Now, dear, how do you really feel? That horrid thief left a bruise beneath your eye. And your spectacles are gone!"

Carina attempted a smile but faltered when it sent a jolt of pain through her bruised face. "I'm well—apart from being a bit sore, that is. I really am sorry I didn't come home last night."

Mrs. Fields released Carina's hands and sat back, waggling her head. "I know, dear, and to tell the truth, I'm simply glad you are safe. Still, if you intend to continue gallivanting around the city with that man, you will have to endure my company."

"That I can do." Carina rested her chin on her fist. "I'm not certain how agreeable Oliver will be to the idea, but that's beside the point. I know you may not believe him, but he really is a good man. He's never attempted to take advantage of me or forced me to remain with him. If anything, I made myself a bit of a pest by following him about."

"I know." Mrs. Fields waved her hand. "I simply couldn't resist giving him a couple of whacks after he worried me so. He doesn't seem a bad fellow, though. Now, tell me, did you get a good look at your attacker? There's a man I'd like to hit over the head with my broom."

"No, I didn't. He was tall, with wide shoulders and a very strong grip. His voice was very low and deep the few times he spoke to me. Oliver said he was dressed in black from head to foot, with not an inch of skin showing." Carina hummed as another memory from the attack resurfaced. "He was also wearing a domino mask, the sort one sees at fancy masquerades."

"Masquerades, eh?" Mrs. Fields perked up. "Do you recall the dance that the other girls went to, the night that you and I talked about your sister? That was a masquerade-themed dance, and it was open to the public. Even if your thief didn't go to the dance, many of the stores near the mill were selling costumes around that time in preparation for the event."

"Perhaps he purchased one recently, then." Carina sucked in a startled breath. "The receipt!"

"A receipt? I suppose he would have one if he bought a mask."

"Not quite. I discovered a receipt the thief dropped when he ran from us the first time. It was from a drugstore near here. Oliver and I intended to visit it, but we were distracted by the livery investigation."

"Oh, how interesting. When you feel better, perhaps we shall journey over and see what the storeowner can recall."

Carina straightened, ignoring the pounding ache in the back of her head. "You're right. I'll talk to Oliver tonight after the mill closes. We can visit the store then."

Mrs. Fields raised a brow. "Not alone, you won't."

Carina couldn't hide her smile at the older woman's words. This investigation was about to get a bit more interesting.

CHAPTER 15

Standing outside the mill gates, Carina waited anxiously for Oliver to emerge. A soft snow had begun to fall during the afternoon, leaving her stomping her feet and blowing on her hands to keep warm. The precipitation had also left a fine white powder upon the shoulders of Mrs. Fields, who had insisted on accompanying Carina out into the cold.

Shaking the snow from her in a manner that reminded Carina of a hen fluffing its feathers, Mrs. Fields pointed toward the mill doors. "At last, here they come."

Indeed, Ella hastened across the courtyard to meet them. The girl pressed Carina into a quick hug, leaning back to examine her face afterward. "Where have you been? When you didn't come in to work today, I very nearly left to look for you. Then Mr. Bricht came upstairs and told Mr. Browning that you had taken ill. Is that a bruise on your face? Where have your spectacles gone?"

Carina laughed. "Ella, slow down. I'm quite all right, I promise. I had a rather unfortunate encounter with a brick wall, but I am mostly returned to health. It's all thanks to Mrs. Fields. Her scones are healing, I tell you."

Ella turned, her face brightening when she noticed the boardinghouse owner. "Oh, Mrs. Fields! It's been so long. How are you doing?" She quickly encompassed the woman in a hug.

Mrs. Fields wrapped her arms around the girl, returning the hug with equal fervor. "I'm doing well, thank you. How are you, dear girl? You're long overdue for tea and biscuits."

Spotting Oliver crossing the courtyard, Carina left the two women to their conversation and met him halfway. "Oliver!"

"Carina? What are you doing here?" Oliver scanned her as he drew to a halt, eyes wide. "You're meant to be resting at home, not gallivanting around the city."

Carina lifted a shoulder. "I felt well enough. Time is of the essence, is it not? The thief knows who we are. If we don't hurry, we may lose sight of him forever."

Oliver nodded, his face sobering. "You're right. I found nothing new here, unfortunately. All the men were present and accounted for at the picker house, and nobody looked as though they had been in a fight. If we base our search on the height of the thief who attacked you, we're left with six suspects in the picker room alone. There are simply too many people to make an accurate guess."

"I know. That's why we should look into our other lead, the receipt. Mrs. Fields said many stores in the area stocked masquerade costumes in preparation for a ball, so our thief could have returned to Robinson's to buy the mask he wore this morning. In addition, we should also see if Mr. Trout sent us any new information."

"A wise idea, Carina." Oliver tucked his jacket around him as a gust of wind whipped through the clearing. "I'm prepared to go if you are."

"I'm ready." Carina gave him a slight smile. "Of course, we won't be traveling alone this time."

Oliver followed her gaze to Mrs. Fields, who had left Ella and was marching toward them with determination on her face. "Oh."

"Sorry." Carina giggled. "She couldn't be dissuaded from coming along."

"That woman frightens me." Oliver leaned closer and lowered his voice. "If we have another run-in with the thief, I may very well send her after him."

Mrs. Fields reached them and lifted one eyebrow. "What are you two whispering about?"

Carina fought to keep the smile from her face. "Nothing of great import, Mrs. Fields. We were simply discussing our plan. Are you prepared to go to the store?"

"I certainly am." The proprietress wedged herself between Carina and Oliver and looped her arms through theirs. "Let's be off."

Meeting Oliver's bewildered expression above Mrs. Fields's head, Carina grinned. "Let's." As they stepped onto the sidewalk, she realized something. "Oliver, where was Mr. Baker? I didn't see him leaving with you as he normally does."

Oliver cast a quick glance over his shoulder. "He was a bit behind me. Timothy wasn't overly happy with my not arriving home last evening. I couldn't tell him what we were doing, so I pushed off most of his questions."

"Don't you think you owe him some sort of explanation? He is your friend, after all."

"The less people who know about our search, the better. At this point, it isn't even a matter of guarding our identities. It's a matter of keeping others safe. If I told Timothy the truth, he might want to help. I can't let him risk his life." Oliver's jaw tensed, his eyes reflecting his indecision. "I have my hands full as it is."

Carina tilted her head, studying him. "You don't have to protect everyone, you know. You can try as hard as you want, but in the end, we are all free to make our own decisions. Something tells me you keeping the truth from Mr. Baker is hurting him more than you telling him ever could."

"I haven't heard you tell Ella what we're doing." Oliver snapped out his reply. "Besides, until I know Timothy is innocent, I can't involve him."

"Children, please." Mrs. Fields lifted her fingers in entreaty. "Stop your bickering. Arguing about things never made them easier. Now, if you would take but a moment to think about it, I believe you'd find the solution to be clear."

Carina sniffed. "You make it sound so simple."

"Dear, it's only difficult if you make it so." Mrs. Fields's reply sounded sure.

"You're right, ma'am. I apologize for bringing conflict." Oliver rubbed the back of his neck with his free hand, an apologetic smile creeping across his face.

Mrs. Fields gave him a reassuring squeeze on the arm. "You're a chivalrous young man who is doing an admirable job of protecting people. Sometimes, however, that will lead to hard decisions. You must approach those situations with patience when they arise. It's the only way you will make it through."

"Thank you. I'll try to remember that." Oliver met Carina's gaze over the top of Mrs. Fields's head and mouthed, "She doesn't hate me?"

Mrs. Fields laughed. "No, young man, I don't hate you. The only thing in this world that I hate is discovering centipedes in my larder. Those little bugs have no business crawling near my food with their little feet. Now, where are we going? My toes are quite frozen."

"Straight ahead and on the right. Our destination is Robinson's General Store, the store listed on the receipt the thief dropped," Oliver explained. "He purchased gloves and possibly a mask."

The business in question looked relatively high-end, with sparkling glass display windows and a neatly painted sign. Not at all the sort of place a knife-wielding criminal would frequent, at any rate. Currently advertised in the windows were tea sachets, cigars, and...

"Look, Oliver. Masks!" Carina pointed. There were several varieties displayed in the window, along with an advertisement for an upcoming winter dance.

Oliver rolled his shoulders back, his eyes sharpening. "That settles it. Let's go in."

A bell chimed over the door as they entered, followed by a voice calling from the back of the store, "Just a moment, please!"

"Look around and see what you can find," Oliver whispered to Carina and Mrs. Fields. "I'll speak to the clerk and see what I can discover. It will look less conspicuous if only one of us approaches him."

Carina murmured her agreement and moved toward the shelves, pretending to examine a box of matches as Oliver approached the counter.

After a few moments, a slim young man emerged from a back room and slid behind the counter. His black hair was slicked back against his head, and his thin mustache, combined with a large nose, reminded Carina of a weasel. "Good evening. What can I do for you?" He twisted a pencil between his fingers.

Oliver stepped forward and removed the receipt from his pocket, setting it on the counter. "I found a receipt on the floor of the mill where I work and was hoping you could tell me who it belongs to so I might return it. It listed gloves as the purchase."

"Gloves, eh?" Brows knitting, the shopkeeper lifted a wooden box from behind the counter and opened it, revealing a number of receipts. "Let me see. One pair of leather gloves... ah, yes. One pair of gloves to Mr. Baker, three nights ago."

Mr. Baker? Carina straightened the matchboxes with a frown. *That can't be.* He was far too short to be the villain who had attacked her earlier. Dread settled into her stomach at a sudden thought. While Mr. Baker wasn't her attacker, he could have been the carriage driver. Had he been forced into it? Was the man really a hardened criminal?

Oliver inhaled a startled breath. "Well, I'll be. He's a good friend of mine. I'll give it back to Timothy, then." His tone was strained, his shoulders rigid. "I don't suppose he bought one of your fine masks as well, did he?"

Mr. Robinson shook his head. "No, only the gloves. He doesn't buy much from me, though he normally stops in to say hello on his way back from the telegram office. Always wiring money to his family so they can repair the house, he is. He's a good man.

Carina winced. *Oh, Mr. Baker. What are you doing?*

~

"*I* see. Thank you for your help." Oliver offered the clerk a tight smile. No wonder Timothy had been so curious to know where he had gone. The man wanted to know if his partner had been caught! Oh, how could Oliver have been so foolish? He would confront Timothy at the soonest possible moment, but first, he would have to confirm his suspicions.

Oliver approached the women and spoke under his breath. "Come, ladies, let us go."

Once they were outside, it was a few tense minutes before anyone spoke.

"What will we do now?" Carina questioned, her voice soft.

Oliver winced. "Well, I suppose I'll have to talk to Timothy.

First, however, I want to see if the shopkeeper's allegations about his wiring money are true."

"How will you do that?"

"Before our fight earlier today, Timothy invited me to attend Christmas Eve service with his family. Tomorrow I'll ask him if his offer still stands, and if it does, I'll go to the service. I'll speak with his family and see for myself whether or not they're enjoying a life of stolen riches." He huffed a sigh. "Even though I've arrested countless suspects, it doesn't make confronting a supposed friend any easier. I don't know why I hesitate to suspect Timothy, especially when the evidence is right in front of me."

"Perhaps Mr. Baker was forced into it," Carina said thoughtfully. "After all, he was not the one who attacked me with a knife. Perhaps he was threatened into helping."

"True."

Would Timothy really take part in such a despicable plot? It didn't seem likely, but it wouldn't have been the first time Oliver had found a seemingly innocent person to be guilty. His stomach churned as he imagined placing his friend on trial.

Could I really do that? Could I incriminate Timothy? The simple answer was yes. If Timothy was an accomplice in the thefts, Oliver would have to arrest him, no matter how much it would pain him to do so. Carina and the rest of the mill workers were depending on him.

As they walked by another row of shops, a quaint little bookstore near the end of the street turned Carina's head. Her feet slowed as they passed it by, almost as if she wanted to go in.

A hint of a smile flashed across Oliver's face despite his best efforts. "Say, do either of you ladies enjoy reading?"

Carina's surprised gaze met his. "I do, yes."

Oliver gestured toward the bookshop. "Shall we make a quick detour, then? There's still time left in the evening."

"Well, I don't suppose it would hurt." Carina was already moving toward the doorway. "A quick peek would be nice."

Oliver met Mrs. Fields's bemused gaze with one of his own.

The older lady spoke in a low tone as they entered behind Carina. "She truly enjoys reading. I've caught her with a book a few times, but she always hides it away once she sees me."

"Why would she be afraid? There's nothing wrong with being educated." Oliver frowned.

Mrs. Fields adjusted the shawl around her shoulders. "I can tell you are from a different world than us, young man. For people like you, books are often treated as decorations, easily found in every home. For people such as Carina and myself, however, a book is a novelty that can only be bought with extra money. Some may never have that extra money to spend. In addition, there's the matter of education. Some could not afford to school their young ones, or even themselves. For Carina to reveal that she can read would be for her to declare that she has an advantage among many of the others in her company. I believe she is afraid of making them feel as though she is boasting."

Oliver watched the young woman before him, who was brushing her hands almost reverently along the book spines. "It's not fair. To you, to her. It isn't fair that some should have to work three times as hard for an item that someone of better birth might get for free and never even care for."

Mrs. Fields shook her head. "It often feels that way, doesn't it? But we are changing. There are people like you, who have good hearts, who help people like us."

Oliver assessed the older woman. "Something tells me you have quite a story of your own."

Mrs. Fields laughed, wrinkles fanning around her eyes. "We all do, young man. My tale is the same as that of many other people in this city. I came here with the promise of a fresh start. It wasn't easy, starting over. I didn't have everything. However, I had what was important." She nodded toward Carina. "Carina has nearly everything, but there is still something missing in her life. Until she finds the answer to the question in her heart, I fear she will never feel whole."

"The answer to what?"

Mrs. Fields smiled, a gleam in her eye. "That is not my story to tell. What I will say is this, Oliver. You have been put here for a reason. You'd do well to remember that."

A wave of protectiveness washed over Oliver as he looked to Carina, with her simple calico skirt and copper-toned hair. "I will." He dipped his head to Mrs. Fields. "If you'll excuse me, I'm going to go speak with Carina now."

Mrs. Fields waved him off, lowering herself into a chair near the front of the store. "Go ahead. I'm going to wait here and warm these old bones."

Once he was certain she was settled, Oliver excused himself and moved to where Carina stood. She had opened a book with a green cover and was quietly scanning the interior, lifting each page as though it was made of gold leaf.

Tilting his head, Oliver could see by the title on the cover that it was a copy of *Pride and Prejudice*. "A bit of a romantic at heart, are we?" he asked with a chuckle.

Carina let out a startled gasp and jumped, nearly dropping the book. "Oliver, you frightened me!" A flush spread across her face, and she quickly tucked the book back onto the shelf. "No, I'm not. I was simply browsing, and the design on the cover caught my interest."

Oliver raised a brow. "If you're going off of covers alone, then I suppose you might like to read..." He paused to view an ornate spine. "*The History of the Roman Empire*?"

Carina set her hands on her hips. "Oh, all right. Perhaps I do like to read Jane Austen. What of it? She certainly knows how to put haughty, rich fellows in their place."

"So the truth emerges. You're taking notes on how to insult me." Oliver sent her an injured look. "That hurts."

Carina shook her head, a smile spreading across her face. "You are strange, you know that?"

"I'll take that as a compliment. Now, how about that book? Shall we purchase it?"

"No." Her face fell. "I don't have the money for it. Not when I have rent to pay and envelopes to mail."

Envelopes to mail? "Ah, a true shame. Why don't you go wait with Mrs. Fields, then? I'll be there in a moment. There's something I'd like to look for."

"All right," Carina agreed, moving to the front of the store.

Walking quickly through the shelves, Oliver selected two books and took them to the counter to purchase. With his items in a paper bag, he joined the ladies at the front door. "Ready?"

They nodded, though Carina looked a bit forlorn. "Yes."

As they left the store and entered the cold night air, Oliver reached into his bag. "Carina, wait."

"What is it, Oliver?" She turned to look at him with her luminous blue eyes.

Oliver pulled one of the books from the bag and handed it to her. "For you."

Carina took the copy of *Pride and Prejudice*, her lips parting in surprise. "For me? But why?"

Oliver shrugged. "Research purposes. How else will you learn of all the best insults for rich, arrogant men?"

Carina hugged the book to her chest, giving him a blinding smile. "Thank you. A dozen times over, thank you."

Oliver tipped his hat, his own smile growing at the sight of hers. "Of course."

"What did you buy?" Carina frowned at the bag and the item it still held.

Oliver reached inside and removed another copy of Jane

Austen's novel. He smiled abashedly. "I thought I would see what all the fuss is about."

Carina laughed aloud. "My goodness, Oliver. You really are something else." Behind her, Mrs. Fields gave Oliver a look of approval. It seemed he had done right by all accounts.

"Oh, Oliver, you must not forget to check for a note from Mr. Trout," Carina exclaimed, her eyes widening in sudden remembrance.

"You are correct. Come, let us get back to the boarding-house." Oliver took the women's arms. Walking quickly, they made it to Lucy's back porch within a few minutes. "Wait here for just a moment," Oliver told them. "I'm not sure what Lucy's policy concerning visitors is." When they had nodded their agreement, he poked his head through the door. "Lucy?"

His boardinghouse owner looked up from where she was cleaning dinner dishes at the washtub. Upon seeing him, she dropped the dishes into the container and advanced on him, soap suds dropping from her arms to the floor. "Oliver Bricht! For land's sake, where have you been? Timothy and I were worried sick about you."

A low shard of pain shot through Oliver at the mention of Timothy's name. "I was...busy. Not to worry, however. I'm quite all right." He cleared his throat. "I have two ladies with me, a Miss Clarke and her escort, Mrs. Fields. Would it be agreeable with you if they stepped in for a moment while I check my mail?"

Lucy waved one soap-covered hand in the air. "You go right ahead. I've got no troubles with them, so long as they're respectful and don't disturb the sleeping boarders."

Oliver thanked her and ushered the two women into the warmth of the kitchen, where it quickly became apparent by their cheerful conversation that Lucy and Mrs. Fields were going to be fine friends.

Leaving them to their chatter, Oliver returned to the foyer

to check the wooden mail rack that hung by the door and grinned when he found a letter waiting in his compartment. "Aha."

"Is it Trout?" Carina asked from behind him, her soft voice making him jump.

"Yes." Oliver hastily opened the letter, scanning it. "My suspicions were correct. June the horse was taken from the livery on the morning you were attacked in the alley. The thieves collected her when Trout's brother stepped out of the stable."

Carina frowned. "I should have thought they would want the knife back. The one the thief used on me was very similar to the one you took."

Oliver slid the cap from his head, running a hand through his hair. "I can only hope Timothy will be able to provide some answers."

Carina inclined her head, but her expression remained troubled. "Be careful, Oliver. We don't know what he's capable of."

Oliver met her gaze, noting the flicker of fear in her eyes. "I will be." If Timothy discovered they suspected him, all could be lost.

CHAPTER 16

"Timothy! Hey, Timothy! Wait," Oliver called, his breath forming clouds in the crisp morning air as he darted across the street. Despite his early start, he'd missed Timothy by an hour, only finding him thanks to a tip from Lucy about a barbershop visit across town. As he caught sight of the man striding purposefully ahead, Oliver's heart raced with a mixture of indecision and anticipation.

Oliver drew up behind his coworker, reaching out a gloved hand to tap him on the shoulder. "Hey, slow down."

Timothy jumped at the sudden contact and turned to look at Oliver, his brows rising. "Oliver? Why are you out here so early?"

"Looking for you." Oliver shifted and tucked his hands behind his back. "I... well, I owe you an apology. I shouldn't have brushed you off like I did."

Boots crunched on uneven cobblestone as Timothy stepped back. "You could have spoken with me yesterday, but you chose to stay silent. Why?"

Oliver met his friend's eyes and was surprised by the genuine hurt in them.

"I was worried about you. *We* were worried about you—Lucy and I, that is. Yet rather than simply assuring me you weren't in mortal peril and didn't need my help, you remained silent. What's happening? Why don't you trust me? I'm your friend, Oliver, and friends are meant to help each other."

Oliver sighed. Here, then, was the moment of truth. "Timothy, I'm sorry. I betrayed your trust as a friend. The truth is, I'm trying to track down the mill thief. I've been getting closer to discovering his true identity, but the search is getting more dangerous as time goes on. I didn't tell you what I was doing because I didn't want you to get hurt. This thief is a dangerous man who will stop at nothing to get what he wants." He was careful to avoid mentioning that he knew of a second thief. If it was indeed Timothy who assisted the thief on the mill heists, the less he thought Oliver knew, the better.

Timothy's eyes had widened at Oliver's declaration. "Searching for the thief? But why? That's dangerous business, Oliver. I would leave it to the police. Better that than have you try to be a hero and get yourself hurt or killed in the process."

Oliver shrugged, feigning nonchalance despite the fact that the jab hit close to home. "It's not a matter of being a hero. You want full wages just as much as I do, no? I simply want to see this thief brought to justice. If it means I have to look for him myself, then I will."

Timothy studied him for a moment longer speaking. "I won't pretend to understand your motives, but I suppose I can understand why you thought it necessary to keep your search from me. I would offer to help you, but it's clear you don't want my assistance."

"I want to keep you from harm. Involving you would be too much of a risk. If anything, you can help me by ensuring that others don't get suspicious of my snooping around. They've known you for far longer than they've known me and trust you. Talking them down would be a great help."

Timothy toed a rock on the ground, nudging it into a pile of slush. "I can do that. I'm not the heroic sort, but I can talk to people well enough."

Oliver grinned. "Splendid. Am I forgiven for not telling you earlier?"

Timothy shoved his hands into the pockets of his wool coat. "The proper thing to do is forgive you, so forgive you I shall." He raised a brow. "Assuming you promise not to hide things like this in the future. We're friends, Oliver, for better or worse. Friends help each other in times of need, and that means I'm going to help you."

"Friends. Yes." Oliver palmed the back of his neck in mock embarrassment. "I don't suppose it would be too late for me to accompany your family to church on Christmas Eve, would it?"

Timothy raised both brows. "Of course not. My family would be more than happy to have you join us. As a matter of fact, my mother will probably make you her honorary son."

Oliver laughed, trying to hide his warring emotions. It wouldn't do to give away his true intentions. "She sounds like a good woman."

"She is the very best." Timothy puffed up with pride.

It hurt knowing he would have to sit amongst these people, all while suspecting them of wrongdoing. Oliver could only hope that somehow, in some way, the evidence was wrong and Timothy was innocent.

～

*C*arina released a long breath and rolled over in bed with a yawn, enjoying the feeling of being able to wake up slowly. Thank the Lord for Saturdays. Stretching her arms overhead, she jolted when they touched something soft that dangled from her bedframe. She pulled the object down, revealing it to be the dress the sister had given her at the hospital.

Carina frowned, running a hand over the fabric. Why had the woman given it to her? It was nice to have a memento from her sister, but the item itself was of no particular use. She shook out the dress and spread it out across her covers, studying the design. It was a rich red color, but the pattern was simple, clearly made for someone who would use the dress for work and not leisure. Carina trailed her fingers along the inside of the collar and sat upright when something brushed her skin. She peered inside and let out a little gasp. The clothing tag! "That's why," she whispered. "The seamstress!"

Darting from bed, Carina hurried to don one of her dresses, pin up her hair, and tie her boots. She raced down the stairs with the dress in hand and nearly collided with Mrs. Fields, who held the daily paper in one hand.

"Good heavens, child! Where are you going so early on a Saturday? You ought to get some extra rest, what with all that's happened these past few days." Mrs. Fields shook the rolled-up newspaper at her.

Carina shifted the dress she held into one hand so she could button her capelet. "I can't, Mrs. Fields. I've just discovered something that may help me find my sister. Do you recall this dress? It's the one I received from the hospital."

Mrs. Fields nodded. "Certainly. What about it?"

"It has a tag with the address of the seamstress. Charlotte clearly went there at some point to buy the garment for her friend. The seamstress may remember her."

Mrs. Fields hummed, studying the garment Carina clutched. "That is a fair assumption. It's certainly worth visiting the address." She raised a brow. "You weren't planning on running off without me, were you?"

Carina laughed. "Don't worry about me, Mrs. Fields. You

stay here and make breakfast for the boarders. I'll be back before you can blink."

Mrs. Fields fisted her hands on her hips and clucked her tongue, a smile crossing her face. "Oh, all right. I'll have griddle cakes ready upon your return. Be quick and stick to the main roads at all times. If you aren't back within an hour, I'll send for the police."

After bidding the kind woman farewell, Carina raced onto the sidewalk and darted down the snow-slicked road with the dress in hand. Vendors hollered from their booths as she ran by, hawking wares that ranged from tart cranberries to holly wreaths. Though the idea of stopping to investigate the booths was interesting enough, the memory of the thief's attack hung close in the back of Carina's mind, and she kept her distance.

Before long, she found herself standing in front of the dress shop, a small building with a few dresses displayed in the storefront. The sign in the window proclaimed the shop was closed, but shadowy figures were moving about inside. Stepping up to the door, she gave it a firm couple of knocks and waited to see if someone would answer.

One of the figures moved from the back of the shop to open the door, revealing a young woman with reddish-gold hair. "Good day, miss. We'll be opening in a few moments, if you'd like to wait."

"I'm afraid this isn't a matter of dress repairs or purchases." Carina swallowed nervously. "I need to speak to you about someone who may have visited your shop. Her name was Charlotte Clarke. I believe she purchased this dress from you."

The young woman took a step back, splaying a hand over her chest. "Charlotte? What business do you have with her?"

Carina's heart jolted painfully. "She's here?" She struggled to see around the young woman.

"I'm sorry, but Charlotte hasn't worked here for months," the employee said, lowering her hand.

Carina deflated, the air leaving her chest.

"She was only with us for a short time, but she was quite adept at sewing. She even sewed pockets into some of our dresses. The ladies positively loved them."

Charlotte had worked as a seamstress? It didn't surprise her. Her sister had been quite adept at sewing. "If she isn't here, where could she be? You must help me, miss. She's my sister."

The girl gave Carina a sympathetic look. "I really am sorry, but we don't know anything else. Charlotte worked here for a very short time, doing dress repairs and the like. She even created that dress you're holding." She gestured to the red dress. "It was the last thing she made. After that, she vanished. Nobody has heard from her since." The young woman pursed her lips. "However, you might check at the boardinghouse where she lived. Perhaps the owner will know more."

"Do you have the address?" Carina straightened, hope rising once more within her.

"Certainly. If you'll give me a moment, I can fetch a piece of paper and write it down."

The helpful employee hurried behind the counter at the back of the room and returned a moment later with a small scrap of paper.

"Here you are, miss." She handed Carina the note and pointed to the left. "If you go down this block, you should find the boardinghouse quickly."

Carina nodded. "Thank you."

"But of course." The young woman leaned against the doorframe, a soft smile crossing her lips. "I'm not certain what circumstances separated you from Lottie, but I do hope you can find her. She was very kind, and a fine seamstress at that. We all enjoyed having her here."

"I'll make certain to tell her. Thank you for all of your help," Carina said gratefully.

Leaving the dress shop, she moved down the road in search

of the boardinghouse. It turned out to be a shabby-looking place, with drooping siding and a rotting porch. Carina winced as she made her way up the steps and promptly put a foot through one of the floorboards. Had her sister really lived here?

Carina knocked on the door and waited until it was opened by a surly-looking woman with twig-like arms and sharp cheekbones. "Good day. I was wondering if—"

"We ain't got no vacancies," the woman snapped, placing dirt-smudged hands on her hips. "You're the third one to ask this morning."

Carina drew herself upright. "I beg your pardon, madam. I'm not interested in a room, but in one of your former boarders. I was told that Charlotte Clarke lived here."

The woman's close-set eyes narrowed in suspicion. "Sure, she did. Hasn't been here for months, though."

Desperation set in. "Please, madam. Where could she have gone? I must find her. I'm her sister, you see."

The woman sniffed and pushed a strand of greasy black hair behind her ear. "What makes you think I would know? I don't bother with my boarders' business. There's twenty-seven of them in here, far too many for me to keep track of. I never was one to listen to sob stories, anyhow. Charlotte came and went just like the rest of them. She paid in full one morning and left with her belongings for who knows where."

Carina struggled to think of a question before the grumpy woman could shut the door. "Wait. Are you certain she said nothing of where she was going? Did she have any friends at the boardinghouse?"

"No and no. She was out all day and in her room all night. The girl never spoke to anyone from what I remember. She visited the hospital on occasion, but that's all I know. I think she had a friend there."

Charlotte glanced down at the dress in her hand. If what

the woman was saying was true, Charlotte's only friend—and Carina's only potential lead—had been dead for months.

"Ah. Well, thank you for your help." Carina fought back tears as she turned away from the boardinghouse and meandered down the road, staring at the dress in her hands. How could her sister have left without a word to anybody? Where could she possibly have gone? What was she to do when Charlotte hadn't even left her a crumb of information?

"Carina? What are you doing on this side of the city?"

The familiar smell of peppermint surrounded Carina. Glancing up, she found a very surprised-looking Oliver at her side. He was dressed in his usual black jacket, though his cap was crooked and his collar was slightly askew. It looked as though he had darted out of bed without a care for his appearance, a thought that made Carina smile ever so slightly.

"Why, Oliver! I could ask the same of you." She held the dress up. "I was looking into something, and now I'm returning home."

Oliver hummed. "I was speaking with Timothy. I apologized to him, and he agreed that I could still come to church with him. It will be a perfect opportunity to investigate his family." He shifted from one foot to the other, discomfort flashing in his eyes. "I did admit to him that I was investigating the thief."

Carina sucked in a breath. "Are you certain that's a good idea? If he really is the thief, then..."

"No." Oliver rubbed his forehead. "I'm not certain of anything. However, I needed to get Timothy's trust back. Telling him about my investigation seemed like the best option."

"I suppose that makes sense." Carina pursed her lips. "Just remember what I said before and be careful, Oliver. I don't want you to get hurt."

Oliver grinned, cocking his head. "Hurt? Who could raise a

fist to this face?" He gestured to his face and chuckled when Carina raised a brow. "Say, since I'm here, would you like me to walk you home? It would be safer that way."

"That would be lovely." Carina's shoulders drooped. "I admit, I haven't felt safe since that thief attacked me."

Oliver's smile fell, and he cast a quick glance at the street around them. "I've been worried as well. We can't be too careful with that brute lurking around."

Carina shuddered. "Don't remind me."

As they started back toward home, Oliver pointed at the dress. "So...what brought you out this morning? Fixing up a dress of yours? The color is quite nice."

Carina hugged the garment to her chest, wishing she had thought to bring a basket. "No. This dress belonged to my sister. I had hoped the seamstress would know where she was."

Oliver moved to stand in front of her, his eyes widening. "You have a sister? What happened to her?"

Carina looked up into his curious gaze as her chest deflated. "Why don't we take a seat? I have a rather long story for you. One I fear I'm overdue in telling."

"Well...all right. Why don't we step inside and get out of the cold?" Oliver turned to the building in front of them, which had *Hotel* painted in large white letters on a sign above the door.

Carina allowed Oliver to take her hand and lead her inside, across the warm lobby to a couple of cushioned chairs against the back wall, where they both took a seat.

"Where to begin?" Her voice echoed in the vast room. Luckily, there were only a few other people in the lobby, and they seemed too interested in their own conversations to care about hers.

"Your sister. What's her name?" Oliver asked softly, removing his cap.

Carina bowed her head, fiddling with the folds of the red

dress in her lap. "Charlotte, though I always called her Lottie. She's three years younger than me, so she would be twenty-three now. The last time I saw her, she was twenty-two." She paused, wiping at the moisture gathering at the corners of her eyes. Then, taking a deep breath, she began her story. She spoke of the letter from the bank, waking up to the smell of smoke, and running from the house with her sister. By the time she reached her mother's death, Carina had to take a moment to gather herself, as tears were rolling silently down her face.

A comforting hand rested on her shoulder, and Carina looked up into Oliver's kind gaze. "I'm sorry," he said quietly, handing her a wrinkled handkerchief.

Carina accepted it with a murmured thanks and dabbed at her eyes. "I'm not normally one to get teary, I promise." As Oliver was about to protest, she cut him off with a wave of her hand. She leaped back into her story, finishing with her visit to the dress shop and her disheartening trip to the boarding-house. Carina kept her eyes trained on her lap, avoiding what was sure to be a pitying gaze from Oliver. "So, in the end, I'm no closer to finding her than I was when I started. The only person Lottie talked to is gone."

Oliver remained silent for a moment, most likely digesting all that she had told him. "You were alone?"

Carina blinked, caught off guard by the strange question. "Well, yes. There was nobody left to look for Lottie but me, so I did."

"That must have been hard. Searching on your own, I mean," Oliver murmured. "You are a very strong woman to have come all this way, Carina Clarke. You've done something incredible."

Carina laughed, wiping tears from her eyes. "My mother used to call me her 'little butterfly.' Delicate, fragile. *Not* strong. I was too frightened for that."

"You mistook her meaning, I think. Butterflies are amongst some of the bravest creatures on the planet." When she gave him a doubtful look, Oliver leaned forward. "Think about it. A butterfly begins its life as a small caterpillar. It must face danger after danger until it can become a cocoon. From there, it changes into something entirely different, something wonderful. It emerges from its cocoon a beautiful creature. Yet without going through a season of change, it never would have gotten its wings and seen the world. So, Carina, I do not think your mother was wrong. You are a bit like a butterfly. You're simply going through your own season of change. If you persevere, you'll emerge as something even more beautiful than before."

"If seasons of change involve losing your family and home, I think I would rather have gone without." Carina sniffed and twisted the handkerchief in her hands. "Still, I thank you for your kind words, Oliver. I never thought of it that way."

"I'm sorry you went through such a horrible event. I want to help you."

Carina glanced up, sucking in a quick breath. "You could help me? Really? The boardinghouse owner said she doesn't know where Lottie went."

"Never doubt a Pinkerton." Oliver sat back with a smile. "I'll help you find Lottie, Carina. I promise. I'll send a friend to Peshtigo to do some searching. Perhaps your sister traveled back there."

Carina relaxed her hold on the handkerchief as a feeling of warmth spread through her chest. *He really cares.* "Thank you, Oliver."

He rose and helped her to her feet. "But of course. Now, what do you say? Shall we deliver you home?"

"Yes, please," Carina said gratefully. She held the sodden handkerchief out in one hand, grasping the red dress in the other. "Would you like your handkerchief back? I'm sorry it got damp."

Oliver closed her fist around the linen. "You keep it." The corners of his mouth quirked up. "Consider it an early Christmas gift."

Carina tucked the handkerchief up her sleeve and ducked her head, for her cheeks were getting hot. What was that curious feeling building in her chest? "Thank you." As they left the hotel and resumed walking down the lane, she chuckled. "You know, it's a bit funny."

"What's funny?" Oliver scrunched his nose. "Is there something on my face?"

"No. It's just that when I first agreed to help you with the investigation, it was because I was hoping you might help me find my sister. The problem was, I could never find a way to ask." She cleared her throat. "I suppose it's not something that comes easily to me. Trusting, I mean."

Oliver grinned, placing his cap on his head. "I don't blame you. I wouldn't trust someone who tackled me either."

Carina shook her head as a smile twitched at her lips. "Thank you for trying to cheer me up, Oliver. I haven't spoken about the events of that night for a very long time, and yet, telling you about it, I feel...whole. As though something broken inside of me has begun pasting itself back together."

"Keeping your pain locked away will never let you heal." Oliver tipped his cap up and winked. "Sometimes speaking about it is the only thing that will give you the closure you need."

Carina fiddled with the dress beneath her arm, stopping only when Oliver tucked her hand securely around his elbow. "If only I could find Lottie. If only we could catch this thief. There's simply too much happening and never enough time."

"We will do our very best, Carina. This I promise you."

Though Carina murmured her agreement, her heart sang a far more cautious tune. She wanted to believe Oliver's words about finding her sister. She wanted to enjoy the time she was spending with him and bask in the feeling of having someone at her side. She wanted to explore that new and curious feeling that appeared whenever Oliver drew near. But that same tiny spark of fear continued to burn in the back of her mind.

The last time a man had made a promise to her, he had broken it. Would this time be different?

CHAPTER 17

*C*hristmas Eve swept through the mill on Wednesday, its arrival urging the workers to pack their belongings and hurry home to their families. Carina witnessed the oncoming celebration with a heavy heart, knowing she would be spending yet another Christmas Eve on her own. Most of her friends, such as Ella and the boardinghouse girls, went straight home for the holiday. Carina, however, had no such family to go home to. She stood in the courtyard and watched the snowflakes twirl to the ground around her, waiting for the rush of people to thin.

"Carina?" a tentative voice asked from beside her. "Are you all right?"

Carina turned, finding Ella at her side. The girl's hair was tucked under a wool hat, and thin mittens covered her slim hands. Ella gave Carina an apprehensive look, and she realized she hadn't answered her friend's question. She adjusted her new spectacles, which she had purchased from an optometrist earlier that morning. "I'm fine, Ella. What about you? Excited to go home and visit your parents, are you?"

Ella nodded, a frown still upon her face. "I suppose so, but what about you? Have you nobody to spend the evening with? You could always come with me and visit my family if you were so inclined." She shifted from one foot to the other. "We don't have much, but I'm sure we could accommodate you."

Carina pulled her capelet tighter around her shoulders. Her friend seemed uncomfortable with the idea of having visitors, and she could hardly blame her. They probably had a hard enough time making enough money to feed themselves, never mind guests. "That's quite all right. I'll see what Mrs. Fields is doing. I imagine she intends to go to church, in which case, I'll most likely join her."

"Oh. Well, that sounds grand." A smile of relief lit Ella's face. "Here I was, afraid that you would be alone again. It wouldn't be a mark of a good friend for me to allow that."

Carina waved off Ella's concern, along with the ache inside her own chest. "You have nothing to fear. Now, before you go, I've got something for you." She procured a package wrapped in brown paper and twine from within her empty lunch pail. "Make sure to save it for Christmas Day, as we always do," she admonished with a laugh. "I know how curious you can be."

Ella giggled. "Guilty as charged, I'm afraid. The same goes for you." She removed a small package from her apron and presented it to Carina. "Merry Christmas, Carina."

Carina accepted the gift with a smile. "Merry Christmas, Ella. Tell your family Merry Christmas for me."

As her friend left the courtyard with a wave, Carina scanned the area for Oliver. He was nowhere to be found, most likely having gone off to church with Timothy. Carina hugged her arms around her chest and began a slow walk toward the gate. "Protect him, Lord," she whispered to the star-dusted sky as she left the mill grounds and turned down the lane.

"*O*liver, are you almost ready?"

The voice drew Oliver from his thoughts. Timothy stood beside him at the picker table with an eager expression on his face. Oh yes...it was Christmas Eve, the night he was to investigate Timothy's family. A sour feeling curled in his stomach, but he was quick to push it down. There could be no sympathy if Timothy was revealed to be working with a criminal.

The reason for his distracted mind lay not, however, with thoughts of Timothy, but with thoughts of Carina. After seeing her home safely the night before, he had hastened to the telegraph office to send a message. Calling in a favor with a fellow detective, he asked the man to find anything he could on Charlotte Clarke. Now it was simply a matter of waiting for something to turn up. It could take weeks or even months, but Oliver was willing to wait if it meant putting a smile on Carina's face.

And if he solved the case before the man found her sister? What would he do then?

Oliver shifted from one foot to the other. He couldn't stay in Milwaukee, not when Pinkerton expected him back in Chicago for a full report. He could, however, give the detective's details to Carina and let the two of them contact each other.

Oliver grimaced as a stab of something that felt remarkably like jealousy ran through his chest. No. He had made a promise to Carina, and he would see it through himself. Somehow.

"Honestly, Oliver, are you even listening?"

A thump on the back returned him to reality. "Sorry, Timothy. I got caught up in my thoughts for a moment."

Timothy nodded, shoving his hands into the sleeves of his jacket. "Thinking of your family back home? I understand. Christmas is one of the few times that mine comes to visit. They save all year to buy train tickets to Milwaukee."

"Really?" Oliver swallowed. "That's nice of them to come all this way to see you."

"That it is. Now hurry up, would you? I don't want to be late." Timothy tossed Oliver's coat at him.

Oliver slid it on and grabbed his lunch pail.

While they passed through the courtyard, Oliver's first instinct was to search for Carina, but she would be on her own for the evening. He could only send a silent prayer for her safety heavenward as they left the mill grounds. He made a mental note to stop by her boardinghouse on Christmas Day to ensure she had arrived home safely.

For a time, they walked in silence. The faint sounds of conversation echoed around them as couples and families meandered down the sidewalk, their cheeks rosy and smiles wide. What would it have been like to participate in such festivities as a child? Oliver had always spent Christmas Eve working or at home. His mother entertained guests on occasion, but his family had never enjoyed the evening's festivities together. The few times it was just him and his parents, they had sat beside the fire for a short time before retiring to bed. There had been none of the caroling or candles or bright holly crowns that adorned other children's heads.

Oliver broke the silence, eager to escape the heavy feeling weighing on his chest. "So, Timothy, tell me about your family. I don't want to meet them without knowing a thing about them."

"Well, there's my mum and my da. Two finer people you'll never meet. Da started working in a steel factory at the end of the war. He's mighty fine at his job. Even his boss has said as much." Timothy's posture attested to his pride in his father. "As for Mum, she makes lovely paintings and sells them. When she's not covered in paint, she's trying to keep it off of my six-year-old sister, Emmy. She's a master at getting into mischief, but she has a kind heart." He laughed. "The last time they were here to visit, Emmy told me she brought a mouse to class. To hear her tell it, the little thing was shivering in the cold. Unfortunately, her teacher didn't see it quite the same way. Emmy faced a stern lecture after that incident."

Oliver chuckled. "She seems like quite a character. I look forward to meeting her."

Back at the boardinghouse, they changed into respectable clothes and combed their hair. Oliver dressed in one of his old waistcoats and suits, smiling at how different the clothing seemed now. In Chicago, he had worn cravats and neatly tailored suits every day, but here it was something few could afford. Oliver topped the ensemble off with his wool derby, the same one he had been wearing when he first met Carina.

Where was she off to on Christmas Eve? Did she have someone to celebrate the holiday with? There was no time to dwell on the matter, for Timothy's footsteps were sounding on the stairs. Lacing his last boot, Oliver hopped to his feet and joined Timothy at the front door.

"Farewell, Lucy. We'll be back in an hour or so," Timothy called.

From the dining room, Lucy waved a cleaning rag at them. "Have fun with your families, gentlemen. I'll see you this evening."

"Gee, Oliver, you look all spiffed up. Where'd you get a fine suit like that?" Timothy asked as they left the building. Unlike Oliver, he wore a simple but clean jacket and his usual brown flat cap.

"I...saved up for it. I wanted to have something nice to wear on the holidays." Oliver ducked his head so Timothy wouldn't see him wince at the lie. How strange it was, when he had never had trouble lying to keep his cover before. It was even more strange when he considered the fact that Timothy was also being dishonest, if not more so.

Oliver cast a sideways glance at his friend. *Well, no matter.* Tonight Timothy's deception would end.

~

*C*arina headed up the sidewalk at a fast clip toward the boardinghouse. With her attacker still roaming free, she no longer felt safe wandering the streets on her lonesome. If the thief needed her for something, it was likely only a matter of time before he attempted to attack her again. The thought sent a shiver down Carina's spine, and she wrapped her arms around her chest.

All around her, the warm lamplights and snow-tipped trees gave the city the look of a Christmas wonderland. The smell of gingerbread wafted from a nearby store, uncovering a memory that Carina had forgotten long ago.

One Christmas when she was very small, her family had decided to bake a gingerbread stable. Her mother had helped her to shape the dough into the form of a donkey and horse, while her father tried to sneak samples from behind. Charlotte had given up midway through and retired to the floor so she could play with her wooden toys. It was one of the few good memories Carina had of her family all together, memories of a time when they had laughed and sang songs by the warm hearth. Memories of the cold nights when her mother had whispered stories to her and the bright mornings when she had helped her father sculpt snow into the shape of a man.

When had she forgotten? It was as if the fire had overshadowed them. Carina hunched her shoulders as a cold gust of wind blew across her face. No. The memories had begun to fade far before then. It was her father's deception and death that had made them dim, replaced by anger and hurt.

Carina followed the warm smell to a little bakery tucked between two larger stores. Pushing open the door, she was met with the delightfully familiar sight of gingerbread cookies, hiding beneath glass cases to protect them from hungry passersby.

An older man in an apron approached, his brown eyes surrounded by an array of soft lines. "Good evening, miss, and a merry Christmas Eve to you. Can I interest you in anything? A warm cookie to take home and enjoy on this cold evening, perhaps?"

Carina felt in her pocket, mentally counting the few extra coins she kept with her for streetcar rides. She wouldn't need to take a ride for the next few days, so there was no harm in buying a sweet. There were no new leads from Charlotte, anyway.

"Might I please have a gingerbread cookie?" She counted out the change to match the price written on a tiny white placard atop the display case.

"Certainly, miss. Any preference on which one?" The employee—or store owner, perhaps—collected a piece of wax paper to wrap the cookie in.

Carina studied the cookies for a moment, her gaze alighting on a familiar sight. "I would love the donkey, if you wouldn't mind."

"Here you are." He plucked the donkey from the case and held it out to her.

After thanking the man and handing him change, Carina accepted the cookie and hurried to the door before he could see the tears gathering in her eyes. Sliding out into the cold, she wiped at her eyes with her free hand. "Silly, silly Carina. Why all of these tears? You haven't cried this much in the past two years."

As she nibbled on the edge of her treat to soothe her raw emotions, the sound of faint music drew her attention. It seemed to be coming from a white chapel on the opposite end of the park—the church where Mrs. Fields attended.

With no other place to go, Carina drew nearer. The closer she got, the louder the singing and organ playing became. Placing the remainder of the cookie in her pocket, she slid one of the heavy wooden doors open and slipped inside as quietly as she could.

A survey of the interior revealed the church to be a small affair, with a few wooden pews on both sides. Stained-glass windows glittered on the walls, their pictures unlit due to the night outside. Gas lamps adorned each pillar, casting a warm glow over the members of each pew. At the front of the congregation stood the pastor at his altar, a Bible spread open before him.

Amazingly, Mrs. Fields sat by herself on a pew near the back. Normally, the woman had several boarders with her, but it seemed this year she was on her own. Carina quietly moved to the pew and slipped in, taking a seat beside her.

The woman jumped at Carina's sudden arrival, her face brightening a moment later. "Carina, dear," she whispered. "What brings you here?"

Carina gestured toward the front of the church. "I heard the singing and remembered you attended church here. I had nowhere else to go, so I decided to come in."

Mrs. Fields squeezed her hand. "I'm glad for that, dear. I must say, you smell quite nice, like gingerbread."

Carina smiled. "I may have made a small detour on the way here."

And maybe this was where she was meant to end up.

~

"Here we are." Timothy gestured to a building of brown brick, a relatively unassuming place in comparison to the towering marble structures on either side of it. While there was nothing glamorous about the church, a certain warmth came from the interior that wrapped around Oliver like a warm blanket.

The massive church of white stone back home had

reminded Oliver of a castle. As a boy, he had been afraid to even speak inside lest he say something too loudly and earn a reprimand from his mother. While he had attended services with his family, he received no real joy in going. Here, on the other hand, there seemed to be something alive and cheerful in the air. Chatter flowed through the doors every time someone entered, and those who waited outside greeted friends and fellow churchgoers with enthusiasm.

"There they are!" Timothy's sudden exclamation made Oliver jump. "Ma, Pa! Emmy, over here!"

Oliver took careful stock of the family walking toward them. Timothy's father was a tall, brown-haired man with strong shoulders and an assessing gaze. His mother stood a good two feet shorter than her husband, with rosy cheeks and dimples. She quickly enveloped Oliver in an unexpected hug, which he returned after a moment of surprise.

"You must be Oliver. Timothy has told us all about you." She beamed. "We're so glad he's found a friend. We do worry that he gets lonely, living here all alone. I keep telling him to find a nice lady, but I'm afraid he's always been shy around women."

"Ma!" The tips of Timothy's ears reddened. "Oliver didn't come here to hear about my romantic woes. I'll find a woman in God's own time, as you like to say."

"Timmy!" A small girl barreled past with chestnut-colored braids flying, launching herself straight into Timothy.

"Emmy. How are you?" Timothy laughed, catching his sister and twirling her in a circle.

"I'm fine. Mrs. Lamb said I'm doing really well in school," Emmy announced between squeals of excitement at the twirling.

Timothy set her down and patted her on the head. "Well now, that's wonderful, Emmy. No more critters in class, I take it?"

Emmy wrinkled her nose. "Naw. Mrs. Lamb said it wasn't safe for them and that they would have a better time outside. I don't believe her, but I'm listening 'cause that's what the Bible says we should do." She caught sight of Oliver. "Who's that, Timmy?"

"That's my friend Oliver. He's coming to church with us for Christmas Eve."

Emmy looked Oliver up and down before nodding decisively. "I'm Emmy Baker." She extended her tiny hand.

Oliver accepted it with a grin and sketched a pretend bow. "Oliver Bricht. Pleased to meet you, Miss Baker."

Emmy giggled. "You can call me Emmy. Nobody ever calls me Miss Baker."

As the beginning notes of a hymn floated out of the church, Oliver cocked his head. "Well then, Emmy, what do you say we go in and take a seat? Service is starting."

"Yes, let's go and get a seat." Emmy tugged on Oliver's hand, her face brightening. "Come on, Mr. Bricht."

Timothy grinned at Oliver. "I do believe my sister has just chosen you over me."

"I'll consider that a compliment." Oliver swept the hat from his head, allowing the girl to pull him into the church.

Inside, Emmy tugged him over to an empty pew and patted the bench. Oliver complied, taking the moment to look around the interior. It was undecorated, with rough wooden pillars and simple gas lamps. There was no frippery or glamor, yet the church had a homey feeling that Oliver's old church lacked.

Just as the church seemed to lack riches, so did Timothy's family. All four of them were wearing simple clothes that were clean but plain. They wore no jewelry or finery apart from the wedding rings on Mr. and Mrs. Baker's fingers. All in all, they gave no appearance of having extra money. Oliver frowned. He would have to ask about their house after the service. Perhaps the stolen money was being used to rebuild what had been destroyed by the fire.

Before Oliver could ask Emmy what she thought of Milwaukee, the room quieted. The organist at the side of the room began a new tune, and the congregation rose as one. Oliver hastily stood with them. A tug on his sleeve brought his gaze down to Emmy, who held a hymnal aloft for him to see, tracing the words carefully with one finger as she sang along. Oliver joined in with a smile, though he had to bend ever so slightly to read the words.

As the song came to a close, the pastor came to the front of the room and motioned for the congregation to sit. Once they were all settled, he opened his Bible. His voice rang out, strong and sure. "Many of you know the story of Jesus's birth. It is a part of the Bible that many of us were told as small children. Yet even those who have heard it a dozen times, such as myself, take joy in the story of our Lord's birth. It was the day that our salvation was born, the day the prophecies were fulfilled. A day of glorious joy and hope."

"I know the story really well," Emmy told Oliver in a stage whisper. "I got to see the older class act it out last Christmas."

"That sounds wonderful," Oliver whispered back.

He had also heard the story of baby Jesus in his manger many a time as a child...and yet it had never seemed so wonderful or so meaningful as it did now. There was an undercurrent of excitement in the air as the pastor described the angel's visit to the shepherds and Mary and Joseph's journey to Bethlehem. The man told the story in such a way that Oliver could almost imagine himself walking alongside them.

Thinking of this difference gave Oliver pause. He had always been a Christian—of that, there was no question. However, what kind of Christian had he been? He had attended church every Sunday and said his nightly prayers. But when was the last time he had opened the Bible in his suitcase and read of his own free will? The people around him seemed eager to be there, not as if church was just another chore to be completed. Oliver turned his hat in his hands, disturbed.

I'm sorry, Lord. I can do better.

When the service ended, Oliver lagged behind the crowd that rushed to get home for the evening. Something about the building made him strangely reluctant to leave. Oliver cleared his throat. "Timothy?"

His friend paused on his way to the door. "Yes, Oliver?"

"Thank you." Oliver tucked his hands behind his back. "It's been a long time since I've truly enjoyed a church service. I hope I wasn't too much of an imposition on your family."

Timothy grinned, fixing his cap back on his head. "Of course not. Thank *you* for coming with us tonight. We enjoyed having you."

Timothy's mother wrapped Oliver in a hug. "Yes, we did. I expect to see you around, Oliver. Next time we visit, you'll have to have dinner with us."

"Yes, yes, please do." Emmy tugged on Oliver's coat sleeve with a mittened hand. "I'll show you my pet squirrel."

"Pet squirrel? I don't recall a squirrel." Timothy's brows furrowed.

"I found him in an alley this morning. He's missing an eye, like a pirate." Emmy put a hand over one eye to mimic an eyepatch. "I might keep him."

"There'll be no keeping squirrels in the house, Emmeline." Timothy's father chuckled, the sound a low rumble. "Run along now." He waved at Oliver. "It was nice meeting you, Oliver."

"You as well, Mr. Baker. Have a Merry Christmas." Oliver sucked in a breath. Oh yes... he had nearly forgotten to ask about their house repair. "Best of luck with rebuilding your home. Timothy tells me it's going well."

Timothy's mother set a hand on Timothy's arm. "We were finally able to fix the roof thanks to Timothy's last payment.

What with that awful theft at that mill, we weren't able to do much building for a while. Timmy tells me they still haven't caught the man."

Oliver shook his head. "I'm afraid not."

By all accounts, Timothy's family was suffering as heavily from the thefts as the rest of the mill workers. If that was the case, why did the robber have Timothy's receipt? Was Timothy hiding the money somewhere, or was he truly innocent?

~

Carina listened in rapt attention as the pastor recounted the story of Jesus's birth, though it was her mother's words that seemed to echo through her mind. She had told Carina the Christmas story every year, a memory that made sadness wrap once more around Carina's heart. Pushing the feeling aside, she worked hard to keep a smile on her face for the remainder of the sermon and the song that followed.

Once the pastor dismissed the congregation, Carina and Mrs. Fields joined the group of people gathering near the door of the church. She met each curious face with a smile as Mrs. Fields introduced her to her fellow parishioners. There were many choruses of "Merry Christmas" and "Have a good Christmas Eve" as they made their way through the crowd.

Mrs. Fields placed a hand on Carina's back and steered her toward the pastor, who stood to the side of the door. "Pastor Green, this is one of my boarders, Carina Clarke. Carina, this is Pastor Green."

The pastor nodded to Carina, giving her a warm smile. "It's good to meet you, Miss Clarke. Mrs. Fields often mentions you. All good things, of course," he added. "How has your Christmas Eve been thus far?"

Carina returned his smile with one of her own, though it

wobbled a bit. "It has been quite nice, Pastor. Your sermon was lovely."

Pastor Green clasped his hands together. "I'm glad to hear it. Have a nice evening, ladies. I hope to see you here in the future, Miss Clarke. We would love to have you."

"Thank you. I believe I will return," Carina agreed softly. Following Mrs. Fields into the night, she removed the cookie from her pocket and resumed nibbling on it until there was nothing left but crumbs.

"Wonderful sermon, wasn't it?" Mrs. Fields asked, a tranquil expression spreading across her face as they strolled the dark street.

Carina hummed her agreement, her mind still twirling between the sermon and her mother. Tears gathered in her eyes yet again, and she quickly averted her gaze to wipe them away.

"Dear? What is it?" Mrs. Fields's voice floated from over her shoulder, and a moment later, the woman's arm came around her waist as she drew alongside Carina.

"It's silly, really."

Mrs. Fields frowned. "Tears are not a laughing matter, dear. Now, let's get inside and sit down. Then you can tell me what's on your mind."

Carina blinked. At some point, they had reached the red boardinghouse door, though she couldn't remember walking up the steps.

Inside, Mrs. Fields removed her coat and scarf and tugged Carina over to the nearest seat. After striking a match, she lit the wood in the fireplace and bustled off to the kitchen. A moment later, she returned with two steaming cups, handing one to Carina. A sip revealed the contents to be hot chocolate.

Taking a seat next to Carina, Mrs. Fields took a drink from her own mug. "Now, then, tell me what's on your mind. You can trust that I won't tell a soul."

Carina slowly unraveled the scarf from around her neck, letting it pool in her lap. "Truly, it isn't anything serious. I was simply thinking of my family. Christmas used to be one of my favorite holidays because we always spent it together. We had the best of times playing in the snow and baking in the kitchen." She cleared her throat. "Of course, it all changed when my father went off to war. Things were never the same after that. We had to focus on keeping our lives from falling apart." She sniffed as moisture burned hot at the back of her eyes. "And now my family is gone. All I have left are memories, and even those are tainted."

Mrs. Fields tilted her head. "Tainted? By the fire?"

"Yes, among other things." Carina stared at the swirling liquid in her mug, wishing she could disappear into its depths. "When my father died, because of the hurtful way it happened, I strove to block out everything I remembered of him. It was easier to forget. Yet, in doing so, I fear I may have destroyed what little I could recall from when our family was whole." She sniffed. "I miss them so much, Mrs. Fields."

Mrs. Fields leaned over to grasp her hand. "Dear, there's nothing wrong with missing your family, just as there's no shame in forgetting. Sometimes the hardest part of grief is trying to remember the good while you're handling the pain. During those times of hardship, it's important for you to understand that good times will come again. Maybe not today, and maybe not tomorrow. But they will come." She squeezed Carina's hand before sitting back. "I promise."

Carina sighed and traced the rim of her mug with her finger. "Sometimes I wonder what my mother would think if she could see me now. The last thing she asked me to do was stay with my sister, and I failed. I lost track of Lottie."

"Now, don't you speak like that," Mrs. Fields said sharply. "You know your mother would never think such a thing. Carina, you tried your hardest to watch your sister. Why, you've never given up looking for her. If your mother could see you today, I believe she would be incredibly proud of you. You've grown into a fine young woman."

Carina gave Mrs. Fields a watery smile. "Thank you, Mrs. Fields." She set her mug down and removed her spectacles so she could wipe her eyes. "I told Oliver this only yesterday, but in speaking about my family, I feel as though something inside of me is healing. It's been broken for a long time, but I didn't realize it until now."

Mrs. Fields nodded. "I'm glad, dear. It wouldn't be right for you to try and face this on your own. I only wish you would have told me all this sooner so I could help."

"Oliver said the same," Carina murmured, staring into the fire. "I'm glad to have both of your help. I only wish Charlotte would have left me some kind of clue as to where she went." She frowned. "I hope she isn't alone on Christmas Eve. I wonder if she's missing our family as well."

"I'm sure she's safe, wherever she may be. She'll come back to you, Carina. I just know it." Mrs. Fields shifted in her chair, the folds of her scarlet dress rustling. "I'm glad to hear that young man has decided to help. What is he doing this evening?"

"He went to church with Timothy's family." Carina pursed her lips. "I hope he discovered something. We can't let this thief go free for much longer."

"True. Especially not when he seems to make a habit of assaulting innocent women." Mrs. Fields sniffed. "The barbarian."

Carina pushed her spectacles up. "Oliver is more determined than ever to catch the person responsible."

"Well, let us hope he finds something soon. I'll pray for his safety." Mrs. Fields gestured toward the fire. "For now, however, let us focus on Christmas. You deserve a break, dear. Hopefully, Oliver will take one as well."

Carina rested her back on the chair, taking a sip of her hot chocolate. "If only I knew the thief would rest as well. Then I wouldn't worry so."

Mrs. Fields laughed. "A life spent in worry is a very poor one indeed, dear. Now, what do you say to helping me bake some sugar cookies? We can string the dried orange garlands on the tree as well."

Carina glanced at the boardinghouse's Christmas tree, a rather small thing that had been covered in a variety of mismatched ornaments. For the first time in a long while, a sense of calm washed over her—a fragile but genuine hope that perhaps, one day, the good memories could be more than just distant echoes and the sadness hanging over her would be gone. She dried her tears and smiled. "I would love to, Mrs. Fields."

CHAPTER 18

*C*hristmas Day had never been a quiet affair, and this year looked to be no exception. Carina grimaced as yet another girlish squeal punctuated the air, followed by the sound of tearing paper. Rolling over in bed, she glanced out the bedroom window. Judging by the dark sky outside, it was far too early to be awake and opening gifts. Still, Carina couldn't deny the tiny thrill of excitement that went through her, just as it had when she was small, at the thought of giving and opening gifts.

When her feet touched the cold ground, Carina shivered. Ella's gift lay unopened on her nightstand, practically begging her to unwrap it. She slid her feet into her discarded stockings and set about doing just that.

Wrapped in a thick layer of paper was a wonderful comb, the handle made of polished pewter. "Oh, my," Carina whispered, running the bristles carefully through the bird's nest of curls that was her hair. Unlike most combs, which caused her hair to frizz when brushed, this one made the thick locks soft and silky to the touch. Carina smiled, knowing her friend must have searched long and hard for such a fantastic gift. She could only hope that Ella would enjoy the new set of ribbons Carina had found just as much.

Carina opened the drawer of her nightstand and withdrew a package of her own. After ensuring that it was still neatly wrapped, she closed the drawer and padded down the steps.

The boardinghouse parlor had been filled to the brim with excited girls, both those who lived there and visitors as well. Wrapping paper lay discarded on the ground as presents were revealed and held up to the light for inspection. Carina caught sight of dresses, cosmetics, and even an engagement ring as she waded through the group in search of Mrs. Fields. Passing by a small cluster of chattering females, she finally caught sight of the dear woman hefting a platter back toward the kitchen.

"Mrs. Fields," Carina called over the noise.

The boardinghouse owner smiled and deposited the tray in the kitchen, advancing on Carina a moment later. "Carina, dear, Merry Christmas! How are you feeling this morning? Can I interest you in a fresh cup of coffee and a treat?" She waggled a cookie at Carina, tempting her with the smell.

Carina accepted the cookie with a laugh. "Thank you, Mrs. Fields, and Merry Christmas to you also. I feel quite well, thank you. I have something for you." She pulled the present from under her arm and presented it to Mrs. Fields.

Mrs. Fields accepted the gift with wide eyes. "Oh, dear, you didn't have to buy me anything. Helping me with the cookies last evening was gift enough."

Carina waved a hand. "Oh, nonsense. Go on and open it."

Mrs. Fields peeled back the wrapping paper, revealing a cookbook Carina had discovered at the same store Oliver had bought her *Pride and Prejudice*. "Oh, my. Carina, this is lovely." The landlady peeked through each page, her eyes brimming with excitement. "This is splendid. I'll be able to make some delightful dinners with these recipes. Thank you, dear. Thank you."

Carina smiled. "I'm glad you like it." Now she had but one gift left to give, though the intended recipient was not present at the moment. "If you'll excuse me, I'm going to get dressed. It's a bit cold to be standing about in my nightgown," she said, tugging on the thin fabric of her gown.

Mrs. Fields nodded. "Of course, dear. Go and get warm. Oh, and don't forget your cookie. We worked hard on them, after all."

"I won't." Carina took a bite of the cookie for emphasis.

Upstairs, she was quick to slide on her warmest dress. As she pulled it over her petticoats, a piece of paper slipped from the fabric and fluttered to the ground. The letter from the hospital! Carina picked it up and slowly lowered herself onto the bed, looking at the unassuming scrap of parchment held between her fingers.

What was her sister doing on Christmas? Was there snow where she was, or was the land green? Had she received any gifts? Turning her gaze toward the ceiling, Carina lifted up a silent prayer for Lottie's safety, wherever she was. If only there was something more she could do to find her sister. Unfortunately, Lottie seemed destined to continually evade her.

A knock at the bedroom door disrupted Carina's thoughts. "Carina?"

Carina recognized the voice as belonging to one of the boardinghouse girls. "Yes, Elara?"

"There's a fellow at the door. He's asking for you." Elara giggled. "He's quite handsome, if I do say so myself."

"Oh, dear." Carina sighed and lifted herself to her feet. Oliver must have braved the horde of females to try and see her. She could only imagine what they were saying to the poor man. After grabbing the remaining package from her nightstand, she rushed past Elara and down the stairs. Carina hurriedly laced her boots and darted to the door, where Mrs. Fields was waiting with Carina's capelet in hand and a knowing gleam in her eye.

"Oliver is waiting for you outside. Don't stay out for too long, now. It's far too cold to be wandering around all day." Mrs. Fields handed Carina the cape. "You can give him a cookie as well. Tell him Merry Christmas for me."

Carina accepted the cookie and tugged the capelet about her shoulders. "I will. Take care, Mrs. Fields. I'll see you in a bit." After slipping out the front door, she closed it softly behind her and turned to face Oliver. He cut a fine figure in a charcoal-gray jacket and blue waistcoat with a cravat tied rakishly about his neck. He held a stovetop hat in one hand, leaving his hair to drape across his forehead in dark waves.

As Carina smiled in greeting, Oliver held out a small square package. "Merry Christmas, Carina. That's a fine pair of spectacles you've got. Brand new?"

She took the package, raising a brow. "Yes, they are. I had to replace them, or else I would be wandering about half blind, and that simply wouldn't do."

Oliver placed his hat on his head. "They suit you quite well, fair lady. Did Mrs. Fields make that cookie you're holding?"

"'Fair lady'? Where'd you get a name like that from?"

"A gentleman always addresses a lady with respect." A mischievous grin crossed Oliver's face. "Even if said lady engages in activities such as falling asleep on haystacks and hiding beneath office desks."

Carina shook her head, fighting the laugh that bubbled up in her chest. "You're terrible. Perhaps I won't give you this cookie, after all." She waved it under his nose in a teasing manner, trying to ignore her accelerating heart rate. *Fair lady.* Nobody had ever called her such a sweet name before.

Oliver's face fell. "Well, now, that really would be tragic. That frosting looks positively wonderful."

Handing Oliver the cookie and his gift, Carina tilted the

package he had given her over in her hands. "Mrs. Fields sends her regards. Merry Christmas, Oliver."

Oliver took a bite of his cookie. "Delicious, just as I suspected it would be."

Carina took the moment to unwrap his gift, revealing a small wooden box. Filled with curiosity, she carefully opened the lid and nearly gasped in surprise. Inside lay a silver necklace with a small butterfly pendant hanging from the chain. Carina lifted the necklace tenderly, running shaking fingers over the pendant. Looking up, she caught Oliver watching her, his gray eyes unreadable. "Thank you," she whispered, not trusting herself to say more.

Oliver nodded slowly, the corners of his lips tugging up in a smile. "You like it? I wasn't sure if you would."

"I love it," Carina stated firmly, securing the clasp and settling the necklace around her throat. "This is the most thoughtful thing anyone has ever given me."

Oliver's eyes revealed his relief. "I'm glad to hear it. It looks splendid on you." Tugging on the twine of the package in his hand, he unraveled it and held Carina's gift aloft. She had chosen a warm scarf for him with wool the color of Lake Michigan on a cloudy day. Wrapped inside the scarf lay a small brass compass, easy to slip into a jacket pocket.

"To keep your sense of direction on your adventures," Carina explained when he gave her a curious look. "With all of your traveling about, it wouldn't do for you to lose your way."

Oliver clicked open the lid of the compass and studied the interior. "This is positively wonderful. Thank you, Carina. It'll be of much help to me when it comes time to track down criminals." He tucked the compass into his jacket pocket and wrapped the scarf loosely around his neck. "What do you think? I find the color quite fetching." He turned from side to side as though posing for her.

Carina covered her mouth to hide her giggle. "You look

dashing, Oliver Bricht. I'm glad my color choice is agreeable with you."

Oliver held out his arm. "Will you walk with me, Carina? There's somewhere I'd like to go if you're amenable."

"Certainly." Carina accepted his arm, falling into step beside him.

As they ambled down the cobblestone walkway, gentle snow began to fall from the sky. It was the type that seemed to hover, uncertain of its destination, before finally settling upon a fencepost or roof. Several flakes drifted down to land upon Oliver's coat and hat, making it look as though he was covered in powdered sugar. Carina must have looked the same, given the fact that snowflakes kept falling onto her spectacle lenses. It was peaceful.

Since Oliver appeared lost in his thoughts, Carina opened the conversation. "How was your Christmas Eve? Was the church service all you hoped it would be?"

Oliver blinked, withdrawing from his reverie. "It was enlightening in some ways and confusing in others. I was introduced to Timothy's family and can confidently say they were some of the nicest folks I've ever met. They didn't look like people of money." His shoulders drooped a fraction. "Not in the least."

Carina tilted her head to the side. "You don't believe Timothy is sending them the money, do you?"

"No. I can't fathom why he would even be involved in criminal operations to begin with. What would Timothy be doing with the money if he isn't sending it to his family or using it for himself? Is he being blackmailed? If so, his family could be in grave danger." He adjusted the scarf around his neck. "I don't know what to do, Carina. I want to help him if he's in trouble, but I don't want to risk giving myself away if he's willingly participating in crime."

"It is a bit of a conundrum, isn't it?" Carina ran a hand over the frost-tipped fence that bordered a yard beside the sidewalk, the icy chill seeping through her gloves. "Did Timothy or his family give any indication that they were under duress?"

A sigh hissed from between Oliver's teeth. "Again, no. They were all so... content. It was as if all the money in the world didn't matter so long as they had each other's company." Longing flashed across his face, quick enough that Carina wasn't even certain she had seen it until he murmured, "Sometimes I wish my family was that way."

"Do you not spend much time together?" Regret immediately tore through her chest as she heard her own words. "Please, ignore that question. That was rude of me."

"There's nothing to apologize for. It was a reasonable question." Oliver tucked his free hand into his pocket. "My parents never put much emphasis on spending time as a family. We attended church on Sunday and visited friends together, but apart from that, we only saw each other in passing. My father was always busy at work, and my mother preferred entertaining company to doing things with me. They weren't bad parents, mind you. I know they did their best." His voice dropped to a whisper. "But it sometimes feels as though they didn't care. As though I wasn't good enough for them."

Carina swiveled, putting herself in front of Oliver and forcing him to halt. "Oliver Bricht, I'm certain they care about you more than anything else in the world. How could they not, when you're doing such marvelous things? Any parent worth their salt would be honored to have a son like you."

A flush spread across Oliver's cheeks. "You don't need to flatter me, Carina."

"It's not flattery. It's the truth." Carina spun on her heel and tugged on Oliver's elbow, prompting them to resume walking. "And even if they weren't proud of you..." She swallowed, contemplating whether or not to say the next words. "I am."

There was a moment of silence as they both let the words sink in. Then Oliver murmured, "Thank you, Carina. It means a lot to me that you would say that." He kicked a rock with the toe of his boot, sending it flying across the snow-covered cobblestone. "Unfortunately, pride or not, I still have no idea what to do about Timothy."

Carina placed a finger against her cheek and straightened as a wave of realization washed over her. "If you could speak to your parents right this second, would you? Would you give them a chance to explain why they've spent so much time apart from you? Would you offer them your side of things?"

"Well, yes."

"Then perhaps you need to do the same with Timothy." Determination built within Carina. "Asking him point blank will offer him a chance to give you the truth. If he doesn't, then we'll simply have to move a bit quicker. But at least it will give Timothy a chance to admit his involvement. If he is being coerced into crime, it will be an excellent escape." Seeing the apprehension on Oliver's face, she patted his arm. "You have to be willing to trust, Oliver. Trust that God will see things through. If this doesn't work, something else will. He'll show us the right way."

"I suppose." Oliver released a long breath, his eyes twinkling beneath the brim of his hat. "You're a wise woman, Carina." He tipped his head toward the space in front of them. "We have arrived."

Following his gaze, Carina let out a small gasp. "Oh, Oliver."

Before them lay a park with a frozen pond in the center. People speckled the ice, each with a pair of skates strapped to his or her feet. A pang of sadness ran through her as a mother helped her young daughter toddle across the pond. Carina could recall the day her mother had helped her do the very same thing, carefully leading her out onto the ice and holding

Carina upright as she found her balance. Carina had kept her first pair of skates for a very long time, until their lack of money forced her to get rid of them for a few pennies.

"Carina? Are you all right? We don't have to skate if you don't want to." Oliver's face mirrored the concern in his voice.

Carina shook her head firmly. "No, I want to skate. It reminded me of my childhood, that's all. It's been a long time since I stepped out onto the ice."

Oliver chuckled, looking a bit embarrassed. "Well, that's more experience than I have. I'm afraid ice skating is not part of my repertoire."

"Well, there's a first time for everything, isn't there?" Carina tugged him toward a wooden shack where a woman was renting out skates. "Don't worry. I had to teach Lottie, and she fell dozens of times. I doubt you could do much worse than her first attempt."

"We live in hope. I don't suppose she was under the age of eight, was she?"

Carina dipped her head to hide her smile. "She may have been four or five."

"Good grief. Well, let us hope I can do better than a small child. Otherwise, my pride may never recover."

After paying the kind lady for the use of two pairs of skates, they found a nearby bench to sit on and put them on. The blades were sharp, just as they should be. Despite the skates feeling foreign after so many years, Carina was quick to ready herself. She carefully stood, then turned to observe Oliver's progress.

Leaning heavily on the park bench, he rose slowly, keeping his legs stiff and spread apart. Once upright, he gave Carina a triumphant smile. "Voilà."

"Done like a true professional." Carina fisted her hands on her hips, raising a brow. "Now the question is, will you make it to the pond without falling?"

A determined look came over Oliver's face at the challenge, and he pushed off the bench, making his way toward the pond with hands outstretched. Carina had to stifle a laugh at the bird-like way he waved his arms in a desperate attempt to keep his balance. In Oliver's defense, however, his strange method helped him to reach the fence surrounding the pond without incident.

"Well done." Carina made her way to his side. "I didn't do nearly as well during my first skate."

Oliver smoothed his hair back from where it had fallen over his forehead. "I'm guessing you were also a child, so I'm not sure how much of a compliment that is. Still, I thank you for your kind words. Shall we?"

"We shall." Carina stepped cautiously onto the ice. It took her several moments to gain her balance, and she skated a few feet for practice before turning about to find Oliver. A giggle escaped her at the sight of his serious face as he took one step, then another, onto the ice. Skating up next to him, she took his arm.

"This isn't as bad as I thought," Oliver said, his brows furrowed in concentration as he matched Carina's pattern of sliding first one foot and then the other. Only a moment later, however, Carina had to clutch at his elbow to prevent him from falling.

"Not so bad, you say?" She laughed. "We'll see about that."

It took several turns about the pond and numerous stumbles and near falls before Oliver was confident, but by their seventh time around, he was able to keep abreast of Carina with little difficulty. "You truly are a quick learner," she said approvingly.

Oliver pretended to sketch a bow, the effort of which nearly cost him his balance. "Why thank you, fair lady. You have to be, in my profession. Are you enjoying yourself?"

Carina took in the moment. The sound of her skates gliding

across the ice. The gently falling snow that drifted lazily through the air. Her warm exhale that created a cloud of white in the air. The solid, reassuring feel of someone's arm entwined with her own. "Yes," she murmured. "I'm enjoying this immensely. Thank you, Oliver."

Oliver grinned. "But of course, fair lady." His expression grew serious. "You deserve to take a break every once in a while. Something tells me it's been a long time since you've been able to fully relax."

"You aren't wrong. And yet I wouldn't trade the last few weeks for the world. I've learned more about the people around me in the past few days than I have in the whole two years I've lived here."

Oliver hummed, his gaze distant. "I'm glad."

"What are you thinking about?" Carina studied him for any sign of emotion.

He shook his head, the clouds in his eyes clearing. "Nothing of consequence. For now, let's simply enjoy the day. I don't want to get caught up in my mind and miss all of this."

Carina arched her brow. "If you say so." She tugged him into a quick spin and laughed when his surprised gaze met her own as they twirled. It took only a moment for them to lose their balance and fall, sending Carina sliding in one direction and Oliver in the other. Sitting up, she adjusted her skirts and called out, "Are you all right?"

"Perfectly fine." He peered at her from where he had slid to a stop a few feet away. "What just happened?"

Snow fell from Carina's skirt as she placed her arms in front of her and rose rather ungracefully. "I was trying to keep you focused on the moment. Is it working?"

A muffled laugh rang through the clearing as Oliver staggered to his feet. "Most assuredly."

After they made several more laps around the pond, the cold air finally drew their skating to a halt. They returned their skates to the shack and set off for the boardinghouse. While she was slightly chilled, the warmth in Carina's chest was enough to make her content.

At length, she broke the comfortable silence. "Oliver?"

"Yes?" He tucked his scarf more securely around his neck.

"Thank you. I haven't had such a nice Christmas in a very, very long time."

As a group of children ran past them, Oliver shifted closer to Carina, enveloping her in the smell of mint. "Of course. I'm glad you had such a nice time. I'm glad you like your present, as well." He patted his coat pocket, where the outline of the compass was faintly visible. "I certainly like mine."

Carina ran her fingers over the metal butterfly that hung around her neck. "I do like my present, very much." She looked at Oliver from the corner of her eye. "Oliver, what will you do when you finish this case?"

He blinked. "You mean when I catch the thieves?"

"Yes."

Oliver frowned and took a step away from her. "I suppose, if I don't receive another assignment right away, I'll go back and spend some time with my parents." He cast a sideways glance at her. "The three of us need to have a conversation that's far overdue. I don't know if it will change anything, but at least I'll know that I tried. Perhaps it will give me understanding on why they've been so distant."

"Oh. I see." Carina held her shoulders stiff, trying to tamp down the disappointment in her chest. Why would Oliver stay in Milwaukee when he had no reason to? It was only a job, after all.

"Of course, my job doesn't end with the thief, you know. I did make you a promise, and I intend to fulfill it. I won't be going anywhere until your sister is found."

Carina glanced up, surprise crossing her features before she could prevent it. "Oh, you don't have to—"

Oliver shook his head firmly. "I'm not going anywhere, Carina," he stated, his voice as clear as the icicles that hung from the eaves of each building. "I always see my promises through."

Always? Carina's posture softened as hope crept back into her heart.

CHAPTER 19

*N*ever before had Carina been quite so unmotivated to go to work. After rolling from bed, she inched her stockings and shoes on, as though that alone would prolong facing the day ahead of her. The mere thought that the thief might attack again made her long to dive back beneath the covers and pretend the world didn't exist. With the mill at stake, however, there was no time to play coward. And so Carina took a deep breath and marched down the stairs.

"Good morning, dear. Breakfast is almost ready if you'd like to sit down," Mrs. Fields called from the kitchen, her voice cheerful.

Carina slid a chair out at the dining table and took a seat amidst the other boarders. True to Mrs. Fields's words, breakfast was not long before coming. After devouring her plate of eggs and bread, she collected her lunch pail, bid Mrs. Fields farewell, and darted out the door before she lost her nerve.

As she walked down the lane, Carina tried to comfort herself with Mrs. Fields's reassurance that she wasn't alone. *Lord, please protect me. Stay with me.* If only she could know for certain they would catch the thief. Then, perhaps, some of the anxiety hanging over her might abate.

"Carina! There you are," a familiar voice said from the right.

Turning, Carina smiled at the sight of Oliver hurrying in her direction. His eyes shone with determination as he fell in step with her, wrapping her arm around his.

"Has something happened? You seem like a man on a mission," Carina observed as they walked briskly down the lane.

Oliver popped a mint into his mouth and chewed for a moment before answering. "Nothing serious. Yesterday simply convinced me that I must confront Timothy as soon as possible about the receipt. I plan to do so over lunch today. With luck, he'll tell the truth, and I'll be able to formulate a new plan based on his answer."

Carina hummed appreciatively. "Well, I'm glad you made a decision about it. Is there anything you'd like me to do while you talk with him?"

"No. Except pray."

What a heartening request. "I can do that."

"Thanks. Otherwise, continue your day as normal. I don't want to alert him to your presence in my investigation. I'll inform you what he says after work."

"All right." They turned into the mill courtyard, and Carina worried her lip. "Be careful, you hear?"

Oliver tipped his cap, a brief smile crossing his face. "Don't worry, fair lady. I'll be fine."

With the plan in place, they parted ways. Crossing from the frigid air into the warmth of the building, Carina moved to unbutton her capelet. She couldn't see Mr. Baker in the crowd, though he could be lurking somewhere nearby. The image of his face mixed with the memory of the tall figure who had attacked her as she advanced up the steps.

Carina found her usual place and set her looms in motion.

As they roared to life, she darted a glance around the room, half expecting a black-masked man to jump out of hiding and attack her.

"Good morning, Carina. How was your Christmas?" Ella's cheerful voice made Carina jump. The girl had a smile on her face and one of the ribbons Carina had given her in her hair. The blue satin seemed to freshen her face, bringing color to her normally pale complexion.

Carina leaned over to inspect the thread on one of her looms. It would need to be replaced soon. "It was wonderful. How was yours? I enjoyed your gift. Why, I used it on my hair just this morning."

Ella squealed. "Oh, I'm so glad. I love my hair ribbons. Why, I have one for nearly every day of the week now." She poked Carina. "Now, did that handsome Mr. Bricht come to visit you on Christmas?" Carina's cheeks must have betrayed her, for her friend giggled. "Oh, you must tell me! What did he say? Did you kiss?"

"Oh, heavens, no. He gave me this necklace." Carina straightened and pulled the chain from beneath her collar, holding it out so the tiny butterfly sparkled and shone in the light. "Then, after we exchanged gifts, he took me ice skating."

"How romantic," Ella crowed, her face delighted. "He seems like a perfect gentleman."

Carina replaced the butterfly beneath her dress, where it would be safe from harm. "He isn't perfect." She glanced thoughtfully out the nearest window. "But he isn't all that bad either." Far from it, actually. The rapid beating of her heart was enough to prove that. At Ella's dreamy sigh, she changed the topic. "Now, what about you? What did you do for Christmas?"

Ella let out an unladylike snort as she removed a finished piece of fabric from one of her looms. "Nothing as interesting as you, I assure you. My family and I sat down for dinner and then opened presents the next day. Quiet and uneventful."

Carina brought the loom to a halt and removed the shuttle, replacing the empty spool of thread with a new one. "That sounds heavenly to me." She slid the shuttle back onto the loom, and it roared to life once more. "I would give anything to have a Christmas like that."

Ella's face fell. "I'm sorry, Carina. I forgot all about your sister. How is the search for her going?"

"Unsuccessful." Carina shifted from one foot to the other, tugging at the fabric of her apron. "I'm waiting for something, anything, to turn up."

Ella patted her hand, her eyes glowing. "I'm certain something will. You just have to give it time."

Carina attempted a tiny smile. "I know. I feel as though I'm not doing enough—that's all."

"Perhaps you need to look at things a different way. You made it this far, after all." Ella settled her hands on her hips. "I'd say you're doing more than enough."

"I know, and I pray every evening for her safety." Carina stepped forward and enveloped her friend in a quick hug. "Thank you for your encouragement, Ella. I needed it."

Ella laughed, her thin shoulders bouncing as she returned Carina's hug. "That's what friends are for, Carina."

As they separated, Carina turned her gaze back to her looms. Though her focus was on the rapidly moving shuttles and the slowly forming fabric, her mind was on Oliver. Would Mr. Baker him tell the truth? Hopefully, but the criminals had already proven they were smarter than Oliver had assumed. If Mr. Baker was, in fact, one of the thieves, he would more than likely lie his way out of the situation.

Something tingled in Carina's nose, and she rubbed it. However, the feeling persisted. As she frowned and switched to scrubbing at her nose with her sleeve, a smell penetrated the air and made her freeze.

No. Please, no.

But there was no denying it, not when the same smell had permeated her clothing and haunted her memories for weeks after that fateful night. The word left her mouth unbidden, a terrified whisper that disappeared amid the clacking machinery.

"What was that, Carina?" Ella leaned closer. "These looms are too noisy."

"Smoke," Carina repeated, this time louder. "I smell smoke."

~

"Hey, Oliver, do you smell anything strange?"

Timothy's question caught Oliver off guard, and he paused his work to sniff the air. He could smell lint, grease, and sweat, but nothing unusual. "No. What are you smelling?"

Standing beside him, his friend frowned thoughtfully. "I can't say for certain, but it almost seems like...smoke?"

Smoke? Alarm coursed through Oliver. Regardless of whether or not Timothy was right, it was worth looking into. "Where's the smell coming from?" No smoke was visible. Still, Oliver couldn't shake the feeling that something had been set in motion.

Timothy frowned, swiveling his head from side to side like a dog on a trail. "I couldn't say, but it seems to be stronger near the door that connects to the main entryway."

"I'm going to check it out." Oliver dusted off his hands as he made his way over.

The knob wasn't hot to the touch, a good sign. As Oliver opened the door, however, his heart dropped. Not only did the smell of kerosene hang heavy in the air, mixed with the woodsy scent of smoke—but a pile of rags burned in the middle of the hall, the flames growing higher by the minute. The fire had already spread across the wooden beams on the walls, the crackling growing steadily louder as the flames advanced on where he stood.

Oliver spun on his heel and ran back into the picker room. "Fire!" he bellowed, waving his arms.

Men halted their work, turning to look at him with alarm in their eyes.

"Fire in the entryway! Help me put it out!"

His cry caused the men to spring from their reveries and leap forward to verify his claim. As one of the men opened the door, smoke billowed into the room, making all present break into coughing fits.

"Oliver!" Timothy exclaimed between coughs, coming to stand next to him. "What happened?"

Oliver shook his head. "I don't know. A pile of rags was on fire in the middle of the entryway." He broke off as his chest seized.

Timothy's brows raised. "Intentional? Who would want to burn the mill down?"

"I don't know, but we can figure that out later. For now, we need to stop this fire."

As Oliver hurried toward the picker table, intent on moving the cotton as far from the blaze as possible, a curse rang out near the door. "The fire has spread to the opening room! The cotton is starting to burn!"

No. And yet, as gasps rang through the room, smoke drifted through the chute that ran between the opening and picker rooms. Horror sank like a stone in his stomach. "We can't save it," Oliver yelled to the workers. "The fire will spread too quickly. We have to get out of the building, and someone needs to get to the fire department."

"I'll go! I know where it is," one of the men agreed. He broke the glass in one of the windows with his elbow and hefted himself through to the safety of the courtyard. The rest of the workers hurried to join him, breaking the windows and jumping through.

Oliver stiffened with a sudden realization. *Carina.* "The second floor! Somebody has to warn them!" He rushed toward the door, but another coughing fit overtook him, he staggered back. Flames roared in the hallway.

Lord, help them.

~

*E*lla frowned, sniffing at the air. "I smell nothing out of sorts." She leaned back to catch the eye of Josephine, who was replacing the thread on one of her looms. "Jo, do you smell smoke?"

The brown-haired woman lifted her head, her brows furrowing. "No, I smell nothing out of the ordinary."

"See? I'm certain it's nothing serious." Ella smiled. "Perhaps some of the thread rubbed against the wood on one of your looms and made it smell. That's happened to me on occasion."

"Oh." Carina shrugged, though the tight feeling remained in her chest. Something wasn't right.

As she bent over her looms to check Ella's theory on the thread, a scream rent the air, followed immediately by shouts from the women who worked the looms near the stairs. Carina's head snapped up. "What's happening?" She craned her neck to see over the machines.

"Fire!" someone cried, the horrible word echoing through the room. "Fire in the mill! Everyone must leave!"

Pure horror invaded Carina, leaving her frozen in place. *Not again.* But there was no denying the truth. Smoke had begun filtering onto the upper floor, creating a thin haze that stung her eyes. The unmistakable smell that followed called forth memories of that horrible night, the night filled with screaming and fear.

Run. The voice broke through the memories and drew Carina out of her shock. *Run, before it's too late.*

Carina tore a portion of fabric from her skirt hem and tied it around her face, grasping Ella's hand. The poor girl looked just as frightened as Carina, her eyes wide and body motionless as she stared at the smoke.

"Come on," Carina shouted over the screams of the panicked workers. Clutching Ella's hand like a lifeline, she dragged her friend toward the people struggling to get down the stairs.

Ella doubled over as they neared the steps, the smoke growing thicker by the minute. "Carina, I can't breathe."

Carina bent and tore another piece from her skirt, handing it to Ella. "Quickly, put this around your nose and mouth."

Once her friend had the makeshift covering in place, Carina charged headfirst into the throng and pushed her way toward the steps. A rush of energy gave her newfound strength, and she managed to reach the top step without a problem. Carina's pace slowed, however, when she glimpsed the lower floor. Flames had begun licking at the bottom steps, hungry fingers of orange climbing up the sides at an alarming rate. At any minute, the steps could collapse.

Carina tightened her hold on Ella's hand. "Hang on, Ella." Together, they raced down the stairs and jumped over the last few steps. Carina's skirt remained miraculously clear of the flames, though her ankle twisted upon landing, sending a jolt of red-hot pain up her leg. There was no time to stop and examine it, so she limped into the crowd of people struggling to exit the building.

Chaos reigned in the courtyard. The torrent of workers rushing from the door pushed Carina and Ella farther and farther into the center until they were able to seek safety beneath their oak tree. Carina watched from the shelter of the trunk, her chest heaving, as the trickle of people exiting the mill began to slow and then drew to a halt. It seemed as though most of the workers had been able to escape the fire unharmed. And, judging by the wail of approaching sirens, help would not be long in coming. Relief flooded her in one great wave.

We'll be all right.

"Carina, you can let go of my hand now. You're hurting me," Ella whispered, breaking into a cough.

Carina gasped, detaching her hand from her friend's. "My apologies, Ella." She hadn't been willing to let go, not after losing her sister.

Ella ripped the covering from her face, her eyes wide. "That was terrifying. What do you suppose happened?"

"I don't know. It seemed as though the fire originated from the first floor." As she continued to scan the courtyard, Carina's stomach dropped. Josephine and the other loom girls huddled near the gates, and most of the picker house men were gathering at the front of the mill to toss buckets of snow on the flames. Only two faces were missing, and no matter where Carina looked, she could not find them.

"Where are Mr. Bricht and Mr. Baker?" Ella joined Carina's search of the clearing.

"I don't know," Carina whispered, fear settling heavily on her shoulders.

$\sim$

"Oliver!" The voice echoed from outside one of the picker room's broken windows, and a man stuck his arm through an empty window frame with a bucket. "Here!"

Oliver grabbed the bucket and wheeled around, running to throw the snow on the flames that had begun to spread across the picker room. He turned to collect another and jerked back at the sight of Timothy standing before him with a bucket outstretched.

"I'll help," Timothy called over the noise of the growing flames, his face determined.

Oliver grimaced but made no move to dissuade the young man. Snatching the bucket from Timothy, he tossed its contents on the flames. Buckets continued to be passed down the line, giving him fresh ammunition to use on the fire. And yet, no matter how much snow he threw on the flames, they continued to grow.

Shaking his head, Oliver turned to Timothy. "There's no use. The flames are too hot and fast. They keep coming back."

Timothy dropped the empty bucket he held on the floor, his face red and dripping sweat despite the frigid temperatures outside. "Let's go, then! Everyone is safe outside."

As they turned to leave, a noise caught Oliver's attention. It sounded almost like...a cry?

"I think there's someone back there!" Darting to the burning hall, he could make out the faint outline of a small woman who seemed to be shielding herself near the crumbling stairs. "There's someone near the stairs," he called. "I'm going to try and get to her. She'll never survive otherwise."

Timothy appeared at Oliver's side, peering down the flame-filled hallway. "Are you mad? You'll burn alive before you reach her!"

"I have to try, Timothy."

Taking one of the remaining buckets of snow, which had melted in the growing heat, Oliver doused his clothing in it. Wrapping the now-wet scarf around his head and face, he gauged the best path to take through the hall. There appeared to be a spot where the flames were smaller.

Oliver took a deep breath, said a prayer, and plunged into the fire. Flames assaulted him from all sides, heat licking his face and hands as he charged toward the faint outline of the woman. The horrible sound of creaking wood told him he had little time.

By the grace of God, Oliver managed to burst into the entryway unscathed. The flames here were less dense as he maneuvered to the woman. A closer inspection revealed her to be little more than a girl. She clutched her black braids in her hands as she huddled against what remained of the bottom few steps.

Oliver approached with hands outstretched. "I'm here to help."

The girl stared up at him with tear-streaked cheeks and pointed to her right foot. "I hurt my leg."

Oliver stooped and quickly hefted her up in his arms.

As he turned, a voice startled him. "Oliver, hurry! The beams are collapsing!"

"Timothy!" Judging by the man's singed shirt, he had followed Oliver through the hall. "What are you doing here?"

"I wasn't about to let you be a hero all by yourself." Timothy tried to smile but failed as a coughing fit overcame him.

Oliver drew the girl close to his chest as a rumbling noise echoed through the flaming building. "Let's go."

They turned and rushed toward the door, dodging flames and falling bits of wood. The girl screamed and clutched at Oliver's shirt as a beam came crashing down, narrowly avoiding them. A few feet from freedom, a sickening crack slowed Oliver's pace. The beam above the door was coming loose, cracks forming in the middle as it sagged.

"Come on!" Oliver ran faster.

Labored breathing told him Timothy was close behind.

Another crack from the ceiling, producing a waterfall of cinders that showered over the door, warned Oliver they were almost out of time. *Lord in heaven, protect us.*

"Oliver, tell Emmy I love her." Timothy's sudden request, shouted over the roar, made Oliver look behind him.

"Timothy, we're almost—"

A hard shove catapulted Oliver the last few feet out the

door, sending him sprawling in the snow. A blinding crash made him throw up his arms for protection. Searing heat burned his hands as the windows exploded, sending shards of glass flying across the courtyard. For a moment after, the world was a blur of light and ringing.

Then hands tugged Oliver off the girl he had sheltered beneath him and pulled them away from the mill. Cracking open his eyes, Oliver could make out the faint outline of the doorway, completely blocked by burning wood and debris. "No," he whispered, struggling to push himself upright.

"Whoa, there, fellow." A man in a firefighter's uniform laid a hand on Oliver's left shoulder. "Calm down. You've had quite a blow."

"Please." His plea came out hoarse. "My friend is in there."

A look of sympathy flashed across the fireman's face, but he quickly masked it. "You just wait right here, sir, and we'll see what we can do. It was a right brave thing you did, getting that little gal out."

Brave? He didn't feel brave. He knew, deep down, that Timothy was gone. He had died saving Oliver, and all because Oliver had wanted to be a hero.

"Oliver." The raspy voice was like dumping cold water on the flames raging in Oliver's mind. Gentle hands tugged him upward, and he found himself facing Carina.

"Drink some of this." She handed him a pitcher of water. "Where were you? I was frightened out of my mind when I got outside and couldn't find you."

Ella rushed up beside them. She stopped and stared at the huddled form of the young girl a few feet away. "Look at her! She can't be older than thirteen, the poor thing. She should be at home with her mother, not in a place like this. She could have died." She turned to Oliver, her eyes brightening. "But you saved her. You're a hero, Mr. Bricht!"

Oliver took a deep swig of water, cooling his parched throat. Upon lowering it, he stared into Carina's blue eyes. The emotion shining there caught him off guard and loosened his tongue. "The girl was stuck near the staircase," he murmured, low enough that only Carina would be able to hear. "Timothy and I ran through the flames to get to her. Beams started to collapse as went for the exit, and…" He swallowed. "Timothy pushed me outside right as the wood fell across the door. He's dead, Carina. He died saving me."

Carina's eyes filled with tears. "Oh, Oliver, I'm so sorry." She wrapped him in a warm hug, and he held onto her like an anchor in a storm.

He blinked back tears of his own. How many times had he calmed grieving mothers after their sons were killed and asked questions of men who had lost their friends for the sake of an investigation? Too many to count. Now that he was in their position, however, his mind was too jumbled to think of any of the reassuring things he had told them.

Gradually, Oliver refocused on his surroundings. Ella had left to converse with a group of women across the courtyard, and Carina still clung to him with trembling arms. She was staring at the flaming building with fearful eyes. While the firemen were working steadily to reduce the fire, the blaze still shone red and orange through the holes where the windows had been.

Realization struck like lightning. "Oh, Carina," Oliver whispered. "I forgot about what happened all that time ago. I'm so sorry. This must have been frightening for you."

Carina shook her head, burying her face in his shirt. "It's all right." The smoky fabric muffled her reply. "I'm just glad you made it out safely. I couldn't handle losing someone else I care about to a fire."

Oliver let out a shuddering sigh. "I did. Timothy didn't." He winced. "The last thing he asked of me was to tell his sister he loved her. How can I do that, Carina? How can I face his little sister, knowing I'm the reason he's dead?"

Carina pushed away from Oliver's shoulder, looking him clean in the eye. "It wasn't your fault he followed you, Oliver. Do you remember what I said? It isn't your job to save everyone. Timothy knew what could happen, and he chose to go through with it regardless."

Oliver gazed at the dwindling flames. "He was a good friend, even when I doubted him." He turned to Carina. "Timothy isn't the thief, Carina. If he was, he never would have followed me into the fire. He never would have sacrificed himself to save me."

"You're right. He isn't a thief." Carina's eyes were filled with honesty. "Timothy was a hero, Oliver. He died a hero."

Oliver released a heavy sigh, the weight of guilt settling over him like a boulder. "I only wish I had realized it sooner."

One of the firemen broke away from the smoldering building, approaching Oliver with his hat in his hands. "Sir, your friend..."

Oliver's shoulders sagged. "I know."

The fireman put his hat back on, sympathy in his gaze. "I'm sorry, sir. We arrived just in time to see what you two were doing, and I have to say, it was very brave. Your friend will have a proper burial as soon as possible."

Oliver nodded mutely, watching as the fireman returned to the scene. His grief was too raw to do anything else, leaving him frozen in place.

Beside him, Carina wrapped her arms around herself. "I wonder what caused all of this. We were upstairs when the fire began and ran downstairs when the steps caught on fire."

A flickering memory latched onto Oliver's mind. "It was intentional." He ground the words out, anger growing in his chest.

"What?" Carina gasped.

"When I opened the door to the hallway that connects the picker room and the entryway, there was a pile of burning rags on the floor. The whole thing stank like kerosene."

Carina clasped a hand over her mouth. "Oliver, we need to tell someone!" She waved over a fireman. "Tell him what you told me."

Oliver repeated the information to the fireman, who glanced over his shoulder with a frown. "We'll look into that. Thank you for telling me, sir. We'll get in contact with the police, and they'll most likely ask you some questions."

How strange it was to be on the other side of the questioning. As the fireman retreated, most likely to contact the police, he turned to Carina. Something had begun burning beneath his skin, growing hotter and hotter until it was roaring in his ears. "The thief set the fire, Carina. I know it was him." He clenched his fists. "He might as well have killed Timothy with his bare hands."

Carina rested a hand on Oliver's shoulder. "We'll find him, Oliver. He'll see jail yet."

Oliver was about to retort that the thief deserved more than jail but paused at the sight of her strained expression. "You're right." The fire sputtered and died within him until all that remained was a cold, empty space. "We will catch him. I'll see that thief brought before a judge if it's the last thing I do."

Carina hugged him once more, and for the time being, Oliver simply held her.

CHAPTER 20

$\mathcal{J}$t wasn't long before the police arrived, and they questioned everyone present multiple times before letting the exhausted workers go home. Carina remained at Oliver's side, knowing that now more than ever, he needed someone to stand by him. She met his eyes only once during the questioning and found them to be a storm of sadness, anger, and fear, behind which was a look of helplessness. It was haunting, and Carina quickly lowered her gaze to their entwined hands.

An ambulance wagon arrived with medics to check over those who had sustained injuries, though none were serious. While some of the mill workers remained out of curiosity to see what the police would find, most were too exhausted to care right then and hurried home.

After the police took Oliver's testimony, they split up to investigate the remains of the entryway. A portion of the second floor had collapsed in the fire, but the back half and most of the first floor still appeared to be intact. With the windows blown out, the mill resembled a large empty shell.

It was impossible to tell whether the building was worth

salvaging, for Mr. Browning hadn't been present during the fire. In fact, he was still nowhere to be seen. Would the mill owner be brave enough to venture out and see what remained of his business? Would he close it down and move elsewhere to start afresh? Until he made a decision, Carina would have to begin searching for new employment.

After a few moments, the police returned from the wreckage. "There's no sign of rags," one of the officers informed Carina and Oliver. "However, we did locate a melted container of kerosene near the picker room. We'll bring in each mill employee to see if we can discover who set the fire. I assure you, sir, we won't rest until the arsonist is caught and your friend is laid to rest."

"Neither will I," Oliver muttered. He nodded to each of the officers. "Thank you. I'm going home now. I have funeral arrangements to make and a telegram to send." He said the words as though each one was a nail in a coffin.

Carina smiled at the officers. "Thank you for all of your assistance." Tugging Oliver from the clearing by the hand, she pushed her way through the crowd of curious onlookers that had gathered outside the mill gates. Once free, she finally released him and settled into a comfortable pace for her still-throbbing ankle. "You don't have to do it, you know."

Oliver blinked as he fell into step beside her. "Do what?"

"Arrange the funeral. I'm sure the police would be willing to contact Mr. Baker's family. They've had to do it numerous times, no doubt."

Oliver shook his head, conviction on his face. "I need to do this. If not for me, then for Timothy. I owe it to him."

Carina studied him from the corner of her eye. Judging by his stooped shoulders and ashen face, the poor man needed a bath and a good, long rest. She could use one, as well. "Well then, we'll look into it tomorrow. For now, you need to rest."

Oliver raised his brow. "'We'?"

"Yes, 'we.' You didn't think I would leave you to face this on your own, did you?" Carina asked, keeping her tone light.

Oliver returned her smile, though his lacked its usual warmth. "Thank you, Carina." His eyes flicked to her stilted walk and he frowned. "You're limping."

Carina shrugged, feigning nonchalance. "Jumping off the stairs took a bit of a toll on my ankle, but it's nothing Mrs. Fields can't fix." The boardinghouse owner was a miracle worker when it came to patching up injuries.

"You should have told me sooner," Oliver admonished gently. "I would have walked slower."

Carina laughed. "It's no worry, Oliver. A twisted ankle is the least of our concerns at the moment." Despite her teasing tone, she was more than relieved when Oliver held out an elbow. She rested her hand on his arm but quickly drew back with a small cry. "Your coat is wet!"

He shot her a quick glance. "I soaked my clothing before running through the flames."

"That was smart of you." Guilt washed through Carina. Her hobbling pace would only hold him up. "You need to get out of the cold as quickly as possible. Why don't you go on ahead?"

"As if I would even consider leaving you, injured and with a criminal on the loose." Oliver's protective frown warmed her insides. "No, and don't hurry either. It's more important not to further injure your ankle. I'll warm up soon enough."

While their progress was slower than Carina liked, it didn't take long for them to reach the telegraph office. She waited with a heavy heart as Oliver purchased a telegram to send to Timothy's family. It was a few moments before he found the words to write down, and each scratch of the pen seemed to age him by a year. After finishing, he handed the telegram to the clerk and rejoined Carina.

"It is done," Oliver murmured as they continued down the road.

Carina patted his arm. "They'll be grateful, Oliver, that you were there for Timothy in his last few moments."

A gust of wind blew past, causing Oliver to shudder. Or was he simply recalling the fire? "It's funny, you know. I've dealt with death before, but it's never felt quite like this. It's one thing to console a person, but entirely another when you *are* that person." He sucked in a breath as if to keep tears at bay. "I've failed, Carina. I failed Timothy, and I failed to save the mill. Hundreds of people lost their jobs in an instant, and it's all because I couldn't catch two men."

Carina prodded Oliver with her elbow, forcing him to look at her. "This isn't over yet, Oliver. What's the saying? We may have lost the battle, but we can still win the war. We'll catch these villains."

"What's the point? Timothy is gone. The mill is destroyed." A freshly stricken look crossed Oliver's face. "And you've lost your job because of me. Oh, Carina, I'm so sorry."

Carina drew her shoulder back. "I'll find another. The problem is, so will the thieves. They'll go on stealing and burning even with the mill being gone. We can't give up, Oliver."

Oliver studied her, emotions flickering through his gray eyes. After a moment of silence, he inclined his head. "All right. I'll keep looking."

"*We'll* keep looking." As they arrived in front of the boardinghouse, Carina tugged on Oliver's hand. "Come with me."

Oliver paused, bringing Carina to a halt beside him. He glanced between her and the boardinghouse with furrowed brows. "Are you certain? I don't want to put you out, and I really should be—"

"Please, Oliver. Even if it's only for a moment. Mrs. Fields will be glad to see you."

After a second of hesitation, Oliver allowed Carina to lead

him to the front porch. Knocking, she waited for Mrs. Fields to open the door.

It soon swung open to reveal the landlady's bright smile. "Hello, dear! Hello, Oliver! What brings you home so early in the day? I don't suppose you've been chasing down that thief again, have you?"

Carina nearly burst into tears right then and there. "Can we please come in? We've had a disastrous day."

The smile fell from Mrs. Fields's face as she took in their sober expressions. "Of course, dear. You two come on in and sit down while I make some coffee."

After settling into a fireside armchair beside Oliver, who hung his coat up to dry, and receiving a cup of coffee from the proprietress, Carina launched into a description of the burning of the mill. By the time she had finished, tears had filled Mrs. Fields's eyes.

"Oh, dear, I'm so sorry." She rose to envelope Oliver in a hug. "I know your friend is proud of what you did. He's in a much safer place now. Don't you fret over him."

A soft smile came over Oliver's face as he hugged her back, and his shoulders relaxed a fraction. "He is, isn't he?" His voice held a note of uncertainty, one that tugged at Carina's heart.

Mrs. Fields released him and placed her hands on her shoulders. "Young man, I know he is. You have nothing to fear." She straightened and looked Carina and Oliver over. "Now, what about you two? Were you injured?"

Oliver pointed to Carina's foot. "She sprained her ankle."

Carina shrugged to allay the alarm that flashed across Mrs. Fields's face. "It isn't all that bad. I twisted it a little while running from the building, is all."

Mrs. Fields bent to examine the offending foot, tutting all the while. "I'll get some ice. In the meantime, I want you to set your foot on the table."

"That would hardly be proper..."

Mrs. Fields's expression made it clear she would not accept an argument. "You must keep it elevated, dear. It will help with the swelling."

As the kind woman bustled from the room with the promise to return shortly, Carina lifted her foot onto the squat table in front of them and turned to face Oliver. "What about you? Are you all right? I should have asked on the way home."

"I am well, though I smell horrible." Oliver wrinkled his nose.

"As do I. And you are beginning to dry out, I hope?" Carina pushed a russet curl from her face. Her bun had fallen loose at some point during the fire, leaving her hair to spring around her shoulders in an unruly mess.

Oliver dipped his head in acknowledgement, but the distant look on his face showed he was retreating into memories of the fire. Carina quickly interpreted the distant gaze, for she had done the same thing often after leaving Peshtigo. She knew what it felt like to think back on memories and wonder if there was anything one could have done differently to save a person they cared about.

"You know, this isn't the first time I've sprained this ankle," Carina informed Oliver as she pinned her hair into a new bun.

Her strange statement seemed to draw Oliver from his memories. "You've sprained it before?"

"Indeed. It was a rather amusing incident, though I didn't think so then. I was about eleven at the time. Lottie and I were walking home from school one day when I heard a rustle, glanced up, and spotted a cat sitting high up in a tree. Lottie begged me to go up and rescue the 'poor creature,' as she called it. So up I clambered in my skirts and went after the animal. I don't suppose you can guess what happened when I finally reached it." She waited until Oliver asked "what?" to continue. "The cat leaped nimbly as could be from the tree, leaving me stranded in its place. I managed to get myself down eventually, but I twisted my leg upon landing. When I managed to push myself upright, there stood Charlotte, holding the cat as though it was her new best friend. She named it Darcy, and the ornery creature lived in our shed for years after. The old cat never did learn to get along with me."

A ghost of a smile crossed Oliver's face. "Not much for animals, are you?"

Carina snorted, adjusting her skirts over her elevated leg. "It's less a matter of me disliking animals and more a matter of animals disliking me."

"Well, they don't have very good taste, then," Oliver said softly. Thankfully, some of the warmth had returned to his eyes. "We'll make it through this, won't we?"

Carina leaned forward, placing her hand over his. "We will, Oliver. That I promise you. It's going to take a lot of time, but something good will come out of this mess. We have to trust that it will."

❧

The funeral was a quiet affair. Carina watched from a distance as Mr. and Mrs. Baker paid their respects along with their young daughter over Timothy's simple coffin. Surprisingly, the family hadn't reacted strongly when they first saw the wooden box. They had instead remained quiet as they paid their respects, though tears rolled down the little girl's cheeks. Undoubtedly, the family's sadness was hurting Oliver more than anyone else. He had been frozen next to Carina throughout the entire procession, seemingly unwilling to get any closer to the grieving family.

When the funeral concluded and the crowd began to disperse, however, Carina gently shoved him forward. "Go and speak to them."

Oliver gave her a stricken look. "What if they're angry with me? I'll never be able to forgive myself."

"Oliver, there's nothing to forgive. Timothy chose to save you, and I know he wouldn't want you to be anxious." Carina gently pushed Oliver's arm. "Now, go and speak with them. They need it."

With a shaky nod, Oliver stepped toward the family that still stood by the gravesite. Carina followed a few feet behind, not wanting to intrude but also unwilling to abandon Oliver.

"Mr. and Mrs. Baker? It's me, Oliver Bricht." Oliver removed his cap and twisted it in his hands.

The kind woman whom Carina guessed to be Mrs. Baker glanced up, her face wreathed, wonder of all wonders, in a slight smile. "Oliver, dear." Without another word, the woman tugged him into a hug.

Shock blanketed Oliver's face, changing into sadness a moment later as he returned the hug. "Mrs. Baker, I'm so sorry about what happened. If I had kept a better eye on Timothy, perhaps none of this would have occurred."

Mrs. Baker grabbed Oliver's hands, looking into his eyes. "Young man, you listen to me. Timothy was as smart as he was kind. He knew precisely what he was doing in following you, so you have no reason to blame yourself." Tears filled the gentle woman's eyes. "What you two did was a heroic thing. My Timmy died saving someone, and I know he died happy. Because of him and because of you, a girl lived to see another day."

"But Timothy didn't. I couldn't save him," Oliver said softly.

Mrs. Baker released Oliver's hands to tug a handkerchief from her pocket. "It was his time to go home, Oliver. Timothy knew it when he pushed you out the door. I can't deny that I'm saddened by his passing, and I always will be. But..." She took a shuddering breath and dabbed at her eyes. "I know he's up in heaven now, smiling down at us."

Oliver turned to the little girl who stood next to the adults. She was dressed in a simple black dress with her brown hair tucked under a bonnet and clutched what looked like a raccoon doll made from a stocking and a few buttons in one hand. He crouched down to look the girl in the eye. "Emmy, I'm very sorry about your brother. He wanted me to tell you that—" Oliver's voice broke, making Carina's heart clench, and he took a moment before finishing. "He wanted me to tell you that he loved you very much."

The girl—Emmy—looked up, tears shining in her eyes. "He asked you to tell me?"

Oliver nodded solemnly. "He did. I promised him I would tell you."

Emmy clutched the raccoon to her chest. "I love him too." She sniffed. "I miss him a lot."

Mrs. Baker swept the little girl into her arms. "Emmy, dear, do you remember what I told you?"

"Yes." Emmy raised a finger and waved it in the air, parroting her mother's voice. "Timmy's up in heaven now."

Mrs. Baker smiled. "That's right. He'll be waiting for us next to Jesus when it's our turn to go home as well."

"He will?" Emmy glanced up at the sky. "Timmy, you'd better be there when I get to heaven!"

Carina chuckled at the demand, drawing the group's attention toward her. "Forgive me. I didn't mean to intrude."

Oliver waved her forward. "This is Carina Clarke. She was present during the fire as well."

"I was." Carina stepped forward. "Mr. Baker was an admirable man. He spoke to me on several occasions, and I always found him to be most kind."

Mrs. Baker fairly beamed. "He was, wasn't he? I'm glad to know my Timothy will be remembered fondly."

"He will," Oliver promised. His face changed into a look of

determination. "We'll find the ones who set the fire, Mrs. Baker. They won't get away with what they've done."

Mrs. Baker studied him with stern eyes. "Well now, young man, you be careful. I don't want Timmy's sacrifice to be in vain." She placed a hand on Oliver's shoulder, her expression easing into something more kind. "It's an admirable thing you want to do, but please remember this. If it's revenge you're seeking, you'll only find disappointment. Revenge does not heal, Oliver. It only deepens hurt. The Lord says, 'Vengeance will be Mine.' You leave it up to Him, all right?"

Oliver's posture seemed to soften as he took in the woman's words. At length, he released a long breath. "While I won't deny that I'd like to administer justice on this culprit myself, it isn't my place to do so. I only want to see him brought before a judge. Then, before the eyes of God and the court, he will face the consequences of his actions."

Mr. Baker stepped forward and placed a hand on Oliver's shoulder, speaking for the first time. "That's good of you, young man. Timothy would appreciate what you're doing."

"I'm glad to hear that, sir." Oliver glanced back at Carina. Thank goodness, some of the twinkle had returned to his eyes. "We'll make sure nobody else will meet the same fate at this criminal's hands."

Carina smiled approvingly as pride spread through her chest—not for herself, but for the man standing before her.

As they bade the family farewell and began walking away, a familiar figure by the back gates of the cemetery caught Carina's eye. "Why, it's Mr. Browning. What's he doing here?"

Oliver replaced the cap on his head. "I'm not certain. Let's go see what he wants."

They closed in on the mill owner, and he quickly caught sight of them. "Ah, Mr. Bricht and Miss Clarke. Might I have a word?"

Oliver raised a brow. "Of course."

Mr. Browning wiped his forehead with a handkerchief. "First, I'm very sorry to hear about Mr. Baker. He was a fine employee. Second, as you are well aware, the mill is currently unusable. The firefighters warned me that the building may not be salvageable. I, however, am far more hopeful."

Carina sucked in a breath. "You mean to reopen the mill?"

"Indeed." Mr. Browning squared his shoulders, tucking the handkerchief in the pocket of his tweed jacket. "I have crews working on it even now. With luck, it will be back up and running soon. I've offered to give everyone back their previous positions, though I'm not certain how many will accept." The man released a sigh. "Truth be told, the reason for my sudden visit is that I'm concerned these thieves will take the reopening as an invitation to return to their sabotage. If they do, we may never be able to keep the mill running. So I have come to ask you, Mr. Bricht, if you plan on continuing your investigation."

Oliver looked to Carina as though seeking her permission. When she gave a subtle nod, he turned back to Mr. Browning. "Yes, Mr. Browning. Miss Clarke and I will do everything in our power to catch these criminals. I assure you, we won't stop until they see justice."

CHAPTER 21

*I*t was strange to awaken without needing to rush from the room. Oliver remained in bed, staring at the ceiling. It was an activity he had done often at home, but after weeks of rising early for work, it felt...wrong. He had taken quite a few things for granted, sleeping in included.

Though Oliver had been on numerous cases, the past few weeks would stick with him far longer than any of the others. Pinkerton would say he was growing soft. In truth, he had never been detached to begin with. He was forever becoming absorbed with being the hero in other people's lives. Perhaps it was time to stop. Perhaps he ought to return home and let Pinkerton send a better detective, one who was calm and calculated, one who wasn't afraid to suspect anyone and everyone. One who wouldn't have been surprised to find evidence incriminating his friend.

One who wouldn't have fallen for a beautiful red-haired loom girl.

Carina... How could he think of leaving without fulfilling his promise to her? The case was no longer a matter of merely proving himself to his father. In fact, it wasn't a matter of Oliver's pride at all. Carina was depending on him, as were Mr. Browning and the rest of the mill workers. It was nice to be needed...but terrifying as well.

Still, Carina had come to mean a lot more to Oliver than he ever would have imagined. He couldn't leave her without finishing what he had started. It would be selfish to do so when he had a life of ease to run back to and she had nothing.

Pushing himself upright, Oliver dressed and made his way downstairs. Lucy, who had been informed of Timothy's untimely death on the night after the fire, had done an admirable job of keeping herself composed throughout the funeral. Yet dark circles were visible under her eyes as he stopped at the kitchen door.

"Lucy?" he asked softly.

The proprietress looked up from the oatmeal she was stirring, quickly masking her frown with a half-hearted smile. "Good morning, Oliver."

Oliver returned her smile as he slid his arms into the sleeves of his jacket. "Good morning. I wanted to tell you I'm heading out to look around. Perhaps there are some other jobs in the area." It was a lie, but he needed a cover if he was to investigate unhindered.

Lucy nodded, the cheer falling from her face. "Best of luck. Oh, poor Timothy. If only that dreadful fire had never happened."

"I know, Lucy. I know." Oliver settled his cap on his head, a spark of determination igniting in his chest. "They'll catch the one who did it, I'm sure."

He left her to her oatmeal and walked outside, pausing when he reached the porch. How strange it was to see the space empty, without his friend waiting to walk to the mill with him. It was something he had taken for granted. He remained there in silence for a moment before ambling down the steps.

His first stop would be the mill itself. While there was

likely nothing left to find, it would be a good starting point. As he walked along the slush-covered sidewalk, Oliver's thoughts turned once more to Carina. Should he ask her to join him? Considering her reaction to the fire, it would likely be best to wait until after he investigated the remains of the mill. She truly was a brave woman to face her fear with such aplomb. It was one of the many things Oliver admired about her.

He drew to a sudden halt. Admired? Yes. He had grown increasingly fond of Carina over the past few weeks, more than any of the young socialites his father had forced him to speak with at events. She wasn't afraid to show true emotion, something the young ladies of his acquaintance were experts at masking. She had stayed by his side throughout the fire and funeral despite the fear she surely felt. Her beauty, while wonderful in its own right, only served to complement her character.

In short, Carina Clarke was a wonderful woman.

Thoughts of Carina eased some of the weight on Oliver's shoulders, though that weight quickly returned when he reached the mill. While mostly intact on the outside, the interior was blackened and collapsed. Charred wood and sparkling pieces of glass littered the patchy snow, along with a few stray buckets left behind by the workers.

Pushing aside memories of running through the fire, Oliver took a deep breath and made his way toward the building. At the sight of people removing debris from the door, he halted in surprise. Ah, yes...Mr. Browning had spoken of hiring cleaning crews.

"Ho, there! How goes it?" he called to one of the nearby groups of men.

One of the fellows halted and turned toward Oliver. "Good day, friend. What brings you here? Looking to help out?"

Oliver stopped before him and raised a brow. "Actually, I'd

be more than happy to help, if you're amenable to the idea. I'd like to be able to get back to work as soon as possible."

The man chuckled and extended a hand. "Fair enough. The name is Christopher Wulf. If you'd be willing to help cart some lumber out of the building, I'd be most grateful."

Oliver shook his hand. "Oliver Bricht."

He wasted no time in following Christopher's directions to the east end of the mill, where workers were systematically removing burnt lumber from the picker room. After rolling up his sleeves, Oliver grabbed the nearest piece of blackened wood, bracing his feet to lift the heavy piece into the air. As he hefted it toward the empty doorframe at the side of the room, he kept an eye out for anything out of the ordinary. There were no more kerosene cans in the hall, most likely having been removed by the police for further investigation. Still, the crumbled remains of the hall left no doubt of the place where the fire had originated.

Minutes turned to hours as Oliver continued to heft charred lumber from the remains of the mill. His boots crunched on broken glass as he dragged splintered beams from the building to the courtyard, all while struggling to tamp down the images that the sight and smell of the wreckage evoked. No wonder Carina had been so frightened the night of the fire. He could hardly look at the crumbling lumber without being reminded of running through the flames.

As Oliver deposited another armful of wood in the back of a wagon, he caught the end of a conversation between two of the cleanup workers.

"After that note, Browning isn't sure if we should keep goin'. He's thinking of selling the mill altogether," one of the men said.

Note? "Is he really?" Oliver meandered closer to the workers.

The one who had spoken nodded, the large hat on his head

flopping. "Sure, he is. I expect he's afraid that whoever did this will come after him next."

Oliver brushed his hands against his trousers, leaving black streaks on the fabric. "Is that because of the note? Was it a threat?"

The man twisted his head and spat a wad of tobacco at the ground next to Oliver's feet. "Yessir. According to Wulf, it said there would be trouble if we tried to rebuild the mill."

Oliver frowned. "And where was this note found?"

The man barked a laugh. "I don't know, fella. You'll have to ask Wulf. He's the one who found it."

"I will. Thank you." Oliver darted toward the spot where Wulf was helping to move another beam. "Wulf, what's this about a note?"

The man called the group of men to a halt and ordered them to release the beam. After carefully lowering it to the ground, he straightened and scratched at his brown beard with a soot-covered hand. "I found it pinned to the door this morning. It said we all needed to stop rebuilding or something bad would occur. Sounds like a whole lot of hot air, if you ask me."

Considering the thieves' previous actions, there was likely substance to the threat. "Where's the note now?"

Wulf swiped at his shoulders with one hand, sending a small cloud of ash into the air. "I've got no clue, sorry to say. My guess is the police took it from Browning after I gave it to him."

Blast. "Well, at least it's gone," Oliver said, affecting nonchalance.

Truthfully, the note only proved that time was running out to capture the thieves. But where to go next? The best course of action was most likely informing Pinkerton of his findings. Perhaps the severity of the criminals' deeds would be enough for his chief to send along an additional detective. Then there would be another pair of eyes to assist Oliver and Carina on their hunt.

Bidding the rather confused Wulf farewell, Oliver made his way toward the telegraph office. All the while, his mind continued to whirl. Why were the criminals so concerned with keeping the mill from being rebuilt? What was their ultimate goal? At first, it had seemed like petty theft, but in light of the new note, something bigger was clearly afoot. With that in mind, what was the villains' true goal? Did the mill have a past Oliver wasn't aware of?

At the telegraph office, he walked straight to the counter and waited for the clerk to emerge from the back.

"Hello, there." A young man walked to the front of the room. "What can I do for you?"

"Good morning. I'm looking to send a telegram."

As he wrote out his message for Pinkerton on the paper procured by the clerk, the man reached behind the counter and straightened with a white envelope in hand. "Mr. Bricht, yes? This came in today for you. I was just about to send it off with the delivery boy."

Oliver accepted the envelope with a word of gratitude and opened the seal, his eyes widening when he read the message within. It was a letter from the detective Oliver had asked to work on Charlotte's case. While there was still no sight of her, the detective had found Willow Deeran, the friend who had pulled Carina to the safety of the river. The letter went on to detail how the detective was planning on continuing his search of Peshtigo and Marinette for any sign of Charlotte Clarke, ending with his promise to send along any evidence.

Oliver couldn't help but smile at the news. While it wasn't her sister that had been found, Carina would surely be glad to know that her friend was alive. After asking the clerk for another telegram, Oliver quickly approved the detective's course of action. He submitted the two telegrams to the man and headed for Carina's boardinghouse. They could both use a moment of celebration.

The wind had begun to pick up by the time Oliver reached his destination, leaving him stomping his feet and blowing on his hands as he waited for Mrs. Fields to answer the door. She soon ushered him inside and called for Carina to come downstairs and into the parlor.

"Good day, Oliver. What brings you here?" Carina asked as she entered the room, her blue eyes wide with curiosity. "Has something bad happened?"

Oliver cleared his throat and swept the cap from his head. "Actually, I come bearing good news. I've just received word from my detective friend that Willow Deeran is alive. She made it out of the river and has taken up residence in the town of Marinette while Peshtigo is being rebuilt."

Carina lifted trembling hands to her cheeks, a smile splitting her face. "Truly? Willow is alive? She has found her family?"

Oliver inclined his head, elation filling him at Carina's happiness. "She's well, Carina. So is her family. It sounds as though they're staying in a temporary home of sorts."

Carina let out a choked laugh. "All this time, I worried. Now I know they both survived." She lowered herself into one of the parlor's armchairs. "I owe my life to her. Had Willow not gotten me to the river, I would have perished in the fire."

"The detective did ask her a few questions about Charlotte." Oliver shifted from one foot to the other. "Unfortunately, she hasn't seen or heard from your sister since before the fire. That being said, she is most anxious to hear from you. The detective has enclosed her address, if you'd like to write to her."

"I would like that very much. If you'll give me a moment, I'm going to fetch some paper." Carina exited the room in a rustle of skirts. A few moments later, she returned with ink, paper, and envelope in hand. Oliver waited while she sat in one of the chairs near the hearth and scripted a long letter, crossing out several words and scribbling notes between the lines.

Seeing Carina's face as she wrote, filled with hope and happiness, Oliver couldn't complain. He would give anything to make her smile like she was.

"All right. I'm finished." Carina finally set her fountain pen down. "May I see the address?"

"Certainly." Oliver handed her the detective's letter.

Carina opened it, frowning as her eyes darted to the top of the page. "Oliver Ramhurst? Is Bricht not your true surname?"

Oliver jolted. He had completely forgotten the detective only knew his real surname. He generally avoided using cover names when sending letters or telegrams to other members within the agency. "Yes, Bricht was part of my cover. Oliver Ramhurst is my actual name."

"Ramhurst." Realization dawned on her face. "Are you related to the Judge Ramhurst of Chicago?"

Oliver winced. The moment of truth had arrived. "Yes. I'm his son."

The detective's letter fluttered from Carina's hands as she stared at Oliver with a slack expression. "All this time, you've been the son of one of the richest judges in Chicago?" She drew a hand to her mouth. "I suspected you were from a respectable background, but this..."

Oliver shook his head. "Carina, you know I could never have used my real name while on a case. Please believe me when I say I never intended to deceive you about who I was." *Please, don't turn away now. Don't leave me too.*

"When did you intend to tell me? Did you ever?" Carina pushed to her feet. "Or did you plan to leave without returning, without seeing or thinking of me again? That's what you detectives do, don't you? You create false lives and false identities that you discard the moment you return home. You don't bother thinking of the people you've left behind. Ugh!" She threw her hands up. "I can't believe I began falling in love with someone who doesn't even exist!"

Oliver rose slowly from the chair and took a step forward as cautious hope spread through his chest. "You...you love me?"

"I don't know anymore." Carina fixed Oliver with a glare, though tears gathered in the corners of her eyes. "I thought you were different. I thought..." Her face crumpled, and she ducked her head.

Oliver took another step forward. "Carina, you need to understand that I never intended on leaving you behind. I made you a promise, remember? The reason I didn't tell you about my background was because I didn't want it to color your opinion of me. I wanted to be known as Oliver, the detective— not Oliver, the son of a judge." He ran a hand through his hair, trying to contain his frustration. "I'm no socialite, nor have I ever wanted to be. I enjoy snowball fights and ice skating. Some of my favorite memories include hiding behind a wheelbarrow full of manure in a horse stall and giving a Christmas gift to the woman I care about. The woman I..." *Love.* For the truth was, he did love her, and he was willing to do whatever it took to prove it to her.

Carina gazed up at him, her face pale. "But you're also the son of a judge, Oliver. And a judge's son should never have been friends with someone like me, much less anything more. For goodness sake, you probably have mansions and suits and a library full of books, whereas I can't even afford one." Her cheeks flushed bright red.

"Don't think that way. Carina, trust me when I say you mean far more to me than any house or fine clothing. I would give it all up in an instant if it meant I could know more people like you. The socialites of Chicago are like statues, cold and unfeeling. But here, people are honest, genuine, not a manufactured version of themselves."

She remained staring at him, misgiving written in every line of her face.

He cleared his throat. "Carina, the truth of the matter is,

you mean very much to me. So much so that I would be honored if you would allow us to grow closer and perhaps one day even court."

"Court? Oliver, regardless of feelings, you should be courting a rich young heiress, not a poor girl like me." Carina's shoulders drooped as some of her bravado fell away.

"Have you heard nothing I said?" Desperation carved an edge to Oliver's tone. "There is no rich young heiress for me. I told my mother I would not marry for money. I have held to that from the beginning, but never before have I met someone I connect with as much as I do with you." He held his hands open. "If you don't return my feelings, I will move on. But please, don't turn me away simply because you fear my father."

Carina nibbled her lip. At length, she pushed her spectacles up her nose and fixed him with a hard look, though it didn't quite shield the hurt behind her eyes. "I need time to think, Oliver. This has come about rather suddenly, and I need to process all you've told me." She rubbed her temples, tension and conflict evident in her face.

Oliver exhaled a deep breath as relief flooded him. She was going to give him a chance. "A wise decision. Shall I return in a day?"

"Yes." Carina drew herself up. "A day should do."

With a bow, Oliver left the room. As he closed the door behind him, he could only hope he hadn't ruined his chances with the woman he loved.

How was he to prove to Carina she was more than enough for him?

CHAPTER 22

*C*arina waited until the door closed behind Oliver to release the sigh that had been building in her chest. For a moment, she simply stared out the window. Then, bending over, she collected the detective's letter from the floor and looked over it again. Sketching Willow's address on the front of her envelope, she startled at the sound of movement behind her.

"Dear? Is it all right if I sit down?" Mrs. Fields hovered in the doorway, concern upon her kind face. She clutched a wooden spoon, as though she had been in the midst of baking.

Carina waved toward the armchair next to hers absent-mindedly. "Certainly. It is your boardinghouse, after all."

Mrs. Fields's skirts rustled as she settled into the chair, though Carina kept her gaze on the letter she was sealing into the envelope. After a moment, the woman let out a sigh. "Carina, I couldn't help but overhear your conversation with Oliver."

Carina stiffened, trying not to let loose the tears threatening to run from her eyes. "And? What of it? I told him to wait."

"I'm not accusing you of anything. I'd simply like to know what you're thinking. You look troubled, dear."

Fiddling with the letter in her hand, Carina cast a sideways glance at her landlady. "I don't know."

Mrs. Fields raised a brow in a knowing gesture. While Carina loved her, the woman saw far too much for her own good. "I won't take that as an answer. You share Oliver's sentiments, don't you? I believe I heard love mentioned once or twice during your conversation."

"In truth, I like him very much." Carina swallowed, recalling her words from earlier. *Love.* Had she really said that she loved him? Memories flickered through her head, ranging from the day he had mistakenly knocked her over to their conversation from a few moments ago. She could practically see his smile, the one he had tried to charm her with after she started asking him questions on that first day.

And it worked, didn't it? That silly man went and made me fall in love with him. Second-to-last, indeed.

Carina cleared her throat. "But my feelings hardly matter. He comes from a wealthy family, and I could never compare. I don't know how to socialize with the elite." She hugged her arms against her chest. "The rich cannot court the poor. It will never bring happiness."

Mrs. Fields studied Carina thoughtfully. "Where do you get the impression that his life is full of the social elite? Why would he be here if he was so focused on attending balls?"

"He must be. His father is an incredibly influential judge, and he mentioned how the man expected him to attend balls, charities, and all sorts of social events. I could never learn to fit into such a world."

Mrs. Fields furrowed her brow. "Did Oliver say he enjoyed them?"

Carina paused, lowering her arms. "Well, no, but..."

"Well, then, I think you have your answer. Oliver's home is not among the wealthy. If it were, why would he take a job that requires him to assume the lowest of positions? Why take a job at all when his father makes enough money to see him happily settled?" She gestured to the room around them. "I believe Oliver's home is right here among the people he can be himself with. Why, he practically said as much himself."

Carina worried her lip. "Regardless of where Oliver wants to live, he's still rich. His parents would never approve of a girl like me, and I would have to meet them at some point. Oliver's not the sort to hide his lady away."

Mrs. Fields leaned back in her chair, her gaze assessing. "Something tells me this runs a bit deeper than Oliver's feelings. You have a resentment in you that I haven't seen before. What happened?"

Did this woman miss nothing? "I've had a bad experience with a rich person before. It nearly tore my family apart." Carina shifted in her seat. "It only served to show me that social classes cannot mix."

"An experience? Only one?"

Carina bowed her head, shame washing over her. "Yes."

"Tell me, Carina, did Jesus judge all men based on the actions of one? Did He not forgive even the ones who wronged Him?"

"Well, yes," Carina whispered, clasping her hands in her lap.

Mrs. Fields's hand came to rest gently on top of Carina's arm. "Carina, it is not fair to judge Oliver because of another person's actions. Oliver deserves to be treated according to his own actions, and from what I have witnessed, he seems an admirable fellow. True, he has made mistakes, but who among us has not? Would it be fair for him to turn *you* away because he had been wronged by a poor person long ago?"

"It would not." She barely got the words out.

Her landlady gave a decisive dip of her chin. "If it is because of fear you hesitate, I can tell you plainly that you have nothing to fear. You can trust Oliver."

Carina discerned the truth in the older woman's eyes. She thought back to the anguish she had seen in her father the night he left. The anguish caused by a heartless woman who thought nothing of what she was doing when she abandoned him. Yet she was only one woman. Not Oliver, but a person he had never known.

Carina's shoulders slumped. "You're right, Mrs. Fields. I shouldn't judge him for the actions of another." She frowned. "But what if he chooses to take me to a fancy event? What if they scorn him for courting a mere nothing of a woman?"

"Carina, you are not nothing. You are a child of God, and if you keep that fact at the front of your heart and mind, there will be no circumstance you cannot face. Treat their scorn with kindness, and they will have no grounds to be rude to you. For you possess something far better than money. You have God on your side, and because of that, you will find friends even in the darkest—or more lavish—of places." Mrs. Fields winked. "Also, something tells me Oliver wouldn't let any insults go past him. He thinks too highly of you. I'm certain he would see to it that you received lessons or instruction of some sort before he brought you into society. He wouldn't abandon you to muddle through on your own."

"That's true." Carina straightened, the first vestiges of hope beginning to rise in her chest. Could there be a chance? Could a woman like her be enough for a man like Oliver? *Lord, if this is the path You have chosen for me, then I shall follow it. If it is not, then show me the correct path.* A wash of peace came over her at the silent prayer, and a soft smile crept across Carina's face. "I think I know what I'm going to tell Oliver."

Mrs. Fields pulled Carina into a hug. "I'm glad. Now, what do you have there?"

Carina lifted the letter still clutched in her hand. "Oh, this is for my friend Willow. Oliver was kind enough to hunt down her address for me. It's been so long since I've heard from her."

"How wonderful!" Mrs. Fields clapped her hands. "Would you like me to walk with you to the post office?"

Carina shook her head. "Oh no, that's quite all right. I'd like some time to think as I walk, if you don't mind."

"But of course. Don't forget your coat, now. It's still quite chilly out there," Mrs. Fields reminded her as she stood and moved toward the door.

Carina murmured her thanks, slipped on her coat, and hurried into the coming evening. Her breath created white puffs of air as she strode along the sidewalk, the glow of the streetlamps slowly growing stronger as the sun sank behind the city. Icicles glistened in the purple light, dangling from fence posts and eaves and falling to the ground with every gust of wind. The cold air swept snow from the sidewalk and formed glittering swirls in the air, tossing stinging snow at her cheeks as she walked.

It wasn't long before Carina reached the small post office. Slipping inside, she took her place at the back of the line and waited patiently to send her letter. At last, the young woman working the register greeted her and took the envelope. "Still looking for your sister?"

Carina counted out change. "Yes. As it so happens, however, this letter isn't for a hospital. It's for a friend who I've just discovered survived the fire."

The clerk accepted the change and envelope, the skin around her eyes crinkling with cheer. "Oh, how wonderful! I'll get this mailed for you. Have a good rest of your evening, miss."

"You as well. Have a Happy New Year's." Carina turned to

leave. As she stepped outside, she startled at the sight of a familiar face. "Ella!"

Her friend grinned, brandishing an envelope with one mittened hand. "Fancy seeing you here! Give me a moment, will you? I feel as though I haven't spoken to you in so long."

Carina folded her arms, though she made no move to leave. "It really hasn't been all that long, you know."

Ella popped inside the post office and reappeared a moment later without the envelope. "I know it hasn't been long, but what with the fire and all, we don't get to see each other every day like we used to."

"True. Have you begun looking for work elsewhere?" Carina asked, following her friend down the sidewalk.

Ella pulled her thin shawl tighter around her shoulders. Her blond hair was pulled back into a loose bun at the nape of her neck, giving her a far older look. The circles under her eyes only enhanced the image. Clearly, the days without work had not been easy for her. "I managed to find employment at a button factory. It's far harder than working at the mill, but at least I'm making an income again. What about you? Have you found work? You could always join me, you know."

Carina hummed, tapping a finger against her cheek. "If the mill doesn't reopen, perhaps I will. However, Mr. Browning is confident he can repair the fire damage."

Ella's mouth dropped open. "Repair the mill? But that's preposterous! Even if they did somehow manage, it would be weeks before we could go back to work. No, I think you're far better off finding a new job. How will you look for your sister if you aren't receiving any pay?"

"Well, you aren't wrong. Maybe I will look for a different job." Carina agreed more to calm her friend than because she was truly considering it.

Ella sighed. "It would certainly be a relief for me if you did. I don't have anyone to talk to at the button factory." She gasped, pointing toward a group of children on the opposite end of the street. "Oh, Carina, look! It's a puppet show."

Just as she had said, a handful of children and adults had gathered around a small wooden stand near the corner of the sidewalk to watch two puppets act out some sort of play, the group's laughter drowning out whatever the puppets were saying.

Ella grabbed Carina's hand. "Come on. Let's watch. I haven't seen a puppet show in ages."

Carina pursed her lips but allowed herself to be tugged across the street and to the edge of the group. Standing on her tiptoes, she managed to catch a glimpse of the puppets over the heads of the crowd. One was a beautiful princess with painted blue eyes and flaxen hair, while the other was a frog with a tiny crown atop his head. Lowering herself back onto her heels, Carina leaned over to whisper to Ella. "It's *The Frog Prince*."

Ella clasped her hands together, excitement on her face. "Oh, how lovely! I adore that story. Come, let us get closer." Weaving her way through the crowd, the young woman planted herself near the booth.

Carina followed with a bemused shake of her head, apologizing to other spectators as she attempted to move past them. By the time she had reached Ella, the princess was leaning down to give the frog a kiss. The corners of Carina's mouth rose as the frog was lowered from the stage and replaced with a handsome prince. The prince and his princess shared a quick kiss amid cheers and a few disgusted faces from the young fellows in the crowd.

While the puppets took a bow, Carina tugged on Ella's arm. "Come now, Ella. It's time for us to get home and out of the cold."

Ella allowed Carina to lead her away, placing a gloved hand on her rosy cheek. "Oh, how romantic. If only something like that could happen to me."

Carina snorted, skirting to the side to avoid a cluster of children. "I highly doubt you would ever kiss a frog. You'd probably run away as soon as you saw it."

Ella giggled. "Oh, well. Perhaps I would. Still, it's nice to think about, isn't it?" She elbowed Carina good-naturedly. "What about you? How is your handsome beau?"

"Well, he was a bit shaken by the fire and was very sad when Mr. Baker died. They were good friends. But he's getting better." She paused, working up the courage to voice her thoughts. "As a matter of fact, he asked to court me earlier today. I told him I would give him an answer tomorrow."

Ella squealed, her eyes sparkling. "Oh, please tell me you're going to say yes! You've never had a beau before—not in all the time I've known you, at least."

"I plan on it." Following her conversation with Mrs. Fields, her short prayer had provided a big answer.

"Oh, how wonderful. Your very own handsome prince." Ella tilted her head, fixing Carina with a mischievous grin. "I don't suppose he knows anyone else in need of a lady friend, does he?"

Carina swatted at Ella's arm. "Oh, hush. You'll find a beau in due time. Then I can tease you like you tease me."

"I only tease you because you hide your love as though it's something to be ashamed of." Ella waved Carina's protest off. "There's no use in denying it, you know. I can see how red your cheeks are. Why, if I knew a handsome detective liked me, I would shout it to the world."

Carina frowned. "I never said he was a detective."

"Didn't you? I could have sworn you mentioned it not long ago." Ella blinked, turning away with a shrug. "Never mind. Will you two go on a date tomorrow?"

Carina allowed the diversion, though something tugged at the back of her mind. "I suppose we might."

They rounded the corner to Ella's apartment building, a

rather shabby place with a sagging porch and fading siding. "Won't you come in for a bit?" Ella asked. "We haven't visited in so long. I can make some tea."

"That would be nice." Carina stepped ahead of Ella, moving toward the door. As she got closer, a whinny drew her attention to the horse that stood in a small shed next to the apartment, its head draped through the window as it perked its ears in Ella's direction. The closer they got, the louder the horse's noises became as it tossed its head and stomped its hooves.

"Oh, hush, June. I'll feed you in a bit." Ella waved her hand, directing Carina in. "Come on, Carina."

June.

Carina peered at the horse, an uncomfortable idea growing in her mind. Up until now, they had assumed the second criminal to be a man. But what if it wasn't?

The second thief had never spoken and always remained in the shadows. The thief had clearly had easy access to Carina's shuttle and lunch pail. The thief knew when she was leaving and returning to the mill.

Carina stumbled backward. She had to find Oliver, and quickly. "I have to go."

Ella frowned. "Do you want a cup of tea first?" She stepped down from the porch. "What's wrong, Carina?"

Carina swallowed. This was *Ella* she was talking about. Her friend would never have something to do with a criminal. *I'm being paranoid, that's all.* Seeing criminals in every face and looking for clues where there were none. Or was she? "Just wondering where you got that horse."

Ella stiffened. "It isn't wise to meddle in other people's business."

"Was it not you who told me to look at things a different way? Well, I'm taking your advice, and I don't like what I'm seeing." Carina spoke softly, tensing in preparation to run.

Ella stepped closer. There was a hardness to her eyes

Carina had never seen before. "I'm sorry to hear that, Carina. I thought we were friends." She nodded, and her gaze traveled over Carina's shoulder. "Let's go."

"What?" Before she could turn around, heavy hands lifted her from behind and tossed her into the dark interior of a carriage.

CHAPTER 23

*H*alf an hour after leaving Carina's boardinghouse, Oliver pushed open the rusty gate of the cemetery where Timothy had been laid to rest and slipped inside. The burial ground was quiet in the coming evening as he made his way past each headstone. The wind had blown the snow away, leaving the names in stark clarity. Fresh flowers lay atop several markers, but he appeared to be the only person present.

Eventually, he reached Timothy's grave. Letting out a gusty sigh, which sent a white puff into the air, Oliver tucked his hands into his pockets. "I've really gotten myself into a rough patch this time, haven't I?"

There was no response apart from the wind in his ears, but Oliver could imagine Timothy's wry expression.

"What was it you called me the first time I mentioned my troubles with Carina? A fool? I'd say it was an apt description." Oliver chuckled. "I seem to have a hard time saying the right thing around her. And now what am I doing? Talking to a gravestone, that's what." He stared down at the simple headstone. "What am I to do, Timothy? What would you tell me to do?"

The distant sound of church bells brought Oliver's head up. Six o'clock, though with the deep indigo sky, it felt more like midnight.

A faint smile crossed his face. "Subtle, aren't you?" Oliver turned toward the cemetery gate. "I believe I'll take your advice." He glanced back at the grave one last time, sitting silent and peaceful in the snow. It would take a long time to get over the loss of his friend, but in that moment, he could almost believe that everything would be all right. "Rest well, Timothy."

Back on the main sidewalk, Oliver set his route for the church he had gone to on Christmas Eve. There was something about the warm, comforting feel of the building he desperately needed. It took several wrong turns and various double-backs before he was able to locate the church. Tugging open one of the heavy wooden doors, Oliver released a sigh at the warm air that surrounded him like a blanket.

The interior of the chapel was silent, though the flickering lamps that cast a glow over worn wooden pews indicated someone was in the building. Making his way down the main aisle, Oliver took a seat in one of the front pews and removed his hat, along with the scarf from around his neck. He dug the compass from his pocket and warmed the cold brass between his palms, turning it over and over so that it shone in the lamplight.

Bowing his head, he began a silent prayer. *Lord, give me guidance on what course of action I should take regarding Carina and the thieves. Show Carina she is more important to me than any amount of money.*

The pew creaked. Cracking open one eye, Oliver found the reverend sitting beside him. "Pastor," he said with a nod. "Good evening."

The man returned his nod. "You can call me Pastor Lane. Please, don't let me interrupt you. I will be here when you finish."

Oliver sighed. "Truth be told, I didn't have much else to say. I'm not terribly good at praying, I fear."

"Prayers are simply like letters or telegrams to the Lord. There's no such thing as a good or bad one. They're important to Him all the same." The man laced his fingers across his stomach.

Oliver's brow quirked. Surprisingly, the pastor was dressed in normal clothes instead of the clergyman's outfit he had worn during the Christmas Eve service. Pastor Lane followed his gaze and shrugged. "The clergyman collars are a bit stiff to wear every day of the week."

Oliver offered a small smile, then turned to look at the cross that hung behind the pulpit, the wood illuminated by the gas lamps below. "How am I to know what I should say? My thoughts are so jumbled, I can hardly form a single request."

Pastor Lane leaned back in the pew. "What's your name, friend?"

"Oliver." Oliver hesitated a moment before finishing. "Oliver Ramhurst." He wasn't entirely certain why he admitted his true name to the man, but something about lying in such a holy place felt incredibly wrong. "I came here for the first time on Christmas Eve."

"It's nice to meet you Oliver." The pastor held out a hand, which Oliver shook. If he recognized Oliver's name, he made no mention of it. "Would you care to talk about the things that are troubling you? It may help you to sort them out."

Oliver took a deep breath and, after a few moments, began his story. He spoke of the thefts, the fire, Timothy's death, and of Carina. When he finished, he was like a bellows exhaling its last bit of air. He fell silent, staring at the cross and waiting for the reverend to speak.

"Well," the pastor began, "I can see why you became overwhelmed. That's a lot for one man to keep inside. I'm amazed you've managed to handle it for this long on your own."

Oliver gazed at the compass in his hands, running his thumb across the rim. "The truth is, Pastor, I can handle thieves and criminals. Why, I've been dealing with them for years. The thing I can't seem to figure out is Carina. Relationships are terribly different from conducting a criminal investigation, as it turns out. There's no planning or unraveling or searching involved. It's all emotion, something I've worked hard to keep far from my job."

Pastor Lane laughed. "Young man, it would appear that you've much to learn about love. It's an incredible gift. We were made from it that we might share it with others. It certainly isn't something to be taken lightly."

"But I do love Carina. The problem is the fact that she doesn't believe someone with money could ever be in a relationship with someone of lower status." And then there was her father... "She's been hurt by a rich person's bad actions before."

The pastor sat back, his brow crinkled in thought. "It sounds to me as though she needs to understand her worth. In the end, we are all the same, regardless of money or status. What defines us isn't the clothing we wear or the manner in which we speak. It's the way we treat others that truly shows who we are inside. If your Carina is anything like your description of her, I would say she is an excellent young woman."

"How do I make her see that? How do I show her she can trust me?"

Pastor Lane smiled, his eyes gleaming in the light of the lamps. "Pray, Oliver. Talk to her and spend time with her. Show her you appreciate her." He winked. "Chocolates may help as well."

"I will." Oliver tilted his head. "What did you do when you fell in love with your wife?"

"Ah, dear Mrs. Lane. I met her when I was a bit younger than you, I imagine. We stumbled upon one another in the park and began talking. We found that we shared the same faith, and the same wit as well." The pastor chuckled. "She's a wonderfully bright woman. We spent most of our courtship simply talking. We also discussed faith frequently. Is your Carina a Christian?"

Memories of Carina's speech from Christmas echoed through Oliver's mind. *Trust in God, Oliver.* "A better one than I," he said, pride coloring his voice. "She's a wonderful woman."

"Well, then, you simply have to tell her that." The pastor sat upright, pointing a finger at Oliver. "And don't forget the chocolates. Most women seem to have an affinity for all things sweet."

Oliver laughed, feeling a bit lighter after unloading his anxiety. "Thank you, Pastor. I'll do just that."

The reverend said a quick prayer for Carina aloud and then clapped his hands together. "Good. One last thing, Oliver."

Oliver halted in the process of wrapping his scarf around his neck. "Yes?"

"A word on your case." The reverend's tone grew stern. "When you do catch this thief—for I am certain you will—do not let a desire for revenge blind you from doing right. You must show mercy, no matter the sin. Justice is not yours to serve."

Oliver studied the pastor's solemn yet earnest eyes. "A wise woman told me the same thing. Fear not, Pastor. It is not revenge I seek."

"Very good." The pastor rose and shook Oliver's hand. "Have a good evening, Oliver. I'll be praying for you and your young woman. I hope to see you more in the future."

"Thank you, Pastor. Have a good evening as well."

After making his way back outside, Oliver held the compass up to the lamplight. It glinted in the warm glow, the needle swaying back and forth as it honed in on north. Oliver studied it for a moment before placing it back in his pocket and starting down the street.

Carina was his true north. If he was to prove his love to her, he had some work to do.

~

A few hours later, Oliver stumbled back to his boardinghouse with a package in hand. Unwrapping his scarf in the foyer, he called out a welcome. The only answer was the clanging of dishes in the kitchen, a sign Lucy was hard at work.

Oliver took the scarf and package upstairs to his room. He opened the door and froze. Clothing had been strewn across the floor, some of the shirts slashed and torn. The lamp lay broken on the bed, the smell of the oil that had leaked into the mattress saturating the air. The drawers of the nightstand had been pulled open and the contents dumped onto the ground.

Oliver hastened to the bed and lifted the corner of the mattress. Thank heavens. His revolver was still there. After sliding the weapon into his jacket pocket, he sifted through the papers on the floor. Surprisingly, they were all intact. An extra note among them, printed in bold, spiky letters, caught his eye.

Leave and never return.

Frowning, Oliver pocketed the note and marched back down the stairs. "Lucy! Lucy, are you there?"

"Yes, Oliver, I'm in the kitchen!"

Oliver strode to the doorway of the kitchen. In the toasty room, Lucy stirred a pot of soup on the stove. "Lucy, have there been any visitors today?"

She paused her stirring and turned, tapping a finger to her chin. "Visitors? No, nobody out of the ordinary."

Oliver crossed his arms and cocked his head to one side. If nobody had entered the building, then the note bearer must have been a boarder. "Did you hear a ruckus upstairs? Have you been in any of the rooms today?"

Lucy raised a brow. "No and no. I was going to do my weekly room cleaning tomorrow. Is there a problem? Has something been stolen?"

"No. My room was ransacked. My clothing is torn, and my belongings have been tossed all over."

Lucy gasped, dropping the spoon with a clatter. "Goodness! Let me take a look."

Oliver led the boardinghouse owner up the stairs and stood back, allowing her to examine the room.

"Terrible, simply terrible. I'll move you to a different room at once." Lucy clucked her tongue, fisting a hand on her hip. "I'll speak with the other boarders this evening. We'll find out who did this, Oliver. Oh, I'm so sorry."

"It's all right." Oliver came forward and touched her thin arm. "Are you certain you have room for me? If not, I can find other accommodations for the time being."

Lucy nodded. "Two rooms opened up today. Arlo and Reuben left, I'm afraid."

Arlo and Reuben. A tall fellow and a short fellow. Oliver's hands dropped to his side as shock ran through him like lightning. "Did they say why they were leaving?"

"No. They simply paid me and left without a word." Her eyes widened. "You don't think they did this, do you?"

Did he? Quite possibly. "Lucy, answer me this," Oliver said sharply. "Did Arlo and Reuben often leave late at night and return early in the morning?"

Lucy twisted her mouth to one side for a moment. "I can recall Reuben doing it more than Arlo, but yes. I always assumed they were out at the bar like most of the other boarders. I never questioned them."

A tall man with a black overcoat and a muscular structure. A wiry man who seldom spoke. Two men who complained and accused others in an effort to cover up their own actions. "Did Reuben possess an overcoat?"

"Yes, he did. He was wearing it when he left, as a matter of fact. How did you know that?"

Oliver sucked in a breath. "Where is Reuben's room? I do believe we've just uncovered the identity of the mill thieves."

Lucy led Oliver to a door farther down the hall and unlocked it. Pushing his way inside, Oliver began inspecting every inch of the space. There wasn't much to find, as the room was nearly barren.

"Oh, this is all my fault. I should have never let them leave." Lucy twisted her apron between her hands. "To think that all this time, they were doing such horrible things behind my back. Why, I even asked Timothy to run errands for them a few times. The poor man probably had no clue what they were really up to."

Oliver froze. "You asked him to get things for them? Things like a pair of gloves, perhaps?"

"I did." Lucy dropped her apron and lifted her hands beseechingly. "I wouldn't have if I had known what they were doing. Oh, Oliver, can you ever forgive me?"

Oliver exhaled. "Of course, Lucy. I don't blame you for their actions. You didn't know." At last, he had proof that Timothy was really and truly innocent. His friend had never been involved with criminals.

As he turned back to his investigation, Oliver discovered a small scrap of paper in the bottom of one of Reuben's nightstand drawers. The handwriting on the note was different from the threat left in Oliver's room, less choppy and more fluid.

She goes tonight.

There was an address at the bottom of the paper, one Oliver recognized all too well. He had been there only an hour ago, after all.

Oliver's heart dropped to the bottom of his toes. "Carina," he murmured.

CHAPTER 24

"*I* have to go."

Oliver darted around the confused Lucy and made for the door. He snatched his scarf from the bed, slipping it on as he raced down the steps and into the cold. The note he placed into his coat pocket, where he could reference it again if he needed. There was no telling how old it was, so for all Oliver knew, Carina could be safe and warm inside the boarding-house. Still, the cold feeling in his chest told him something was horribly wrong.

Did they intend to use Carina to lure him in? If so, that would at least reassure him they were keeping her alive.

Oliver skidded around the corner, ran to the door, and knocked several times. He had just raised his fist for another knock when the door creaked open.

"Oliver! You're back already?" Mrs. Fields blinked wide eyes at him. "Why, I thought you were meant to come tomorrow. Has something happened?"

Oliver took a deep breath. "I'm sorry, Mrs. Fields, but this is incredibly important. Is Carina home?"

Mrs. Fields shook her head. "No, I'm afraid not. She went

half an hour ago to the post office. She should be home soon if you'd be willing to wait."

Blast. "No, I haven't got time to wait. I need to find her as soon as possible. I'll look for her at the post office. Goodbye, Mrs. Fields."

Mrs. Fields frowned. "Oliver, dear, slow down. What's the matter?"

Oliver looked the boardinghouse owner in the eye. "I fear Carina is in terrible danger. The thieves have made her their next target."

"Good heavens." Mrs. Fields gasped, her hands flying up to her cheeks. "Are you certain?" At his nod, she whirled around. "Give me a moment, and I'll go with you."

True to her word, Mrs. Fields emerged a few seconds later with a coat and hat on. Oliver lengthened his strides to keep up with her as she set a surprisingly fast pace for a woman of her age. It took them only a few twists and turns to reach the post office. Pushing the door open, Oliver quickly scanned the room, his heart sinking. Carina was nowhere to be seen.

"Excuse me, ma'am?" He advanced on the clerk who stood behind the counter. "Did Carina Clarke come through here recently?"

The young woman placed one hand over the other on top of the counter. "Well, yes. She came here not long ago to post a letter. Who's asking?"

Oliver sighed in relief. At the very least, Carina had reached the post office unharmed. "My name is Oliver Bricht. I'm a colleague of Miss Clarke's." He drew himself up. "Did you see where she went after leaving here?"

"I'm afraid not. I was helping a customer, but I believe I heard her talking to someone outside. I think they left together and went to the right." The clerk gestured in the general direction. "Is she in danger?"

Talking to someone? Dread filled Oliver. "Thank you for your help, ma'am. Don't worry. We'll find Carina." *I hope.*

Oliver exited with Mrs. Fields beside him and strode down the sidewalk, drawing to an abrupt halt at a crosswalk shortly after. There was no sign of Carina in any direction. "Blast. Where could they have gone?" he muttered, running a hand through his hair.

Mrs. Fields carefully studied the three different lanes. "Carina still had a limp. Would that have affected her footprints?"

"Yes, but far too many people have walked through here. I'd never be able to pick her boot prints out in all this mess. We need a different plan."

"Do you have any idea who could have taken her?"

Oliver snapped his fingers. "Reuben and Arlo, two men from my boardinghouse. If we can discover where they went, perhaps we'll find Carina." He whirled around. "We have to talk to Lucy. She was the last one to speak with them. Perhaps she'll have some clue as to where they've gone."

As they hurried back toward Oliver's boardinghouse, he sent up a hasty prayer for Carina's safety. *Please, Lord, let her be all right.*

~

"*L*ucy? Are you still here? We need your help!" Oliver charged back into the boardinghouse like a raging bull.

The landlady peered around the corner of the kitchen doorframe. "Oliver, is that you?"

"Yes. Sorry, Lucy. I didn't mean to frighten you." Oliver lowered his voice as he drew to a halt in front of the frightened woman. "I need your help. My friend Carina has gone missing, and I fear she's been taken by Reuben and Arlo. Lucy, I need you to think. Where could they have gone? What do you know of them?" He gestured to Mrs. Fields, who came to stand beside him. "Mrs. Fields, whom I believe you remember, has come along to provide assistance."

Mrs. Fields smiled encouragingly and walked over to pat Lucy on the arm. "I'm sorry you had such a fright. Have Arlo and Reuben ever acted violently before?"

"No. Reuben may have been loud, but he was always polite. Arlo was so quiet and unobtrusive. I had no idea they would do something so dastardly. To think I was harboring kidnappers and arsonists!" The poor woman looked as though she might faint. "As I said, they gave me no indication of where they were going when they left. Now that I think about it, they never said where they were from either. I brushed it off as them being surly."

Oliver's hopes sank. Clearly, his landlady didn't know anything helpful. "That's all right. Why don't you take a seat while I look through the rooms again?" There had to be something he missed, some sort of clue that would hint at where they'd gone.

Lucy took a deep breath. "No. I'll be all right. Would you care for some help in your search? It's always good to have an extra set of eyes."

"If you wouldn't mind, that isn't a bad idea."

"I'd be more than willing to help. To think of a poor, innocent girl in the hands of those two..." The woman shuddered. "Besides, they're the reason Timothy is no longer with us. They deserve to see justice."

Lucy and Mrs. Fields followed Oliver up the stairs, where Lucy unlocked the two rooms. While the women went into Arlo's room, Oliver went back over every nook and cranny of Reuben's room, whom he suspected to be the more dastardly of the two, but it quickly became apparent the man had been thorough in removing every sign he'd been there.

Oliver sat back on his heels and put his head in his hands with a frustrated groan. "Where are you, Carina?"

"Oliver, I found something!" Lucy rushed into the room, causing Oliver to glance up. "Arlo didn't do nearly as good a job of cleaning out his things. There was a receipt for a pub hidden under his bed." She waved a small paper over her head. "He was always out late drinking and doing Lord knows what else. If you were going to find him anywhere, it would most likely be at a place like this."

"Brilliant!" Oliver hopped to his feet and accepted the receipt from Lucy. The name at the top of the paper read, *Mariner's Lakeshore Pub.*

"Hang in there, Carina," he muttered. "I'm coming."

CHAPTER 25

The rattling of wooden wheels was the only sound audible inside the dark carriage.

After being shoved inside by the large brute, whom Carina had no doubt was her attacker from before, the door had been slammed shut and the carriage began moving. Despite pounding on the door with her hands, shoulders, and even knees, it refused to yield. The windows were also sealed shut, leaving her without an escape route.

Instead, she'd devoted herself to finding a viable weapon to protect herself with. Unfortunately, the cushions wouldn't do her much good, and the bottom of the seats were plain and wooden. In a sudden moment of inspiration, Carina managed to pry a large splinter from the seat and hide it in her sleeve. It was the last thing she was able to do before the carriage slowed to a halt.

The door shrieked open, revealing Ella and a rather formidable-looking man who was dressed entirely in black.

"So we meet again," Carina said dryly as the man pointed a dagger at her, directing her out of the carriage. "Was one murder not enough?"

They stood in an empty warehouse. Large wooden beams stretched from one side of the ceiling to the other, with gas lamps that dangled several feet above Carina's head. There were windows, but they were covered in dust and darkened by the night. A set of barn doors provided the only entrance and exit.

In front of her, the tall man sneered. "One dead body should have been enough to keep you away. Besides, the fire wasn't meant to kill anyone. The fact that Timothy ran back inside was the result of his own foolishness."

Carina bristled. "That doesn't excuse what you did. Why *have* you done this?" She pivoted to pin her former friend with a hard stare. "Ella, why would you be party to murder, theft, and arson?"

"Stand guard." Ella waved the tall man toward the door without answering Carina. "I'll watch her until the detective gets here." She removed a small derringer from her apron pocket and pointed it at Carina. "Don't move."

Carina folded her arms. The glimmer of fear in Ella's eyes hinted that the woman wasn't likely to shoot her—but then again, nothing about Ella could be counted on. "I'm not. You still haven't answered my question, Ella. Why are you doing this? You're setting a trap for Oliver, aren't you? But why? Why not run far from here?"

Ella curled her lip. "And leave him to discover our identity? I think not. Besides," she continued, her face relaxing ever so slightly, "we aren't stealing from anywhere else. For your information, we weren't interested in money to begin with. Not that it matters to you, little miss high and mighty."

"Then why? I don't understand. Make me understand." Carina held her palms up. "What would drive you to do this?"

Ella released a shuddering sigh. "When I was sixteen, I had a younger brother. We all adored his antics." She smiled, her gaze focused far away. "He used to make little animals out of sticks and twine to give to me. But then Father lost his job." Her face darkened. "We all had to take up work if we wanted to survive. I went to the textile mill, and Frankie came with me to work as a bobbin boy. For an eight-year-old, he felt very grown up to be doing a job alongside the adults. Things were going well until one day the woman in charge wasn't paying attention, and the drawing frame malfunctioned while Frankie was trying to retie thread onto one of the bobbins. He was crushed beneath the machine and died a few hours later." Her jaw tightened. "There was nothing the doctors could do to save him."

"Oh, Ella..." Carina held her hand out.

The tears that had been gathering in Ella's eyes disappeared, and she waved the pistol to keep Carina in place. "Frankie shouldn't have been allowed to work at the mill, and he's not the only one. Dozens of other children have died while working under conditions like this. Think about the girl that was trapped during the fire. She was thirteen, Carina. Thirteen!"

"And so you took it upon yourself to shut down the mill."

Ella nodded. "It was supposed to be simple. Take the money allotted to the employees and eventually, they would leave to find work elsewhere. If enough people left, the mill would be forced to shut down. But then your detective came in and started sticking his nose where it didn't belong. I realized he was undercover when I came upstairs and discovered the two of you searching through the office. We tried to warn you away, but you wouldn't listen."

"You sabotaged my shuttle and put a venomous snake in my lunch pail." Carina ground out the accusation, betrayal lashing her. "It seemed less like you were trying to warn me and more like you were trying to kill me."

Ella grimaced, a flash of guilt crossing her face. "I didn't want to kill you. I knew I could have alerted you to the danger before you got hurt."

"That's no excuse." Carina pressed her hand to her chest. "Ella, I truly am sorry about your brother. I know what it feels like."

How had she never heard of Ella's brother before? Because she hadn't really asked the girl anything about her family. Guilt assailed Carina. Maybe it wasn't too late to make Ella see the light. If she could only get past the anger, perhaps she could find the cheery girl she had counted a friend. And, if she could, there was still a chance for her to escape.

Carina continued, twisting the fabric of her skirt in her hands. "You know what happened to my mother and sister. I could have chosen to get angry. I could have chosen to blame the farmers for burning the fields. But I knew that wouldn't bring them back. Ella..." Carina looked the young woman in the eye. "Seeking revenge on the mill will not bring you peace for your brother's death. What killed your brother was an accident and nothing more."

"An accident that was caused by a rich man's greed!" Ella stomped her foot. "Jamieson was willing to put children to work so long as it lined his pockets. Frankie never would have been in the mill if it wasn't for him."

"But Browning is not the same mill owner, as evidenced by the changes he made when Jamieson died. There's nothing to avenge, Ella." Carina softened her voice. "Your little brother wouldn't like to see you doing this. I know it and you know it."

Tears streamed down Ella's face as she clutched at the handle of the gun with shaking hands. "Someone has to pay for what happened. It isn't fair that his death should go unnoticed."

"Revenge will not bring notice to Frankie's death. He can be remembered fondly, without anger attached to his memory. You can find peace another way. It isn't too late. Be honest with yourself, and I think you'll find you don't want to do this."

Ella hesitated, her arm wavering. "The fire wasn't my idea," she said softly, her brows drawing together. "Neither was trying to sabotage you. I never wanted violence, but he insisted upon it." She gestured to the man near the door with his back to them, keeping watch.

"Who is he to you?"

"My older brother, Reuben," Ella murmured with a glance toward the door. "He began working at the mill before Frankie died. He's a bit...harsher in his ideas. His anger runs deeper than mine, though sometimes I wonder if Frankie's death isn't the only thing that drives it."

"Ella," Carina whispered, daring to take a step forward. "You can leave all of this behind. All you have to do is come clean and start over. Please. I know there's good in you."

Ella tilted her head and parted her lips, as though considering Carina's words. Then, glancing over Carina's shoulder to where Reuben stood, her face went blank. "I'm sorry, Carina, but it's a bit too late for that. Things have been set in motion, and with luck, your detective will follow the clue Reuben left to the proper place. Once he makes his way here, he'll be...properly dispatched. Then we can leave and nobody will be the wiser."

"And what of me? Do you plan on dispatching me as well?" Carina drew herself up. "Will you do it yourself, or will you have someone else do it for you?"

"Stop!" Ella jabbed the derringer into Carina's side.

"I won't! Not until you see reason. Even if you manage to kill Oliver and me, others know what's going on. They won't stop until you've been caught. Turn yourself in while you still have a chance."

A flicker of something that looked remarkably like guilt flashed in Ella's eyes. "There is no chance for me."

Carina studied her friend's face. Could it be possible Ella blamed herself for what happened? "Yes, there is. There's always a chance for forgiveness. You simply have to ask for it."

"Shut it!" Warring emotions played across the young woman's face.

Carina drew a breath to speak again, but something hard hit the back of her head, and she descended into peaceful darkness.

~

The pub was a dingy little place, the type of hole in the wall few would take notice of. A faded sign with a fishing boat on it confirmed it to be the *Mariner's Lakeshore Pub*, the place listed on the receipt Arlo had left behind. A lot hinged on the likelihood of one or both of the criminals being present. If they weren't, Oliver would be in for a long wait. Still, Lucy had seemed fairly confident Arlo and Reuben would show.

"They went out nearly every evening after work," she had told Oliver as they were traveling to the pub. She and Mrs. Fields had both insisted on accompanying him to this dismal section of town—against his protests that it was far too dangerous, especially at eight-thirty in the evening. "I didn't know exactly where they went, but they would return late at night smelling of alcohol."

Leaving the intrepid little ladies waiting across the street in front of a dry goods store, Oliver stepped into the main room of the pub. The faint lighting and lack of windows made it hard to identify the men who hunched over the bar and grouped around the tiny tables near the back wall. Raucous laughter filled the air as he moved closer to the bar, the sound originating from a group crowded around a pool table tucked in one of the corners. The room stank of cigar smoke and alcohol. Everything appeared to be covered in a thin coat of grime, though that didn't seem to bother the customers. Upon closer inspection, the counter itself was covered in chips and scratches, with several large spill stains permanently fixed on the wood.

Approaching the bartender, Oliver affected what he hoped was a casual smile and tossed a bit of change on the counter. "Good evening, sir. One pint, please."

The bartender, a tall man with bushy eyebrows, snorted and swiveled around. "Sure thing, *sir*." There was a sarcastic tone to his voice as he turned back with a pint of golden liquid in one hand. "Here you are. For your information, most of these fellows leave their manners at the door. You'll be more likely to survive among them if you do the same."

"Ah. I'll keep that in mind." Oliver took the glass and raised it in a mock salute. Rather than drink the beer, he hunched over the glass like many of the other customers, using the position to cast surreptitious glances at the face of each. As he gazed down the bar, a familiar head of hair caught his eye.

Arlo.

Oliver kept his face calm and expressionless and his fists from clenching, though it took everything in him to not rush straight over and throw the scrawny man against the nearest wall.

The group by the pool table broke out in a flurry of shouts, the noise escalating as curses filtered through the air. The bartender set his glass down with a heavy hand and left the counter to break up the arguing men, his threats joining the din and providing the perfect opportunity to speak with Arlo.

Moseying over to where the man sat hunched over his drink, Oliver planted a hand on the bar to catch his attention. Arlo jumped in his seat before looking at Oliver, his gaze blurred from the effects of several drinks.

Smiling, Oliver gave Arlo a friendly but rather hard pat on the back. "Arlo, old friend! Where have you been? We missed you at dinner, and then Lucy told us you had moved out."

Arlo's face drained of color as recognition dawned in his

eyes. "Oliver." His hands trembled as he removed them from around his drink and tucked them in his pockets. "What brings you here?"

Oliver laughed, then dropped his voice to a sharp whisper. "I believe you know why I'm here. Why, it's written all over your face. Seems as though you've gotten mixed up in some tricky business, eh, Arlo?" He leaned closer, leading the man to shrink beneath his gaze. "Tell me where you've taken her, and the judge might reduce your sentence."

Arlo's brows tented in confusion, though his shoulders twitched. "She? Who is *she*?"

Oliver clenched his fists to prevent himself from doing something rash, like knocking some sense into the drunk man's head. "The woman you kidnapped. Where is she? Where is Carina Clarke?"

"I don't know anything about a woman. I came here because Reuben asked me to meet him. He was supposed to be here an hour ago, and he never showed." Arlo held up his hands. "I swear it!"

"If that's the case, why did you leave the boardinghouse so abruptly, and without a word to any of us?"

Arlo's face reddened. "I may have run into some troubles with gambling. With me being out of work and all, I couldn't pay off my debts, and it made a few people angry. I needed to clear out before they discovered where I lived. Reuben said he would come with me and help me out. I assumed he was doing it because he was a good friend." He frowned. "What's going on? Did he do something wrong?"

Oliver huffed a breath. Regardless of whether or not the man was telling the truth, the police would want to speak with him. "Come with me," he said coldly. "Don't give me trouble, or I'll be back with the police before you can blink."

Arlo swallowed and stood, swaying for a moment before he regained his center of balance. "All right. I'm telling you, I don't know what you're talking about. I didn't kidnap anyone."

"But Reuben did." Oliver propelled Arlo toward the door. "And you're good friends with him, which makes you a suspect. If you really are innocent, then you have nothing to worry about. If not, the police will determine your fate."

Arlo shuddered. "Look, the only thing I know is that Reuben was going to meet me here so he could tell me about some new business venture he thought would help me pay off my debts. Some building he bought that he wanted to show me. He said we would be rich by the end of the month."

Oliver froze, his hand still gripping the smaller man's shoulder. "Keep talking."

"He said we could use the building for shipping, but he wanted my opinion on what cargo we should export. I'm guessing it's some sort of warehouse down by the docks. If he really kidnapped a lady like you're saying, couldn't he have taken her there?" Arlo fiddled with his hands. "That's really all I know. Please, let me go."

Oliver walked Arlo outside and did just that, though something wasn't adding up. If Arlo was innocent, who was working with Reuben? And where was he? Reuben hadn't showed up for his meeting, which was telling.

Arlo twitched and scuffed his shoes on the ground. Oliver would keep an eye on the man, but in the meantime, he had a far bigger lead. Where would he search for records of the sale of this warehouse? Or should he go straight to the docks and start looking for the building? It was an option, but by the time he searched through all the buildings, it could very well be too late.

After Arlo ambled off, the women approached Oliver, and Mrs. Fields placed a comforting hand on his arm. "Dear, you look as though your head is about to explode. What happened?"

Lucy shuffled even closer. "Yes, what?"

As Oliver explained, their expressions grew serious. When he finished, Lucy remained silent for a few moments before suddenly brightening.

"I know what to do!" she exclaimed. "Reuben's monthly rent payments all originated from the same bank. If he uses it for all of his business, shouldn't the record of his purchase of the warehouse also be recorded there? If they have the purchase record, they should also have the building's address."

Oliver grinned. Getting the building's address would be far faster than searching through the docks at random. "Lucy, you're a genius. Do you know how to get there?"

Lucy tugged the sleeves of her coat down over her thin, wrinkled hands. "I know where the bank is. However, even if it keeps late hours today, it will be closing soon."

"That won't be an issue." Oliver would find a way to get the records, no matter the cost. Carina's life depended on it.

CHAPTER 26

*T*he next time Carina awoke, the sky outside the windows was completely devoid of light. The lamps on the warehouse ceiling lit the room in a faint glow, enough that she was able to see that she was alone. Was it the same night, or had a day gone by? It was impossible to tell.

Shifting where she lay, she found her mitten-clad hands were bound in front of her with rope. Her feet, too, were wrapped tightly. The pounding headache in her temple indicated she had been dealt a hefty blow, though her vision remained clear and her spectacles were still on her face. Carina shivered as a gust of wind rattled the windows outside the warehouse, goosebumps racing across her skin. Thank heavens she was wearing a thick dress and scarf.

Where had Ella and the brutish Reuben gone? Somewhere in the carriage? Had they managed to lure Oliver away? Fear rushed over Carina, and she began trying to inch her boots off to create slack in the rope. After a while, she was finally able to slide her footwear off, giving her the space she needed to free her feet from the rope. She released a sigh of relief as feeling rushed back into her toes, wiggling them several times before pushing her feet back into the warm boots and standing to look around.

Her limbs sluggish in the cold, Carina walked slowly to the barn doors. She tugged on them as firmly as she could with near-frozen hands, but they remained stubbornly shut.

Filled with resolve, Carina turned toward the closest window. A quick examination proved that it not only was firmly sealed shut, but also that the glass panes were too small to allow for escape.

There has to be a way. I can't be trapped in here.

As desperation began to set in, Carina whirled around and searched for an object to throw at the glass. Locating an adequately sized rock on the ground, she managed to awkwardly pick it up and toss it at the glass. It bounced off with a *plunk* and landed back on the ground. *Drat.* Undeterred, Carina continued her efforts until finally the windowpane cracked and broke.

Peering outside, Carina made a quick study of her surroundings. Unfortunately, it was almost impossible to tell where she was when the outside of the warehouse was completely dark. The only visible sign of life was a faint cluster of lights that shone in the distance—from another warehouse, perhaps? If she squinted, she could see the faint outlines of long rectangular buildings surrounding the warehouse she was in. The air was still and silent, though she could hear the faint sounds of the city somewhere behind her.

Carina pursed her lips. Where on earth had they taken her? The docks, perhaps? It would make sense, given the number of buildings. "Hello," she called into the stillness. "Can anyone hear me? Help me, please! I've been kidnapped!" Her voice faded into the silence, unheard and unanswered.

No. Not unheard. She sent up a quick prayer. *Lord, You can hear my pleas. Please, help me to get out of here. Help me warn Oliver before it's too late.*

Filled with new determination, Carina turned back toward the door. Walking around had warmed her somewhat, allowing her to move a bit faster than before. There had to be a way to make the door open. Perhaps she could pry it open with something.

Carina's gaze lit on the faint outline of a loose floorboard. *Aha.* She marched over, dug her mittened fingers beneath the wood, and pulled. It moved a measly few inches before settling back in place.

Frowning, Carina tried again. This time, the board moved a bit higher before clattering back in place. After several more tries, the board finally broke free from the rest of the floor.

Falling back onto her hind end, Carina held the board up like a victor brandishing a trophy. "Hurrah!"

Her still-bound hands made the effort somewhat tedious, but Carina managed to stumble back to her feet and headed for the door. She placed the board between the door and the wall and drove it downward in an effort to break the lock. After trying that for several moments, she switched tactics to prying the door open.

The door groaned and slowly bent farther and farther from the wall, renewing Carina's energy as she gave it one last shove. There was a crunch as—to her horror—the board broke instead of the door. She was left holding half of the plank, the other half remaining wedged in the door.

"No," Carina whispered, sinking to the ground in defeat.

Apart from trying to break the wall itself, she had no other options. She was completely and utterly trapped, with no way to save Oliver. How foolish! A cleverer person would have escaped ages ago. Yet here she sat, with a broken board, a bump on her head, and shivering limbs. Some detective she was. She was all alone on New Year's Eve, the final day of a terrible year.

Well, not entirely terrible. She had met Oliver and deepened her friendship with Mrs. Fields. Carina touched the butterfly charm that hung around her neck—a reminder that she had changed. That she was loved and knew what it was to love in return. What a shame that it could very well all end here.

Moisture gathered in Carina's eyes, but she quickly brushed it away. There was no time for crying, much as she longed to simply let the tears run down her face and then take a good nap.

"What am I to do, Lord? Wait and accept my fate?" Carina whispered.

She studied the half of the board still in her hands. Nails stuck out of the end and sides, making the plank a rather formidable weapon. Placing one of the jagged nail heads between the threads of rope still around her hands, Carina sawed her hands back and forth until it snapped. Rubbing her sore but free wrists, she blinked.

Was the board all she had left? Was she to resort to violence as Ella and Reuben had done? She frowned, thinking hard. "No." Carina wouldn't hurt them if it could be avoided. Still, if things became truly terrible, it would be good to have a weapon to defend herself with.

Carina flinched at the sound of footsteps drawing nearer to the building. *They're coming.* There was no time left to consider her options. Standing, she hid the plank behind her back. "My life is in Your hands," she whispered.

~

"I'm sorry, but we're closing now. You'll have to return tomorrow." The bank teller barred the door with one thin arm, his mouth pressed into a disapproving line. The man's graying hair and thick glasses gave Oliver the distinct impression of an owl—and a very disgruntled one, at that. He had appeared in the doorway as Oliver and the women approached the bank, intent on keeping them from entering the building.

"Sir, this can't wait. Not when a woman's life is at stake." Oliver stepped up to the man and squared his shoulders. "We need to review some transaction records. We won't be leaving until we get them."

The teller raised a brow. "And why should I show you highly confidential records?"

"Because I'm a detective with the Pinkerton Agency, and if we don't get access to those records, someone might die." Oliver removed his badge from his pocket and showed it to the teller, never breaking eye contact with the man.

"A Pinkerton," Lucy murmured from behind Oliver. "That would explain quite a bit."

The teller returned Oliver's stare for a moment before grumbling something indistinct under his breath. "Very well. This way, please."

Following the man down a hallway on the right, they soon emerged into a large room filled to the brim with wooden cabinets. "Who are you looking for records of?" the teller asked as he crossed over to the filing system.

Lucy spoke from behind Oliver. "Reuben Weston."

"Just a minute." The teller bustled into the rows of cabinets.

Mrs. Fields, who stood beside Oliver, frowned. "Weston? Why, that's Ella's last name."

Oliver jolted. "Ella? Carina's friend?"

"Yes. This Reuben must be a relation of hers."

Oliver's mouth ran dry. Could it be? "Ella is the second thief."

"What? But she's such a sweet girl!" Mrs. Fields's expression went slack. "She would never do such a thing."

"It must be. If she's related to Reuben, it would make sense. The second thief was far shorter and never spoke." And she was so close to Carina, Oliver had never suspected her.

The teller returned holding a few sheets of paper against his chest. "Here are all the transaction records, banking records, and deeds we have for Reuben Weston. The most recent paper is a deed for a warehouse, which he purchased with a loan. Mind you don't mix up the papers or remove them from this room."

Oliver tugged the paper from the teller's hand and quickly reviewed the contents. He grinned at the sight of the building's address, printed at the top of the deed in bold ink. "Wonderful. Thank you, sir. We'll be leaving in just a moment. Could I borrow a pen and paper?"

The teller scurried from the room and returned a moment later with the requested items. After scrawling the address twice onto the piece of paper, Oliver returned the file and the pen to the disgruntled man. "Thank you. Have a good night."

"What's the plan, Oliver?" Mrs. Fields whispered as they hurried from the bank. "How are we going to get our Carina back?"

"We can't risk even a minute, not when we don't know for certain what they want with her." Oliver turned to face the ladies. "I'll head for the docks right now. In the meantime, I need you two ladies to run and fetch the police." He ripped the paper in half. "Tell them to get to this location as quickly as possible." He handed one of the addresses to the women, keeping the other for himself.

Oliver frowned. The only unknown variable in his plan was the second thief, presumably Ella. How motivated was the girl to participate in crime? He had to assume she was dangerous and watch for her as well, in the event they tried to ambush him. He tapped his coat pocket, feeling for the revolver he had concealed within. He would try to avoid causing anyone harm, but with Carina's life at stake...

"You be careful, you hear?" Mrs. Fields patted his arm.

"Yes. Be careful, Oliver," Lucy agreed, her face creased in worry.

Oliver's heart swelled with gratefulness. "I will. If...if I don't see either of you again, I want to say thank you for all your help. I know Carina would be glad to know so many people care about her safety."

Mrs. Fields stepped forward and set a hand on Oliver's shoulder, her brows tenting over determined eyes. "Oliver Bricht, you had better return in one piece, or else I'll be after you with my broomstick. Go, get our Carina, and get yourself safely out." Despite her scolding, Oliver didn't miss the way her voice wavered.

"I'll do my best." Oliver released a heavy breath, anxiety tugging on his heart. "Now, let's be on our way. We have thieves to catch."

CHAPTER 27

*T*he barn door slid open with a thunderous clang, the sound echoing through the empty building. Carina took a few cautious steps backward and made certain the board was concealed behind her as Reuben entered the warehouse, with Ella trailing close behind. The man had a terrible coldness in his eyes, visible even in the limited light. As he scanned the interior of the building, his gaze met hers, and a smile crawled across his face.

"Well, would you look at who finally woke up? Did you enjoy your beauty rest? Ella was afraid I hit you too hard." He laughed, the sound harsh and grating. "Not that I care, but she still seems to hold some sort of tender feeling toward you. Since she is my little sister, it wouldn't be very nice of me to take away something she cares about." His eyes narrowed. "Of course, once the detective is caught, that may change."

Carina lifted her chin, though she made no effort to answer.

The horrid man tilted his head, studying Carina's ropeless feet. "It seems you do have some wits about you, after all. Unfortunately, we can't have you running out on us. We want to make this a New Year's Eve your detective friend won't forget."

Carina tensed, grasping the board tightly behind her back. She would have only one chance to use it, for Reuben would quickly realize she was hiding something behind her. As the odious man drew closer with a length of rope in his hands, she spoke. "That detective you speak of has a name. It's Oliver Ramhurst. Are you too afraid to say it?"

Reuben raised a brow. "Ramhurst? Well, I didn't expect to be killing a judge's son, but I guess there's a first time for everything. Who knows—perhaps it'll make the front page of tomorrow's paper."

Just as he was about to reach her, Carina swung the board and caught Reuben upside the head. He let out a roar as she dropped the wood and raced toward the open door.

Ella stood frozen, clenching the derringer. Amazingly, the girl kept the gun pointed at the ground.

Someone tackled Carina from behind, slamming her to the ground.

"Not so fast." Reuben's sour breath fanned her face.

Flipping over, Carina attempted to punch the brute, but her fist only glanced off his shoulder as he hauled her to her feet and tied her hands behind her.

"Stupid females," he muttered, grasping her arm and forcing her back toward the center of the room.

Once there, he released her, and she turned to face him. Blood ran down the side of his cheek from where the nails in the board had scratched him. Carina allowed herself a small grin of satisfaction. At least her attempt hadn't been entirely in vain. The only downside was that she now had a throbbing fist and an incredibly angry adversary.

"I'd kill you right now if I didn't think you'd be useful." Reuben cracked his knuckles in what Carina assumed was an attempt to frighten her. "And you!" He whirled on Ella, who still stood near the door. Ironically, she was wearing one of the hair ribbons Carina had given her for Christmas. "What good is having a sister if she isn't helpful when I need it? Get over here and watch this slippery little eel so I can deal with Ramhurst." He practically growled the last word at Carina. "You see, I can say his name as many times as I want. I'm not afraid of some prissy detective."

Carina scoffed. "Oliver would never be so foolish as to walk directly into your trap."

Reuben snorted. "That's what you think. I've planned things rather well, if I do say so myself. I suppose he thinks he's quite smart, having discovered from Arlo that I purchased a warehouse. What he doesn't know is that I asked Arlo to meet me there because I knew the detective would show up. All it took was one well-placed receipt. The detective wouldn't be able to resist following my little breadcrumbs to the pub, not when his lady love was in danger. From there, he'll go to the bank, locate the address of the warehouse, and come searching." He spat the words with enough contempt to make Carina physically recoil. "What your rich little detective doesn't realize, however, is that he's going to the wrong warehouse. The one I purchased is full of nothing more than rotting timber, left behind by some dismantled lumber company."

Carina stepped back as a wave of uncertainty washed over her. "If that's true, where are we?"

"In a warehouse I didn't have to buy." Reuben shrugged. "Deeds won from gambling don't have to be filed with the bank." He grinned, though it was more a baring of the teeth. "So you see, your detective will waltz in thinking he has everything figured out, when in reality he'll be walking directly into an ambush."

"You're wrong." Carina battled the panic rapidly building in her chest. Would Oliver really be so foolish as to rush in without a plan? Would he fall for Reuben's trap?

Reuben laughed. "I don't think I am, and judging by the look on your face, neither do you. Now, if you'll excuse me, I have a detective to ambush." He snapped his thumb and fore-finger. "Ella, get over here and be useful for once. Keep watch until I return. I'll take care of her after that."

Ella finally broke free from her trance, moving forward on unsteady feet. She looked uncertain about the whole deal, as though something had changed since the last time Carina had seen her. The dark circles under her eyes had grown larger, making her look tired and frail.

"Are you sure about this, Reuben?" Ella questioned, the derringer dangling lazily from one hand. "Killing a judge's heir would get us executed if we were caught. We could take the left-over money and go. We could force Carina and the detective to keep quiet."

"Have your brains gone soft? We can't let them go free, Ella! They'd be after us with a posse the moment they walked from the building. If you want to start a new life, then we're going to have to take care of all the loose ends." Reuben gestured to Carina. "That includes her."

Carina remained silent, studying the siblings. Something was changing, creating a glimmer of hope in her chest. She could try to convince Ella to let her go, but first, Reuben had to leave. Carina couldn't chance being knocked unconscious again.

After a moment of tense silence, Ella sighed and stepped forward. "As you wish, Reuben."

Reuben grunted and released Carina's arm, giving her a push forward. "Don't let her out of your sight. I'll be back." With that, the tall man stalked from the building.

A minute later, Ella spoke. "You'd better not talk to me again about changing my mind. If you do, I'll shoot you." Though her words were harsh, her voice trembled. A single drop of sweat trailed from her hairline down to her chin, leaving a wet track on her cheek.

Carina raised a brow, trying to appear unruffled even

though her hair was in utter disarray, her head was pounding, and there was dirt smeared all over her dress. "Something tells me you've never used that before."

Ella frowned and gripped the weapon tighter. "Regardless of whether or not that's true, it doesn't take a genius to figure it out. I won't have much of a problem hitting you at this range."

Carina shrugged, trying not to show the fear that dripped down her spine. "Fair enough. May I ask why you don't want me to speak of an opportunity for you to turn your life around? It's only words, after all. If you are as hard as you claim to be, I would think such talk wouldn't bother you."

Ella slashed her free hand through the air. "Be quiet. Your voice is annoying, like a fly buzzing in my ear."

Carina allowed a small smile to creep across her face. Despite the insult, the way Ella shifted from one foot to the other revealed she was unnerved. "Well, if you think I'm annoying, you'll find the guilt to be much worse."

Surprise flickered across Ella's features and disappeared in an instant. "Why should that matter? I can handle guilt."

"It isn't just guilt. It's God that's talking to you, warning you that the things you're doing are wrong." Carina shrugged. "The only difference is whether you choose to listen to Him or not."

Ella furrowed her brows. "I want nothing to do with God. He killed Frankie, and for that, I'll never forgive Him."

Carina studied Ella. "Aren't you doing the same thing right now? You're threatening to murder me." She nodded her head toward the gun. "Yet, rather than being angry at you, God is offering to forgive you."

"I don't want His forgiveness. He killed Frankie."

Apparently, Ella was so trapped in her own convictions that she was deaf to anything else.

"God didn't kill Frankie," Carina said quietly. "He brought Frankie home. We all have a time when we must go home, but that home is where we choose to make it." She tilted her head.

"I don't want to see you create your own demise, and neither does God. Please, don't do this to yourself. You know it can only end in ruin, for you'll never be able to stop running. I can see it in your eyes."

Tears filled Ella's eyes. "How can you say you care for me when this is what I am? When this is what I've become?" She gestured to the derringer in her hand, her voice cracking. "I'm a monster."

Carina took a step forward, trusting Ella wouldn't harm her. True to her guess, her former friend remained in the same slumped-over position. "We cannot choose to be human, Ella, but we can choose to be monsters. You still have that choice. There is still time to make things right."

Indecision and raw pain flashed across Ella's face as she bit her lip. "Make things right? That's impossible."

"Nothing is impossible. There is still time." It would be so easy to scorn Ella for what she was doing, but something told Carina to stay and help her friend, to show her mercy. For it was clear by the look on the woman's face that nobody had shown it to her before.

Ella wiped at the tears streaming down her cheeks, letting out a tiny sniff. "What about Reuben? I can't leave my brother. He may not be the best person, but I love him regardless. I can't run to save myself without at least trying to save him too."

Carina exhaled a long breath. She understood loyalty to a sibling. "Talk to him, Ella. You are his sister. Make him see reason as I did with you. It is his choice whether or not he listens. If he doesn't, then at least you'll know you tried."

"He didn't used to be this way," Ella whispered, her voice sad and broken. "When we were younger, Reuben used to be happy and carefree. But when Frankie died, it was like all that was good and decent within him died too. He became angry and violent, choosing drinking and gambling over his family. He hardly even speaks with me anymore, and when he does, it's never in a kind tone." She tucked a lock of hair behind her ear, the blond strands damp from her tears. "I fear he may never listen. His heart is hard." Ella looked up at Carina. "But I have to try, don't I?"

Carina winced as pins and needles spread through her bound hands. She was running out of time. Oliver could arrive at the docks any minute. "That's good of you. Now you are faced with a choice, Ella. Will you help me, or will you listen to your brother and allow your life to be destroyed?"

For a moment, Ella remained silent, staring into Carina's eyes. Then she straightened and moved to Carina's side. "I'll help you. Maybe it's because you were so nice to me. Maybe it's because I can't pull the trigger. All I know is, I can't stomach the idea of letting you be killed." She made quick work of untying Carina's hands and stood back, pinning her with a hard look. "But I don't want to hear any more talk of the Lord. I..." A riot of emotions flickered over her face. "I'll sort that out on my own. You've said enough."

Carina rolled her wrists to return the blood flow to them and attempted a small smile. "Thank you, Ella. Now, where is this warehouse Reuben bought? We don't have much time. If we don't hurry, your brother and Oliver are both in danger of being killed."

Ella ducked her head abashedly. "Well, I don't exactly know."

Carina sent her an incredulous look as the throbbing in her head began to worsen. "You don't? Why ever not?"

"Reuben was afraid I would be a liability." Ella smiled ruefully. "By the looks of it, he was right."

Carina began pacing back and forth, the loose curls around her face bouncing with every step she took. "Well then, what do you know?"

Ella tilted her head. "Well, the warehouse is somewhere close by. It was owned by a lumber company, so there may still be a sign on the building. It should also be directly on the water, because Reuben told me there was a spot for docking and loading boats."

"In that case, we'll have to check each building until we find it. I can only hope we locate it before anyone gets hurt."

Ella grimaced, holding up the derringer. "I won't use this on anyone, but if worse comes to worst, I won't let Reuben get himself or anyone else killed. The sight of it should be enough to get his attention."

Carina searched Ella's eyes, finding them to be truthful. "Very well. Let us go while there's still a chance."

They raced out the barn door, Carina's still-healing ankle protesting the rapid movement. Once in the open, she drew to an abrupt halt and glanced from one side to the other. "Drat. Double drat. It's too dark to see anything!" She groaned, trying to make out the details of the building next to them. Just as she was about to inquire whether or not Ella possessed a lantern, a brilliant flash of light illuminated the air. Carina gasped as a flower of colored light bloomed in the sky, followed by a large boom.

"Fireworks! They're setting them off to celebrate New Year's Eve," Ella exclaimed from beside Carina. "Reuben was hoping Oliver would show up tonight. He thought the noise would be a good cover for his ambush."

Thank You, Lord. "In that case, we have to hurry." Carina used the light of the next flash to study the building next to them.

"I think it's this way!" Ella collected her skirts in one hand and took off toward the right.

With no other viable options, Carina followed her, running as fast as she was able. Would they be in time?

CHAPTER 28

*W*ith Carina's compass in hand and the address lodged in his memory, it wasn't long before Oliver located Reuben's warehouse. He ducked behind a building that had a good view so he could study the site without fear of being spotted.

Large piles of logs lay stacked around the exterior of the building and near the open door. While they would make a good cover, the stacks would also be an excellent place for Reuben to try and ambush him. No lights were shining within or outside the warehouse, so Oliver would have to enter the building blind. It was a risky move, but without knowing where Carina was, it was one he would have to take.

Whispering a silent prayer for safety, Oliver drew his revolver and set off toward the door of the dark warehouse. Snow crunched under his feet, each footstep like a gunshot. There would be no hiding his approach from Reuben, not when even the ground seemed to be conspiring against him. Cold air bit at his cheeks and neck. By the time he reached the warehouse, his face was practically numb.

As he halted a few feet from the door, a firework exploded

in the air, the light making Oliver flinch. Any other time, the beautiful colors might have brought him joy.

Another firework joined the first, the flash of light illuminating a shadowy figure that stood inside the warehouse. Perhaps the fireworks might be useful, after all. Though a familiar black overcoat covered the man's tall frame, his face and white-blonde hair were exposed, along with the gun he held in front of him.

"Hello, Oliver." The voice echoed from within the building, deep and cavernous.

"Reuben! Fancy meeting you here." Oliver skirted in a quick zigzag motion toward the left of the doorway, making him a harder target for Reuben should the man decide to use his gun. He kept his own revolver clutched at his side, ready to fire the moment he knew for certain Carina wasn't close by. Once he reached the wall of the warehouse, he peered around the corner of the open door, searching the darkness for the woman that should have been there. *Where is she?*

A laugh echoed from within the warehouse, followed by a loud bang. Oliver ducked back as a bullet whizzed past him. "Funny you should say such a thing when it's you who's intruding on my property." Reuben's smug statement blended with the exploding of fireworks.

He would gain nothing by losing his temper, infuriating as the man might be. "And how did you come upon enough money to buy a warehouse, I wonder?" Oliver fought hard to keep his voice calm. "Does the seller know you paid them with stolen goods?"

Reuben snorted. "That wouldn't have made for very good business, Oliver. I think even you know that. Though you don't really have to conduct business, do you? I suppose being the son of one of the wealthiest men in Chicago has its benefits."

"Let's get back to the reason I'm here." Oliver glanced once more around the corner, and a flash of frustration ran through him at the blackness within. Another bullet shot through the doorway, only a few inches from his head, and he jerked away from the opening. "Where is Carina?"

Reuben laughed again, the sound completely devoid of warmth. "Why don't you come here and find out? Or are you too much of a coward to face me? I would expect nothing less from a dandy."

Oliver inched toward the open doorway. If Carina was close to Reuben, the criminal could kill her or use her as a shield before Oliver got to them. "I could say the same of you, Reuben. After all, wasn't it you who took an innocent woman rather than facing me directly from the start? That was a bit of a low tactic, don't you think?" A firework illuminated Reuben again, revealing that Carina was nowhere near him. Oliver nearly sighed aloud in relief and raised his gun. "As a matter of fact, everything you've done thus far has been quite cowardly, under the guise of night."

"What I did was nothing less than genius. How do you think I managed to get away with everything? Certainly not by doing it in broad daylight. Besides, I got you to come here, didn't I?" Reuben scoffed. "Not only that, but I tricked you. Carina isn't even in the building. We get to face each other man to man."

Oliver froze at the edge of the doorway, the gun poised in one hand. "What do you mean?"

"This was nothing more than a decoy. Ella has Carina nearby, and at my cue, she'll shoot. As a matter of fact, since the girl has outlived her usefulness, I might as well signal Ella to go through with it now." Reuben raised his arm.

"No!" Oliver fired his pistol.

The gun flew from Reuben's hand, and the man bellowed, doubling over.

Oliver raced into the building and slammed into Reuben with his left elbow, bringing them both to the ground. Reuben smashed a fist into his arm. His weapon flew from Oliver's hand, landing somewhere in the darkness.

Reuben reared up to punch Oliver again, but he managed to dodge the blow and slid out from underneath the larger man. Kicking Reuben's knees, he sent the criminal tumbling to his back with a thud. Oliver brought his arm back in preparation for a jab, but his attempt was thwarted when Reuben's feet connected with his stomach, propelling him into a nearby woodpile. Logs clattered loudly around him as he struggled to catch his breath, wincing at the pain in his side as he rose.

Where were the police? It couldn't have taken all that long for the women to find them and show them the address. *Please, Lord, speed their steps. I need help.* Reuben was far bigger and stronger, though that didn't mean Oliver wouldn't fight to the end to bring the criminal down.

As though summoned by Oliver's thoughts, Reuben launched himself out of the darkness and landed another quick blow to Oliver's shoulder. Avoiding another flying fist a moment later, Oliver managed to land a jab of his own on Reuben's nose. There was a sickening crunch as blood began to pour down the man's face, mingling with that from a few smaller scrapes.

Reuben reared back with a cry, his face contorted with anger.

Using the distraction to his advantage, Oliver tackled Reuben's waist in an attempt to flip him onto his back. Unfortunately, the action only sent the two of them to the floor, where they desperately struggled to stay out from underneath one another.

"None of this would have happened if you had stayed away." Reuben snarled, his fist slamming into the dirt as Oliver rolled aside to avoid the blow. "Because of your meddling, an innocent person died."

Oliver gritted his teeth, copying Reuben's move and kicking

the man in the stomach. He used the moment of freedom to leap to his feet, though Reuben did likewise a second later. "I didn't kill Timothy. You did. If anyone should be blamed for murdering innocents, it's you."

"You're right. It *was* my choice, and now I'm choosing to kill you." Reuben growled, charging toward Oliver.

Bracing for impact, Oliver jolted at the sound of a gun firing. Reuben heard it as well, freezing a mere foot from Oliver.

"Stop it this instant, or I'll fire again," a feminine voice cried.

Ella stood a few feet away. The girl was trembling despite her bravado, pointing the gun not at Oliver, but at Reuben. Behind her, partially cloaked in shadow...

"Carina!" Relief flooded Oliver at the sight of her. She smiled at him, looking tired but none the worse for wear. While he would have liked nothing more than to rush to her side, doing so would give Reuben an opportunity to go free.

"Ella, what are you doing? You knew the plan! Point that stupid thing somewhere else so I can finish this. Better yet, shoot him and we can leave." Reuben's chest heaved, and his clothes were torn from the fight.

Oliver took a step away from the man but froze when his foot nudged an object on the ground. His revolver! Slowly, he bent and collected the weapon.

"I won't." Ella held her gun higher. "I won't allow you to destroy your life like this."

Reuben laughed, though the man twitched when Ella adjusted the gun. "Has that woman been filling your head with promises of love and forgiveness? It's too late for that, Ella. This is what we are now." He gestured to the warehouse around them. "You can say it however you want, but we're criminals through and through."

"But we don't have to be. We can be better than this. We can make a new life for ourselves like I wanted. All we have to do is stop and we can start over. Please, Reuben, you're my big brother. You're my *family.*" Rawness and pain radiated through the woman's voice.

There was a moment of tense silence, as though the stars themselves were waiting for Reuben's answer. His eyes narrowed in derision. "What about Frankie? I suppose he means nothing to you? He was your brother too."

Ella shook her head, tears streaming down her cheeks. "Frankie is gone, but you aren't. No revenge is worth losing your life over, and I should have known that from the start. Please stop fighting. We can start over. We don't need revenge to guide our lives any longer."

"Ella, you're a fool." Reuben spat a mouthful of blood to the side, making Oliver's stomach twist. "I don't have time for this. Put the gun away and leave this place. I'll deal with Clarke and the detective myself."

Ella planted her feet, holding the gun steady. "I can't let you do that."

There was a flurry of movement at the door of the warehouse. "Police! Put your hands in the air!"

Oliver released a sigh of relief. Finally, help had arrived.

Reuben let out an outraged cry and bolted forward, but Oliver darted in front of him and trained the revolver on his chest. "I think not."

As the police took Oliver's place, commandeering Reuben's weapon, Oliver rushed to Carina and wrapped her in a tight embrace. His aching limbs protested the movement, but he wasn't about to let go for even a second. "Are you all right? I was so worried."

Carina returned the hug with equal fervor. "I'm all right, Oliver. They didn't hurt me."

"You nearly scared me to death when I came to find you and you were gone." Oliver didn't break his hold on her even as the police escorted Reuben from the building. "Never do that again."

Carina laughed softly. "I'll do my best to avoid getting kidnapped in the future, but I can't make any promises." She released a long breath. "I'm so tired, Oliver."

Oliver leaned back, scanning Carina for injuries. There was no doubt she was cold, for she was shivering beneath his arms. Apart from that, however, she seemed unharmed. Her hair hung in loose curls around her shoulders, and her eyes shone clear and blue in the flashing light of the fireworks.

Oliver shrugged out of his jacket and set it around her shoulders. "We'll get you home. First, however, I must know— how did you escape?" He listened as Carina gave him an abridged version of her capture and subsequent escape. When she had finished, he gave her a bright smile. "Carina, you're brilliant. Why, I hardly did a thing."

"Lies. Fighting Reuben was incredibly brave of you. I saw you trading blows with him when we snuck in through the side door. It was impressive, if a bit frightening."

Oliver grinned. "You should have seen me tackle him when I first ran in the building. I believe it's the first time I've ever done it effectively." He glanced toward the door. "We should go outside. There's someone who would like to see you."

Carina tugged his jacket tighter around her shoulders as a shiver wracked her frame. "All right. Give me one moment, please." She turned to the place where Ella had been, but the space was empty. "Ella?" she called out, glancing around the building.

Oliver followed her gaze to the open side door and shook his head. "I suppose she ran out once the police came in. Should I send someone after her?"

Carina stared at the gaping doorway, her eyes surprisingly sad. "No. I don't believe she'll trouble us or anyone else again. She wanted revenge. Without it, she'll be forced to face the emptiness that's left inside."

"Perhaps she'll turn out a better person because of it." As

Oliver spoke, he took Carina's arm, tucking it securely into his elbow as though they were out for a stroll in the park.

Carina hummed, casting one last glance at the place where her friend had stood. "I certainly hope so."

She allowed him to lead her outside, where the officers were attempting to place handcuffs on Reuben's wrists. The man struggled against them, shouting blistering curses all the while. Only the fireworks that still exploded in the air interrupted his tirade.

"Carina! Oh, my dear! Thank goodness, you're all right." Mrs. Fields rushed forward and enveloped Carina in an embrace. Why the woman had decided it was a good idea to come along was a mystery, but Oliver could hardly complain as the boardinghouse owner bundled Carina in a quilt she had brought. His smile of approval turned to surprise when Mrs. Fields turned and hugged him as well. She released him a moment later, grasping his elbows. "Oh, Oliver. You brought Carina back to us. Thank you. Thank you so much!"

Oliver gave the woman a lopsided smile. "Actually, Carina mostly escaped by herself. I simply kept Reuben at bay until the police arrived."

"You did wonderfully, Oliver. I wouldn't have escaped without you." Carina came to stand beside them. "Here, you can have your jacket back. Thank you for letting me borrow it."

As Oliver slid the coat back on and pocketed his revolver, a shout caught his attention. He whirled as Reuben broke free from the officers and grabbed a gun from one man's holster. Turning, the madman aimed it straight at Carina. "I'll finish what I started!"

"No!" Oliver pushed Carina aside.

A shot rang through the clearing. Time seemed to slow as the bullet slammed into his chest, sending Oliver flying through the air. He hit the ground with a thud, lying with his eyes shut as he waited for pain to overtake him. While he had anticipated feeling fear over dying, peace flowed through him. He was prepared to meet the Lord.

Only, the pain he was expecting never seemed to come.

"Oliver! Oliver, can you hear me?"

His eyes fluttered open.

Carina was leaning over him, her face pale and her red curls dangling like a curtain over her shoulders. "Please, please be all right."

Oliver blinked. "Why am I not dead? Or at least in pain? I felt the bullet hit my chest."

Carina stuck her hand into the front pocket of his jacket and pulled out a badly dented compass. A compass that had stopped the bullet from hitting his heart. She let out a breathless laugh, tears falling from her eyes and onto his chest as she held the compass out for him to see. "You kept it with you."

Oliver's lips curved into a weak smile. "Of course I did. Why wouldn't I, when it was a gift from you?"

Carina's eyes sparkled with something more than relief. She leaned in closer, and before Oliver could process what was happening, she pressed her lips to his own. The kiss was soft and tender, a fleeting touch that conveyed more than words ever could.

For a moment, the world seemed to pause, and the only sound was the beating of Oliver's heart. He was frozen, caught between wonder and fear that movement would break the spell holding them both in place.

A firework split the air, and Carina pulled away. "I'm sorry. I don't know what came over me..."

Oliver pushed himself up and tugged Carina into a fierce embrace, burrowing his nose into her curls and silencing her nervous words. "Don't apologize." He inhaled the faint scent of lavender. "There's nothing to be sorry for. Nothing at all."

Carina sniffed, burying her face in the shoulder of his

jacket. The action sent a twinge of pain running through Oliver, but he hardly cared.

"I thought I lost you." Carina's voice was muffled by the fabric of his coat. "I thought you were gone forever."

"I'm not going anywhere, Carina." Oliver rested his cheek on her head as a smile tugged at his lips. "I promise."

CHAPTER 29

*C*arina awoke to the whistle of a kettle. Rolling over in bed, she sighed in satisfaction at the feeling of having a warm comforter wrapped around her.

After returning home last evening, Mrs. Fields had promptly ushered Carina into the bathtub and, from there, straight to bed. She had been quick to fall asleep, thoroughly exhausted from the events of the night. The memory of Reuben and Oliver fighting hadn't left her mind for a long time, haunting her dreams along with Ella's pale face. In addition to the nightmarish memories of the fight, another image had also remained bright in her mind—one of her lips touching Oliver's. The thought alone was enough to make heat rush through Carina's cheeks, though she couldn't quite regret her impulsive action.

Carina slid from bed, dressed in a simple gown, and slowly made her way down the steps and into the kitchen, where Mrs. Fields was already hard at work.

"Carina, dear, welcome to the new year! How did you sleep?" The woman abandoned her cooking to envelope Carina in a hug.

"It is New Year's Day, isn't it? It's hard to believe it's 1873." Carina returned the woman's hug before pushing back to look her in the eye. "To answer your question, I slept quite soundly. Last night was exhausting."

"It was, at that. Now, why don't you have a nice slice of bread and butter? Oliver ought to be by soon, so you'd better eat something."

Carina took the bread and promptly devoured it, speaking only once every last crumb was gone. "Is he all right? Did he see a doctor?" She wiped a butter smear from her cheek with one finger. "He looked to be in bad shape when he left. Reuben did a number on him, the poor man. Why the police decided to question us right then, when he was clearly injured, I'll never know."

Mrs. Fields chuckled, handing Carina a hot cup of tea. "Well, you could hardly expect them not to ask questions after a man tried to kill you. Luckily, Lucy ushered him straight to the doctor's office after they saw us home. She stopped by early this morning with a lovely loaf of bread and informed me he has only a few cuts and bruises. That compass truly did save his life."

Thank the Lord. Carina took a sip of her tea, her shoulders rounding at the delightful flavor. "This is delicious, Mrs. Fields. How long ago did Lucy stop by?"

"Oh, about seven, I would say."

Carina nearly dropped her cup. "Good heavens! How long did I sleep?"

Mrs. Fields spun around to face what looked like a pot of oatmeal and took to stirring it. "It's ten now. Don't worry about it, dear. You had a very long night."

A knock at the door interrupted their conversation.

"Well, that was fast." Mrs. Fields abandoned the oatmeal and bustled to the door.

A rather worried-looking Oliver stood on the stoop. He

wore a rumpled cotton shirt and a half-buttoned jacket that made it look as though he had run through a strong wind. His ruffled hair only served to enhance the windblown appearance, making Carina stifle a laugh.

"Good morning. Is Carina awake? If not, I can always return—"

Carina stepped up beside Mrs. Fields with her teacup in hand, effectively cutting him off. "I am here."

The worry left Oliver's brow, replaced by one of his bright smiles. "Ah, Carina! Happy New Year's Day. How are you feeling?"

She adjusted her spectacles to hide the way heat stole across her face at the sight of him. "I'm well enough now that I've had time to rest. What about you?"

"Considering I was shot, I feel wonderful." Oliver twirled his cap in one hand. "As it so happened, I was wondering if you wanted to accompany me to the mill so we can tell Mr. Browning the good news. Only if you feel well enough, of course," he hastily added. "After that, we should stop at the police station and give a full statement. They'll want to hear all about how you thwarted a gun-toting madman. Of course, if you aren't up to it, I'll let them know you need more time."

Carina set her free hand on her hip. "I wouldn't want to miss getting credit for my daring escape, would I? Give me a moment to fetch my coat." She turned to Mrs. Fields and held out her teacup. "Would you take this, please?"

"But of course, dear." Mrs. Fields clasped the cup, a twinkle in her eye.

Carina scurried up the stairs and into her room. A few moments later, she returned with her coat buttoned to the collar and joined Oliver on the step. "Let's be off, then."

"Don't stay out for too long," Mrs. Fields called as they walked away. "I'm baking a pie."

"We won't." Once they turned the corner, Carina released a

snort. "I think the dear woman is afraid to let me out of her sight."

"Can you blame her?" Oliver tucked his free hand into his pocket. "The last time she did, you were kidnapped."

Carina blew out a sigh. "No, I suppose not."

The familiar scent of mint wrapped around her, and she touched the butterfly charm that hung around her neck as the memory of their kiss burned in the back of her mind. She swallowed, recalling his promise from the previous evening. *I'm not going anywhere.* Had he really meant it? He could have easily said it in the heat of the moment. "Oliver... what will you do now? You caught the criminals responsible for the mill theft. That means your work here is finished. Where will you go now?"

Oliver studied the building they walked past. "Well, I expect I'll need to remain in Milwaukee in case they call upon me as a witness for Reuben's trial. Once that's finished, I'll report back to Chicago and see if Pinkerton has another case for me."

"Oh..." Carina bit her lip as emotions warred in her chest.

"Carina." Oliver's voice was soft, but it drew her attention. Looking up at him, the intensity in his gaze took her by surprise. "I'm not going to leave you behind."

Carina's heart skipped a beat. How had he known what she was thinking? "You...you won't?" She hated the fragility of her voice, the way it wobbled as she spoke.

"No. I made you a promise to find your sister, and I never break my promises."

Was that the only reason Oliver wanted to stay? Obligation to fulfill a promise? Had the warmth she had seen in his gaze the previous night been a figment of her imagination? Had it been a mistake for her to let her emotions take over?

Oliver's steps faltered as he sucked in a quick breath. "Carina, come with me."

Carina blinked and paused beside him. "Beg pardon?"

"Come with me to Chicago. Consider it a three-day holiday. You can stay at my home and meet my parents." The enthusiasm in Oliver's voice increased as he spoke. He touched her elbow and resumed their walk. "They'll love you. You'll get to see the city while I check in with Pinkerton. If word comes about your sister, it will be sent to my family's address. After that, we can both come back to Milwaukee and wait for Reuben's court date."

Carina fiddled with her dress, twisting the fabric between her fingers. "I don't know. If I did come, I wouldn't want to stay at your parents' home. Not when they don't know a thing about me."

Oliver rested a hand on her shoulder. "Oh, nonsense. You'd be my guest." His eyes sparkled. "It's important to me that they meet the woman I care about. Will you at least consider it?"

The woman I care about. Warmth bloomed in Carina's chest, and the tightness in her chest eased by a fraction. "I will." Her mind flickered to Oliver's previous words. "Oliver, what's going to happen to Reuben? He's awful, but he is Ella's brother. She would be devastated if he died."

Oliver's jaw twitched. "Considering the conversation I had with the police last night, I don't think Reuben will receive much grace. The evidence isn't in his favor. In the end, it will be up to the judge to decide his fate. He'll have to answer for his actions, and there's nothing you or I can do about that."

Carina studied Oliver. "Well, regardless of what happens to him, it's admirable of you to extend him mercy. Most people in your position would be eager to see him spend his life in jail."

"I would be lying if I said I didn't abhor what he's done," Oliver admitted with a shrug, "but I know Timothy would want me to forgive him. The fact is, Reuben will receive proper justice. If not in this life, then surely, in the next."

"Very true." Carina's steps slowed as the mill loomed before them.

The exterior of the building displayed new windows, while the courtyard had been cleared of rubble. Considering the last time she had seen the mill, it was a far sight better. There was hardly any sign of the disaster that had befallen it.

Mr. Browning stood near the front of the building with his back to them, gazing up at the white letters that had been painted in bold strokes across the brick. *Browning Mill.* The man's posture betrayed his pride.

Oliver cleared his throat as they drew abreast of the man. "Mr. Browning. Happy New Year's Day."

The man turned, wariness and hope evident in his gaze. "Mr. Bricht, Miss Clarke. Happy New Year's to both of you."

Oliver held out his hand, which Mr. Browning shook. "Thank you for coming to meet us."

"Of course." The mill owner stuck his hands back in his pockets. "What did you wish to discuss? Make it quick, if you please. I have to get back to my family for breakfast."

Oliver grinned, glancing briefly at Carina. "Mr. Browning, I am proud to say that the thieves have been apprehended and placed in prison. The Weston siblings will not be stealing from your company any longer."

Mr. Browning's mouth dropped open. "You are certain it was them?"

"Indeed. Thanks to the work of Miss Clarke, we know for certain they are the thieves."

Carina pursed her lips. "He is too modest. Mr. Bricht also did quite a bit of work."

Mr. Browning raised a brow, studying Oliver's bruised temple. "I can see that. In that case, I thank you both. I wouldn't have been able to reopen the mill had it not been for your diligence." He turned to Carina. "Miss Clarke, you are more than welcome to resume your former position when the time comes."

"Thank you." Carina bobbed her head, trying to tamp down

the disappointment in her chest. While she should have been grateful to have a secure job, the idea of returning to the loud, stuffy rooms made her shudder.

"With that said, I do need to get back to my family. My hands may freeze if I stay out here any longer." Mr. Browning doffed his hat, a brief smile crossing his face. "Well done, detectives. Thanks to you, I'll finally be able to rest well at night. Enjoy the rest of your holiday." He lifted a hand in farewell before making his way toward a carriage waiting outside the mill gates.

Oliver took Carina's arm and looped it through his own. "Would you mind stopping at my boardinghouse on the way to the police department? I need to fetch something from my room."

Carina blinked. "Certainly. I'm in no rush."

It took them only a short time to reach Oliver's boardinghouse, whereupon he darted inside with the promise to return shortly. Carina enjoyed the brief moment of silence in his absence. A gentle snow cascaded toward the ground, the snowflakes fat and lazy as they settled like a blanket on the sidewalk. It was the first day of a new year, the time when many people decided to make changes in their lives. Sometimes frightening changes, but changes they would see through.

Am I ready to make a change? Carina glanced at the door Oliver had disappeared into. Her lips twitched as warmth bloomed in her chest. *Yes. Yes, I am.*

Oliver reemerged from the boardinghouse, shutting the door behind him with a bang. He darted down the steps and presented Carina with a wrapped bundle.

"What's this?" Carina took the package from him and turned it around in her hands.

"You could consider it a bit of a New Year's gift, I suppose," Oliver said, putting his hands in his pockets. "You can open it."

Peeling the paper back, Carina gasped at the sight of brand-new copies of Jane Austen's books, tied together with a velvet ribbon. "Oh, Oliver! This is incredible. Thank you!"

"To be entirely honest, I intended to give them to you a bit ago. I nearly forgot about them until this morning, when I was cleaning my room and discovered the package beneath my nightstand." The tips of Oliver's ears reddened as he tucked his chin. "I know most ladies seem to prefer roses and chocolates, but I thought you might enjoy those more."

Carina beamed. "Oh, I will." She hugged the books to her chest and took a deep breath. *Here goes nothing.* "In fact, I'll enjoy them on the train to Chicago."

Oliver's head whipped up. "Really? You'll come?"

"Yes. It's only for a few days, and I'd love to visit another state."

"Amazing! I can't wait for you to meet my parents. They'll be impressed once they hear of your heroic escape."

Carina grimaced, biting the inside of her cheek. "About that... I'd like to stay in a hotel, if you wouldn't mind." She wanted to be at her best when she met Oliver's parents, and that meant finding somewhere to freshen up before going to meet them.

"Are you certain? You wouldn't be putting them out." Seeing Carina's expression, Oliver placed a comforting hand on her arm. "Very well, then. Let's get to the police station and then back home so you have time to rest and pack. I'll pick you up at ten tomorrow morning to drive us to the train station. Does that sound all right?"

Carina nodded. "Perfect."

A new adventure awaited, far from her life as a mill girl.

∾

"*M*rs. Fields? I'm back!" Carina called from the foyer, clutching her new books tightly to her chest as she shut the door behind her.

The proprietress appeared from the kitchen and bustled over, scrutinizing Carina's gift. "What do you have there?"

"Oliver gave me the rest of Jane Austen's novels. Now I have my very first complete set." Carina could almost dance a little jig right there in the foyer. "Aren't they simply splendid? They're brand new."

Mrs. Fields took in Carina's flushed cheeks and grinned knowingly. "Indeed, they are. I don't suppose anything else of interest transpired, did it?"

"Oliver asked if I would go to Chicago with him for a few days," Carina said slowly. "He wants to introduce me to his parents. I believe he wants their approval before he...well..." *Before he asks to court me.* A sliver of anxiety jabbed at her chest. What would they think of a girl like her?

Mrs. Fields studied Carina. "And what did you say?"

"I told him I would like to go. I've never left Wisconsin before, and I think a trip away would be nice. Of course," Carina hurriedly added, "I won't be staying for long. There's the matter of the court case and my sister and all sorts of other things."

"Oh, posh. Those things can wait. If you return Oliver's feelings, you should go with him and meet his parents." Seeing Carina's apprehensive expression, Mrs. Fields waggled a finger in the air. "Now, don't you go getting anxious on me again. You are a fine young lady, Carina Clarke, as any person with good sense can see. If his parents choose not to like you solely because of your background, then shame on them."

"I'm afraid I'll feel out of place among so many fancy people." Carina clutched the books even tighter. "I know nothing of their customs."

"My dear, simple manners will get you a long way with people like Oliver's parents. The rest will come with time," Mrs. Fields said with a wink.

Carina's face flushed.

Mrs. Fields chuckled and placed a hand to her cheek. "Ah, young love. My husband and I were the same when we met. He always knew how to make me blush." She turned and started for the kitchen. "Now, we'll need to pack a few days' worth of dresses. I would recommend bringing your nicest one for the day you meet Oliver's parents."

"'We'?" Carina echoed, confusion lacing her tone.

"But of course. You can't go without a chaperone." Mrs. Fields smiled mischievously.

"But who will watch the boardinghouse?" Carina followed Mrs. Fields through the kitchen.

"Lucy mentioned she has a daughter looking for work. I expect the girl would be more than willing to take over for the few days. I'm not about to let you go on an adventure into society all by yourself." Mrs. Fields's face shone with determination.

As the woman bustled around the kitchen, seemingly intent on packing a week's worth of supplies, Carina reached up to touch her butterfly pendant. Time to spread her wings.

Would this *adventure* prove to be all that Oliver promised, or would she crumble beneath the pressure?

CHAPTER 30

*T*he whirring of the train wheels slowed and then finally stopped as the locomotive drew to a halt in front of the bustling Chicago depot. Glancing out the window, Oliver folded the newspaper he had been browsing and placed his stovetop hat back on his head. He had decided to wear a suit for the trip back, as his mother would expect it. Still, it was rather stiff and uncomfortable in comparison to the cotton shirts he had grown accustomed to wearing. He intended to change back into something simple as soon as he was done meeting Pinkerton and his parents.

Oliver cleared his throat. "Ladies, we have arrived."

Seated across from him, Carina lowered her copy of *Sense and Sensibility,* her eyes wide and anxious. "Truly? I haven't even reached the halfway mark in my novel."

"Train travel does seem to be growing faster and faster, doesn't it?" Oliver chuckled as she put her book away.

"It does at that. Why, the last time I took a train, I felt I could have walked faster," Mrs. Fields agreed from the seat next to Carina. "Of course, the last time I took a train was over ten years ago." Oliver had been all too glad to hear that the kind woman would be coming along as an escort. While he would do his best to make Carina feel at home during her visit to Chicago, having a familiar face would probably make her more comfortable.

After he helped Carina rise, Oliver assisted Mrs. Fields in standing and collected their luggage from the storage rack above his head. "Right this way, ladies." He carefully maneuvered the carpet bags into the walkway and from there out onto the depot platform, with the women trailing him. "Welcome to Chicago." He set the luggage in a neat stack on the wooden floor and waved his arm. "What do you think?"

Carina halted beside him, shielding her eyes with her hand as she glanced around. "Well, it's a bit noisy but not all that different from Milwaukee." She tucked her book under one arm, giving Oliver a smile. "But it's nice, being able to see something new. I can't believe I'm in an entirely different state!"

Oliver laughed. "Wait until I show you around. There's quite a bit to see. First, however, I have to find a carriage. I'll return shortly."

It took him only a few minutes to locate and pay for a carriage to deliver them to the Pinkerton Agency. Oliver helped the ladies board and lifted the luggage in behind them. He took a seat on the bench opposite Carina. She was looking out the window in wide-eyed excitement, all the tiredness from the past day gone.

"If it's all right with you ladies, I had planned on finding you a hotel and then leaving to stop by the detective agency. That will give me time to speak with Pinkerton while you two settle in. Once that's accomplished, we can explore a bit of the city."

Carina turned from the window, a frown tugging at her lips. "I had hoped to see the agency. Would that be possible?"

Oliver grinned. "Certainly. I'm sure Pinkerton would love to meet you, especially with all the help you gave me."

They sat in pleasant silence for a few moments until the carriage began to slow.

"Pinkerton Detective Agency," the carriage driver called, bringing the vehicle to a halt.

Oliver hopped down, then held out a hand to assist Carina and Mrs. Fields. After ensuring that the carriage driver would wait for them to return, they entered the large brick building that housed the detective agency.

"My goodness," Carina whispered as they walked through the foyer and into a room with rows and rows of desks, drawers, and typewriters. People bustled to and fro, some with empty hands and others clutching briefcases that no doubt contained case directives. All were in a rush, as though their next destination could be their last.

Oliver halted in front of Pinkerton's office and removed his hat, knocking on the door. Once Pinkerton called out from inside, Oliver opened the door and strode in with the two ladies close behind. "Good afternoon, sir."

Pinkerton's brows shot up. "Ramhurst! I hadn't expected you back so soon. I was glad to hear of the results on your case. It was two siblings working together, eh?"

"Yes, sir. Thanks to the help of these two ladies, both thieves were unmasked. Browning sends his thanks to the agency," Oliver proudly informed him.

A broad smile crossed Pinkerton's face as he came to his feet. "Well, well. Congratulations are in order for all of you." He tilted his head, studying the women who stood silently behind Oliver. "Who might these two lovely ladies be?"

"Ah, forgive my manners. May I introduce Miss Clarke and Mrs. Fields?" Oliver stepped aside, giving his boss a clear view of the women.

"Pleased to meet you both. I don't suppose you'd be interested in a job at the detective agency, would you?" Pinkerton chuckled, bowing over each of their hands in turn.

Carina hummed, her face glowing with barely contained excitement. "Who knows? Perhaps I will someday."

"Well, a position will be open for you should you want it." Pinkerton moved back behind his desk to address Oliver. "Ramhurst, give the judge my regards. I'll contact you with a new case soon." He made a shooing motion. "Now, go and enjoy your free time while it lasts. Show these two ladies around."

"I plan on it. Thank you, sir. I'll tell my father you send your greetings." Oliver replaced his hat and turned, holding the door open for Carina and Mrs. Fields. Once they were all through, he closed the door behind them and spun to face the women. "Well, then, shall we find a hotel?"

"That would be lovely." Carina's gaze flicked among the men and women at work in the room. "Did Mr. Pinkerton mean what he said about giving me a job? Do ladies really work as detectives?"

"Most certainly. Women have the same job as men here, going undercover and solving crime. The first woman to be employed here, Miss Kate Warne, if I recall correctly, even helped to thwart a plot to assassinate Lincoln back in 1861." Oliver forged a path back through the building and out the front door, with ladies following close behind. "I think you'd make a fine detective, by the way," he commented as they walked toward the carriage waiting at the edge of the boardwalk. "You should consider Pinkerton's offer. You'd certainly be able to see the world with a job like that." She could be his partner as well, though he didn't voice that.

Carina hummed thoughtfully. "True. I will think about it."

Stepping back into the carriage, Oliver gave the driver directions for a nearby hotel where his extended family often stayed while visiting. While rather simple in appearance, it was clean and well-kept.

Once they arrived, Oliver helped the women unload their bags and deliver them to the porter who waited near the front door. Then they entered the lobby and approached the front desk.

"Good afternoon. May I please get one room for two nights?" Oliver asked the clerk. "It will be for these ladies. You can register them under the name Oliver Ramhurst."

The clerk wrote his name on the hotel ledger, along with a room number, before fetching an iron key from the wall behind the desk and setting it on the counter.

Carina spoke in a low voice, her brow knit. "Oliver, you really don't have to pay. I have enough funds to cover two nights' stay."

Oliver shook his head, already handing the clerk the proper amount of money. "I insist, fair lady. After all, you just helped me solve my biggest case. And you must allow me to show you around the city." He swept the key from the counter and tucked it into Carina's palm. "Even the zoo."

Carina raised a brow, a smile tugging at the corners of her mouth. "A park full of animals? All right, that seems a fair trade." She closed her fist around the key. "You spoke to your mother, correct?"

"Indeed. I wired her before we left Milwaukee, and I'll speak with her tonight, as well. Dinner has been arranged for six o'clock tomorrow, which gives us plenty of time beforehand to visit the zoo and a few of my other favorite spots. Does that suit?"

Carina fidgeted. Oliver waited for her response, not wanting to pressure her to accept. Finally, she straightened her shoulders, determination shining in her gaze. "Yes, I would like that very much."

~

"**O**h, Oliver, isn't that otter simply darling?"

Oliver laughed as Carina pointed from where they stood at the edge of the enclosure. Snow drifted around them as she tugged on Oliver's sleeve, bringing him closer until he was only a few inches from her.

"Just look at it. Why, I do believe it's my new favorite animal. It has snow on its nose!"

Oliver grinned at Carina's enthusiasm. For someone who proclaimed they weren't overly fond of animals, she had taken to the zoo nicely. His guess that she had never been to one before had been correct—hence, his reason for bringing them there. Luckily, the cold weather had kept most people from venturing out, which made it far easier to see the animals.

"Are those zebras really from Africa?" Carina asked as they wandered over to an enclosure, with Mrs. Fields a step behind. "They look so unusual. I've seen drawings of them, but it doesn't compare to real life. They make such odd noises."

"Yes, they are from Africa, and yes, they are a bit strange." Oliver glanced at his pocket watch. "Unfortunately, we're coming up on five, so we may have to finish touring the zoo at a later time. Shall we go so you have time to change for dinner?"

Carina accepted his arm, casting one last look back at the zebras. "I suppose so." Was her reticence more from regret...or dread?

He gave her arm a reassuring squeeze. "It will be a lovely evening." Or so he prayed.

After flagging down a carriage near the side of the road, Oliver gave the driver directions to the ladies' hotel and helped Carina and Mrs. Fields in. Once there, he waited about forty-five minutes in their lobby until they descended in their best dresses.

"You take my breath away," he told Carina as he escorted them back to the waiting hired vehicle.

As the carriage rolled into motion, Carina placed her spectacles in the faded reticule dangling from her wrist and twisted the folds of her dress between restless fingers. The gown's emerald-green color made her carefully pinned hair and shining eyes seem even more vibrant in the waning light of day. Even if she was dressed in rags, however, Carina would still be the most beautiful woman in Chicago, both inside and out. Oliver's heart was practically bursting with pride at the thought of introducing such a fine woman to his parents.

Reaching over, he gently tugged the dress from her grasp and took her hand in his own. "They're going to love you."

"Are you certain?" Carina's gaze drifted to their entwined hands, red dusting her cheeks. "I don't want them to think I'm taking advantage of their son."

"I won't allow that," Oliver murmured, running his thumb over her knuckles. "I asked you to come to Chicago, Carina. I offered to pay for everything. Not the other way around. All you have to do is be your normal, radiant self." He tapped his pinkie on her reticule. "That also means you don't have to hide your spectacles if you don't want to."

Carina took in a shuddering breath. "Very well. I would prefer to keep them off, if you don't mind."

A smile spread across Oliver's face. "I have no care, so long as you feel comfortable."

The carriage turned onto the family's driveway, giving Oliver a view of the house. Was it really only two months ago he had left for Wisconsin? It felt as though he had been away for years.

Beside him, Mrs. Fields let out a soft gasp. "My, but that is a beautiful home."

The carriage drew to a halt in front of the house, and Oliver hopped down and helped Carina and Mrs. Fields descend.

Thanking the carriage driver, he took Carina's arm and led her carefully up the front steps.

"It's so grand," Carina whispered, turning her head to look at both sides of the building.

"It is my father's home, Carina. Not mine." Oliver waved his hand, gesturing to the house. "This is not my dream. I want a chance to travel the world."

Carina straightened, a bit of confidence blooming in her eyes. "Traveling the world does sound more exciting."

Oliver winked. "That it does."

At the door, they were greeted by Jack. "Greetings, Mr. Ramhurst. Welcome to the Ramhurst residence, Miss Clarke and Mrs. Fields. Your presence has been much anticipated." He held out a thin arm, inviting them into the foyer.

"Thanks, Jack." Oliver slid the scarf from around his neck and handed it to the butler, along with his coat and hat. Turning to Carina and Mrs. Fields, he gestured for them to also divest of their wraps.

"Goodness. The ceilings are so tall," Carina murmured as she slid the capelet from her shoulders and handed it to the butler, who hung it on the coatrack beside the door.

"Mrs. Ramhurst will see you in the parlor. Please, follow me." Jack's shoes clicked smartly on the glossy floor, echoing in the cavernous hallway as he set off.

Oliver and the others trailed behind the stout man. Oliver made sure to slow his pace, giving Carina and Mrs. Fields time to look around.

The butler paused in front of the parlor door and cleared his throat, waiting to speak until the three of them were positioned behind him. "Introducing Mr. Ramhurst, Mrs. Fields, and Miss Clarke."

Oliver led the way into the parlor, where his mother sat on her floral couch. She wore a spotless blue dress embroidered with tiny white flowers and trimmed with lace. Her hair had been pinned to perfection. As they entered the room, she rose. "Welcome back, Oliver, dear." She moved forward to kiss his cheek. Turning to Carina and Mrs. Fields, she curtsied in one effortless movement. "It's a pleasure to meet you. I'm most excited to make the acquaintance of the woman whom Oliver favors."

"I've been eager to meet you as well, ma'am. Oliver speaks very highly of you." Carina attempted a curtsy of her own, though it was a bit less graceful than his mother's.

She raised a brow, though she didn't comment on the clumsy movement. "That is good to hear. Won't you have a seat?"

Oliver assisted Carina and Mrs. Fields in settling on the couch across from his mother before lowering himself into his favorite armchair.

Mother sank gracefully onto her couch. She rested her hands demurely in her lap, her posture the picture of perfection. "Miss Clarke, Oliver tells me you assisted him in his most recent case. Is that true?"

Oliver's jaw tightened. He hadn't told his mother much about Carina, for she had been entertaining the family of a politician when he arrived home the previous evening. He had settled for telling her only the barest details, stressing his admiration of Carina. It seemed that now his mother wanted the rest of the story.

Carina glanced at him, her brows drawn together.

Oliver inclined his head a fraction, enough that his mother wouldn't be able to notice. *It's all right.*

Carina relaxed ever so slightly and turned back to his mother. Starting from the beginning, she spoke of meeting Oliver at work, helping him with his case, and eventually, catching the thief. Mother's face grew more and more surprised as Carina went on. By the time she finished, Mrs. Ramhurst had gone completely still.

Carina turned back to Oliver, eyes wide and anxious. Oliver shook his head. His mother was simply processing the outlandish story in its entirety. Was she concerned that a man had shot at him? Or was she more worried about the fact that he had been alone with an unmarried woman on multiple occasions?

Finally, Mother spoke. "Did my son really leap in front of you to save you from a bullet?"

Carina shifted, adjusting the folds of her dress. "Yes, ma'am. It was incredibly brave of him."

"And did you really run all the way to the warehouse to try and warn him?"

Carina blushed. "Yes, ma'am."

Oliver's mother hummed. "How courageous of you." She gave Oliver a measured smile. "May I speak briefly with you in the adjoining room?"

Oliver opened his mouth with a concerned glance at the guests, but his mother had risen and moved toward the rear portion of the double parlor. He followed, whispering to Carina, "I'm sorry. Please excuse us a moment."

Mother slid the pocket door closed behind them, walked to the center of the rug, and faced him. Before he could ask her why they had abandoned their guests, however, she lifted a hand. "Please, allow me to speak."

Oliver swallowed and dipped his head. Surely, this unexpected behavior could not bode well.

"From the beginning, you were determined to court and marry for love and not money. Now, what I wasn't expecting was for the woman you chose to be a loom girl." Mother tilted her head, studying Oliver.

"Mother, I—"

"Hush. Let me finish. I wasn't expecting that woman to be a loom girl." Mother's expression softened, and the corner of her mouth lifted. "But your story tells me you two truly care for each other. Oliver, it is no secret to me that you have no wish to join the social elite. I know you don't care for entertaining guests or dancing at balls. Why, some days, I envy your ability to make that decision." She cast an almost longing look toward the closed door. "The social groups that allowed us to live such affluent lives are the same groups that kept me from watching you grow from boy to man, something I have long regretted." She lifted her chin, turning her gaze back on him. "That is why I will try to make it up to you now. In light of what Miss Clarke has told me, I'd like you to know that I approve of her. She seems like a very fine woman, finer than many of the young women your father tried to get you to speak with." She raised a brow. "I expect that you will follow the proper rules of courtship, of course. Courting a woman of a different social standing is unusual, but that is no excuse for improper behavior."

Oliver beamed, relief flooding him. "Thank you. It means a lot to me that I have your blessing." He whooshed out a sigh and whispered, "I love her, Mother."

"I can see that." Mother held her hand out in the direction of the door. "Now, go and tell her what I said before she fears I'm disowning you. Your father will be home shortly, and I'm afraid he may be a bit harder to convince. You can at least assure her I approve of her first."

Thanking her once more, Oliver returned to the front parlor and grinned at Carina and Mrs. Fields, who stared at him with drawn expressions. He spoke in a murmur to Carina. "She adores you."

Carina seemed to deflate on the spot. "Oh, thank goodness. I feared the worst."

"What did I tell you? All you had to do was be yourself."

They smiled at each other, Carina's cheeks blooming red as she gazed at him from behind her spectacles. Adorable. Her gaze shifted to his mother, who rejoined them, sat down, and adjusted her skirts around her.

Before anyone could speak again, however, the front door creaked open. Heavy footfalls approached in the hallway, and Oliver winced.

Father.

Now came the real test of how his future would play out.

CHAPTER 31

*T*he judge swept into the room, his mere presence seeming to command respect. His finely tailored frock coat draped around him like royalty, his stiff posture enhancing the image of a king entering his court. Sharp silver eyes the same color as Oliver's peered around the room until they landed on Carina. She held her shoulders straight as the man's imperious gaze narrowed, assessing her.

"Good evening, sir. It's so nice to see you again. It isn't as though I've been gone for months." Oliver's voice, laced with amusement, interrupted the tense silence and brought the judge's gaze away from Carina. She released a tense breath as he passed her by, moving instead to stand in front of Oliver.

"Welcome home, son. I'm sorry I didn't greet you yesterday evening. I was attending an event being hosted by a city official, as I'm sure your mother mentioned." Judge Ramhurst's voice was deeper than Oliver's, with a commanding ring to it. No doubt, more than one criminal had crumbled under his stern gaze and harsh tone.

The judge turned toward Carina and Mrs. Fields and

executed a short bow. "And whose acquaintance do I have the pleasure of making this evening?"

"These two fine ladies are Miss Clarke and Mrs. Fields." Oliver's mother rose and glided over to rest her hand on her husband's arm. "They've come for dinner, dear. At Oliver's invitation. I believe I mentioned it to you two days ago, when he first sent a telegram."

One of the judge's bushy gray brows lifted. "Invited them, did he? It must have slipped my mind. Forgive me." He returned to his assessment of Carina. "Which part of town are you from? I don't believe we've met before. I'm sure I would have remembered."

Oliver stiffened. "They aren't from Chicago, Father. They're from Milwaukee. I met Carina during my work there."

"Calling each other by your Christian names, are you? If you met while working on a factory case, truly, further conversation is pointless." The judge glared at Oliver. "Although I would like to know what possessed you to issue an invitation to our home. Is there some *reason* I should be made aware of?" His pointed glance at Carina's midsection left no room for misinterpretation.

Carina's face went up in flames.

"Father, stop." Oliver's voice was harsh enough to bring silence, his tone rivaling his father's in severity. His eyes fairly spewed brimstone as he came to stand in front of Carina. "You have no right to speak about Carina in such a manner. She is a woman of integrity who is as intelligent as any of the socialites you pushed my way at events, if not more so. I would never compromise her or any other woman in such a manner, and it appalls me that you think me capable of such. I invited Carina to Chicago under the impression that you would welcome her as the dear friend she is to me. After all, is it not you who proclaim to judge all the same, whether they be rich or poor?

Why then do you scorn her? Because she does not flaunt money like the rest of the Chicago elite?"

Carina's heart raced as her gaze darted between the man in front of her and the judge. The intensity in Oliver's voice and the way he shielded her filled her with both gratitude and disbelief. *He really thinks that of me?*

The judge's face reddened. "I'll thank you to watch your tone, son. I am not scorning her, but a person from her station cannot be involved with one of Chicago's future judges."

"I am not a judge, Father, nor will I ever be." Oliver drew himself up. "It has never once been in my plans to study law. I am a detective, and that is all I want to be."

The judge sputtered and fell silent. Finally, he shook his head and turned to leave. "Then you are no son of mine." He strode from the room with his coattails flapping behind him.

Carina gasped, clapping a hand over her mouth. Oliver's father had turned away his son, and all because she had agreed to come to Chicago. Her shoulders slumped, and she hugged her arms to her chest. She had been right to assume his parents would never accept someone of inferior standing.

A warm hand clasped her elbow, and the smell of peppermint surrounded Carina as she looked up into Oliver's eyes. "Don't fret, Carina," he murmured. "My father isn't mad because of you. He's always wanted me to be a judge, but that's the first time I've told him I want nothing to do with it."

Carina sniffed. "Oh, Oliver, I'm so sorry. This wouldn't have happened if I had stayed away."

"Don't speak like that. Those words have been at the back of my mind for years. Having you at my side simply gave me the courage to finally say them." Oliver released a long breath, rubbing his neck with one hand. "The truth is, my father will never be proud of me. So long as I'm not a judge, I'll never be the son he wants."

"Oh, Oliver, that isn't true." Oliver's mother came up beside him, her expression gentle. "Your father is very proud of your work, though he has a hard time finding the words to tell you." She looked at Carina. "Carina, darling, don't take my husband's reaction to heart. He was surprised by the quick turn of events, but I know he'll come around. I, for one, think you are a very fine woman."

Mrs. Fields, who stood next to Carina, nodded her agreement. "Yes, don't mind the judge. You know he wasn't speaking the truth."

Carina dropped her arms to her side as some of her embarrassment fell away. "Thank you." She glanced at the doorway. "Shouldn't someone go and speak with him?"

Oliver ran a hand through his hair in an agitated manner. "I suppose I should. You three can stay in the parlor while I find him or move to the kitchen for dinner, if you prefer. The food will get cold if we wait much longer."

Carina tapped on Oliver's elbow, drawing his attention. "Oliver, you remember what happened to my father. One of my biggest regrets about his death was the fact that I never attempted to offer him reconciliation after he confessed. If I had the chance, I would go back and forgive him a dozen times over, if only so he would die knowing I still loved him." She fisted a hand over her chest. "Time is too short, and life is too fragile to risk letting your father go like this. Talk to him with an open heart."

Oliver studied her face, his expression softening. "I will. I'm glad to know a wise woman like you, Carina. Will you wait here for me?"

"Of course. I'm not going anywhere until you return." Carina tilted her head. "The hotel is too far away for me to walk, anyways."

A smile graced Oliver's face, though it quickly vanished. "True."

As he left to find his father, Carina sent up a prayer that he would be able to reconcile with the man before it was too late.

~

A quick search of the house revealed that the judge was nowhere to be found, so Oliver moved outside to check the stables. His father had always had an affinity for horses, something Oliver found a bit out of character for the stoic man. As he had suspected, the man was in the middle of the long building, stroking the nose of one of his favorite stallions. His back was to Oliver, but the way he stiffened showed he had heard Oliver's footsteps approaching.

Oliver halted a few feet away. Carina's words hung heavy at the back of his mind, taming the anger that he longed to unleash on the man who had done so little good in his life. "I never wanted to be a judge, Father. Had you paid attention, you might have realized that sooner. I'm sorry I sprang it on you with guests in attendance, but I don't regret what I said."

The judge continued stroking the horse's nose. "All these years, all of these things I built were for you. This house, these stables, a good reputation. All so you would never have to see poverty in your life. Yet you chose to go to the poorest slums and work among them. You chose to befriend the beggars over the very people you grew up with. Why?"

"Because those so-called beggars are more real than any of the socialites here. They don't treat each other differently based on money or status. They don't treat love like a business transaction." Oliver took a breath. "They don't treat faith like it's a ritual."

Father dropped his hand, turning to look Oliver in the eye. "What do you mean?"

"Here, going to church and reading the Bible are treated like a chore. We're expected to come, sit, listen to a few words, and then leave. There's no real life or joy in any of it. But those people..." He gestured toward the house. "They know what it means to have a relationship with the Lord. It means more to them than money or status. They celebrate it as though they're rich." Oliver straightened his shoulders. "Father, I've learned more living among people like them than I have in all the years I spent growing up here. Not only that, but I've become happier, as well."

The judge studied Oliver. After a moment, he turned back to the horse. "I'm sorry to have failed you in such a way. I thought I was doing the right thing in giving you all of this. I suppose I was wrong to want what was best for my son."

Oliver clenched his fists. "The only thing I ever wanted was a father who was proud of me. A father who cared about me more than he cared about his social standing."

The judge remained still as Oliver continued.

"I didn't need wealth or houses or any of this. All I needed was a father to be there for me. I brought Carina here not because I needed your approval, but because I wanted it as a son. I came here because I foolishly thought you might be happy I found a woman I truly want to court. In that, I suppose *I* was wrong." Oliver released a sigh, his shoulders drooping. "If you want nothing to do with me, very well. Know that while I'm sorry I cannot be what you want me to be, I'm still your son. I'm proud of my father regardless of whether or not he returns the sentiment. But my father's dreams and accomplishments are his own. They are not mine, nor will they ever be. I, too, want to help people, but not in a courtroom. My calling is to be *among* the people I am helping, even if that means giving up a life of luxury." Oliver drew himself up. "And that will never change. Goodbye, Father."

As he turned to leave the stables, his father called out. "Oliver. Son, wait."

Oliver halted and turned around, waiting as the judge came to stand before him. The older man's eyes searched his, and something in his father's expression seemed to break.

"All this time, I thought I was doing what was best for your future. I thought I was preparing you for success, to live a life where you would never want for anything. But, in doing so, I suppose I disregarded what was already there. And now the boy that once tried to follow me to the courtroom grew up. He has aspirations of his own that are vastly different from what I originally expected." The judge dropped his gaze to the ground. "In a way, that frightens me. I felt so certain that my plan was the only one my boy would ever want. It would appear I was wrong." He again met Oliver's eyes, and he tucked his hands behind his back. "For that, I must apologize. I'm sorry for not paying more attention to your victories instead of your losses." His jaw tightened. "In the end, I was worried you would run off and never come back again. I feared that you would make mistakes I could not be there to fix. I was afraid, Oliver. Can you forgive me?"

Oliver exhaled. Could he? Looking at the man before him, he saw behind the bravado and the fine clothing to the father he had longed to follow ever since he could walk. The father he had wanted to make proud from the day he knew the meaning of the word. "Yes, Father." Oliver took a step forward. "I can. I understand your fears, and I only wish you had told me sooner. I would never leave you and Mother. You are my family, and that will never change. As for mistakes, while we all make them, I was taught well." He crossed his arms. "However, loving Carina is not one of them. I plan to court her, if she'll allow it. She means a lot to me, Father."

"If social standing truly doesn't matter to you..." The judge drew himself up and dipped his chin. "I will not stop you. You are happy, and in the end, that is what counts the most. I may not be completely happy with the arrangement, but I suppose I will grow used to it given time."

Elation filled Oliver, bringing a smile to his face. "She is a good woman, Father. You will see that once you talk to her."

"Well, then, why don't we rejoin them? We seem to have abandoned the womenfolk inside." The judge hummed. "My mistake."

"You know, it was Carina who told me to come and find you," Oliver informed him as they started back toward the house.

"I suppose you expect me to apologize, do you?" With a rueful glance at Oliver, the judge adjusted the collar of his coat. "Well, let's get it over with. It's not often that I do this."

They followed the sounds of conversation into the dining room, where the women were sitting around the table. When they saw Oliver and his father, the talking came to an abrupt halt. Carina's eyes moved quickly to Oliver, and he gave her a reassuring wink.

"Ahem. It has been brought to my attention that I have been...well, less than courteous." The judge coughed. "For that, I am incredibly sorry." He turned to Carina, a hint of regret in his gray eyes. "Young lady, I owe you an apology for my hasty words. I fear that in the heat of the moment, I spoke rashly. Oliver speaks very highly of you. I never should have doubted his judgement."

Carina inclined her head, relief evident on her face. "Thank you, Judge Ramhurst. I forgive you, but truly, I can understand what a shock it must have been to hear all that information at once."

"I'm glad you can forgive me." The judge gestured to the empty seat at the head of the table. "May we join you?"

"But of course!" Carina held her hand out. "Do sit down. It is your table, after all."

As they slid into chairs, Oliver selecting a seat next to Carina, he leaned over to whisper in her ear. "Thank you."

"There's no reason to thank me." Carina replied in a hushed voice, her eyes twinkling. "I'm simply glad things were resolved."

"So am I, Carina. So am I." Oliver pressed his lips together to contain a smile. Now only one thing remained for him to do.

CHAPTER 32

"*C*arina, dear, the porter gave me a message for you."
The summons from Mrs. Fields came from the adjacent sitting room the next morning.

"Coming," Carina called, stabbing one last pin into her hair. Hurrying into the adjoining area of their suite, she found her older friend waiting with a paper in hand.

"Here you are, dear. My guess is that it comes from Oliver." Mrs. Fields chuckled, handing Carina the note.

Carina opened it and scanned the interior with a smile. "You are correct. He says his parents had a wonderful time meeting us and send their regards."

After Oliver and the judge had returned to the house, they had enjoyed a pleasant dinner of roast chicken. While Mrs. Fields bustled off to the kitchen to question the cook on what she called "a most excellent recipe," Carina had spoken to Oliver's mother and discovered that they shared a love of reading. They had conversed for another hour before Oliver suggested they go back to the hotel. What a relief to learn his parents had been left with a favorable opinion of her.

"Oh, it also says here that Oliver wants to meet us in the hotel lobby at ten-fifteen. Is that agreeable with you?"

Mrs. Fields nodded, a grin tugging at her face. "Oh, certainly. I wonder what your young man has planned for today."

Carina laughed. "Who knows? Shall we go downstairs and find out?"

A few minutes later, they descended to the lobby. Oliver stood waiting at the foot of the stairs, dressed in a plain navy jacket and thick trousers similar to what he had worn in Milwaukee. He looked as handsome in worker's clothes as he did in the fine suit he had worn the day before.

Oliver bowed as they came down the final flight of steps. "Good morning, Carina. Sleep well?"

"Very." Carina drew to a halt in a swirl of skirts and set her hands on her hips. "So, Mr. Tour Guide, where are we going today?"

Oliver straightened and held two fingers in the air. "I have a couple of destinations, but both are surprises. If you'll follow me, there's a carriage waiting to take us to the first."

Carina gasped in mock dismay. "A surprise? That's not fair."

"I'm afraid you'll simply have to trust me." Oliver took her arm and winked. "I promise you'll like where we're going."

Carina rolled her eyes but smiled, nonetheless. "All right. I trust you."

Outside, they clambered into the waiting carriage and trundled off to the first mysterious destination. When the vehicle finally slowed to a stop, Oliver hopped out and helped Carina down. To Carina's surprise, Mrs. Fields decided to remain in the vehicle.

"I trust you two will behave yourselves." She waved them off with a chuckle.

Carina couldn't help but raise a brow at the woman as she

stepped foot on the sidewalk. Did the proprietress know more than she was letting on?

"Right this way," Oliver said, gesturing forward.

Carina hurried to follow Oliver as he strode down the sidewalk. "You don't have to walk so fast, you know. Which building are we going to?"

Oliver pointed to a large brick structure at the end of the road. "That one."

As they drew closer, Carina read the sign and gasped. "Truly?"

"Indeed." Oliver held the door open. "After you, fair lady."

Entering the building, Carina gazed around in amazement. Books covered the walls from floor to ceiling, ranging from slim novels to thick tomes. The air was quiet and faintly musty, hinting at the many stories that were kept within the building's walls. Tall ladders reached to the top shelves, inviting visitors to climb up and seek the novels that waited beyond their reach. Carina watched in delight as a man used a ladder to glide from one end of a shelf to the other. "My goodness, they have wheels!"

"That they do. What do you think?"

"I think this is the most splendid library I've ever visited." Carina twirled in a quick circle, unable to contain her excitement. "I don't believe I've ever seen so many books in one place before. Could we look around?"

"But of course. It would be foolish to come into a library and not look." Oliver gestured toward the shelves. "Lead the way."

Carina hastened to the nearest shelf and began browsing the myriads of book spines. "Oliver, come look at this. It's Charles Dickens! I've never had a chance to read his books."

Oliver appeared behind her shoulder, peering at the book in her hand. "Ah, *A Tale of Two Cities*. A good novel, if I do say so myself. My parents own a copy, if you'd like to borrow it."

Carina gasped. "Truly? I would love to, assuming they wouldn't mind."

"I'm certain they wouldn't."

They spent half an hour milling about, enjoying the vast variety of books the library had to offer, and even taking a ride on one of the ladders before Oliver suggested moving on. Returning to the carriage, they discovered Mrs. Fields fast asleep against one of the seat cushions. Carina stifled a giggle as the carriage began moving and the dear woman released a tiny snore, though she didn't wake.

They stopped at a cafe for a quick bite of lunch, and then it was on to the second destination. When the carriage slowed to a stop once more, they descended, leaving Mrs. Fields to her nap. Once on the ground, Oliver instructed Carina to close her eyes.

"Why do I need to close them?" Carina questioned, though she did as he had asked.

Oliver carefully guided her from the carriage, the warmth from his hand seeping into her elbow. "I want it to be a complete surprise."

There was a creaking noise as they entered a building, one that was surprisingly warm. Oliver moved her quickly through another door, into a room that smelled like flowers and spring. Water trickled nearby, but the rest of the room was silent. Except...was that a gentle fluttering?

"All right. You can open your eyes," Oliver murmured, his voice near her right ear.

Slowly, Carina opened her eyes. They were in a brightly lit room filled to the brim with tropical plants of every variety. The water Carina had heard belonged to a small fountain that sat in the center of the plants. And perched on every leaf and flower were...

"Butterflies," Carina whispered.

They flew through the air in a multitude of colors, ranging

from yellows and oranges to browns and blacks. Some were as large as her fist, while others could have fit on her little finger. Some hid deep in the safety of the plants, while others soared freely through the air.

"Oh, Oliver. This is amazing," Carina covered her mouth, afraid to speak lest she disturb the quiet atmosphere of the room.

Oliver stepped back, gazing around. "I'm glad you think so. This room is kept at the same temperature year-round so the butterflies stay healthy. The nectar from the flowers keeps them fed." He gestured to the nearest plant. "You know, if you get closer, one might land on you."

Carina moved next to a cluster of flowers, causing some of the butterflies to leave the plant and flutter through the air. Some chose to rest on other flowers, while one landed directly on Oliver's right shoulder. Carina stifled a laugh, pointing at the little black-and-white insect. "You've made a friend."

Oliver glanced down, a smile breaking across his face. "So I have." He nodded to Carina's dress. "And so have you."

Looking down, Carina gasped at the sight of the beautiful butterfly on her skirt. Its vibrant yellow color and long wingtips identified it as a swallowtail. She hadn't had a chance to see one since she was a child running through the fields in Peshtigo. "It's beautiful."

"It is, and so are you."

Carina swallowed. "Oh, I wouldn't say that."

"It's true. Carina, you are beautiful, both inside and out. From the start, you astounded me with your quick wit and kind heart. Even if I didn't make the best first impression." He flashed her a grin. "I would gladly fill a room with butterflies and books if it made you smile. I'd go to the farthest reaches of the jungle if you wanted to know what was at the end." He took a quick, deep breath. "In short, I would love nothing more than to court you, Carina Clarke."

Carina studied Oliver, from the unruly lock of hair that had fallen across his forehead to the snow-dampened tips of his boots. Oh, how she had come to love him. "Had you told me that two months ago, I would have said you were stark, raving mad." She tilted her head, the corners of her lips twitching up. "However, while I once said you were the last person I would ever marry, my sentiments seem to have changed. You may be impulsive, particularly when it comes to knocking people over, but you were also willing to give your life to save me. In a crowd of people, it's you who I always seem to look for. In times of crisis, it's you who I want to ensure is safe. So, yes, Oliver Ramhurst. I would love to be courted by you."

Oliver's gaze softened, a mixture of tenderness and relief shining in his eyes. He took a step closer and reached out to touch her hand, sending a flutter through her heart. "You have no idea how much that means to me."

Carina's breath hitched slightly, her heart racing as she looked up at him. In that instant, surrounded by rushing water and the gentle flutter of wings, it was as though they were the only two people in the world. Oliver's thumb brushed lightly against the back of her hand before he leaned in, his eyes never leaving hers. His lips met hers in a kiss that was soft and tentative, filled with all the emotions they had for so long held close to their hearts.

Carina ducked her head and buried her face into Oliver's jacket so he wouldn't see her blazing cheeks. "Oh, my."

Oliver wrapped Carina in a hug and planted a kiss on her forehead. "My fair lady. My Carina," he murmured into her hair.

Carina looped her arms around him, enjoying the scent of peppermint that came from his jacket. "You're scaring away the butterflies, you know."

Oliver's laugh rumbled in her ear. "The ones in the air or the ones in your stomach?"

"Both." Carina lifted a brow, glancing toward the door. "Why do I get the sneaking suspicion that there's a reason why Mrs. Fields is peering in?"

"I may have informed her of my plans for today. She told me she would wait in the carriage, but I suppose her excitement must have gotten the better of her."

Carina walked to the door on Oliver's arm, making sure she wasn't carrying any winged stowaways before she slipped outside.

"Oh, what did you say?" The words poured out of Mrs. Fields in a rush, and the dear woman clasped her hands together as though barely containing her excitement. "If you said no, I need to have a word with you."

Carina glanced at Oliver, who gave her a bemused smile. She turned back to Mrs. Fields with a giggle. "Of course, I said yes, Mrs. Fields. You have nothing to fear."

Mrs. Fields squealed and pulled Carina into a tight hug. "Oh, my dear, I'm so happy for you. You two suit each other so well."

"We do, don't we?" Carina touched the butterfly charm that hung around her neck. "We do," she whispered. If only Charlotte could be here to see it...

"What are you thinking about?" Oliver touched her arm. "You have that look on your face. The one when you've got something on your mind."

"Oh, I was thinking of Charlotte. She would be happy for us —and a bit jealous too." Carina laced her fingers through Oliver's as they began walking back toward the carriage. "She always said she would be the one to court a man first because I spent too much time reading books and working. I suppose she was wrong, wasn't she? If only I could see her now, to laugh and celebrate and tease her mercilessly."

"We will find her, Carina. You and I will do it together, as partners."

"Partners in the business sense or in the relationship sense?" Carina asked wryly.

"Both would be excellent." Oliver lifted their entwined hands and kissed Carina's knuckles. "When we do find your sister, she'll be in for quite the surprise."

Carina leaned against Oliver's shoulder, soaking in the warmth that radiated from his coat. *When we do.* She liked the sound of that.

EPILOGUE

"*I*t feels as though we were in Chicago for such a short time," Carina told Oliver as their carriage pulled to a stop in front of the train station.

Oliver grinned. "Well, you could always consider becoming a detective. Then you'd get to stop by the city every once in a while. We'd also get to visit all sorts of places together."

Carina studied his face. "Perhaps I will. It sounds far more interesting than standing over a loom all day. I'll send a telegram to Pinkerton once we're back in Milwaukee."

Mrs. Fields cleared her throat from beside them, a wry smile on her face. "Only if you promise to come and visit this old woman in between your travels. I do need company every once in a while."

Carina bent to kiss the woman who had become like a mother to her on her cheek. "But of course, Mrs. Fields. Besides, I would send you plenty of letters while I was away."

They stepped out into the melee of the train station, where people were rushing about on their way to other destinations.

"Carina, dear, our train is this way." Mrs. Fields pointed over the crowd.

Carina followed the proprietress with Oliver close by her side, and after a few moments, they reached the train. The locomotive sent white puffs of smoke into the air, a sign that it was prepared to take her home. Or at least, to what she currently considered her home. Looking at the people who stood next to her—Oliver in his navy jacket and Mrs. Fields in her plain gingham—Carina knew she would feel at home wherever they were. More than that, she would feel loved.

A shout caught her attention. Swiveling, she spotted Oliver's mother running toward them in a rather unladylike manner with the judge close behind. Both of them were dressed rather shoddily for people of their station, giving Carina the impression that they had rushed straight from breakfast to the station.

"Mother, what are you doing here?" Oliver gaped at his mother as she reached him and pulled him into a hug, her lavender skirts swishing around them.

"You didn't think I would let you leave without saying goodbye, did you?" Oliver's mother reached up to adjust her enormous purple hat with one hand, holding an envelope aloft with the other. "Besides, this came in the mail for you this morning. I thought it would be easier if we delivered it to you before you left as opposed to sending it back to Milwaukee."

Frowning, Oliver took the envelope and studied it. "It looks as though it's been forwarded from an address in Marinette, though it's seen better days." The ink on the envelope was faded and smudged, as though it had been dropped in a snow pile before reaching him. "I suppose my detective friend must have mailed it."

Carina pressed closer. The detective friend investigating Charlotte?

Oliver tore open the top, tugged the letter out, and scanned it with sharp eyes. "I don't believe it."

"What? What is it?" Carina asked, her heart pounding in her chest.

"Well, I can't quite make out the bottom few lines because of the water damage, but I can read the top. My friend says he's found some extremely important evidence in Peshtigo." Oliver met Carina's eyes. "According to him, it may be enough to find your sister."

Carina took a startled step back, air flooding into her lungs. "Find Charlotte? He really believes it?"

"Yes. He wants you to come to Peshtigo as soon as possible."

Carina nodded, her thoughts racing. "Of course, I'll go. Oh, Oliver! To think that I might finally be able to bring her home." She wiped at a tear as it rolled slowly down her cheek, unable to contain the intensity of her emotion. "I've waited for so long."

"*You'll* go? I think you mean *we'll* go, Carina." Oliver squeezed her arm. "I wouldn't miss this for the world. Assuming you'll have me along."

Carina beamed, joy crashing over her as the shock began to wear off. She finally had a lead on her sister! "Certainly, I will."

"I wish you all safe travels." Oliver's mother cast Carina a smile and a wink as she enveloped her son in another hug. "Oliver, dear, do make sure to come and visit us soon. Bring Carina along as well. We would love to have her."

From behind her, the judge cleared his throat. "Yes, son. Don't stay away for long. We miss you at home." His countenance softened ever so slightly. "Before you leave, we want you to know that we're proud of what you're doing." Catching sight of his wife's raised brow, he coughed. "In other words, *I'm* proud of you. I'm afraid I've been rather lax in saying it."

Oliver grinned and wrapped his father in a quick hug, causing the judge's brows to raise. "That's all right. Thank you, Father. I'll certainly visit soon. We both will."

After waving a final goodbye to Oliver's parents, they stepped up to the door of the train. Oliver offered his arm. "Shall we, my fair lady?"

Anticipation tingled through Carina. Her sister was waiting for her, and Carina was going to find her. What once seemed so out of reach was no longer impossible, and it was all thanks to the man the Lord had brought to her side.

"Yes, my dear sir," Carina said, taking his arm. "We shall."

AUTHOR'S NOTE

I originally intended to base Carina's story around the Great Chicago Fire of 1871. However, when I began doing research, I was surprised to learn that more than one fire occurred on October 8, 1871. At the same time the Great Chicago Fire began, residents of a Wisconsin lumber town called Peshtigo found their town being consumed by an inferno. Witnesses described what appeared to be a "wall of fire" descending upon them, accompanied by winds nearly as strong as a hurricane. The terrified citizens of Peshtigo had only a few minutes to seek shelter in open fields, root cellars, and the Peshtigo River before the firestorm roared through. Many burned where they stood, while others drowned in the bitterly cold waters of the river.

By morning, the fire had died down, leaving behind a charred wasteland. Those who survived the night walked to the nearby town of Marinette, which had been only partially damaged by the flames. Once there, they waited until help arrived from Milwaukee, Green Bay, and the surrounding cities.

An estimated one million acres of land were completely razed, and over twelve hundred people lost their lives. This makes the Peshtigo Fire the deadliest fire in American history.

Its origins are still unknown, though historians suspect it was most likely caused by a combination of dry conditions, high winds, and controlled burns. Loggers and farmers often piled up large amounts of slash—leftover tree and agricultural material such as branches, logs, and dead plants—which they would then burn to clear land. Although these fires typically died out quickly, it is possible that one rekindled and rapidly grew out of control.

Oliver's story is centered around the Pinkerton Detective Agency, which was at its peak from the 1870s to 1890s. Led by Allan Pinkerton, the Pinkertons were well known for their private investigating and security services. Their missions included preventing strikes in factories and mills and pursuing various robbers, including Butch Cassidy and Jesse James. The Pinkerton Agency was also known for being the first private investigation agency to employ women detectives, the first of whom was named Kate Warne. Hired in 1856, she went on to help thwart a plot to assassinate Abraham Lincoln and was soon after placed in charge of Pinkerton's Female Detective Bureau.

Though certainly fascinating, butterfly rooms—or butterfly houses, as they are more commonly called—did not begin appearing until the 1900s, making the one in this story fictitious. There are a multitude in existence today, particularly in larger cities such as Milwaukee. They are certainly worth a visit.

If you would like to see more of Oliver and Carina, feel free to follow along with my writing journey at avrieswan.com. For those of you who are on Pinterest, you can follow the link on my website to find a board based around their story.

Did you enjoy this book? We hope so!
**Would you take a quick minute to leave a review where you
purchased the book?**
It doesn't have to be long. Just a sentence or two telling what
you liked about the story!

Receive a FREE ebook and get updates when new Wild Heart
books release: https://wildheartbooks.org/newsletter

If you love historical romance, check out the other Wild Heart books!

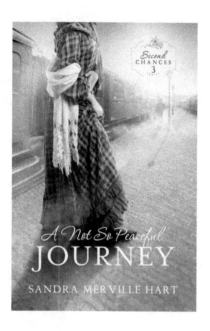

A Not So Peaceful Journey by Sandra Merville Hart

Dreams of adventure send him across the country. She prefers to keep her feet firmly planted in Ohio.

Rennie Hill has no illusions about the hardships in life, which is why it's so important her beau, John Welch, keeps his secure job with the newspaper. Though he hopes to write fiction, the unsteady pay would mean an end to their plans, wouldn't it?

John Welch dreams of adventure worthy of storybooks, like Mark Twain, and when two of his short stories are published, he sees it as a sign of future success. But while he's dreaming big with his head in the clouds, his girl has her feet firmly planted, and he can't help wondering if she really believes in him.

When Rennie must escort a little girl to her parents' home in San Francisco, John is forced to alter his plans to travel across the country with them. But the journey proves far more adventurous than either of them expect.

~

Ranger to the Rescue by Renae Brumbaugh Green

Amelia Cooper has sworn off lawmen for good.

Now any man who wants to claim the hand of the intrepid reporter had better have a safe job. Like attorney Evan Covington. Amelia is thrilled when the handsome lawyer comes courting. But when the town enlists him as a Texas Ranger, Amelia isn't sure she can handle losing another man to the perils of keeping the peace.

Evan never expected his temporary appointment to sink his relationship with Amelia. Or to instantly plunge them headlong into danger. But when Amelia and his sister are both kidnapped, the newly minted lawman must rescue them—if he's to have any chance at love

A Heart's Forever Home by Lena Nelson Dooley

A single lawyer whose clients think he needs a wife.
A woman who needs a forever home...or a forever family...or a forever love.

Although Traesa Killdare is a grown woman now, the discovery that her adoption wasn't finalized sends her reeling. Especially when her beloved grandmother dies and the only siblings she's ever known exile her from the family property without a penny to her name.

Wilson Pollard works hard for the best interest of his law clients, even those who think a marriage would make him more "suitable" in his career. And when the beloved granddaughter of a recently deceased client comes to him for help, he knows he must do whatever necessary to make her situation better.

As each of their circumstances worsen, a marriage of convenience seems the only answer for both. Traesa can't help but fall for her new husband—the man who's given her both his home and his name. But what will it take for Wilson to realize he loves her? Will a not-so-natural disaster open his eyes and heart?

www.ingramcontent.com/pod-product-compliance
Lightning Source LLC
Chambersburg PA
CBHW070919140325
23252CB00006B/13